ROSEBLOOM

A Novel by Christine Keleny

Hope you enjoy
the book !
Thanks
Christine

CK Books

Although this novel was written around real events and places in history, the story and its characters are fictional.

No part of this book may be reproduced, scanned, or distributed in any printed or electronic form without permission. Contact: CK Books, P.O. Box 214, New Glarus, WI, 53574
www.Rosebloombook.com

Library of Congress Cataloging-in-Publication Data

Keleny, Christine
    Rosebloom : a novel / by Christine Keleny.

        p. : maps ; cm.

    Includes bibliographical references.
    ISBN: 978-0-9800529-0-9

1. Young women—Middle West—Nineteen thirties—Fiction. 2. Excursion boats—Mississippi River—Fiction. 3. Runaway teenagers—Middle West—Nineteen thirties—Fiction. 4. Historical fiction. 5. Bildungsromans. I. Title.

PS3611.E4464 R67 2007
813/.6
                                                    2007940706

Cover artwork: Earl Keleny, www.EarlKeleny.com
Interior graphics: Kelly Anderson, www.sentialdesign.com

To my parents:
My father, who gave me my
love of the written word,
and my mother,
who never said never
in anything I tried.
I love you both.

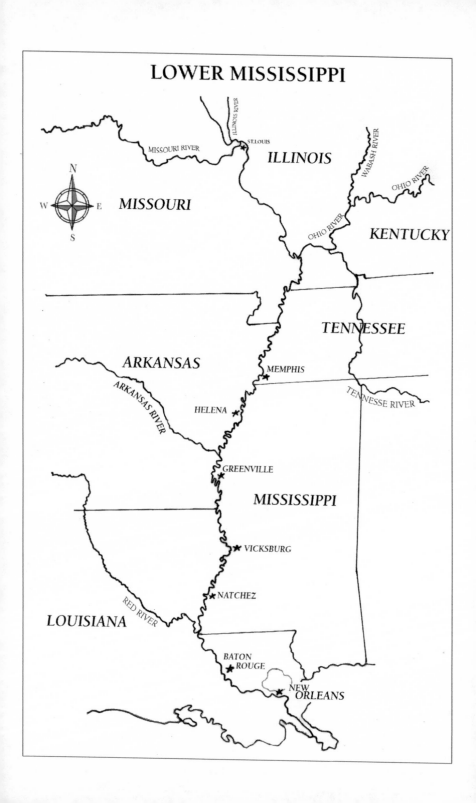

ঙ Acknowledgements ଔ

As any writer who has a family, I have to first and foremost thank my family—Andrew, Aaron and Rachel—for all their patience and understanding while I spent many hours over the many years researching and writing this book.

Then there is Sir Adam (Seeger) who was brought into my life at just the right time; always there to answer those odd questions with his seemingly infinite knowledge base and to find just the right web site to answer my frequent, peculiar questions. His polite editing style was an amusement and a great help. But most of all, I appreciated him as a fellow writer who gets as excited as I do by a well written sentence.

My other two editors and consultants, Jane Carlson and Robin Zenz, not only lent me their skill with grammar and punctuation; they were great resources for my constant questions of what to include and what to leave out of my story.

I need to thank the helpful people at the many libraries and museums I have visited over these many years—their skill at finding reference material in their large well of information is a skill I wish I had but am so happy I can easily access. Pam Brown at the Savanna Railroad Museum. The folks at the Wisconsin Historical Society—one of my favorite places in Madison. The public librarians of Prairie du Chien, St. Louis, New Orleans, and most especially New Glarus, the latter who never flinched or asked me what I was up to when I excitedly took out such titles as *Call House Madam* and *Storyville: New Orleans...the Notorious Red Light District.* Betty Gordon and Annie Blum of the Mercantile library at the University of Missouri - St. Louis, who gave me the names of my wonderful Capital steamer authorities: Henry Evans and Mary Otte. Henry built an exact replica of this wonderful old steamer and saved me when I had given up on finding anything more than a few exterior pictures of the beautiful boat. You were a life saver Henry! Mary Otte is a very pleasant woman of 94 who actually worked on the Capital and remembered a lot of the little details that help make my story that much more real.

I want to thank the Army Corp employee I met on the excursion boat my husband, daughter and I took during the 2004 reproduction of the Grand Excursion (one of the many events, places and people who, I have no doubt, were put in my path to help me write this book). He put me on to a wonderful book I would recommend to any Mississippi river lover: *A River We Have Wrought.*

Then there is Dorothy Brown, the church clerk at the Antioch Baptist Church in the Ville, St. Louis, who was able to give me some details of the workings of this beautiful, historic church. I was blest by being able to attend a service in the church's beautiful new sanctuary, which gave me some good material, and more importantly, gave me a wonderful feeling for the caring, welcoming Antioch community. And there is the other St. Louis contact that was dropped on my doorstep: Louise Bryce. With her kind heart and generous spirit she helped fill in the details of life in St. Louis in the late 1930s, when she was a teenager.

Sister Mary Elise Antoine of St. Gabriel's Catholic Church, and the friendly couple Marilyn and Earl Rybarczyk in Prairie du Chien (and their niece Angela Gasior who set up my meeting with them) where of great help to me. Through them I was able to learn what life was like in Prairie those many years ago. Marilyn and Earl's daughter and son-in-law were also nice enough to give me a tour of their auction facility in Prairie, which was the old *Metro* theatre mentioned in my story.

I want to thank my brother Earl Keleny for his willingness and expertise in helping me develop a book cover that is a wonderful representation of my story—Dad is smiling about our collaboration, I'm sure. And Bill Martinelli, who did the wonderful graphics for the cover—his addition put the icing on the cake. I want to thank Kelly Anderson for the beautiful job on the inside graphics and lastly Kira Henschel and all the folks at Goblin Fern Press who educated me and held my hand along the path to publication. I couldn't have done it without her.

ℬ 1 ℭ

R ose Marie Krantz was a beautiful baby—a beauty she would come to find was as fragrant and as prickly as the climbing rose bush just outside the window by her crib. But just now, it was growing without restrictions on a small south west Wisconsin farm amidst the valleys and buttes of the driftless, unglaciated upper Midwest.

~ ~ ~

Rose was given her name by her father, because it was his wife's middle name, and because of the rose-shaped, pink birthmark on the back of her right shoulder. It was a favorite spot he would kiss when he caught her running in the farmyard on those hot Wisconsin summer days. It would turn her into a squealing, writhing little cherub, curly auburn locks softly caressing his skin as she tried to break free. It's hard to tell if that was why she was her father's favorite, but being a favorite child in a large family didn't mean much, especially after the depression hit. Rose was turning eight that year, and her sixth and seventh siblings had just joined the family. By then the specialness of children had worn a bit thin, not to mention the money, clothes, and free time.

Michael was the oldest in the family. He was the quiet, studious type who did his chores without question but yearned for the hours he could spend behind a book. He could only go to school part-time since his help was needed at home. Both of his parents knew, however, the only way for a young man to make it in this tough new world was to get an education, so they let him go as much as they could.

Second in line was Gertruda, though everyone called her Gerty. She didn't have Rose's beauty, but she was stubborn and clever—two helpful qualities in a large farm family. Gerty was the second mother of the house, and she ran it with precision—something her mother lacked. She resented being the oldest girl. Frequently she had to be in charge of her younger siblings, since her mother always needed help, and Rose seemed to get away from most of the house chores somehow, or at least that's how it seemed to Gerty. Gerty had gone to school through the ninth grade, but once the twins came along she was needed at home; the luxury of school would have to wait.

Rose was number three. She was a rosy-cheeked child with a twinkle in her eyes and a skip in her step, which gave away a spirit that couldn't be suppressed; she wanted to do and learn about everything she came in contact with. After she started walking, she would follow her father around the farm asking him "why?" so many times, he would call out for his wife to take the small urchin before he started to yell. When she was old enough to know about school but too young to go, she would follow Michael as he did his chores, asking for stories about the things he had learned that day at school. She was mesmerized by it all: English, math, science and especially geography; she loved to hear about the places and people from far away. No one knew at the time, but Rose's future was engrained in her very soul.

Next in line were Margaret and Katherine, both of whom were girls with a capitol "G." The twins, Sean and David, were both all boy and kept the girls in the family busy trying to keep them out of trouble. John—number eight in line—was a blessing to the family with his quiet, reserved manner. Child number nine was due in December.

The farm they all grew up on wasn't large—about one hundred acres—consisting of the typical two-story, white farm house, a small barn to house the plow horses, their feed, the dog in the winter, and the passel of wild farm cats every farm is blessed or cursed with, depending on who you talk to. There was a corn crib for animal feed, an out building for equipment, a small chicken coop, and a pen for those years it was profitable to raise pigs. In early twentieth century Wisconsin, when Grandpa Krantz started the farm, it was not the fashion to raise milk cows, so when Rose's father took over the farm he didn't keep cows either, despite most of his neighbors doing so.

Rose's father had worked the farm with his parents, who had spent all they had to purchase it. Grandpa Krantz had come over to "the land of opportunity" on a ship from Germany. He worked in the coalmines of Pennsylvania to earn enough for a down payment on a small farm. He then moved to the harsh, but beautiful southwest Wisconsin rock hills which were told to have reasonably priced land and a good German community to support you. There he met his wife Christine, and as in all good Catholic homes, they started a family. As it turned out, Rose's father Karl ended up being their only living child, so it was assumed he would take over the farm. Karl had wanted to go on to high school and take up a trade, but when he met his beautiful Irish wife, Lilly Rose O'Leary, soon after his father passed, he didn't see a way off the land. It was the fastest way to support a family, and his mother would have been heartbroken if he had tried. So he stayed, married his red-haired beauty, and kept his mother happy with grandchildren in her waning years. Rose's mother Lilly grew up in a large family of mostly girls, so when she met this strong, handsome German she decided she would follow him wherever he went.

Watching Lilly, a person could tell immediately where Rose inherited her spirit. It wasn't from her quiet, no-nonsense father; she received her love of learning from him. Lilly was the well that poured out the spirit into each of her children—some more, some less, but all were left with her watermark. She was also the cog in the family wheel that kept it all going and going with flair. She had a song on her lips and a lightness of heart which made even the most everyday, mundane chores easier to tolerate for everyone. Along with this spirit came a stubbornness which even surpassed her husband's. The Irish were as devout Catholics as the Germans, and they accepted children as blessings from God. But, "Saints preserve us," by child number nine, Lilly had decided the blessing needed to stop, no matter what Father Kelly at St. Mary of the Hills had said.

As Rose grew, so did her love of adventure and the great "out there." Once all her chores were done—the beds made, wood piled in the kitchen, breakfast dishes washed, animals fed—Rose was free to go.

There wasn't much supervision of the older children during their free time—there wasn't the time or the need. If they were old enough to wander off the farm, they were old enough to take care of themselves and each other. So Rose, her best friend Silus, and at times various younger siblings, built forts, found caves, and played cowboys and Indians, like Jack Armstrong on the *All American Boy* radio show. As they matured, so did their games; they became detectives like *Inspector Dawson Haig* in the series *Yu,an Hee See Laughs* from the Prairie du Chien weekly, *The Courier*, which they would snatch up as soon as Rose's father was done with it.

To continue to feed her hunger for knowledge of life beyond the farm, on quiet evenings just before bed, Rose would pull out books on different countries and of different cultures and read well into the night. She would get these books from the small library at her one-room school house or from the larger library in Prairie du Chien. The Prairie librarians, knowing Rose's propensity for these types of books, kept track of new acquisitions and always pointed them out to the extremely appreciative Rose.

Rose's desire to travel was cemented when her school took a trip during their last week of school to the Villa Louis—the stately Dousman family home on Saint Feriole Island in Prairie du Chien. Rose was in eighth grade, and the plan was for her to go onto high school at St. Mary's Academy—an all girl's school in Prairie. She was to go for at least for one year, boarding at an elderly Aunt's in town in exchange for some work around her home. Rose wasn't so keen on the whole idea, and after she visited the ostentatious Dousman home, she lit upon a plan of her own.

It was 1936, and the home had just been opened to the public as a historic landmark. Rose's teacher, Miss Turner, thought it would be a great opportunity for some hands-on learning so close to home, plus a fun trip to celebrate the end of the school year.

The class slowly stepped up to the cream brick, two-story home built in the Italianate style. Miss Turner attempted to gather the young, male stragglers who were still trying to skip stones across the artesian spring-fed pond, which flanked the south side of the house, despite her entreats to the contrary.

The builders of this stylish home had the foresight to use the earthen Indian mound, which was the site for one of the buildings of the first Fort Crawford, which was razed in 1832. This had saved it many times over from being filled with Mississippi mud, unlike the rest of the island. Before 1828 the island had been a bustling community, boasting a firehouse, hotel, school, and grocery store. Now there were only a few old buildings left, besides the large Dousman estate.

The young, exasperated teacher finally herded everyone into the narrow, glassed-in porch, which surrounded more than three-quarters of the first floor. Rose decided the curator, Charles Minney, obviously didn't like children. He never once lost the scowl which seemed to be permanently affixed to his face.

After Miss Turner's threats to the class and assurances to Mr. Minney that no one would touch anything in the home, they were let into the large entry-hall through tall, wooden doors consisting largely of cut glass.

"The first home on this spot was built by Hercules L. Dousman in the early 1840's," Miss Turner explained as the children, including Rose, stood slack jawed at the obvious opulence which surrounded them and that very few in Prairie were accustomed. Most assuredly, everyone in Rose's school either lived on farms, or had parents who made a living with their hands.

"Mr. Dousman worked for and ran the John Jacob Aster Fur Co. in the upper Midwest, though he made most of his money in real estate. He built his home close to the Mississippi River because, at the time, Prairie du Chien was the major fur trading center for the upper Midwest." Miss Turner paused a moment in slight anticipation.

"Does anyone remember what Prairie du Chien means in French?" she asked hopefully.

Rose looked around at her classmates, and after a sufficient silence she spoke up.

"Field of the dog."

Miss Turner smiled knowingly at Rose. It wasn't just the fact that Rose was the oldest in her class—she was to turn sixteen in August—it was that Rose thoroughly enjoyed learning and went out of her way to learn the little details about the subjects Miss Turner taught. She was going to miss Rose.

"This home was build by Hercules' only son, Louis, in 1870 with bricks transported all the way from Milwaukee. He and his wife, Nina, moved here from St. Louis after Louis' mother, Jane, died."

As they wandered from room to room, Rose saw first hand a lifestyle she had only read about in books. It was a beautiful, Victorian style home with many luxuries, such as radiator heat, indoor toilets, and ornately decorated rooms.

Rose couldn't believe what she was seeing. She whispered to her friend Marsha, "There's a fireplace in every room!"

"Louis and Nina," Miss Turner continued, "had five children— four girls and a boy—four of whom are still alive today."

She pointed to the statues which filled the rooms and the richly painted portraits of the various Dousman family members that hung on the patterned, wallpapered walls.

"The two oldest girls, Violet and Virginia, have overseen the renovation, and the gracious donation, of this home to the town of Prairie."

As Miss Turner spoke, Rose marveled at the beautiful furnishings and the life-style that went along with them. There were stables which once held thoroughbred horses, a pool to swim in, a whole separate house to entertain your guests in, with billiards or dancing, and even a small golf course.

At the end of their tour, Rose sat on one of the wicker chairs in the wrap-around porch. She pretended she was reading a book as a maid set a glass of iced lemonade on the table beside her.

"Danka, Margaret," she said to the young German girl, using one of the few German words she had learned from her grandmother.

Rose learned from Miss Turner that the Dousman's frequently brought young foreign girls home from their travels to work in the family home.

Her brother Michael sat a chess board down in front of her.

"You wanna play?" he asked.

"Come along, Rose," Miss Turner cajoled, as she looked at Rose from around the corner of the house, breaking Rose out of her day-dream. Rose didn't play chess, but she imagined the Dousman girls knew how to play. She knew they didn't have animals to feed and clean up after, wood to haul, or dishes to do.

Trailing the class, Miss Turner affectionately put her arm around Rose's shoulder. Rose was going to miss the friendly, young teacher as well.

"Where did the Dousman children go to school?" Rose asked.

"Well, what I've been told is they went to grade school at St. Gabriel's in town, but I think at least Louis went to high school out east."

"I didn't think folks with such style would go to school around here."

"They learned some of that style from their parents. Louis and Nina developed their taste for fine art in St. Louis, where they lived when they were first married," Miss Turner explained.

"I want to visit St. Louis, for sure!" Rose said with a smile of self assurance.

"I'm sure you will, Rose. I'm sure you will," Miss Turner replied with confidence.

As they joined the group on the other side of the pond, Rose glanced at the river just past the mansion. A barge, four sections long and three deep, was moving slowly along the Mississippi. She stopped in mid stride. Her expression brightened even more. *That's how I'll make it to St Louis, I'll stow away on a barge!* Rose thought.

~ ~ ~

Ever since her parents had announced she would be going onto high school, she was trying to think of a way to get out of it. With her somewhat skewed, teenage logic, she had come to the conclusion that once she was in school it wouldn't be long before she would be pushed toward marriage, and Rose wasn't ready for either yet. She also decided, with the ninth sibling on the way the family would be better off with one less mouth to feed. Now she had found her way out. And so the planning began.

The idea was to start out after everyone was asleep, walk to town, and try to steal onto a barge as it docked along the river for supplies. But, like any good adventurer, Rose was flexible and willing to change course when the opportunity for something better presented itself, which it did—fortunately for Rose. Rose thought her barge plan was a good one, but being a young girl, she had no idea of the position she would have been putting herself in on a barge run by men who tended to be rowdy and unkempt.

Rose knew a little about barge life from a few men who had worked on barges and had come by the farm looking for work. One of the few times Rose sat still, other than to read, was when they had visits from these passersby. Her mother always seemed to find a little something extra to share with these poor ramblers, despite Karl's feeble objections. "It was the Lord's way" she would frequently say (though Lilly stressed the Lord and family came before strangers, and in that order). Most if these men would oblige a cute, young girl's questions about their travels. After these visitors had stopped, Rose would dream for many nights and imagine many games with her friends, of these curious and strange places.

Her plans changed, however, when she read an ad in *The Courier.*

Friday, June 14th
Capitol Steamer De Luxe
"Pride of the Mississippi"
featuring: Sidney's 11-Piece Novelty Dance Band
"Mississippi Serenaders"
in the Dreamy, Rainbow Dancing Palace
Tickets—75 cents
Prairie Du Chien 8:30   McGregor 9:30

Just below the ad for passengers was another looking for help. *That would be even better,* Rose thought. *I wouldn't have to worry about being caught, and I could earn a little money along the way!* Rose wrote down the name of the steamer company and the person she was to ask for and stuffed the paper into the breast pocket of her overalls. She would make the call in town when she went to sell eggs that next Saturday. She couldn't take the risk of making the call from home since the operator on the party line, and most likely some of her neighbors, would listen in and spoil her plans.

~ ~ ~

When Rose had turned nine her father felt she was old enough to take on a little more responsibility, so she was put in charge of the chickens. With this new responsibility came the benefit of going along to town every Saturday to sell the eggs. Her father gave her a small share of the profit, which allowed her to put a little money in the bank and keep the rest for an occasional show in town with friends, or to buy ice cream at *Prairie Dairy,* the town creamery, for the two favorite men in her life: her father and Michael. When Saturday arrived, the three left for town as usual. That is when Rose set her new plan in motion

They set up their egg stand at the corner of Blackhawk and Minnesota Streets, right in front of the *Prairie City Bank.* Since the family kept their money there, the manager didn't mind Mr. Krantz setting up shop out front. Karl liked this spot, because most folks came to the bank on Saturday to do their financial business and would easily pick up a dozen fresh eggs with the little extra change in their pocket.

"Dad, I have to go to the bathroom," Rose suddenly declared.

"That's fine, Sweet Pea," was his only reply, as he continued to take the eggs out of the wooden crate.

Rose headed for the gas station two blocks away. She knew they had a pay phone there she could use. She opened up the door to the phone booth and stepped inside. She reached inside her overalls and pulled out the well-worn piece of paper with the steamer company name and contact on it. She looked at it again, though she really didn't need to; she pretty much had it memorized. Just looking at the piece of paper would start her imagining all the exotic places she would go and all the interesting people she would meet there.

After the operator put her through, Rose spoke with a woman at the Streckfus Steamer Company in St. Louis. She was told to be at Feriole Island at three in the afternoon that next Friday with a reference in hand, to meet Mrs. Baas.

"Reference, how am I going to get a reference?" Rose asked herself. On top of that, Rose wasn't really sure what a reference was. Now she really *did* have to go to the bathroom.

As she sat on the toilet in the small, white-tiled room, all kinds of thoughts went through her pretty little head. Getting away from the house wouldn't be that hard, but she'd have to think of some way to bring a few extra clothes with her. Then there was the walk into town. It would take a while, but she knew the way; that would be a piece of cake. It was the reference she was worried about. She would have to figure it out later—she had to get back to the egg stand.

"Why were you gone so long, Miss Rose?" her father asked.

"Oh, they were working on a real neat car in the garage, and I kinda got caught up watchin'em work."

This excuse seemed plausible to her father since Rose would stand and watch him many times, or even help, while he fixed the truck or house generator. For a girl, she had a surprising interest in engines.

When her father stood up for a short walk to stretch his legs, Rose got Michael to explain to her what a reference was. She even managed to get him to write one up for her later that evening. She hoped that would be good enough. Rose was unusually quiet the rest of the afternoon and on the way home. Her father was concerned about Rose's unusual silence and asked her if there was something wrong. His questioning brought her back to reality and away from her plans to get on the boat.

Rose didn't want to alert her father to anything, so she asked him about the Fort Crawford surgeon William Beaumont, and his digestive experiments on the American Fur Company employee who was accidentally shot in the side. It was an interesting story, because the wound healed in such a way as to leave a hole for the good doctor to insert small sacks of various foods into the man's stomach, then remove them a while later and record what he had found. Rose liked this story because it was kind of disgusting and interesting all at once.

Karl was a history buff, and Rose knew he would go on for hours about the local history. Rose had heard many a time how Nicolas Perrot established a trading post there in 1685, making it the second oldest white settlement in Wisconsin's history.

The doctor is story was the perfect distraction. Nothing more had to be said.

Rose began mulling over her plans again as they bounced along the gravel road toward home. The more she thought about it, the more unsure she became that she could pull this off without someone finding out—especially Michael and Silus.

~ ~ ~

As Rose was walking home on one of the last days of school, Silus started asking questions. It was one of those unusually warm spring days, the afternoon sun heating their backs as they walked slowly along. They had taken off their shoes to let their toes stretch out in the tender new grass. Rose much preferred being barefoot and was glad for the opportunity to start to toughen up her feet for the coming summer. She rarely wore shoes in the summer— only on Sundays or for special occasions like birthdays or funerals. Rose's mind was wandering as they walked, not thinking about her feet but the plans for her departure. Silus woke her out of these musings by asking her a question.

"Somethin' the matter, Rose? You've been awfully quiet lately."

"Nah, I was just wondrin' what I'm gonna do this summer, is all," Rose replied, telling a half truth.

Rose had to be extra careful with Silus since he was the first to know when she was lying. Besides, some of her brothers and sisters were walking home with them, and she didn't want to let on anything to them either.

Rose knew she had to execute her plan soon after the school term was over, or Silus would figure out what was going on.

~ ~ ~

It was a warm, lazy afternoon the day of Rose's departure. Rose stood just inside the kitchen screen door, looking out at the hazy scene the screen created. There wasn't a cloud in the clear blue sky, and the cicadas were singing an early summer song promising more sun and heat in the days ahead. Her Mother was at the line hanging laundry. The sheets and clothes were taking up the warm breeze, floating easily on the currents and casting an undulating, muted light on the woman standing there in her simple work dress and apron. The four-year-old, John, lay underneath in the grass, giggling as he swatted at the clothes which playfully moved above his head.

Rose's stomach was full from dinner—the midday meal was always the big meal of the day at the Krantz farm—so she was ready for her long trek into town. But as she stood there, stomach distended, eyes wide in anticipation, she decided her second helping of potato salad probably wasn't the best idea. Her stomach was trying to decide, along with her heart, if this trip was the right thing to do. Rose had to finish her goodbyes, and it wasn't going to be easy.

She stepped through the screen door, listening to the drawn-out squeak as the spring stretched out to accommodate the passer by, then the slap of wood meeting wood as it quickly pulled the door back into place. Rose had never really paid much attention to the sound before, but today she opened and closed the door with a touch more purpose than usual. This was in contrast to the normal way she left the house: flying out the door, anxious to get out of the house and onto better things.

Rose stood on the edge of the porch. Max, the family dog, was at her feet looking up expectantly, waiting for the signal that they were heading out. Rose felt his head nudge her leg. She looked down and smiled at the large, black, furry mass she lovingly called "Bear". She called him this because his small, dark brown eyes and short snout reminded her of a real black bear. She knelt down, setting the bundle she had prepared for the trip next to her and dug her hands into the soft, black fur around his neck. She had so many great times with that dog. He was a constant companion on any of her jaunts away from the house.

Rose looked up and out over the farm yard. She saw her father—tall, thin, and well built; and Michael—just as tall, but a bit stockier, his muscles less defined. They were standing by a large pile of wood; cutting it up for her mother to use in the kitchen stove. They had their shirts off and their bodies gleamed with sweat, even in the shade of the barn where they were working.

Early summer wasn't the best time to cut wood, but it had been a particularly cold winter, and they had gone through more wood than usual, so they didn't have much choice. Rose had helped her father drag the logs to the yard the day before with their horse, Tucker, and she wished she was helping them now. Her plans were looking a little less enticing right at the moment.

Rose stood and picked up her bundle. She adjusted the cap on her head, took a deep breath to prop up her courage and harden her resolve, and stepped off the porch into the sunshine of the day. She had no way of knowing she wouldn't be seeing that porch again for some time to come.

~ ~ ~

Rose walked over to her mother first, taking a moment to bend down to tease her brother, John. She straightened up and stood looking at her mother. Her back was to Rose as she worked in that very familiar yellow calico dress and apron. Rose noticed how beautiful she was: trim and neatly dressed, not in new clothes or shoes, but always clean and neat. Her hair was the prettiest shade of red, cut just below her shoulders, with the same wave Rose struggled with each morning. But her mother's hair always seemed to sit nicely in place or was easily pulled up when working in a hot kitchen. Rose didn't inherit that gift, despite Gerty's attempts at training her to style it. Gerty, Margaret and Kate would spend hours trying to put up each other's hair in different styles. Rose would look over Gerty's shoulder while Gerty studied the outdated fashion magazines her girlfriends shared, but Rose just didn't understand what all the fuss was about. And when Gerty offered to put up her hair, or paint her nails, she would run out of the room as quick as she could.

"I'm heading over to Marsha's, Mom."

Rose stepped closer and gave her Mother a sudden, awkward hug. Lilly blinked and froze for a moment. Rose was not one to show physical affection, and she was just staying overnight at a friend's. She held Rose away from her by her shoulders, looking into her face with a questioning glance. Perhaps her tomboy was starting to grow up. She took advantage of the unusual mood and pulled Rose back in close.

"Well, you be havin' yourself a good time, Miss Rose, and behave like the young lady I know ya are," she said in her soft, Irish brogue. "You must be rememberin' you're a guest in their home. Ya need to be polite," Lilly finished, squeezing Rose across the shoulders before she let go.

Rose smiled at her mother. "I will, Mom."

Rose didn't resist the contact as she might normally have done; she drank in the softness of her mother's body and subtle scent of Lilly of the Valley, which her mother always wore—her one indulgence. A scent which, in the past, she would only get a hint of in the small moments her mother would grab her as a young girl to give her a quick squeeze, or when she pulled her close to her side as they sat on Rose's bed at the end of the day. Rose always looked forward to this time of day; it was her special time when she had her mother all to herself. That was when her mother would always say, "Tell me about your ramblin', Miss Rose."

Gerty may have been Lilly's savior at home, but Rose was her wings. Watching Rose, Lilly saw her own reflection of many years ago. She enjoyed watching herself through Rose's eyes; discovering the wonders that "God put on this good, green earth," as Lilly would say. Gerty wasn't mistaken when she felt Rose got away with things; both her mother and father held Rose with loose reins.

Rose turned, rustled John's hair, and walked toward her father and Michael. She let out a sigh of relief; her mother hadn't questioned her somewhat uncharacteristic behavior, but this next goodbye would not be so easy.

"Wow, you guys are working hard; you've got quite a bit done already," Rose commented, trying to act casual.

They stopped what they were doing and looked up, welcome for the small break.

"Where you off to, Munchkin?" Michael asked, eyeing the parcel she was carrying.

"Oh, I'm staying over at Marsha's tonight," she replied, looking down and kicking the gravel at her feet.

Rose was silent for a moment, not knowing what to do next. She knew she wouldn't see them for a while, and she didn't want to go away without hugging them, so she decided she just had to do it. She reached out to her brother and grabbed him around the middle as quickly as she could, then she let go, ran around to the other side of the wood pile where her father stood, and grabbed him around the middle too.

"Well, I never," was all her father could say, a bit befuddled. Each evening Rose would give her father a good night kiss on the cheek, but rarely did he get a hug out of her. Karl was a man of few words and not outwardly affectionate himself, so he didn't say anything else as Rose released her grasp.

"Well, I gotta go," Rose said abruptly; then she turned quickly and walked away, not wanting to look at either of them for fear they would question her about what had just happened. Karl and Michael looked at each other in bewilderment. Karl went right back to what he was doing, but Michael turned to watched Rose walk up the drive. That was a little too odd for him to shrug off so easily. Then he noticed she was wearing shoes. He wasn't sure what she was up to, but he knew his sister well enough to know something was going on. He assumed he would find out about it later. What he didn't know was, it wouldn't be until much later and under circumstances which neither he nor Rose could have ever predicted.

~ ~ ~

As Rose headed down the driveway, Max ran quickly past her. Rose called the dog back and made him sit down in front of her. She had one more goodbye to go. She had said goodbye to Gerty, Margaret, Katherine, and the twins earlier. She was surprised at the strange desire she had to hug her siblings, but she couldn't get herself to do it. It would be too out of character and make Gerty suspicious. Rose just told them she was staying at a friend's and that she would see them later. Not that they cared much, but Rose wanted to say something to all of them before she left. The last to go was Max. Rose knelt down in front of him, setting her bundle on the ground. She took the dog's head in her hands and looked into his soft, brown eyes.

"Now Bear, where I am going you can't come. I need you to look after the family for me. You're in charge of that now. I'm going away for a while, but I'll be back before you know it," she said, looking at him seriously.

She bent further down and gave him a hug. Max wasn't use to that either, but he didn't mind. He didn't move a muscle.

"You stay, Max," Rose commanded as she stood up and motioned with her hand for him to stay.

"Stay!" she said firmly; then she turned and walked away.

Rose had taught Max many tricks and "stay" was one of them, so he dutifully sat there as Rose walked out of the end of the driveway and out of sight. A few moments later, he slowly jogged to the end of the driveway and laid down next to the road.

❧ 2 ☙

'Ignorance is bliss.' It is a well worn phrase which is most notably true when you are a teenager on your first real venture away from home. But unfortunately, that also means the inevitable opening of one's eyes to the sometimes harsh reality of the way things really are, and *that* can change a person forever. How far we fall, how well we bounce is never known until we get there. It's one of those prayers parents say to themselves each time their child steps out the door: have I prepared them well; will they know what to do? No one could tell Rose what was ahead for her or how she would react to it. She wouldn't have believed them if they had.

~ ~ ~

Rose's friend Marsha lived on the way to Prairie du Chien, so it wouldn't look strange to anyone that Rose was walking in that direction. But it felt a little strange to Rose as she came up to their long driveway only to walk on past. She looked behind her, sure someone must have discovered her plan and was standing there ready to drag her home. She looked out over the dry, empty, gravel road. When no one appeared, she sighed and turned back toward town.

"Well, this is it," Rose said as she took one large step past the drive and started toward town. "I'm headin' to St. Louie!"

She was half excited, half hoping someone from her family would have shown up. Her lie was sitting uncomfortably, right next to the potato salad, and both were coming up for a vote.

The sun and the walk were warming Rose as a bead of sweat rolled down the side of her face, so she stopped under the shade of a large oak tree to rest a minute.

Crawford County was a beautiful place: steep hills and deep valleys bunched close together, preserved this way for thousands of years after the glaciers had missed this small area in the upper Midwest, in a time so long ago. Those hills and valleys often had a farm nestled inside them, or perched on top of them, with farm fields framed by rows of trees and rocks. Cattle dotted the landscape, most of whom were now lying down or standing in the shade of a tree, as Rose was doing. Not that Rose really appreciated what she saw. It was all she knew, so it's quiet beauty passed without a gaze. She did, however, appreciate the shade of the tree and the support its rough trunk gave her back as she rested her head against it. She was getting a little sleepy in the warmth of the day, so she lifted her head and gave it a small shake.

Rose took off her cap, set in on the ground next to her and opened her bundle, pulling out an oatmeal cookie which her Mother, Gerty and Margaret had made the day before.

Cooking was one of many things her mother had tried to teach Rose. It wasn't that she couldn't do it—she just wasn't interested in learning how. Eventually, to Rose's satisfaction, Lilly gave up trying. But Rose surely enjoyed whatever food was put in front of her. These oatmeal cookies were one of her favorites. She savored the sweet, dry taste in her mouth. Rose didn't dally too long, however; she knew she had to make it to town by three. She wrapped up her bundle, flipped on her cap, and finished her cookie on the way to town.

The road to Prairie followed a ridge which eventually wound its way due west to a stretch that went straight down to the river basin. As she got closer to town, the hills closed in on each side of her, with a creek following close on one side and a rough, limestone rock wall on the other. When Rose approached town, she could see the flat land which spread out from the tall, tree covered bluffs on each side of her. The east edge of town hadn't spread out to the bluff yet; it ended a couple short blocks west of the rail road tracks at Ohio Street, less than a quarter of a mile in front of her. But the land from Ohio Street to the river was filled with buildings and homes. The road that she took to town was very familiar to Rose; she had ridden on it many times with her father and Michael. If they turned right on New York Street they were off to the cannery. If they stayed straight on Bluff they were going to the bank, the creamery, or the garage.

Once in town, the county road she was on became Blackhawk Street. Not too long ago, the town had changed the name of the street from Bluff to Blackhawk. Rose figured they did this to try and take advantage of the history of the area, though she never quite understood why they wanted to be remembered for the massacre of the Sauk Indian tribe. Rose could never quite get used to the name change anyway. It was always Bluff to her.

As she walked into town there wasn't as much of a breeze as there had been up on the ridge, and Rose began to sweat even more. She took off her cap and pulled her handkerchief out of her back pocket to wipe her forehead. Then she stuffed her hair up underneath the cap as she put it back on her head. She had wanted her mother to cut her hair shorter, but her mother had told her, "No girl of Lilly Krantz is gonna to be lookin' like a boy." And there was no arguing with her mother.

Today Bluff Street wasn't as busy as on the weekends, but surely, Rose thought, someone she knew would stop and question why she was in town all by herself. So Rose pulled her cap lower on her forehead and only looked up when she was crossing a street.

The first building she came to was the gas station where she had made that fateful phone call to set this all in motion. On the other side of the street, just a block off Bluff, was the bakery which she loved to stop at. They always had a piece of cookie or doughnut they were willing to give a polite, young girl. Unfortunately, she didn't have time for that today. The clock on the Peoples State Bank said two-fourty. She had to keep going. Bluff went straight west down to the river, passing over a small canal which separated and created Saint Feriole Island, or as it was called locally: the Fourth Ward. She passed by The Metro movie house. There was an Andy Hardy movie playing, with Mickie Rooney as the star. Rose decided she wanted to see that one. The Prairie Creamery was across the way, as was the fire department. And just before Main Street, on the right, was her favorite haunt: the town library.

After Rose crossed Main Street she could smell the river—that distinctive wet, green smell of a large amount of water. First she came up to the canal, stopping for a brief moment to look over the edge of the small wooden bridge. The water was a bit browner than she remembered. It looked like watered down milk chocolate. A few men sat or stood just below the bridge fishing. Rose didn't dally long. Keeping due west she headed straight for the river.

It wasn't but a minute before she noticed the white rails and posts of the large paddle wheeler, Capitol, moored just across from the old Dousman Hotel. The Capitol was the largest remaining stern paddle wheeler on the river, measuring 256 feet in length and 50 feet wide, with large, red paddles which ran the length of her stern. She was a four story vessel, mostly white. It had gingerbread above the walkways and shapely, flat wood rails below. The second floor was partially enclosed with windows, which were open to try and catch the afternoon breeze. The third deck was an observation deck. It was partially covered on each side by five large life boats—the only excursion boat at the time to have such a feature. Just above of this deck was another closed—in area which was narrower and shorter than the decks below. Rose found out later, it was a second cafeteria and could be heated on cold spring or fall nights. There was also an eating area and cafeteria on the first deck. The fifth floor—the Texas deck—was smaller still. This was were some of the crew were quartered. It was enclosed except for the small windows which ran along each side, one for each small cabin. It was topped with a square, domed pilot's house with an ornately designed roof which peaked in the middle like a Middle Eastern tent. The engine pipes were tall and black and stuck out of the Texas deck in front of the pilot house with dark, gray smoke gently billowing out of their ornate tops.

Rose beamed. It was the most amazing boat she had ever seen—at least at that moment. She had rarely seen bigger vessels pass by the island on their family excursions to town and seeing one up close—one she would soon be working on—made it larger than life. The excitement made her pick up her pace.

~ ~ ~

It was a few minutes before three when she stepped anxiously onto the wide, metal gang plank held in place by a thick cable and boom attached to metal rigging on the bow of the boat. The boat looked huge up close.

People were very busy on board the paddle wheeler—moving things here; tightening things there. Rose stood on the deck thinking someone would notice her and help her out, but when no one did, she picked out a gentleman who looked fairly friendly and asked him where she could find Mrs. Baas.

"Mrs. Baas?" the man replied in a strange Southern accent, "Don't know no Mrs. Baas," he continued in a belligerent tone.

Rose pressed on. "I answered an ad in the paper for help and was told to meet Mrs. Baas on the boat at three o'clock. I think they said she's the cook."

The man finally looked at her with a vague look of understanding.

"Oh, you mean Grandma B. She's down there," he answered, pointing down the side of the boat. Then he went right back to work.

Rose thought she better not bother this fellow for any more details. It appeared to Rose that he needed a nap. She tentatively stepped around him. *Grandma B.*—that was a nice thought, working for someone's grandmother. She walked up to a large, mahogany staircase in the front of the boat with shiny brass kick plates along its whole length. There was a placard at the top with the name of the boat carved into it painted in gold letters. Just behind the staircase was the coatroom. Rose stepped tentatively around the coat room, the fuel bunkers, and the large boilers that supplied the steam to the engines in the stern of the vessel. She came to an open area which was filled with tables and folding chairs, called the Green Room. Boxed ferns decorated the middle of the room with paper lanterns and ceiling fans overhead. On the opposite side of the room she could see a cafeteria line where passengers could buy food. She had never seen anything like it, and she wasn't exactly sure what it was. She would find out later that the Capital was the first steamer to employ such a service, modeled after a restaurant in New York City—the Streckfus family was always looking for ways to incorporate modern improvements on their boats. A big grin spread over Rose's face as she gazed at the spectacle. *Silus would never believe this*, she thought to herself. She could hardly believe it herself. She took a deep breath and made her way toward the back of the boat.

Just before the engine room was a doorway which was open and busy with men carrying wooden boxes of fresh vegetables, cheeses, fruits and glass bottles of wine and beer. It was obviously the kitchen; there was food stacked everywhere there was a free space. Rose could see that the room ran about thirty-five feet long, and was a touch wider than her own kitchen at home. There was a large gas stove on the left side of the room, with six burners, four ovens and a stainless-steel counter on each side which held pans of freshly baked buns. Along the front of the burners ran a stainless steel counter, approximately twelve feet long with a small, steel counter perched above it along the front edge. There was shelving below this where the aluminum and blue-enameled cookware was stored. On the right wall was shelving where metal cans or glass jars of dry goods were kept, with more counter space below. This is where some girls were currently busy working. In the far end of the kitchen—separated by what appeared to Rose was a large ice box—was where the dishes were washed and kept. A large man, as dark as pitch, stood working at two large stainless-steel sinks cleaning out some pots. He was sweating profusely, or maybe it was dish water which dripped from his face. Rose couldn't quite tell.

The people who were unpacking boxes of fruits and vegetables and moving things about were all young women—young colored women. They were all thin looking. Some were short and some tall, but all were wearing short-sleeved, calf-length house dresses and white aprons. They appeared to vary in age from about her sister Katie's age—eleven years—to Gerty's seventeen.

Someone tapped Rose on the shoulder. "Excuse me," the young girl said.

Rose stepped into the room to get out of her way. "Oh, sorry," Rose replied.

The girl quietly stepped passed Rose with obvious disinterest.

Where was Mrs. Baas? Rose wondered. Again, no one stopped what they were doing to help her. The youngest of the girls looked up her from her work emptying crates and stared at Rose. She didn't smile or seem very approachable, so Rose decided she should speak to someone a little older. She walked up to the young lady who was folding white napkins. Rose noticed how the napkins looked extra white against her very black hands. Rose cleared her throat.

"Umm, could you please direct me to Mrs. Baas, I mean Grandma B.," she said, correcting herself, not wanting to make that mistake again.

"Grandma B.!" The young lady yelled over her shoulder so loudly, it made Rose wince.

"What you want, girl?" a deeper voice yelled back as a small woman stepped out from behind a stack of crates.

Rose's eyes widened as she looked at the short, thin, black women who stood somewhat stooped in front of her. She was wearing a house dress similar to the one Rose's mother wore, except the calico pattern was more faded. Her skin was a medium, cocoa brown and looked smooth and soft in places, but a bit like it was over-sized for the wearer—hanging from under her arms and chin. Her large breasts didn't seem to fit her small frame either. They sagged almost to her waist. It took Rose a moment to remember why she was there.

"You must be Mrs. Baas," Rose declared as she stuck out her hand in greeting.

Mrs. Baas ignored the gesture.

"Did da boat company done send ya?" she asked, looking Rose up and down as if she were buying a piece of used furniture.

"Yes, ma'am. My name is Rose Krantz," she replied with a smile.

The smile was not reciprocated. Mrs. Baas just looked straight at Rose with a pair of tired, deep set, brown eyes.

"Good! Da last joker dat come in here thought he could just waltz right in without talkin' to da boat company first. Don't take no men in my kitchen 'sceptin' Jeb here," she explained, gesturing to the man washing a large kettle. "Dey sees ta dat."

Then she turned and waddled slowly away on her thin, bowed legs. Rose's arms dropped to her side. She stood staring at this small lady walking away from her. Mrs. Baas looked even shorter and thinner from the back. Rose would have thought she was a child, except she was slightly bent over and had quite a few gray hairs mingled with the black. Mrs. Baas finally turned her head slightly and looked at Rose out of the corner of her eye.

"You comin', girl?"

Rose quickly stepped up next to the old woman.

"Ya's ever worked in a kitchen befo?" Mrs. Baas asked.

"Just at home, ma'am."

Mrs. Baas turned around quickly and gave Rose a stern, squinty look.

"Now listen here girlie, ya'll can stop callin' me ma'am. I ain't nobodies ma'am. Call me Gram'ma B. like everyone else do, ya hear!" she ordered, shaking her thin, bony finger at Rose.

"Yes, ma'am, I mean Grandma B. I have a reference right here."

Rose fumbled to get the piece of paper out of her breast pocket and show it to the grumpy old woman.

"Reaference, I don't need no reaferance. That's for dem city folks at da boat company. I can tells if a person's any good by da look in der eyes."

At that, she squinted at Rose, coming uncomfortably close to her face.

"Dat's where ya can see a person's soul, deep in der eyes."

Then she stepped away from Rose, appearing satisfied.

"It looks like you're an okay sort a girl. You ben brought up right, dough you ain't seen much, dat much I can tells, but dat's all da better," she chattered on. "You got somethin' else ta wear besides dem overalls? I'll be needin ya ta go out and serve the folks once day get here, and ya can't be wearing no overalls and cap."

She turned away from Rose with a small grin on her face. "Won't day be surprised ta see a white girl servin'em," she said under her breath.

"You mean I got the job?"

"I wouldn't be askin' 'bout your clothes 'cause I care how your mama dress ya!"

"Yes, ma'am, Sorry…Grandma B., I brought one of my church dresses, just in case."

As they were talking, one of the girls in the kitchen timidly stepped up to Grandma B.

"What you want, Lavenia?" Grandma B. snapped.

"Somebody's here askin' 'bout da job."

"Tell'em it done been filled." Grandma B. turned her attention back to Rose.

"Why don't you go puts da dress on den. Da toilet's out dat door and up dem steps. Right next ta da soda fountain," Grandma B. said, pointing to the door Rose had first walked through. "Don't ya dawdle none; ders a lot dats needin' ta be done yet 'fore da paying folk arrive."

Rose turned and headed out the kitchen door and up the narrow steps on the side of the boat which led up to the main ballroom. This deck was more open than the room below, with the supports off to each side, leaving forty feet or so totally free of obstructions—perfect for dancing. The soda fountain at the back of the room ran the width of the boat, with an opening on each side for the men's and women's toilets. Right in front of this, facing the room, was a large staircase which led to the third deck. The dance floor was made of light-colored, wood planks that shined from a new polishing, and there were wooden benches all along both sides of the long room, just under the windows. The dance floor had Japanese silk lanterns down its center, and on each side, ceiling fans, which Rose would find were a God-send on hot evenings when the dance floor was full of people. In the middle of the room on the left was an area boxed in by railings where the black musicians were setting up their instruments. At the far end of the ballroom, on each side, were counters where patrons could buy candy and popcorn on one side, or cigars and cigarettes on the other. At the head of the mahogany steps, which Rose had first spied when she stepped onto the steamer, was a small area canopied by a color–filled dome, held up by six white pillars—a fitting entrance to the rainbow dance floor.

Rose viewed the expansive scene in haste. She didn't want to get Grandma B. more perturbed than she already was. Rose thought she seemed like an okay sort of lady and probably quite pretty at one time, but she wondered if everyone on this boat needed a nap. Grandma B. sure wasn't like either of her own grandmothers. Her grandmothers were always smiling, wanting affection, and readily giving out something good to eat. Rose realized she wasn't at home anymore, that was for sure.

The women's room was all white, like most of the rest of the boat, with eight toilets enclosed in stalls and small windows above. The sinks were opposite this, built into a long counter with a stool in font of each sink, and an ornate, gold mirror hanging over the top, which seemed a bit out of place. Rose was surprised to find that the toilets weren't flushed with water, they just emptied onto the large paddles and the river below. Rose changed in a flash, then stuffed her overalls and cap in her bundle. She stopped to look at herself in the mirror, flattening down her hair as best she could. It was cut in a bob for the summer, so the curls tended to make it stand out from her head. She frowned at her reflection, disappointed she couldn't wear her cap.

She made her way back to the kitchen and started searching for Grandma B. again. Grandma B. found her.

"Der you is." Grandma B. stopped and stared at Rose. "Girl!" she declared, looking at Rose as if she just stepped out of a flying saucer. "What did you done do witch your hair? We has ta do somthin' 'bout dat later. Here, put on dis here apron." She handed Rose a crisp, white apron, like all the other girls were wearing. "I needs ya ta cut da cheese."

The other girls snickered at Grandma B.'s statement as Rose would normally have done had she not been so afraid of who had said it.

Grandma B. instructed Rose how she wanted the cheese cut just so, then abruptly left to continue with other preparations. It wasn't long, however, before Rose heard Grandma B. yell out.

"Damn! Dose boys ain't no good for nuthin'. I done told'em ta get me my roast, and days done bring me a turkey. Dat ain't no good. I can't use no turkey. Does roustabouts don't know der head from a howe in da ground."

Rose turned and was staring at her in wide-eyed amazement. She had never heard a woman swear before.

"Girlie, what's your name agin?" she asked, pointing at Rose.

"Rose, ma'am," she said, forgetting Grandma B.'s instructions because of the tone in her voice.

"Didn't I tell ya ta call me Gram'ma B.?" she asked, shaking her head. "Never mind. Come over here. Take dis here turkey and give it ta Peta. He's standin' out der somewheres. Tell'em I need a beef roast not no turkey. Go on now, git. I ain't got time for dis nonsense!"

She pointed Rose to the door after dropping the big, cold, semi-wrapped bird in her arms, grumbling indistinguishably.

Rose stepped out of the kitchen door, looked up and down the side of the boat, but she didn't see anyone. Then she spied a group of young men standing on shore. They looked up from their conversation as she made her way toward them.

"Are one of you Peter?" Rose asked without hesitation.

"I'm Peter," a stocky, blond-haired young man said with a smile. "And who might *you* be?"

"I'm Rose. Grandma B. wants you to take this back to the butcher shop, and get her a beef roast instead. And you better hurry up," Rose added, placing the bird in his arms. "She's not in a very good mood!"

"I ain't afraid of that old, black biddy," he said with a sneer. "She's always in a bad mood. But you…" he continued, smiling and stepping closer, "*you* I like."

He put the turkey easily under one arm, reached up and touched Rose's hair. Rose didn't even hesitate; she came down hard on the front of Peter's foot, and when he bent over from the sudden, unexpected assault, she flicked the underside of his nose, sending his head up and back—a little trick she had learned from the boys back home.

The other young men stood around Peter laughing, but he wasn't amused. His white-hot stare seared the back of Rose's head as she turned smartly and walked away.

"I'll get back at that pretty one, one way or another," he said under his breath.

~ ~ ~

Once back in the kitchen, Rose went back to her work quite sure of herself for what she had done. *He won't bother me again*, she thought to herself. *Imagine that, touching my hair*. No boy she ever knew at home would ever try such a thing, and she was sure this guy wouldn't try it again either.

About a half hour before the boat was to leave the dock, passengers started arriving. One of the kitchen girls was standing in the doorway which looked out onto the walkway down the side of the boat, so Rose thought she could take a chance and have a look. Rose had caught this girl's eye a few times while they worked in the kitchen. She had a strange feeling that she had met her somewhere before, but she knew she couldn't have; she rarely saw colored folks in town. She figured, at the very least, they would become friends.

She stood behind the girl, looking over her head as best she could, not saying a thing. They couldn't see much, since the passengers moved quickly out of sight and up the stairs to the dance floor above them. The young girl finally noticed Rose was standing behind her, and she looked a little annoyed.

"I gotta go pee," she yelled passed Rose back into the kitchen.

"Then hurry up, girl!" Grandma B. yelled back.

The young girl looked silently at Rose, smirked and quickly left the room.

"I have to go too," Rose called back to Grandma B.

Grandma B. shook her head, disgusted.

"Go on den."

When Rose stepped up to the dance floor, the young girl was standing next to the staircase that led to the third deck looking out at the crowd. Couples were sitting or standing while they talked and laughed with each other. Rose stared intently; her attention was strangely drawn to the women and what they were wearing. Her mother wore nice dresses to church each Sunday, but not as nice as what these ladies wore. These ladies had on calf-length dresses in muted colors of predominantly tan, burgundy, or gray, with soft, light fabric which flowed gently as they moved. Some had padded shoulders that stuck out further than their real shoulders obviously did.

Their hair was also done up. The prevailing style was short, with a side part laid tightly against their heads, and curls at the bottom or wavy all the way down. Rose particularly liked the ladies who wore hats. Her Mother's fedora hat was plain compared to what these ladies had on. Many wore hats which fit snuggly on their heads, with a petite brim that sliced diagonally across their forehead and a smart ribbon and bow for style. They looked more like the ladies in Gerty's fashion magazines. When these ladies sat, they sat on the edge of their seats, legs crossed, while they drank colorful drinks and talked with the handsomely dressed gentlemen in suits and ties.

"I'd give anything to be sitting in there," Rose said out loud. The young girl turned and looked at Rose. She was a pretty girl, Rose thought, with lighter-colored eyes than Grandma B., but the same medium brown skin, which—unlike Grandma B.—fit her just fine. Rose figured she was about fourteen or so. Her hair was cut short, and from this close Rose could see the tight curls. She had the strange inclination to reach out and touch it; it looked so springy.

"Maybe you, but not me!" the young girl replied. "I don't see no colored folks on dis here boat 'ceptin us who's does the work, dat is."

Rose hadn't really noticed before, but she was right. None of the people she saw in that room were black. Rose's cheeks turned a light pink, and she hastily changed the subject.

"I'm Rose, what's your name?"

"Lilly Mae," the girl replied in a small, mousy voice.

"Hey, that's my mother's name! But she's Irish and doesn't put the Mae on the end of it. I live just a few miles up in those hills. I took this job because I wanted to see some other towns besides Prairie before I had to go on to high school. Where are you from?" Rose rattled off.

"I'm from Na Orlins."

"New Orleans," Rose's eyes widened. "I'd love to visit New Orleans! How come you're so far away from home?"

"I got eight brothers and sisters, and I'm the oldest, so I had ta take dis here job ta help my Mama out."

"Doesn't your daddy work?"

"My daddy ain't around no mo'," she answered, looking down at the ground.

Rose had done it again. This time it was a little harder taking her foot out of her mouth, and it left a bitter aftertaste on top of it.

"Oh. Sorry," was all she could think to say.

Rose was rescued from misspeaking a third time by the yell of Grandma B., calling them both back to the kitchen. Once back at work, Rose was pleasantly surprised how she enjoyed talking with Lilly Mae. She didn't usually like talking with other girls much, but Lilly Mae wasn't like most of the girls Rose knew—she was different somehow, but Rose wasn't quite sure how. It took a while before Lilly Mae relaxed a bit and actually spoke more than a word or two in reply. That didn't seem to bother Rose though; she just kept talking and asking her questions until finally Lilly Mae offered a little information of her own. It turned out Lilly Mae was actually sixteen and had been working on excursion boats up and down the Mississippi for over three years. She captured Rose's attention on that fact alone. Rose was eager to find out about the river-boat towns she had visited, especially St. Louis and her home town of New Orleans.

And for some reason, working in Grandma B.'s kitchen didn't seem as bad as working in the kitchen at home. Grandma B. sang as she worked, just like her mother always did, so it made her feel more at home. Music was a staple of the Krantz–O'Leary home. Her mother had taught the children to sing as well. When the family, minus Karl of course, preformed *Amazing Grace* at special church services, there wasn't a dry eye in the place. Mostly though, her mother liked to sing Irish tunes from her childhood like *Just a Little Bit of Heaven* or *Tis Irish I Am*.

The songs Grandma B. sang were different. Most of them were religious songs, but with a sorrowful feeling and a melody which was unlike anything Rose had ever heard at St. Mary's. They made Rose want to move and hum along.

~ ~ ~

The evening flew by all too quickly. Rose would steal a minute or two, when Grandma B. was distracted, to watch the couples dance and the band play. Rose discovered then why they called it the Rainbow Dance Floor; as the musicians played, hidden lights all around the room slowly changed color. It was a magical effect.

The music was similar to the big band music her mother and father would listen to on the radio at home, but it was so different listening to a live band play. The young musicians moved and swayed as they played. At times they seemed to just push the music out of their bodies with all their heart and soul. Rose particularly liked the sound of the saxophone player; he was able to bend and twist the sounds with precision. When they played a slower tune, the saxophone spread out a sweeter, more haunting melody. During these slow songs most of the couples stood up to dance, slowly shuffling together on the dance floor, bodies close in silent, swirling affection. Rose could see her parents in their living room holding each other, moving gracefully in a small circle in the center of the room.

Her mother loved to dance. Rose remembered one Christmas morning in particular when her father and Michael had surprised her mother with a radio. They had discovered it at the town dump and fixed it up so it worked quite well, good enough to pull in Benny Goodman on Sunday nights. If their parents weren't listening to F.D.R's *fire side chats*, it was the whole family listening to the comedy of Burns and Allen, or the big band sounds of Benny Goodman or Artie Shaw. This is when Lilly would sweet talk Karl into dancing with her. It was quite against his nature, but he couldn't refuse his Lilly. Sitting on the floor, the kids would make a space for their parents as they sat smiling up at them, feeling the warm glow of family and the love which surrounded them. No worries could touch them on those nights in front of the radio. Rose sighed at the thought.

Boy, Mom sure would like to be here tonight, Rose thought with a smile, leaning her head against the side of the stairway.

Throughout the evening Rose had gotten quite a few compliments about how pretty she looked or the color and wave of her hair. Grandma B. had put some of her hair product on Rose's hair, so it had a slight sheen and didn't stick out quite so far. Rose had never thought herself to be particularly good-looking, but she had never spent much time thinking about that sort of thing either, so the sudden attention by these strangers was at the same time pleasing and uncomfortable. She caught another glimpse of herself in the bathroom mirror later that evening; the muted light softened her features. *Maybe I don't look that bad,* Rose thought to herself as she looked in the mirror, periodically changing profiles, trying to look serious, mysterious and older all at the same time.

When the last of the passengers and band members had left, and the girls had finished cleaning up the kitchen and large dance floor, Grandma B. came up to Rose shuffling her feet, her head hanging low.

"Ya did okay, girlie, for da first time in my kitchen." Grandma B. put her hand on Rose's shoulder and leaned into her a bit. "I could sure use your help more often if 'in you's interested. My last girl done got herself pregnant and had a baby, so she had ta quit, so I's lookin' for a permanent replacement."

"Oh, I'd like that very much!" Rose replied, perking up a bit.

She had never realized how much work it was standing in a kitchen and serving people for almost eight hours straight, but if it kept her on this boat she'd make the sacrifice.

"Where we going next?"

"Well, first we's headin' up river ta La Crosse and Winona. I know da Elks is sponsorin' da boat outta Hasting, and da Shriners outta St. Paul. Den we's head down agin, makin' our way back ta St. Luey."

That was all Rose needed to hear. She was finally going to see St. Louis. She couldn't wait.

"Ya bunk with Lilly Mae here, since ya two seems ta be hittin' it off so well. Lilly Mae, show dis here girlie where ya'll gonna sleep."

Rose wondered if Grandma B. would ever call her by her name. That really didn't matter though; she was going to St Louis. She followed Lilly Mae up the stairs to the fifth deck: the Texas deck. The women and the officers stayed here. The deck hands had their quarters in the hold, below the main deck, a place the women weren't allowed or ever wanted to venture. There was a long hall in front of them which ran the length of the deck, interrupted only by some steps which led up to the pilot's house. Their room was little bigger than a large closet, with two small, metal beds in the outside corners and a small window in between.

"You can have that one," Lilly Mae said, pointing to the bed on the right side of the room.

Lilly Mae opened the door of the small closet behind the door.

"You can put your bundle in here if'in you want."

"Okay, thanks."

Rose stuffed her bundle into the locker, then fell on her bed and promptly fell asleep. After Lilly Mae had changed out of her clothes, she covered Rose up and got into bed herself.

~ ~ ~

Rose's dreams that night were of sweet music and couples dancing. One of the gentlemen she had seen on the dance floor had just asked her to dance when, suddenly, she was woken out of her bliss-filled sleep by a rough hand covering her mouth. She was so disoriented with her surroundings and the hand over her mouth, it took her a few seconds to yell out and try to move the big, grease-smelling hand away. The room was dark, but her eyes quickly accommodated to the darkness. All she could see of the large figure hovering over her was a black form. It wasn't until the person sat on the edge of her bed that the pale blue moonlight coming through the window lightly illuminated the face. Her eyes widened in recognition and shock.

❧ 3 ❧

Rose knew, even at a young age, true adventures were ones taken alone. But what she didn't realize was that true adventures were usually risky and took you away from the watchful eyes of family, friends and your community. Rose had no idea that soon she would be crying herself to sleep, longing for at least one pair of those vigilant eyes.

~ ~ ~

It took Rose a while to figure out what was happening. Once he spoke, she knew for sure she wasn't dreaming. It was Peter, and he had a sinister smile on his face.

"Now we'll see how smart you are, little girl," he said.

He grabbed her right arm and pinned it to her side by leaning into her, freeing up his left hand. Rose tugged even harder on the hand which held her mouth. He hardly seemed to take notice of her efforts. Then he did something Rose did not expect; he reached down and started to fondle one of her breasts through her dress, his heavy body pressing her hard into the bed to keep her from moving. This made Rose inhale deeply as the strange feeling took her by surprise. The smell of grease from his hand burned in her nostrils.

Oh, my God! Why was he doing this? She squirmed and kicked, trying to get away from his grasp, but he had her pinned tight to the bed, and her free arm wasn't strong enough to push him away. He began to lean down, moving his face closer to hers as he took his hand off her chest and started to move it down her body. Rose froze, eyes wide, not knowing what to do next. With his face so close to hers, another smell made its presence known. She had come across this smell before—a sweet, bitter kind of odor, like old fermenting fruit which had gone bad.

Yes—she remembered. Once, one of the strangers who had stopped at the farm had smelled like that. Her mother seemed particularly anxious for the man to leave, which seemed unusual to Rose at the time. After the man had left, Rose asked her mother what was the matter. She told Rose that the man had been drinking, and "…one can never be trustin' a man who's been drinkin'."

Peter had been drinking. In fact, Peter was drunk, and now he was trying to lift up Rose's dress! Realizing what he was trying to do, Rose began to fight him again, this time with renewed vigor, kicking and punching him as hard as she could. He leaned his body on her legs as best he could to stop from being kicked.

"Whew! You're a feisty one ain't ya? Now listen here girl, there ain't no use fightin' 'cause you ain't gonna…"

Then for some odd reason Peter stopped talking. He turned his head slightly as if he had heard something behind him. Rose didn't know what was going on, so she stopped too. He turned his gaze back to her with a strange, wide look in his eyes. Slowly, he sat upright then stopped again. His hands didn't move. Rose heard a clicking sound come from behind Peter's back.

"Don't make a move ya piece a river scum. I'll blow a hole in ya so wide ya can see right through, and don't ya think I won't. I knew ya was no good the minute I saw ya. Now, let dat girlie go!" Grandma B. commanded.

Peter slowly removed his hands from Rose's mouth and thigh. Rose lay petrified, unable to move. Grandma B. stepped out from behind Peter. She was in her night gown, but she had a huge shot gun in her hands, and she was aiming it straight at Peter. Behind her, Rose could see Lilly Mae cowering in the corner.

"Now stands up and turn 'round real slow like. We're gonna take a little walk ta da captin's cabin. Now, move!" Grandma B. pushed the barrel of the gun in his back, moving him forward. She looked sort of humorous, that little, thin old lady holding that huge shot gun. But she didn't strain or hesitate a moment. Once they were out of sight Rose suddenly felt sick to her stomach. She ran out the door and onto the boat deck; leaning over the rail, she lost all of Grandma B.'s good roast beef, and then some. As she stood there hanging her head over the side of the boat, the blue-white reflection of the moon on the water below started to blur. The tears came fast and furious. She felt an arm go around her, and she turned quickly to face the obscured face of Grandma B. just inches from hers. She fell into her arms as her body heaved and sobbed.

"Now, ya let it all out, sweet Rosie girl. Dat scum ain't gonna be botherin' ya no mo, Grandma B. done seen ta dat."

Rose hadn't even noticed that Grandma B. had called her by her name. She wasn't thinking about that; she couldn't even comprehend what had just happened, and she didn't want to think about what would have happened if Lilly Mae hadn't woken Grandma B. Her crying started with renewed gusto just at the thought. The next thing she knew, she was at the side of her bed. Rose laid down, and Grandma B. covered her up. Rose curled up on her side, the tears coming less heavy now, interrupted only by large heaves as she tried to take in air. Grandma B. gently caressed her back as a soft, sorrowful song of the type Rose had never heard floated in the air above her.

> *Go ta sleep ya little Babe, go ta sleep ya little Babe,*
> *ya mama's gone away and you're daddy's gonna stay,*
> *don't leave nobody but the Babe.*

Rose closed her eyes, thinking only of home and her family— the gift of sleep eventually giving her relief.

> *Go ta sleep ya little Babe, go ta sleep ya little Babe,*
> *everybody's gone in the cotton an the corn,*
> *don't leave nobody but the Babe.*

~ ~ ~

The girl who woke up in that bed the next morning was a different girl than had fallen into it the night before. The shocking reality of the cruelty, which we as humans are all capable of, had dealt Rose a strong blow; a blow that would change her forever.

Rose didn't talk for many days. She probably would have gone home if the boat hadn't been so far away. But she wasn't even sure she could do that. She was different, and she knew it. She felt it best to stay on the boat for now.

Rose avoided the men who worked on the boat as much as possible and kept mostly to herself. Grandma B. didn't make her serve the passengers on the next couple excursions; she kept Rose busy in the kitchen. Rose didn't even want to watch. Lilly Mae went out of her way to talk with Rose, but she didn't get much of a response. Rose's demeanor didn't go unnoticed by Grandma B. either. When this had gone on for about two weeks, much longer than Grandma B. thought it should, she decided she better have a talk with the girl.

Rose sat on her bed with Grandma B. sitting next to her. Grandma B. took Rose's hand in hers and began to speak.

"Rosie girl, I brought ya in here 'cause we's got ta have a little talk. All dis mopein' 'rounds gotta stop. I knows what ya'll is goin' through. I knows 'cause it done happen' ta me too, septin it was my own husband."

Rose looked at Grandma B. in amazement.

"Dats right. It was a long time ago, though. Took me a while, but I finally smartin'd up and left da sorry sack of you-know-what. But never ya mind about dat. I ain't tellin' ya dis so you feel sorry for me. I's tellin' ya dis so ya can see dat us women, well, God done made us strong so we can survive such things. I survived, and ya'll survive too."

"But I'm so scared, Grandma B., scared it will happen again or even worse!"

Tears welled in Rose's eyes as she started to feel that familiar ache in her stomach.

Grandma B. brought Rose to her chest, laying her head on that warm, soft place, her small, thin arms circling around her. The tears slowly streaked down Rose's face as Grandma B. held her close. After a minute or two Grandma B. could feel Rose's body change and stiffen.

"I wish I were a man," Rose declared. "I'd beat that Peter to a bloody pulp!"

Grandma B. lifted Rose upright by the shoulders and looked her straight in the eyes. Her nose and eyes were red, but there was a hardness there, which Grandma B. knew all too well.

"Where ya be hearing such talk, and from such a sweet girl too?"

"I hate him Grandma B. I hate him so much!"

"Now ya betta be lettin' go a *dat*, Rosie girl. Hate's a powerful thing. I's seen it suck the life right outta folks who don't know no betta. It'll fester inside ya and keep growin' 'tills it eats ya from the inside out!"

"But I hate him for what he did to me. I just don't feel the same anymore. How am I ever going to face my family?"

Tears began welling in her eyes again. "He took that all away from me!" Rose spat out, clenching her fists.

"Well, that's only if ya let him."

Rose looked at Grandma B., puzzled. Then she unclenched her fists.

"Let me explain somethin'. When dis done happen to me, ya wouldn't believe it, but once I was away from dat good for nothin', I started to feel sorry for da fool. Dat was all he knew—get drunk and beat up on da only ones in his life dat love him. Now, I's sure he has his reasons why he got so mean. God don't make us mean to start, ya know. Even though I felt sorry for'im, I didn't need ta go back ta see if he'd figure it out. I wasn't gonna let him ruin my life, no-sir-re. So it was me. I decided what I was gonna do, and I did it. You's a strong girl, Rosie; I can tell and a smart one too. Don't ya let dat no good river scum decided how ya gonna be livin' your life."

Rose looked into her lap and nodded her head slowly in recognition. Grandma B. was right; she was letting what Peter had done to her run her life. She hadn't stepped off the boat or hardly left her cabin, except when she had to work. She didn't want to keep living like that!

"An' another thing. Ya ain't done nothing wrong neither, septin maybe pickin' a fight wid the wrong kinda trash. Da boys done tol' me what happened. Girl, ya gotta learn who ta pick your fights with and when it's best ta just walk away. No goods like dat Peta, he ain't worth your time."

Grandma B. looked off into the distance.

"It's kinda strange thing" she said, shaking her head softly. "God done made us a wonderful place, but what I can't figure out is why he gives us the bad along wit' da good. Best as I can figure is, it's kinda like cookin'; ya don't know what sweet really tastes like 'tils ya had somethin' bitter. And Lordie girl, ya done had yourself a mess a bitter."

Rose sighed as the tears made their way back into her eyes. Grandma B. brought Rose back to her chest, rocking her back and forth softly. Rose hardly made a sound. She was thinking about what Grandma B. had said to her, when Grandma B. lifted her up and handed her a handkerchief.

"Now, I's got an idea. We's be puttin' up in Savanna real soon. The captin, he's got friends der, so we's gonna be der for a whole day 'fore we load up ta go out agin. I wants ya and Lilly Mae ta take dis here money." Grandma B. reached inside her apron pocket, pulled out some bills and placed them in Rose's hand. Rose's face brightened as she looked at the money.

"Now, ya earned it." Grandma B. smiled, "I talked ta Mary, and she gave ya a little advance. Ya go and buys yourself somethin' real nice."

Rose looked up at Grandma B. and smiled. She grabbed Grandma B. around her neck and squeezed as hard as she could.

"Lordie, Girl!" Grandma B. said as a small smile came across her face.

"I'm gonna find Lilly Mae and tell her!" Rose exclaimed as she ran out of the cabin. Rose left Grandma B. sitting on the bed, gazing out of the window. Slowly, a more somber look over took her smile. She sighed, looked down in her lap and lightly touched her forehead, chest, right shoulder then left. She hoped her prayer would be answered.

~ ~ ~

Rose took Grandma B.'s words to heart and tried to busy herself exploring the boat. She found out how the huge engines converted coal to steam to move the large red paddles, and how the Capitol's state-of-the-art water filtering system turned the brown river water into something clear and drinkable.

Rose was more sensitive to sudden noises now, but the only time she became anxious was at night. At Rose's suggestion, Lilly Mae readily agreed to keep their cabin door closed and locked despite the warm, sticky August nights. That midnight encounter had shaken Lilly Mae almost as much as Rose.

It took quite a few days, and a number of excursions, to make it down to Savanna from St. Paul. When they passed by Prairie du Chien, Rose suddenly realized she hadn't written to her family yet. All they had so far was a note tucked next to the sugar jar in the pantry. She knew her mother wouldn't look there until the morning after she left, when she would start baking again, like she always did right after breakfast. Her note didn't give them any details about where she was going, but she did tell them she would write to let them know she was all right. Rose got some paper and an envelope from the captain, but she had to promise him she would come and find him after she was done with her letter. She happily agreed. The captain had noticed she was feeling a little better, and he wanted to do a little something for the poor girl. He felt partially responsible for her incident, since he was the one who hired Peter on, despite Grandma B.'s protests.

Rose sat on the large, metal, triangular frame on the front of the paddle wheeler, which moved the gang plank up and down. She hung her feet over the edge in order to get a good view of the river while she composed her letter. It was her favorite spot on the boat; it made her feel like she was piloting the large vessel.

The afternoon sun was shining in a cloudless sky. The sweet, warm, August river air caressed her face and filled her nostrils, her lungs, and her soul, while the boat slowly lumbered down stream. This kept her cool as she looked out over the placid scene. Rose sighed. All that could be heard was the constant humming of the engines way below her. Rose didn't even notice them anymore; it was just a part of her now. A small smile made its way across her face as she looked out over the wide road of water in front of her and the green covered landscape which enveloped it. It was called the muddy Mississippi for a reason, but from a distance it looked as blue as any inland lake; its surface reflecting the blue sky above.

Rose liked how desolate it felt between the towns they passed; it felt like they had stepped back in time and were on an expedition with LaSalle, or Joliet and Father Marquette, exploring the river for the first time. There wasn't a building in sight. Trees and shrubs covered the islands, with steep hills or bluffs on each side. Occasionally, rocks poked their heads out of the greenery which seemed to hold in the water on either side.

Sometimes there were large flat areas on each side of the main channel with quiet, haunting backwaters leading this way and that, calling to Rose to come explore. But the Capitol, she was meant for larger water, and she was making her way on one of the best.

If the Mississippi could talk, it would go on for hours about the different vessels and the myriad of people who have lived and died on her watch, from the birch canoes of the Natchez or Sioux Indians, to the massive, now extinct log rafts the white man used to strip the upper Midwest clean of timber for a growing country. And now these metal monsters: barges pushed by large tugs which could haul many a ton from St. Paul to the gulf of Mexico. Except for the occasional fishing boat they'd come across, Rose felt as if the Capitol owned this great river, and she felt privileged to be on her.

They had just passed Guttenberg, a small town just south of Prairie du Chien. The town was laid out about twenty feet up off the river and was as flat as Prairie. Like Prairie, Guttenberg was nestled between the river and a tree-covered bluff just behind it.

All you saw from the river was a single line of shops with homes sitting as book-ends on each side.

Rose liked passing these small towns. There were always children running up to the water's edge to wave at the boat as it floated by. Rose always waved back. It reminded her of their family picnics when they would see the boats go by and wave at the river folk too. If you were lucky, you could even get the boat to blow its whistle by making a pulling down motion with your arm. All the kids would jump up and down and cheer if they got a boat to whistle. It was such a shrill, loud sound, echoing off the line of trees on the other side of the river, making the sound even more haunting, and sending any perching bird into flight. Rose was still smiling as the pleasant memory left her, and the river came back in view. She began to write:

My dearest family,

I'm sorry it has taken me so long to write. Lots of things have happened since I left home, so I haven't had much time to write. I have seen many wonderful sights and met many nice people and a few that were not so nice, but I'm doing fine. I really miss you all, and hope you are not worrying about me. I'm not sure when I will be home, but I will write you whenever I can. Please tell Silus that I am fine, and I'm sorry I couldn't tell him what I was planning. I didn't want to get him into trouble. Give a hug to Max for me. I love you and miss you all!

Your Rose

Rose folded the letter, kissed it, and placed it in the envelope. She decided she would mail it when she and Lilly Mae went into town. She could hardly wait.

~ ~ ~

Rose found the captain as she had promised. He wasn't in his office, which was just off the dance floor toward the front of the boat; he was up in the pilot house. She had covered almost every inch of the Capitol, but she had never been there. Once at the top landing, she peered inside. The room was square in shape and had windows all around it. The captain was standing holding a beautifully finished, walnut wheel that stood as tall as his chest, with handles pointing out of the spokes, just like she had seen in books of sailing ships. Behind the wheel was a round device on a chrome post which looked like a small drum on its side with a couple leavers coming out of it; it was the Cory Signal device used to signal the speed to the engine room below. Just behind the captain was a table covered with charts and an open log book. A stool sat in front of this, a rocker off to one side, and a radiator for the few occasions the pilot needed heat. Rose was surprised to see the captain here. She didn't know he could pilot the steamer.

The captain was dressed in a clean, neatly pressed, navy blue jacket and pants and a blue captains cap. He looked so official standing there. Rose contemplated turning around and going back down, but just at that moment he noticed her standing there and motioned for her to come in with a wave of his hand and big, warm smile. She opened the door slowly, stepping into the small, bright room.

"Welcome, little lady! I'm so glad you made it. Pull up a stool and have a seat," he said with a grin.

Rose pulled the tall stool up and sat a few feet away from where the captain was standing.

"I bet you've never been in a pilot house before, have ya?"

"No sir, I haven't."

"Oh please, call me Captain Roy." He nodded and gave her a wink. "It's quite a view from up here, isn't it?"

"It sure is," Rose replied, craning her neck to look farther out of the windows.

"Well, this here boat, she used to be one of the hundreds of packet boats that ran up and down these waters in the late 1800s. That was before she was converted into the excursion boat you're workin' on today. She's seen many a port along this here river, I'll tell you that right now."

Rose remembered seeing paddle wheelers in the river at Prairie. Being a port town, there were always things coming and going from the big water, "the mighty Mississippi" Michael explained to Rose when she was quite small. Prairie du Chien was the closest big town her family had, and when her mother was looking for some material for the kids' clothes or her dad needed a part for the tractor, they would pile the lot of them into the pickup truck—Mom, Dad and the little ones in front, the rest in the back—and head down the windy, cool valley road to town. After the family errands were done, they would frequently have a picnic on the banks of the river, right next to the foundations of the old Fort Crawford army fort on Feriole Island. It was a great place to see things on the river: paddle wheelers, clammers, or fishing boats, and the strange folk who ran them, going slowly up and down the milk-chocolate river.

Rose had never dreamed she would ever be on one of them. But here she was, and in the pilot house to boot. Rose had a million questions but wasn't sure she should ask. She looked up at the kindly face. The captain was looking out over the water ahead. He had deep wrinkles on the sides of his eyes, so she thought she might as well try one or two. She started with a question which had bothered her for sometime.

"Why do people call boats and the river 'she'?"

The captain looked at Rose with a sideways glance, not answering right away so he could ponder the question.

"You know little lady, that's a good question. I'm not really sure," he said. "That's the way it's always been, I guess. But if I think about it a bit, maybe it's because, like yourself, ladies deserve respect. The Capitol here, well, she deserves our respect too. She's an old girl and needs a little finesse to manage her on these ever-changing waters. But handle her just right, and she'll see you through most anything. The river, well, she pretty much demands our respect. No matter what the Corps does to her—and they've done a lot over the many years I've been workin' her. She can never be ignored or taken for granted. Any fisherman or riverboat captain will tell ya: the quietness of these here waters, well, that's just an illusion. You can't let your guard down one minute. This grand old waterway can't be predicted or tamed."

"The Corps? What's the Corps?"

"The official name is the Army Corps of Engineers. It's the government agency that's in charge of the river. Though I must admit, even though they've put their two cents into what's happened to this great river over time, there've been many more players in on the changes than just the Corps. And the biggest change is yet to come. Remember what you saw as we were passing Gutenberg?"

"Yah, I noticed them working on something in the river. It looked like they were making a big dam."

"That's right, it is a dam, with some locks attached to it too. But the dam isn't there to hold the water back completely; it's there just to help control the water level. Mind you, they're planning to put twenty-four locks and dams all along this upper Mississippi, from St. Paul all the way to Rock Island. They're proposing to make a channel nine...feet...deep!" he said with an air of amazement. "That's so the barges can run their goods almost nine months of the year. Imagine that! I can remember summers not that long ago when the water was so low, even a paddle wheeler like the Capitol here couldn't run, and she draws only five feet."

"Draws, what do you mean, draws?"

"Oh, that means how far under the water the hull of a boat goes. Barges, they typically draw seven foot or more fully loaded, so they need more water to run during the dry season."

"You said they're building locks along with the dams; what's a lock?"

"Well, ya see, the river bottom in the Upper Mississippi keeps dropping as we go down stream. In fact, there was quite a large falls at Rock Island at one time, and some at Keokuk too. That is, before they blasted most of it away. The locks'll take boats up or down to the different water levels that'll be created when the dams go in. That's how they'll keep a channel nine feet deep. And below Rock Island you're gonna be surprised at how different the river looks. But that's mostly because of the wildlife refuge."

"Yah, my dad told me about that. He likes to hunt and fish, so he thought President Coolidge was smart to do that. He said there's a lot of garbage that gets dumped into the river, and that makes it hard for the fish to survive. He thought it might make them figure out something else to do with their junk."

"Yup, he signed that in 1924, to be exact; I remember the day. There was a lot of fightin' going on about that decision too. But spending most of my born days on this here river, I have to agree with your dad. Unfortunately, the refuge hasn't stopped the cities from dumping into the river, but these dams might. Their sewage won't be able to run down-stream like it does now. Ya know, things don't last forever. It's like anything, if you don't take care of it, sure as the world, you're gonna lose it. That's why the clammers are pretty much gone. They can't find enough clams. All you see are piles of empty shells with holes punched out of 'em, outside the boarded-up button factories."

"We've got some of those in Prairie, outside the old Iriquois factory on the Island. We use to play with the shells when we were kids, but ya had to be careful not to cut yourself on'em, though. That factory's closed too."

"The refuge supporters aren't sure what's going to happen with all these locks and dams they've planned, but time will tell. They'll keep a close eye on things, that's for sure. This nine foot project, this is going to change the upper Mississippi like nothing else has. Personally, I think it was mostly the depression that made Hoover fund the plan. He knew making all those locks and dams would put a lot of people to work. You can't blame'm for that.

"Course, it isn't going to harm the farmers either. They could use a little help. Prices to ship their grain by rail can be pretty costly these days. The railroads got a pretty sweet deal goin' along the river here. They're allowed to charge more to move grain and such off the river for higher than anywhere else in the country. They claim they have to compete with the riverboats. But the truth is, the riverboat and barge traffic ain't changed for years. That's why the farmers and business people pushed so hard for the nine foot channel. They want to change all that."

"Sounds pretty complicated."

"It's a lot of politics little lady, a lot of politics."

They both sat quietly for a while, looking out over the expansive waterway—Rose, in awe of the new found beauty; Captain Roy, comforted by a familiar friend stretching out for miles in front of him.

"Looks like they tried to build a dam here too, but stopped," Rose said, pointing to a low pile of rock and brush jutting out into the river, "Look, there's a bunch of them along here." Rose leaned forward, straining her neck to see a bit further down river.

"Those are called wing dams. That was the last plan the Corps had to deepen the river. They were never meant to hold it back. As you can see, those dams narrow the river down and that puts more water in this smaller channel," the captain explained, expertly holding the large wooden wheel with his leg while he formed a channel with his hands to demonstrate his point. "This makes the water move faster and takes a little bit more of the river bottom along with it as it travels down stream. That keeps the channel deeper than it normally would be. Pretty nifty, huh?" He smiled broadly. "That project started in 1878, and would you believe, there are over 1,900 dams like that along the upper Mississippi?"

"Wow, that's a lot! But you said 'the upper Mississippi'; what do they do in the lower Mississippi?"

"The river below Rock Island doesn't drop like the upper river. They don't need locks or dams to keep boats moving down there. They have some wing dams too, but they use snag boats and dredgers mostly, and so do we."

"What's a snag boat?"

"You're full-a questions aren't you; Grandma B. was right," he chuckled. "Look there, see that log over there?"

The captain pointed to a log which was bobbing in and out of the water. It looked like someone was pulling at it from below, but it was too slippery to get a good hold of and they kept losing their grip, allowing it to bob back up again.

"That's what we call a 'preacher'; it's bowing to the parishioners."

The captain bowed up and down, holding out his hand to shake the pretend hands in front of him.

"If it's still and has branches on it, it's called a sawyer."

"You mean like Tom Sawyer? Is that where Samuel Clemens got the name?"

"You mean Mark Twain?"

"Mark Twain is the pen name that Samuel Clemens used."

"Well, I'll be. I didn't know that. Now see there, you taught me somethin'."

Rose smiled in satisfaction.

"Do you know that mark twain is what the river men would call out to the pilot when the boat was in twelve foot a water?" the captain explained.

"Well, I'll be. I didn't know that! Now see there, you taught me somethin'," Rose replied teasingly.

They both smiled at her little joke.

"See that log over there? That one's stuck in the bottom. You can tell by the way the water moves around it. We call those 'planters', but the ones you really have to look out for are the 'sleepers.' They're the ones that lay sleeping underneath the water, and when you least expect it, they wake up and rip a hole right through your hull. That's what snag boats are for: pulling out all those pesky logs that slow ya up or lay ya over for repairs."

"How long have you been in the river boat business, sir?" Rose asked, looking at the white and brown hairs which poked out from under his cap and the ones in his matching salt and pepper beard. Looking at his uniform up close, she realized it was more worn than she had noticed before.

"About thirty some years, I reckon. I started out as a cabin boy with my brother Joe about 1900, haulin' freight with my father in the summer. After a couple years of high school, I became a steward. I got my mates license when I was twenty one and an engineer's license a year after that. Then, with a bit more work, I eventually got my captain's papers, and my father gave me the command of the Sidney. A lot of things have changed over the years, 'ceptin' my love of this river; she's in my blood, she is."

"Captain, have ya seen Rose?" came a muffled voice out of no where. "Grandma B.'s lookin' for her." Rose looked around to try and find where the voice was coming from. Rose spied the speaker close to the ceiling just to captain's left. He reached for a small microphone on a wire.

"She's up here with me," he said into the microphone, turning to wink at Rose. "I'll send her down."

Rose slowly slid off the stool. She had lost track of time; Grandma B. would be mad.

"Thanks so much, Captain Roy, but I better get back to the kitchen."

"Well, I hope I didn't bore you too much with all my river talk. I tend to get carried away sometimes, especially with such a willing listener."

"Oh, I wasn't bored at all. I love listening to you talk about the river, really. Thanks a lot!" Rose closed the door to the pilot house quietly and quickly made her way down the steps to the kitchen.

⁓ 4 ⁓

Being almost sixteen, Rose's first time away from home had its advantages; it could easily distract a young girl who had just had her world turned upside down. Living in the moment still came readily for such a girl, and each new day had the potential for good things to happen.

The world Rose still knew and believed in was a world where everyone who knew you or knew your family looked out for you. In Rose's world, even people she didn't know would help each other. They would help bring a crop in if they had heard so-and-so two farms down was sick, or round up loose cattle which were wandering out on the road from any farm they might pass. Who knows when you might be the next one to need a little help. But it was more than that; it was just what you did; you looked out for each other and they looked out for you. Rose didn't realize as she opened her eyes to a new day, that this blind optimism, this assumed good in all mankind—until proven otherwise—could be a curse as well as a blessing.

~ ~ ~

When Rose woke the next morning, she immediately knew something was different, though it took her a minute to figure it out. The motors on the boat were silent; the boat had stopped. Rose jumped out of bed and shook Lilly Mae lightly until she woke.

"Lilly Mae, the boat's stopped. We must be in Savanna. Hurry up and get dressed!" She continued talking as she pulled Lilly Mae's clothes out of the closet, throwing them on top of her. "You know what that means—we're going to town!"

Rose dressed in a flash, leaving Lilly Mae behind, and ran out to the rail to see what she could see. The bright sun of the new day was just cresting over a large hill which lay three or four blocks from the river's edge. It nearly blinded her, so she had to shield her eyes to see. She heard foot steps on the wooden planks just below her. Leaning out over the rail, Rose spied Martin, one of the engine men.

"Martin, Martin, is this Savanna?"

"Sure 'nouph is, Rose," he said with a smile on his face. He was heading off the boat like everyone else. Word had spread quickly on their little floating island; they were going to be tied up all day. They didn't get a chance to put their feet on solid ground very often, so everyone wanted to make the most of the shore time. Rose ran back in to hurry Lilly Mae along.

~ ~ ~

"Rosie, if'in ya don't start chewin' your food, you're gonna choke. Now slow up, girl," Grandma B. ordered.

Rose took a last big gulp of the food that was in her mouth and took a deep breath.

"Town ain't goin' no where, child. It'll still be there five minutes from now."

Rose smiled at Grandma B. She sounded like her mother just then. Rose took another bite of her biscuits and gravy, chewing with exaggerated, halted movements.

"Now, ya girls, you be careful. Mind what ya says and where ya goes. Ya don't know 'dese folks none."

Rose finished before Lilly Mae, of course, and was waiting just outside the kitchen door checking out what she could see of Savanna with a discerning eye. She was also mulling over what had happened of late. Rose had thought it through; she had let her guard down, and she wasn't going to let that happen again. She was going to be watchful of young, strange men, how she interacted with them, and what she said to them, until she was good and sure they were okay. With this decision tucked smugly away, she was ready to take on the world again.

Lilly Mae finally stepped outside.

"Great! Let's go," Rose said, heading for the bow of the boat. Then she stopped abruptly.

"I almost forgot somethin'. I'll be right back."

Her voice trailed behind her as she ran back inside the boat. A few minutes later, she came back with a letter in her hand.

"Almost forgot my letter."

Rose tucked it gently in the breast pocket of her overalls, adjusted the cap on her head, and walked quickly off the gangplank with Lilly Mae trailing behind.

Looking left, Rose spied one of their first opportunities for exploration.

"Wow, look at the bridge," she said in amazement. "That looks neat!"

Just north of town was a high arching, metal bridge which spanned the Mississippi. To their right, down stream, sat a large building on stilts built right on the river bank. The sign out front said *Savanna Boat Club.* Rose thought that would be a good place to start, but she had something important to do first.

"I've got to mail my letter first off, but then we can do what ever we want," Rose said to Lilly Mae.

Rose stopped.

"Look at that hill, Lilly Mae!"

Rose pointed due west to a small, tree-covered bluff she had spied before breakfast.

"I wanna check out what it looks like from up there, for sure! I wanna see if they have a book store too. I'm just dying to read a good book," Rose rattled on. "I bet there's a great view from on top of that bridge. Maybe we can check that out later!"

Lilly Mae rolled her eyes. Rose started for town with Lilly Mae trailing aways behind, not sure of what she was getting into with this chatty white girl. She had to pick up her pace more than was natural to keep up. From the boat landing, the girls walked straight east on Murray Street one block until they hit Main Street. Rose spied a couple of shops she wanted to check out later, but first, the post office. It took a while to find it; Rose finally had to ask someone where it was. She mailed her letter and set out to explore the city with her somewhat reluctant companion.

Two blocks further east of Main Street, between the Presbyterian Church and the grade school, they came to the base of the steep hill.

"Neat!" Rose exclaimed. "Look at all these steps."

Rose smiled as she looked up at the series of steep, cement steps, which seemed to stretch to the heavens. Or at least that's what Lilly Mae thought. Lilly Mae stood at the bottom, looking up in dismay. Rose didn't hesitate; she bounded up the celestial ladder.

"Com'on, Lilly Mae," was all Lilly Mae heard as she put her head down for the climb.

Rose stopped about three quarters of the way up to catch her breath. It was higher than she thought. Lilly Mae had already stopped about half way up, bent over and panting.

"Com'on Lilly Mae, or you'll miss it!"

"Miss what—my funeral?" she said under her breath.

She didn't have enough air to breathe, let alone speak. Head still down, she waved at Rose to keep going. Without hesitation, Rose turned and headed up the rest of the way, going a bit slower this time.

Lilly Mae got to the top, only to find a road and another set of steps which, of course, Rose had already climbed. Lilly Mae turned around and sat down on the top step next to the road. She looked out over the town and the river which held it in place, chest heaving slowly. It *was* a nice view; she had to admit that.

Once she had caught her breath, she crossed the road and climbed up the last flight of steps to where Rose was sitting.

"Isn't it great up here? You can see for miles," Rose mused, leaning back on outstretched arms.

The city sat at their feet, three to four blocks wide and a mile or so long, with a thin stretch of river to the west. On the other side of the river was a quarter of a mile of backwaters, then farm fields as far as the eye could see.

"I'd love to live in one of these houses; to wake up every day to this glorious sight would be a dream," she continued.

Lilly Mae looked right, then left of where they sat. There were small, neatly kept houses with equally small, neatly kept yards on each side of them. *It would be great to live up here,* thought Lilly Mae, but it wasn't anything she could even contemplate for more than a few seconds. She lay down in the grass and closed her eyes.

The sun was making its way across the mid-morning sky as they sat enjoying the view—Rose, of the lush green country which spread out for miles at her feet; Lilly Mae, of the underside of her eyelids. Rose sat straight up with a start.

"Let's go, Lilly Mae," she said. "The days a wastin'."

Lilly Mae sat up slowly and followed Rose back down the multiple steps back into down town.

When they got back to Main Street, they turned left. The building on the corner was a large, three-story, brick building called the Radke Hotel. Rose looked inside the lobby window. It was a wide, open room with a high, tin ceiling. The main desk sat against the back wall and was made of darkly stained wood which matched the woodwork which surrounded the rest of the room. The floor was laid with small, octagon mosaic tile, with green and maroon tiles placed among the white to look like flowers. It reminded Rose of a quilt her grandmother made, called the flower garden. In the next building, attached to the hotel by double glass doors, was the Townhouse Restaurant. It had the same tin ceiling and octagon tile as the hotel, but in a slightly different pattern. *Maybe we could have dinner there later on,* Rose thought as she looked inside. Lilly Mae stood next to Rose, looking up and down the street nervously. Rose noticed her apprehension.

"What's the matter, Lilly Mae?"

"Never been in this town bafore," she replied in a quiet tone.

"There isn't anything you have to be afraid of. I'm sure folks around here are nice. Besides, it's the middle of the day; nothin's gonna happen in the middle of the day!"

Lilly Mae's expression didn't change.

"Hey, look—a book store!" Rose said excitedly, pointing across the street.

She grabbed Lilly Mae's hand and they headed across the street.

Rose stopped in front of the store. It was just what she wanted: a used book store. She walked up the steps and opened the large glass door. There was a bell attached to the door that rang as she opened it. Rose looked behind her, noticing Lilly Mae hadn't followed.

"Com'on, Lilly Mae," Rose said, motioning her to follow.

Lilly Mae stepped heavily up the two cement steps and stood in the doorway just behind Rose.

There was an elderly man sitting in the middle of a square, wooden counter just inside the door. He looked up when the two girls walked in. Lilly Mae noticed his brow wrinkle and eyes narrow slightly as he pushed back the glasses which were perched on the edge of his nose. Rose noticed the musty smell in the stagnant air and the large quantity of books; they were everywhere. The man stood up and faced the girls.

"May I help you?" he asked, not taking his gaze off Lilly Mae.

"We're just looking, thanks," Rose replied, glancing up at his face, hesitating only a moment before she started making her way down the tall, dark aisles.

Lilly Mae stepped up right behind her, keeping her eyes on the old man long enough to confirm that, yes, he was still looking directly at her.

The well-worn, dusty wood floor squeaked under their feet as they moved slowly from stack to stack. Rose turned right and headed down one of the aisles labeled "Fiction." Lilly Mae took a quick look behind her before she followed. The old man was leaning his head slightly over the counter, eyes fixed on Lilly Mae.

"Rose, I don't like this place. Maybe we should go."

"I know. It smells funny, but look at all these books! Isn't this great?" Rose exclaimed, oblivious of her friend's consternation.

Lilly Mae didn't reply, she just kept close to Rose, periodically turning to look behind her while Rose slowly walked along. Rose was gazing up and down at the rows of books, stopping every step or two to pull one out and examine it in more detail.

"What kind of books do you like to read?" Rose asked casually.

"I…I don't like readin' much."

"Well, maybe you just haven't found the right book. It really does matter what book it is. I know—here's a great one!" she proclaimed, pulling another book off the shelf. "This is one of my favorites."

Rose turned the book face to Lilly Mae so she could read it: *Ethan Frome and Other Short Fiction* by Edith Wharton.

"Looks okay, I guess."

"Oh, it's great; the first story's got a great twist. We can read it together if you want. We used to do that all the time at home. In the winter we'd read almost every night. Those of us that could, of course, but everyone got a turn picking what book we would read. We were one of the first families in our area to get electricity, ya know. We don't have it running to our house from a pole on the road, like they do in the city. My Dad rigged up a motor to the house and ran the wiring so that most of the rooms have a light hanging from the ceiling. We would start it up most nights to read or listen to the radio programs. Ya ever heard Gracie and Allen? They are *sooo* funny."

Lilly Mae shook her head. "Never had no radio, only seen'em in the store."

"It was a great way to pass the time, especially when my mom made us work on tie-quilts to sell at the church bazaar, or while we mended clothes. I was pretty rough on my pants, and mom got tired of mendin'em herself, so she taught me how to do it. It was fun—the reading part, I mean. My brother, Michael, he was the best. He'd make up all kinds of voices for the different characters."

"You girls need any help?" came an unexpected voice from behind them.

Lilly Mae jumped up and reeled around all at the same time. She stared at the old man, the whites of her eyes in plain view. She took a step closer to Rose, swallowing hard to get her heart back down into her chest. Rose had seen the shop keeper enter the aisle out of the corner of her eye, so he didn't surprise her as he had Lilly Mae.

"Yup, I think we found just the book," Rose replied, walking past Lilly Mae and handing the book to the old man. "It's a great book. You ever read it?" Rose continued talking to him, heedless of Lilly Mae's distress.

As they stepped out of the book store and onto the sidewalk, Lilly Mae gave a sigh of relief. The bright light of mid-day shone down on them both. Lilly Mae closed her eyes and pointed her face into the sun to let it soak in. Rose looked up and down the street, trying to decide which way to go next. Then her stomach growled.

"Excuse me," Rose apologized. "Maybe we should get something to eat. You hungry, Lilly Mae?"

"Sort-of" was her quiet reply.

"Let's go back to that hotel restaurant. I liked the look of that place."

Rose turned and headed back across the street, slowing up just long enough for Lilly Mae to catch up.

Rose climbed the steps of the hotel restaurant, and again, Lilly Mae didn't follow. "Come on, Lilly Mae!"

Rose rolled her eyes and went back down to the side walk to grab Lilly Mae's hand. This time she didn't budge.

"What's the matter?"

Lilly Mae looked past Rose to the front of the restaurant then back at Rose again. "They don't let colored folks in there."

"Whatta you mean?"

"See the sign."

Lilly Mae pointed at a small sign in the front window. *Coloreds round back*, was all it said.

"That's just plain stupid. I heard about this kind of stuff happening in the south, but I didn't think it happened around here."

Rose stopped talking a minute and looked back at the restaurant; then she looked back at Lilly Mae.

"Well, it's a nice day, anyway, how 'bout we have a picnic on that hill. That'd be a great place for a picnic!"

"You ain't getting me up that hill a'gin, no-sir-re!"

"Okay then, how 'bout at the park by the boat. I noticed they've got a great park right next to the river."

"That'd be okay, I guess."

"I'll go in and order us a couple sandwiches. My treat. Ya know, for helpin' me out that night—on the boat," Rose finished, looking down at the ground.

"Ya don't have ta…"

"Yah, I do. I'll be right back."

She turned quickly and went inside.

~ ~ ~

The girls sat on the beach by the rivers edge, the warmth of the soft sand melting their backsides in place. The river was not very wide at this point, maybe a half a mile across, but the moist air that wafted gently across their skin was enough to keep them cool, despite the lack of shade. Both girls dug their now bare feet deep down in the sand, down far enough to cool their toes in the river water which kept the deep sand wet. They swatted at the occasional mosquito, as the small fighter pilots aboard these almost invisible bombers noisily flew around their heads.

Keeping the sand out of their food was a trick, and the small gritty crunches they heard as they ate illustrated their inability to do so. They sat quietly facing the river, slowly eating their sandwiches. The river was quiet; not another vessel in sight. Rose hadn't said much since she had gone into the restaurant to get the sandwiches. Lilly Mae knew something was on her mind; Rose was never quiet for this long.

"Lilly Mae," Rose started slowly. "I never did thank you for what you did for me that night." Rose stopped a moment and looked down at her sandwich. "I don't know what Peter would have done if you hadn't gotten Grandma B.," her voice straining to get the last words out.

Rose held her lips tight, but not quite tight enough. A small tear escaped and ran down her cheek; the wound was too fresh. Lilly Mae hesitated only a moment, then reached over slowly, placed her hand on top of Rose's hand, and squeezed it gently, switching her gaze to the slow moving river in front of them. She had known other girls back home who had bad things happen to them. It was never talked about much, but the girls never seemed the same after that. She didn't know what happened to them inside; what made that wall that no one wanted to look over. She was too afraid to ask. She was just glad she had gotten Grandma B. before something worse had happened to Rose. Lilly Mae figured no girl, white or black, deserved a life carrying that weight around.

Rose sniffled and wiped the water from her eyes with the back of her hand. Lilly Mae pulled a handkerchief from her dress pocket and handed it to Rose. It was always something she kept with her, out of habit. There were never a lack of noses to wipe when you had small brothers and sisters hanging on you.

"Oh, thanks, but I've got one," was Rose's runny nose reply.

Rose pulled a handkerchief out of a pocket in her overalls and blew her nose. She took a deep breath, and the two gazed back out over the water. They sat that way for quite a while, two young girls, straddling the seemingly deep ravine between the known world of make believe and living day-to-day of their childhood, to the unknown world of men and the seemingly endless responsibilities which signified adulthood. They weren't sure they would be able to make the jump or even if they wanted to try. Each one came from a very different world, but they shared the common bond of sisterhood. Knowing they didn't have to speak, they were lost in their own thoughts, and comfortable in the shared silence of a gendered fellow.

After a time, Rose leaned closer to Lilly Mae and put an arm around her shoulders. Lilly Mae stiffened at the unaccustomed gesture but then made herself relax when she realized Rose wasn't going to let go. *This white girl ain't so bad,* Lilly Mae thought to herself. *Even though she does talk an awful lot.*

Rose finally broke the silence, "Let's go back to town. I noticed they have a movie theatre an' I'm dying to see a movie."

Rose stood up, brushed herself off, and reached a hand down to Lilly Mae. Lilly Mae looked at the white hand in front of her, looked up into Rose's face, and reached up to meet it.

"Com'on, let's go!" Rose called back to Lilly Mae as she rushed out ahead of her toward town.

Lilly Mae rolled her eyes. *Some things never change,* she thought.

~ ~ ~

They had walked three or four blocks before Rose spotted her target. The sign above the over-hang read *Orpheum Theatre.* Rose ran up to the billboard just outside the doors.

"Hey look, it's a Shirley Temple movie, *Little Miss Marker.* Ya wanna go?"

"Sure!" Lilly Mae replied with some enthusiasm.

She also liked the movies. Besides, it would keep Rose from going into more strange places, and she was all for that.

"My treat. I insist!"

Lilly Mae thought about arguing with her, but she knew better. Besides being a master of conversation, Rose was pretty good at persuasion. Rose opened one of the heavy doors and they stepped inside.

Once inside, the girls were amazed by what they saw. The carpet was a strange half circle pattern, in various shades of maroon and orange, and the walls were covered with a textured, maroon wall paper. Straight ahead of them was the concession counter with velvet curtains hanging on each side to cover the doorways which led into the theatre. On each side of that were wide stairs which led back toward the entrance, turning up and out of sight. Under each stair case was a door. The door on the right said "manager;" the one on the left said "coat check." Both doors were closed. The room was lit by opaque glass sconces in the shape of a fan along the side walls. They channeled most of the light out the top of the fan, illuminating the maroon-covered wall just above it.

As they gazed at their opulent surroundings, the young lady on the other side of the counter spoke, startling them both. They hadn't even noticed her standing there.

"May I help you?"

"Oh, yah. We want to see the movie. When does it start?" Rose asked.

"It starts in about twenty minutes, but they always run the news reels before the movie. Those start in about fifteen minutes."

"That's okay," Rose replied, shoving fifty cents across the counter to the girl.

"How 'bout a strawberry vine, Lilly Mae?" Rose asked, spying the candy just behind the ticket girl.

"Okay, but I'll pay."

Lilly Mae had her money out and across the counter before Rose could even protest. She didn't want this white girl to think she couldn't afford to treat her as well.

They each took their tickets and licorice and headed toward the curtained door to the theatre. There was a young man in a crisp, overly tight uniform standing next to the curtain. He opened it as they got a little closer, and turned on his flashlight. Lilly Mae stopped at the base of the steps as Rose continued on toward the doorway. Rose stopped and looked back at Lilly Mae.

"Where you goin', Lilly Mae?"

"Up to the balcony," she replied in a slightly hushed tone.

"I think we'd get a better view from down here."

"No coloreds allowed on the main floor," the young man interjected.

"What! What do you mean?" Rose questioned.

"Those are the rules," he shot back.

Rose looked at him with a furrowed brow.

"Well, then I'll just come up in the balcony with you, Lilly Mae," Rose said decisively as she started up the steps.

Lilly Mae stepped up to Rose and grasped her arm to hold her back. She whispered to Rose so the young man couldn't hear.

"You better not, Rose. You might not be welcome up there. Not all colored folks likes white folks, and I don't know how these here coloreds are."

Rose looked at Lilly Mae with a questioning stare.

"Not like me? They don't even know me!" she replied, not being quiet at all.

Rose knew of some folks in Prairie who didn't like colored people, but they were usually folks who didn't like most everybody, so she never paid much attention to them. Actually, Rose hadn't seen many colored folks in Prairie; no coloreds lived in town, so it was just those who were passing through on occasion. And even though some of the other colored girls on the boat weren't especially friendly, she just figured that was the way they were. She had no clue they might not like her just because she was white. Rose's heart sank and her shoulders along with it.

"Okay, Lilly Mae, if you think that's best."

Lilly Mae nodded in agreement.

"We'll meet right back here after the show is over, okay?" Rose continued, as if somehow that would make it better.

"Sure Rose, right back here."

Lilly Mae turned and headed up the stairs. Rose watched her turn the corner and walk out of sight.

Rose gave the usher a stern look as he led her into the dark theatre with the beam of his flashlight guiding their way. It took a few seconds for her eyes to adjust to the dark room, but once she could see, she was momentarily distracted by the scene that lay before her.

"This is even more beautiful than the lobby!" Rose said to herself.

She followed the young man slowly down the aisle, which was lit by small lights on the side of each seat; her head looking right then slowly panning left so as not to miss any feature. In front of her was a stage which spanned the width of the room. On each side of the stage were gold velvet curtains pulled back in the middle by a thick, gold cord and tassel. The same gold curtain was draped in waves across the top. Covering the screen was a large, maroon velvet curtain trimmed with a huge fringe. There were large, dimly lit chandeliers on each side of the curtain and small twinkling lights in the dark ceiling above imitating stars in a night sky.

It was a large theatre, with at least twenty seats in the middle and four on each side. Rose stopped short and quickly turned around to look up. She had walked out from under the balcony and she wanted to find Lilly Mae. It took a while, but she finally found her sitting about one quarter of the way from the front row. Rose waved her arm at Lilly Mae. Lilly Mae lifted her hand slightly and waved back, looking right and left to see who was watching, then she sank down into her chair. Rose turned around and sighed. She was directed to a spot in the middle of the theatre by the young man. Rose sat down, staring blankly at her licorice sticks.

Before long, the large curtain rose, and the news reel began to play.

"The Summer Olympics—1936, the games that will go down in history, not just for the likes of Jessie Owens, *The Tan Cyclone*, who brought home an amazing four gold medals, or the fact that these were the first games ever broadcast on the miracle of television, but more so for the fact that we were in the games at all."

Rose had read in *The Wisconsin State Journal* at the Prairie library that a man named Hitler had taken over Germany as a kind of dictator. Since the games were to be held in Germany this year, some of the other countries, including the United States, were thinking of boycotting the games. She wasn't sure what all the fuss was about, but she knew the United States had decided to participate anyway.

After the news reel finished, Rose looked up again into the balcony. Her eyes couldn't make out Lilly Mae's face in the darkened theatre, especially after looking at the bright screen. She turned back around and slunk down in her seat. *Maybe we should have just skipped the movie*, Rose thought to herself. The screen came alive again, illuminating Rose's face. Rose automatically put a piece of licorice in her mouth and began to chew, not really noticing the sweet, red taste.

Every so often, when the movie got slow, Rose would turn around and look briefly up at where Lilly Mae was sitting. *I can't believe they wouldn't let her sit down here.* Thoughts started spilling out of her head. *I remember Miss Turner telling us about such things, but I didn't think that it happened around here. And what's the problem with me sitting up there! I haven't done anything to anybody. They don't even know me.* She shook her head slowly. *They don't even know me!*

The thought just wouldn't leave her.

~ ~ ~

When the movie was over, Rose immediately got up to leave, not bothering to sit and read the credits or mull over the good and bad parts of the movie, as she normally would have done back home. She had to squint as she stepped out into the lobby; the light seemed so bright compared to the dark theatre. There was Lilly Mae, standing expressionless at the bottom of the steps. Rose searched her face closely. *She doesn't look upset*, Rose thought. Rose didn't know what to say, so she didn't say anything.

As they stepped outside, the warm air enveloped them like a blanket. They hadn't realized the theatre was air conditioned.

"Whatta'ya wanna do next, Lilly Mae?"

"Maybe we should go back to the boat," she suggested.

Lilly Mae had had enough of town. She had never ventured into Savanna before, even though the boat had stopped here many times. She knew better than that. Grandma B. always sent the boys for supplies. She knew it was best not to go where you didn't know the folks, especially if you were a colored and a girl. Everyone knew that.

"Augh, not yet!" Rose whined. "We haven't seen half of town."

"Rose, ain't you got no sense? We don't know these folks. A white girl and a colored girl walkin' 'round together, well…folks might not like dat so well."

Rose was rendered mute. She had never thought of it like that before. They didn't let coloreds into the restaurant, and they had a segregated movie theatre. Maybe there were folks in town who *would* give them a hard time. Then Rose's expression changed to one of determination.

"But wait a minute, Lilly Mae; they can stop us from sitting together in the theatre, and they can stop us from eating together in the restaurant, but there aren't any signs on the street. We can walk together wherever we want!"

"They don't need no signs, Rose," Lilly Mae said quietly. "Dats just da way it is."

Rose's shoulders sank again. "Ahh, come on, Lilly Mae. It's the middle of the day, and Grandma B. said we don't have to be back 'til four." Rose pointed to the clock on the bank a few blocks down. "We've got two hours to kill."

Just then they heard the loud, long call of a train whistle. It sounded close as it echoed off the buildings all around them.

"Come on, let's find the train," Rose called out as she took off running.

She waited for Lilly Mae to catch up, then she headed toward the water; Rose remembered crossing the tracks when they first got off the boat. The whistle blew again, this time even louder. As they passed the last building, they could see the towering locomotive bearing down on them, black-gray smoke belching out the top of the single stack. The intimidating, round, black engine roared past with its huge, spoked wheels spinning with seeming ease under the horizontally revolving arms. The coal car was next, and behind that were box cars as far as they could see. The ground vibrated under their feet; their clothes and hair blew every which way as the wooden and metal cars swayed and rocked, rushing by on the normally rock-solid track, which now reluctantly undulated from the fast moving load. Lilly Mae stepped back. Rose stepped back too; the power of it was both intimidating and awe inspiring. They stood there for what seemed like forever, watching the cars whizzing by. Rose tried to count the cars, but there were so many she lost track. Rose liked waiting for the caboose so she could wave at the man who always stood at the back of the train. He didn't disappoint her; he smiled and waved back.

"At home I'd watch the trains go by when my dad, Michael and I went to the cannery with cabbage. Boy that was a stinky job, but dad said that Germans really liked sauerkraut, so we'd grow cabbage almost every year. Anyway, there was a track right across the road from the cannery, but the trains never went that fast in town," Rose said.

"That was neat!"

Lilly Mae nodded in agreement.

"I know what we can do. We can go back up the hill and start reading our story. That would be a great place to read." Rose looked hopefully at Lilly Mae. "Nobody will bother us up there," she added for emphasis.

"Not up them steps agin, no ma'am. Dat's way too much work."

"Well, how 'bout we walk up the road then. Remember the road that's at the top, just below the last set of steps? I know it ran down toward the south side of town some where, so we could just walk up the road instead of the steps. It'll be a nice walk too. How 'bout that?"

"Well, I sappose," Lilly Mae replied reluctantly. She wasn't keen on the idea, but she figured it was one way to keep them out of trouble. But it was an awfully long way to go. She never understood why some white folks took walks for no good reason. A lot of folks would do it along the riverfront in New Orleans, too. She couldn't see expending all that energy for no good reason. Whenever *she* got some free time she preferred to take a nap, or maybe play marbles or jacks, or even watch the riverboats go by. But walking—there was no sense in it. She should have figured Rose was one of those "walkin' whites."

~ ~ ~

Once at the top of the hill, Rose pulled the book out of the bag. Her face beamed as she ran her hand over the cloth cover. Opening a book for the first time was like traveling to a different place without ever leaving the farm. Rose liked that. If it was a particularly good book she would travel for hours on end, coming back home only because she was hungry or because one of her siblings was calling for her. This book was one of Rose's favorites.

Gerty had given it to her to read after she had read it. Rose was excited to share it with Lilly Mae.

"Do you want to start or should I?" Rose asked.

"Oh. Umm, you can start."

"Okay."

Rose opened the cover slowly, creasing the first page back carefully. She started to read.

"*I had the story, bit by bit, from various people, and, as generally happens in such cases, each time it was a different story…*"

At the end of the first chapter Rose stopped and handed the book to Lilly Mae.

"Your turn."

"Um, I like ta listen ta *you* read. You keep goin'."

"I like listening too. It's easier to imagine what's going on when you're listening. That's the fun of it. You read next."

Rose shoved the book into Lilly Mae's hands.

"Yeah, I remember listen'in to my Gram'ma tell stories," Lilly Mae replied with a long, lost look in her eyes. "Now that woman – she could tell a story! She practically raised us kids 'cause Mama was always off working one job or another. Gram'ma took in laundry, and she'd tell us all kind a stories when we would hep her wit the washin'. Gram'ma didn't need no book though. She knew all kind a stories just by heart." Lilly Mae said, prattling on uncharacteristically. "Man I wished I could remember some of dem stories."

Rose looked puzzled at the unusually loquacious Lilly Mae.

If Rose didn't know any better, she would have sworn Lilly Mae was stalling.

Lilly Mae looked down at the book and stared. She opened it up, and started to slowly read.

"K-Kapta two. As da-dan-dankers po-pored out of thee hall, Froom, dr-dro-dra... Ah, Rose, I can't read worth a tinkers damn."

She closed the book hard in frustration.

Rose blinked her eyes at Lilly Mae. After a moment, she reached out for the book, not saying a word. Lilly Mae gladly gave it back to her.

"I only been through the third grade, and we only just got started readin'."

Rose sat stone faced, looking at Lilly Mae, trying not to act surprised, when suddenly her face lit up.

"Lilly Mae! I've got a great idea! How 'bout *I* teach you to read? I was teaching my little brothers and sisters back home, and Miss Turner said I was a natural-born teacher."

Lilly Mae looked at Rose. She had always wanted to read. And as she thought about it, what did it really matter if it was a white girl teaching her? No one back home would know. Wouldn't her mama be proud if she came home and could read the paper to her? Or maybe she could even teach her brothers and sisters to read.

"Sure Rose, that'd be nice," she replied tentatively.

"We'll start right away—tonight. We'll have to pick up a different book though; this one's a bit hard to start with."

Lilly Mae stood up, brushed herself off and reached her hand out to Rose. Rose looked at the brown hand in front of her, looked up into Lilly Mae's face, smiled, and reached up to meet it.

৪৩ 5 ৪৩

The wider world, with its blind prejudices, was slowly creeping into Rose's flowered wallpaper world. Instead of just the occasional derogatory comment she might have over-heard in town back home, there were now places where certain people couldn't eat and places where certain people couldn't sit – white or colored. Soon she would discover just *being* wasn't allowed, and that…, that went against Rose's grain and all she knew deep down to be true. A stand had to be taken, despite the risks.

~ ~ ~

When they had made it back down to Main Street, Rose stopped suddenly with a blank look on her face.

"I almost forgot! I wanted to get Grandma B. something for…, well, you know what for."

Rose scanned the store fronts. She spied a sign on top of a long building which had windows all along the front. Just below the sign was a large red and white stripped awning which ran the length of the building. The sign read:

5-10-$1 and UP MARTH BROS. 5 -10-$1 and UP.

"That looks like a good place. Let's try there."

Rose headed down the street with Lilly Mae trailing behind, as usual.

Once inside Rose stretched her neck up, trying to look over the aisles to see what she could see. She passed by aisles of kitchen supplies. *No; she doesn't want something for work.* She passed aisles of note paper and stationary. *Um; I'm not sure she can write.* She passed aisles of sewing items. *Nope; too much like work too.* Rose was standing looking down the aisle of shoes when someone tapped her on the shoulder. Rose jumped a foot forward and swung quickly around.

"Oh, I'm sorry my dear. I startled you. May I help you girls?" the elderly lady said in a pleasant tone.

Rose sighed, recovering from her surprise.

"Well, I'm looking for a gift. A gift for-for my Grandma."

"Come right over here. I've got just the thing," she said as she turned and headed toward the back of the store.

Rose looked at Lilly Mae and shrugged her shoulders. She didn't know what to call Grandma B. She really wasn't her grandmother, of course, but she wasn't exactly a friend, and she knew her too well to be considered an acquaintance, so grandma it was. The store clerk led them over to a glass case. Inside it were embroidered handkerchiefs and white gloves.

"Oh, well, my-grandmother, she's not the white glove type, and she probably has lots of handkerchiefs."

Lilly Mae nodded her head in agreement. Rose looked to the left and noticed something which Grandma B. *might* like. Her eyes lit up.

"How much do those cost?" Rose asked.

"We have these all along this shelf and a few smaller ones in the case underneath."

The elderly lady took one of the larger items off the shelf and placed it on the glass case in front of Rose and Lilly Mae. Rose looked at the tag: $14.95.

That's a bit too much.

"How 'bout one of those smaller ones?"

The clerk pulled one out of the case and set it on top: $8.95.

That'll use up most of the money I've earned so far, but that's ok, Rose thought. "I'll take this one, please."

"Shall I wrap it up?"

"Yes, please, and I need some of your note paper and envelopes too."

Once outside, the girls headed back to the book store to pick out a book for Lilly Mae. As before, Lilly Mae stood on the sidewalk while Rose stood waiting for her at the front door.

"I'm gonna wait here," Lilly Mae declared.

"Don't you want to help me pick one out?"

"Naw, you know more 'bout books then I do. You pick out somethin'."

Then she turned and sat on the step, hoping that would end the discussion.

Rose just shrugged her shoulders. "Okay, you hold the packages then," she said, setting them on the step next to Lilly Mae. Then she turned and went inside.

The old man was surprised to see Rose again and asked if she had forgotten something. Rose told him she hadn't, but she needed one more book. She headed straight for the fiction section again. She wanted something that would keep Lilly Mae interested, so she decided on a mystery.

"Agatha Christy, *The Murder of Roger Ackroyd*, that'll do" she said softly as she pulled a book from the shelf and headed back to the front of the store.

As Rose stood at the front door looking out, she noticed a group of young boys with their bikes gathered on the sidewalk. Then she realized, she didn't see Lilly Mae. She quickly pushed through the door and down the couple steps to find out what was going on. The boys were all gathered around something. She made her way through the boys and bikes to see what was going on. There was Lilly Mae, standing at the corner of the building with one of the tallest of the boys standing in front of her. Rose took him to be thirteen or fourteen and not a year more. He turned around when Lilly Mae looked at Rose standing behind him.

"Whatta *you* want?" the boy asked, obviously annoyed by her presence.

"I want you to leave her alone."

"Whatta you care what happens to this darkie?"

Rose narrowed her eyes and stepped closer to the boy, just inches from his face.

"This *girl's* name is Lilly Mae, and she's my friend."

"Friend! Friend! Huh. She ain't nothin' but no nigger," the boy spat back at Rose.

That was it. That was the last straw. This was one fight Rose wasn't going to back away from, no matter what Grandma B. or her mother had told her. Besides, this kid was shorter than her. She figured she could take him.

"Say that again, and I'll make you eat those words."

"She ain't nothin' but a *nigger*," he repeated slowly, puffing himself up as best he could.

"I warned ya," Rose replied. "You asked for it!"

Rose stepped past the boy and set the book on top of the pile Lilly Mae was already carrying.

"Hold this for me, would ya?"

Rose turned back and stepped up uncomfortably close to the boy's face. She stealthily placed one of her legs around the back of one of his, leaned in even closer and easily pushed him down over top of it. He scrambled to get up, but she kicked out one of his hands from underneath him, then jumped on top of him, pinning his arms with her legs.

"Let me up, you cow!"

"Not until you apologize to my friend."

"I ain't apologizing to no nigger!" he snarled back.

Rose grabbed his nose and began to twist. The boy started to cry out in pain. Lilly Mae, seeing her chance to escape, started to slowly make her way around the two on the ground.

"Ooow…Mikey, help me!" the boy called out in a nasally voice.

Rose looked up and saw two of the boys who were watching start to put the kick stands down on their bikes. Lilly Mae saw it too. By now Lilly Mae had made her way to the edge of the ring of boys, as they stood and watched the scene. She set her foot up on the first boy's bike and pushed as hard as she could. The boy wasn't watching her, so it took him by surprise, and he fell right over, right on top of the boy and the bike next to him, who promptly fell on the boy and bike he was standing beside; each boy and bike falling on the next, toppling over like a set of dominos. Lilly Mae covered her wide open mouth with her hand. She couldn't believe what she had done. Rose and the boy on the ground couldn't believe it either. Lilly Mae didn't wait around long to find out what was going to happen next; she ran over to Rose, grabbed her by the straps of her overalls, and pulled her off the bully.

"Com' on, Rose. Let's get outta here!"

Rose watched Lilly Mae take off down the street. She quickly started up after her, down the block and around corner, toward the river and the large, white paddle boat sitting motionless on the river's edge. The girls didn't stop or look back until they fell in an exhausted heap on Rose's bed. They laid there giggling and panting—white legs and brown arms in a jumbled, wiggling heap.

When they finally settled down, they untangled themselves and sat on the edge of the bed.

"Boy, Lilly Mae. I couldn't believe what you did to those boys!"

"I don't believe it either. I didn't mean to knock'em *all* down. I just wanted ta get one or two of'em, so'es we could get away. One against three ain't no fair fight."

"I think you're right, Lilly Mae. I coulda' taken that one kid, but not all three of'em. Thanks."

Lilly Mae smiled. She wasn't sure what to say. She'd never had a white girl stand up for her like that, or call her a friend. Maybe all whites weren't as bad as her grandma had said they were. She'd have to wait and see about this one.

"It's probably after four; we better get down to the kitchen," Rose said.

"Yeah, we don't want the old girl to gets her undies in a bunch," Lilly Mae replied glibly.

She stopped and stared at Rose with her eyes wide open, realizing what she had just said. Then she covered her mouth and started to giggle. Rose started to giggle along with her. She couldn't believe this quiet, little thing could say something so funny. Rose put her arm around Lilly Mae's shoulders, and they headed for the stairs. Lilly Mae put her arm around Rose's waist. The two girls giggled all the way down the hall. Then just before they started down the stairs, Rose stopped and turned back down the hallway.

"I almost forgot the package for Grandma B.," she yelled back to Lilly Mae.

She ran back into the room and got the package off the bed. She hoped Grandma B. would like it.

~ ~ ~

"Where ya girls been? Ya lookin' awful pleased wit' yourself," Grandma B. said as they stepped into the kitchen. "Come over here and wipe dat monkey-faced grin offen' your faces. I be needin' dese here onions peeled."

Rose just stood there facing Grandma B. with her hands behind her back. Lilly Mae stood just behind her. Neither one could stop smiling.

"What's a matter wit you two anyways. Ain't ya heard what I says?" Grandma B. continued, even more annoyed.

Rose pulled out the package from behind her and held it out to Grandma B., not saying a word.

"What's dis here nonsense?" Grandma B. said, wrinkling up her face at the package in front of her.

"It's for you. Lilly Mae and I, we picked it out."

Grandma B.'s face immediately softened, and her jaw went slack. She couldn't remember when anyone had given her a gift when it wasn't Christmas. And her birthday was in July—peak boating season—so she was never home on her birthday and hadn't received a birthday present in years. She looked up at the girls' faces. Rose's eyes beamed; she was so excited, she could hardly keep herself in her skin. Lilly Mae was also smiling, but she wasn't looking at Grandma B., she was looking at Rose. No one had ever given her credit for doing something nice when she really hadn't done anything at all.

There was no pegging this white girl on what she'd do next, Lilly Mae thought.

"Go ahead," Rose continued as she placed the package in Grandma B.'s hands. "Open it."

Grandma B. looked at the package again, then looked back at Rose. She didn't say a word as she pulled up a stool to sit down. She untied the white cotton string and slowly unfolded the stiff brown paper.

"Well my word—a radio! Girl ya ought not be buying me things. Dat money I done give you was for ya to buy somethin' for ya'self."

"Oh, this is for me! Now I don't have to listen to your singin' anymore."

Grandma B.'s expression suddenly changed from soft to hard, then in an instant, soft again.

"You so funny, I forgots ta laugh."

"Come on, let's plug it in!" Rose said, as she grabbed the radio off Grandma B.'s lap. She plugged it in and started turning the big round dial on the front. The sound squeaked and moaned as she ran through the different channels until she finally found one that came in and clear and strong.

"...and what a sound that was, yes-sir-re folks, you ain't heard jazz until you heard Duke Ellington. And you can't talk about legends without talkin' about The Mills Brothers. And here they are singin' *You're Nobody Til Somebody Loves You.*"

The smooth, milk-chocolate, three-part harmony flowed into the room, and Rose couldn't help but nod her head along to the music.

You're no-body 'til some-body loves you,
You're no-body 'til some-body cares.

Before long her foot was tapping and her hips started to sway. She looked up at Grandma B. She was smiling and nodding her head to the music. She strutted up to Grandma B., circling around her as Rose jerked her arms and legs up and down in stiff, awkward motions.

You may be king, you may posses the world and its gold,
but gold won't bring you - happiness, when you're growin' old.

Grandma B. huffed at the sight and shook her head.

"Ya look like a chicken tryin' to get a date," she teased.

"And you can do better?" Rose replied, feeling her oats.

"Darn right I can, honey child, you watch!"

At that, Grandma B. slid off her stool and started shimmying around the room. Her hips moved this way as her shoulders moved that; her arms hung out from her sides, caressing the air softly as her legs moved her small frame effortlessly in perfect time with the music.

> *The world still is the — same,*
> *you'll never — change it,*
> *as sure as the stars — shine a-bove.*

The rhythm had caught Lilly Mae as well, and she was moving in her own little circle amid the trays of breads and boxes of cheese and vegetables. She wasn't as smooth as Grandma B., but she didn't miss a beat. Rose looked at the two women dancing, and a grin the size of Texas came across her face. She started snapping her fingers while she studied Grandma B. carefully, trying to imitate her movements.

The other girls in the kitchen came over to see what all the commotion was about. It was quite a sight. Rose quickly caught on to what Grandma B. was doing, and the three danced the whole song like they were the only ones in the room.

> *You're no-body 'til some-body loves you,*
> *so find yourself some-body to love*

When the song finally ended, Grandma B. flopped back on the stool, a long lost glow emanating from her face.

"Whew, girl! I ain't dance like dat in years. Ya done caught on right quick ya self!" Grandma B. said smiling, still floating in the healing pool of living in the moment.

But it didn't take but a moment, and her countenance changed.

"Now, enouph'a dis here nonsense, we's got work ta do. Shoo now—go on. Ya'll get back ta work," Grandma B. said, waving all the girls away, the subtle glow still detectable in her face.

Rose and Lilly Mae looked at each other and smiled; Grandma B. was back to the hard-shelled, sharp-edged woman they all knew and loved. But it was fun while it lasted. Grandma B. turned around and reached up to the radio to turn it down, but for some reason, she didn't quite make it; she stopped half way and remained there, motionless. A few seconds later she grabbed at the front of her dress, trying to clutch at the deep, sharp pain which shot straight through her and stole the air out of her lungs. She sat down hard on the stool and leaned on the counter, not moving a muscle. Rose and Lilly Mae rushed over to her side. Some of Grandma B.'s soft brown color had drained from her face, and she had a slight glean of sweat across her forehead.

"Grandma B., are you okay?" Rose asked anxiously, afraid she already knew the answer.

Rose's voice was a small, sweet sound in Grandma B.'s ears, a sound just out of reach of her reply.

"Lilly Mae, go get the captain! Quick!"

❧ 6 ☙

Rose didn't realize how much her world was hanging by a thread—a black, kinky thread, mixed with a touch of gray—which had woven its way, unbeknownst to Rose, into her heart. She discovered this the minute Grandma B. sat mute on her kitchen stool. What she had taken for granted at home amongst her family, she had transferred to this small, crumpled figure. Rose had the makings of strong glue brewing inside her, but right now it was in small bits, not fully mixed or hardened. Seeing Grandma B. in obvious pain, unable to move, was pulling and stretching all of Rose's soft spots, and they were on the verge of breaking. The fate of this small, seemingly uncommon woman, whom Rose had come to rely on, needed mending itself. But who was going to do it? Were the pieces too old and worn to hold together? Rose's insides trembled at the thought.

~ ~ ~

Rose and Lilly Mae stood just outside Grandma B.'s cabin door, listening as the doctor was giving Captain Roy his recommendations for her care.

"Now, she needs to rest at least a week; then I doubt she'll be able to work to full capacity. At her age, I'd give her a good month of part-time work before she should even try and push herself. She had quite a significant episode. You need to keep an eye on her. Another episode like that and I doubt…."

The two men walked out into the narrow hallway and noticed the two girls standing there. The kind looking physician smiled at the girls then continued giving orders to the captain, not completing his last sentence.

"The pharmacy on Main is closed, but I'll have a prescription dropped off first thing in the morning. I've given her something to make her comfortable for tonight, so she should be good until then."

"Well, thank you, doctor. We appreciate you comin' down so quickly." Captain Roy shook the doctor's hand, and they headed down the hall.

Rose saw this as their chance to slip into Grandma B.'s room. They stepped tentatively inside the room, but they could never have anticipated what they saw. The cabin was the same size as the one they shared, but it had only one bed in it, in the far right corner, just where Rose's bed stood. Opposite was a desk which was neatly piled with papers. The shelves above it held two or three books, one of which was a bible and all kinds of unusual items: shells, uniquely shaped pieces of driftwood, tins from baking products, a small black cloth doll…. But what surprised them the most were the pictures; the wall next to Grandma B.'s bed was covered with them. There were black and white pictures of every shape and size, some in frames, some just stuck straight to the wall. They were pictures of people, colored people of all different ages: family portraits with people wearing stiff looking clothes and somber faces, baby pictures of small, round-faced children with big dark eyes in their Sunday best, a couple standing in front of a church, children playing on a beach.... Rose and Lilly Mae stood gawking, their mouths hanging open at the sight.

"Ya'll gonna suck down a fly iffin' ya keeps your mouth open like dat."

Grandma B.'s voice startled the girls. They had almost forgotten why they had come. They looked down at the petite, looking women propped up in the small, metal bed. She had regained her color, but she looked a little thinner somehow, more frail.

"Don't just stand der like bumps on a log, go ahead, sit-down!"

The girls immediately sat, tentatively perching themselves on the edge of Grandma B.'s bed. It was decided ahead of time that Rose was going to do all the talking. Lilly Mae didn't even want to be there; she was too afraid of Grandma B. to venture into her room, but Rose had cajoled her into coming for moral support. But if Lilly Mae was pressed, she had to admit, she was concerned about Grandma B. too.

"How are you feeling, Grandma B.?" Rose asked.

"I's doin' all right, child. Little tired though, prob'ly from dat medicine da doctor done give me."

"What happened?"

"It's jus the good Lord remindin' me who's boss. I's afraid the Baas heart done caught up wit' me. My daddy and his daddy befor' him all met der maker on account a der heart."

It had never entered the girls' minds that Grandma B. could have died. The thought of this made both Rose and Lilly Mae sit up straight, eyes as big as saucers. Grandma B. noticed their apprehension.

"Ya'll don't need ta be worrin' none. I ain't goin' no where any time soon. I just needs ta rest here a bit, an I'll be back in my kitchen in a day or two."

"I heard the doctor say you couldn't work for at least a week!" Rose corrected her.

Grandma B. waved that notion away with her hand and a puff of her lips. "*Puff,* Dat doctor, he's use to tendin' ta white folks. I gots things ta do. I can't be sitting 'round relaxin' when der's work needin' ta be done."

"Well, all the girls, we've got things figured out for this evening, and if you tell us what to buy and what needs to be done, we can handle the rest of the excursions for as long as need be. We already talked with the captain about it, and he thought it would be okay," Rose explained eagerly.

"Well, it sounds like ya girls gots it all figured out, all right," Grandma B. replied slowly, shutting her eyes for a moment.

The drugs were pulling her down into her bed against her will. The great pain in her chest was now more of a ghost-like ache; the medication helped that sink further down as well. That she didn't resist.

Rose stood, and Lilly Mae followed her lead. Rose stepped up a little closer to the head of the bed and said in a quiet tone, "Grandma B., we gotta get back to the kitchen."

Grandma B. sleepily opened her eyes at Rose's tender voice.

"We'll come back up in a while to see if you need anything."

Just then, Rose felt something hard nudging her in the back. She turned around to see Lilly Mae holding out the radio.

"Oh yah, Grandma, we brought up the radio for you to listen to, so you wouldn't get too bored."

Rose took the radio from Lilly Mae, set it on the desk and plugged it in. She turned it on, and the mellow sounds of Glenn Miller's *Moonlight Serenade* floated into the room. Grandma B.'s eyes closed again. She took a deep breath and pulled the sound into her chest. It seemed to help sooth the ache inside her almost as well as the medicine had. A subtle smile made its way across her face. The girls smiled along with her. They turned to go, when Rose was startled by Grandma B.'s firm grip on her arm.

"Thanks for da radio, Rosie girl," she said softly as she looked deeply into the young girl's bright blue eyes.

They sparkled back at her. Rose touched Grandma B.'s hand and squeezed gently.

"You're welcome, Grandma B."

~ ~ ~

It took some effort and a little scolding from Captain Roy, but the girls in the kitchen managed to keep Grandma B. in bed for about four days. Rose made up a schedule when each girl was to visit Grandma B. and keep her occupied. Some of the girls could read, so they would take turns reading Rose's book to her.

Grandma B. gave Rose a list of the items they needed for supplies, and Rose would send the boys shopping in Rock Island or Keokuk—some of the other stops along the way. Rose gave everyone strict orders not to tell Grandma B. when they were taking on passengers, so as not to worry her. But most of the girls caved in fairly easily to Grandma B.'s demanding questions, so she knew most everything that was happening on the boat, just like she did when she was in the kitchen.

Day five rolled around, and Grandma B. appeared in the kitchen just as the girls were serving the crew breakfast. Rose walked over to her with a stern look on her face and her hands on her hips.

"Grandma B., you're not supposed to be up!" she scolded.

"Ya put me off long enough, Rosie girl. Don't think I don't know what ya'll been up to!"

"Well, since you're here, you might as well have breakfast with us." Rose walked over to the large dining table and pulled out Grandma B.'s chair. No one had the gumption to sit in it while she was gone, so it sat empty. Grandma B. slowly walked over to her chair and sat down, holding onto the table for support. Glances went all around the table as they all watched her labored movements. They sat in silence as they passed the food around the table to Grandma B.

"Who done made dees here eggs?" Grandma B. barked out after she had taken a few bites.

Lavenia, the young lady Rose first had talked to when she walked into Grandma B.'s kitchen those many weeks ago, froze in her seat.

"I did, Grandma B.," Lavenia finally admitted in a sheepish voice, eyes fixed on the plate in front of her.

"Well, least someone done paid attention in my kitchen. Lilly Mae, hand me one of does biscuits an' da butta too."

Rose smiled; that was the closest thing to a compliment Grandma B. could give. Lavenia sighed and timidly returned to eating. Rose was glad to have Grandma B. back in the kitchen, even though she probably shouldn't have been there. It never felt quite the same when she was gone.

Grandma B. worked in the kitchen all morning, though she sat down most of the time, and when she did get up and move, it wasn't in her usual whirling dervish fashion. She hadn't forgotten how to give orders, however; there were more of those flying around the room than ever before. No one complained, though; it was nice to have things at least partially back to normal. After the dishes were cleaned up from dinner, Rose thought Grandma B. looked especially tired. She was determined Grandma B. should rest.

"Grandma B., we're not taking on any passengers this evening, how 'bout I read you a bit out of my book? We left off at a really good part."

Grandma B. looked up at Rose, knowing what she was up to but not really caring.

"I got some paperwork ta do in my cabin. Guess I could do dat after we reads a while. All right, let's go up."

Rose was surprised how quickly Grandma B. had agreed. She had a few other excuses up her sleeve, which she didn't even have to use. On the way up to her cabin Rose discovered why. Grandma B. *was* very tired; she stopped two or three times, and she had to use the wall of the hallway leading to her room to help prop herself up as she went along. Once in her room, she plopped herself down on the bed, her hand resting on her thighs as her chest heaved up and down.

"Hand me dose papers, child, and my spectacles too," Grandma B. finally said, after she had caught her breath.

Grandma B. had worked up a sweat, so Rose opened the small window to let the slightly cooler river air sweep into the room.

"It's a bit warm in here Grandma B. Do you mind if I open the window?" Rose lied.

"Dat's fine," Grandma B. replied, motioning her confirmation with her hand without looking up from her papers.

"I'm gonna go get my book," Rose said, and she hastily left the room.

Rose stopped just outside the cabin door long enough to hear Grandma B. let out a large sigh. She wasn't so sure of Grandma B.'s prediction that she was going to be all right. *If she had another spell...*, Rose wiped the remainder of that thought out of her head. Rose had a feeling she knew why the doctor stopped talking the other day when he saw her and Lilly Mae. Rose hurried to her cabin so she could quickly get back to check on her. While she was gone, Grandma B. had propped herself up in her bed and was looking at the papers with heavy lids. Rose pulled up the desk chair next to Grandma B.'s bed and gazed up at the gallery of black faces looking down at her.

"Grandma B., can I ask you a question?"

"'Course ya can, honey child," Grandma B. said, setting down her papers and resting her head back against the wall behind her.

Since her attack, Grandma B.'s hard veneer had softened a layer or two when she and Rose were alone.

"Who are all these people?"

"Dat der's my family. See dat one in da middle, da one wid da six kids, dose be my kids."

Rose raised her eyebrows as she strained her neck to look at the picture. She didn't even know Grandma B. had any kids.

She had never talked about them. She stood up for a closer look. Just as Rose suspected, the young colored woman in the picture was trim and quite lovely. She wore a simple-looking dress with a delicate, white collar, a belt around her waist and a stylish hat on her head. She was standing behind a young colored man who was sitting in a chair. He wore a suit and tie and was just as trim and handsome as his wife.

"You were stylin', Grandma B.!"

"Stylin'? I suppose I was. It was a picture for da church directory an, a'course, they hav' ta be makin' a little money, so they cons ya inta buying a picture for home."

"Is that the man that you left?" Rose asked a little tentatively.

"No, dat der is my second husband, Martin. God rest his soul. He was a good man fo he done got his self killed in da mine."

"Oh, I'm sorry, Grandma B."

"Never you mind, child. It was a long time ago."

"How did he die?"

"He was killed when a tunnel caved in," Grandma B explained. "Dat was in Galena. Dats where I met 'im. I worked in the kitchen on a ore boat outta Galena. I met him one night when we was out on da town."

"Where's Galena? Have we passed it yet?"

"Yeah, we done passed it a while back. It's up da Fevre River, just south a Guttenburg but on da Illinois side."

"Oh yeah, I remember seeing that river, but it looked too small for a riverboat."

"Yeah, it's too bad. They had to dredge it regular ta keep it open, but in 1885 when I started workin' on da river, I'd guess der was three hundred or four hundred paddlewheelers comin' and goin' from dat town a year. It was the biggest stop north a St. Luey." Grandma smiled as her mind took her back those many years before. "It was a hoppin' place all right!"

"So is that where you lived once you got married?"

"Not on your life, child. Too much a minin' town; too rough to bring up chill'ins right. We lived in St. Luey, where I grew up, and Martin, he came home every month or so for a few days."

"Wasn't that kinda hard for you, raising six kids mostly by yourself?"

"Not really; when your man be gone most of da time ya can runs things like ya likes'em, and not have ta argue like ya hear alotta dem do. Martin, he weren't home long enough ta get into much of a row, an' when he was gone, I could do things the ways dey oughta be done. You'll find dat out for yourself one day."

Rose smirked at the thought of being married, not giving it much import. "Weren't you afraid, livin' by yourself?"

"Heavens no, girl! I gots lots'a family down dere, an we all looks afta' each otha. And da other good thing was, da other fellas knew I was taken so day done left me alone. Most of da time, anyway."

"Is your family still in St. Louis?"

"Sure 'nough. Got fifteen grandchilds and a few great-grandchilds too!"

"Can I meet'em sometime?"

"I don't see why not."

Rose's whole body brightened at the prospect. She really wanted to see St. Louis, and meeting Grandma B.'s family would be an interesting addition to the trip. She wondered if they would be much different from her own family. She could not know how different their lives were from hers.

"Now, 'nough a dis here family talk. Let's find out whats goin' on in dat der book," Grandma B. ordered, pointing at the book in Rose's hands.

~ ~ ~

Over the next four weeks they traversed up and down the winding, wet, brown highway, from Davenport to Burlington, on the Iowa side, or Keokuk down to Quincy, Illinois.

The town Rose was most anxious to see was Hannibal, Missouri, where Samuel Clemens lived as a boy. It was just as Rose had pictured it. Like most of the river towns, it was longer than it was wide, with Main Street just a block off the river running north and south. This town didn't have a bluff behind it as many did, but once you got a block west of the main drag, the town started to slope up away from the river basin. Running down each side of Main Street were narrow, two and three-story, quaint, brick shops. Just off Main were four buildings furnished in the era of Mark Twain, toting signs such as "Mark Twain Boarding House" and "Becky Thatcher House." They even had a fully furnished law office which was reported to have been used by Mark Twain's father.

They had a whole day layover in Hannibal, and Rose managed to pry Lilly Mae off the boat to check out the town, including a trip to the post office to drop off another letter. Rose tried to write to her family about every other week, so when they stopped anywhere long enough to pick up supplies, Rose would always volunteer to go into town so she could mail her letter. This would also give her a chance to do some exploration. This time when

Rose suggested finding a store which sold books, Lilly Mae was a bit more enthused to join her. Rose had been working with her on her reading skills, and Lilly Mae was anxious to get another book to read; they had read the Agatha Christie book twice through already. Rose told Lilly Mae the coffee-table version of *Huckleberry Finn*, in anticipation of their stop in Hannibal, and she was so taken by the story that they decided they would try and find it at their next layover.

Rose was more conscious of how folks reacted to her and Lilly Mae after their experience in Savanna; trying to shy away from any possible trouble. She had decided getting into another fight might not be such a good idea.

The girls also made a trip to a local clothing store. Rose needed to get something else besides the one dress and overalls she had been wearing. One of her two pairs of socks had a big hole in them, and she didn't have anything to mend them with. Her pants were getting a little short, to boot. If she were home, she knew Silus would be asking her when the flood was coming. So Rose picked out another simple dress, a tee shirt, and a new pair of tan slacks, which she thought were a little more stylish than the overalls. When she was trying on the tee shirt and slacks, she decided she had to break down and buy a bra—something Gerty had tried to get her to do a couple years ago. The flap of her overalls covered up her chest well enough, but with just a tee shirt on, Rose decided she stuck out a little too much in the front. She even convinced Lilly Mae to buy a new dress.

The two girls had a time, laughing and making fun of themselves and each other as they tried on various outfits. Their friendship was growing, as all good friendships do: slowly and with care taken on each side, learning what made the other laugh, and shying away from the things which dampened a good conversation, telling secrets late at night when the lights were out and learning those little things that made the other person smile. All these things would help them in their experiences ahead, experiences which would pull and strain at the closeness they were fostering.

The next day the boat was a flurry of activity. Captain Roy had explained to everyone the night before that they were taking on some important passengers the next evening, so the place needed to look ship-shape. That was the same day Grandma B. woke out of a disturbing dream. Grandma B. felt it was a premonition, and Grandma B.'s premonitions were rarely wrong. This one made her particular edgy, because it was about herself.

The guests that evening were especially important to everyone on the Capitol because they were friends of the Streckfus family, so Captain Roy wanted to make a good impression. This made everyone on the boat anxious, especially Grandma B., mostly because they were to serve a regular sit-down dinner with table cloths and fine china. These additional supplies had been borrowed from a sister boat, the J.S. Deluxe, which had dropped off the items the night before. And to top it off, things weren't going well in the kitchen. Grandma B. had burned the dinner rolls, and the champagne the captain had ordered didn't arrive when it should have. The captain had come down to the kitchen to check on the preparations.

"Grandma B., you know how important these people are. We have to put our best foot forward," Captain Roy said, as the smell of burnt bread filled the air.

"Yes'um, I knows. I be doing the best I can," she replied in a subdued, curt tone, looking him straight in the eye.

"Well, I'll leave you to your work then," he said and left the kitchen without further comment.

He knew getting Grandma B. more upset wouldn't help his cause, so leaving well enough alone was best for now.

Grandma B. was mumbling under her breath as she lifted the heavy tin of flour off the floor to start another batch of buns, when she stopped suddenly. The tin hit the floor with a loud, dull clunk, and everyone close by turned to see what had happened. Grandma B. was leaning on the table, hand to her chest. She slid slowly to the floor as her legs lost their will to hold her upright. Lilly Mae was closest to Grandma B., so she rushed over to her side. Rose was on the other side of the kitchen and hadn't heard Grandma B. drop the tin.

"Grandma B., what's da matter?" Lilly Mae asked, anxiously. "Rose, Rose, come quick! I think Grandma B.'s having another attack!"

~ ~ ~

Grandma B. was looking down at the floor and was unresponsive as Rose ran up to her. She knelt down next to Grandma B. and looked into her face.

"Lilly Mae, go get the captain!" Rose ordered.

But Lilly Mae was stymied in her mission. Grandma B. had gotten hold of Lilly Mae's dress and wasn't going to let go. Grandma B. looked up slowly into Rose's face with that hauntingly familiar, pale brown color, and sweat on her brow. But there was another pain in Grandma B.'s face which wasn't there the first time Rose had seen Grandma B. this way.

"Ya can't...tell...da captain," Grandma B. whispered in a halting voice.

"But you need help. The doctor said...." Rose couldn't complete the sentence or the thought.

Grandma B. let go of Lilly Mae's dress and pulled Rose down close to her face.

"If they finds out...I'll lose...my job," she said slowly, trying to pull in air. "I's got to make it...ta da end a dis season. I can't lose...dis job. I just can't!"

There was a desperation in Grandma B.'s eyes and in her voice which Rose had never seen or heard before, and she realized how important this was to her. She knew then, she would do whatever Grandma B. wanted. Despite this, there was still a nagging deep down inside which told her that what she was about to do would end up wrong.

"What should we do?" Rose asked Grandma B. in resignation.

"I's got some medicine left...in da top drawer a my desk...."

Lilly Mae didn't say a word, she ran out of the kitchen, up and back down the many flights of stairs in just minutes, her heart pumping almost as fast as Grandma B.'s was.

"Here...it is," Lilly Mae huffed out, holding the bottle out to Rose, trying to catch her breath and talk at the same time.

Rose had gotten Grandma B. a glass of water, so she took one of the pills out of the bottle and handed it to her. Grandma B. put the pill into her mouth with some difficulty. She tried to take a drink of the water, but her hand was shaking too much. Rose grasped Grandma B.'s hand around the glass to steady it and guided it to her lips.

Grandma B. sighed and leaned back against the counter, eyes closed, with a tense look on her face. It took a good ten minutes before they attempted to get her off the floor and onto her stool. She was still a bit pale looking, but the furrow had eased out of her brow. The whole kitchen was gathered around her, talking in hushed tones.

"Now, ya'all…don't say a word a dis to da captain, ya hear!" Grandma B. barked out as best she could.

"We won't tell anyone, Grandma B.," Rose reassured her, as the girls all shook their heads in silent fear.

Their fear was not just from Grandma B.'s words but, mostly, from a feeling they all shared; the feeling that the rock which was so steady and firm in their lives looked, at this moment, like it was breaking. And the uncertainty of that thought sent a chill through every girl in the room on that hot August afternoon.

Rose and Lilly Mae were Grandma B.'s hands and legs the rest of that day. They didn't argue with each other or complain about all that needed to be done, they just took turns taking orders from Grandma B. and divvying out tasks to the other girls. If any of the men on the boat came in and questioned what was going on, they kept them away from Grandma B. with any excuse they could think of. It turned out Lilly Mae was particularly good at making up stories, just like her grandma in New Orleans. The men never caught on.

Luckily, the evening went off without a hitch. It turned out to be a good thing Rose and Lilly Mae had purchased new dresses; all the older girls were required to serve the guests, which was a new experience for Rose. She took her cues from Lilly Mae and Lavenia and, as with most things, caught on with ease; keeping the champagne and water glasses full, serving from the left, picking up from the right. After the guests had left, Captain Roy wandered into the kitchen to compliment Grandma B. on a job well done. Rose saw him come into the room and hurried over to meet him, wiping her hands on her not so white apron.

"I'd like to speak to Grandma B. Where is she?"

"She is up in her room, captain. This evening was a little hard on her, so we told her we would clean up, and she could go up and rest."

He had no idea how true that statement was.

"There isn't anything wrong, is there?"

"Oh, no!" Rose assured him. "She's a bit old, ya know. She gets tired by this time of night."

"Well, I can understand that. I'm a bit tired myself. Entertaining important people is not my cup a tea. It can wear you down more than you might think."

At that moment it dawned on Rose how little the captain knew about how hard the people on this boat worked. His life and his stress were on a different level than theirs. He had the stress of making a good impression for the passengers, working with the main office, and making sure everything was kept ship shape by the crew. Their stress was of a more physical nature: waking up early to cook meals for the crew, keeping the boat clean and in working order from top to bottom, going to bed late after cleaning up after the crew's dinner or after the passengers had left; with rarely a rest in between. He really didn't have any idea. She also realized, if she hadn't been working on this boat for the last two months, she would be in the same ignorant state. Rose just smiled back at the captain and nodded her head in recognition.

"Well, tell the girls that we'll put up a whole day in Louisiana before for we take on another group on Sunday, kind of as a thank you for a job well done. I think we could all use the rest."

"Thank you, captain! A truer statement was never said!"

Even if he didn't understand their lot, he did have a kind heart. She couldn't fault him for that. He turned and left Rose and the others to clean up.

~ ~ ~

Grandma B. was never the same after that night. She moved much slower and tired easily. She was always the last to arrive in the morning and the first to go to bed at night. She couldn't lift anything heavy or make it the whole day without an afternoon nap, so the whole kitchen crew had to take up the slack to keep Grandma B.'s secret. Luckily they only had two more weeks in September before they were done for the season. The Capitol only plied the upper Mississippi. Other boats like the Natchez and J.S. Deluxe worked the lower river year round. Once it started to cool off further up river, the Streckfus Company took the Capitol to New Orleans for the winter to be overhauled before starting the winter excursions along the New Orleans river front. Grandma B. had been taking the winter months off after she had turned seventy, five years earlier.

Grandma B. and the kitchen crew managed to keep the extent of her infirmary away from the captain for the most part. He suspected she wasn't well, however, when he caught a glimpse of her walking to her cabin one evening, propping herself against the wall with her hand as she walked. In addition, he noticed she was always sitting whenever he entered the kitchen. The service to the passengers never faltered, however; so he decided not to mention it to anyone else. He too realized there was only a short time left in the season, then Grandma B. could take a much needed rest.

To keep up Grandma B.'s expected level of service, Rose and the other girls worked harder than they ever had. They rose a bit earlier and went to bed a bit later, falling into bed and to sleep within minutes of their heads hitting their pillows. The whole kitchen staff was counting the days to the end of the season. Rose was counting the days as well, but for a different reason; soon she would be in St. Louis.

As they worked together in the kitchen, Rose would needle Grandma B. for information about St. Louis, and as long as Grandma B.'s patience lasted, she'd supply it. Rose learned that most of Grandma B's family lived in a part of St. Louis they called "The Ville." She had moved there in 1910 from the Mill Creek Valley area of St. Louis, where she grew up. She moved there because the Ville had the only black high school in St. Louis at the time, and she wanted her children to go to high school. In fact, all of her children had finished high school—something she was quite proud of. Only one of her children was at home yet—her youngest daughter, Grace and her family. Grandma B. liked having them there because they looked after her home for her when she was gone during the riverboat season.

Grandma B. talked about her experience at the 1904 Worlds Fair, at a place called Forest Park. It sounded wonderful, taking up acres and acres of land with a zoo, amphitheater, art museum, golf courses, tennis courts, and even paths for people to ride their horses.

Grandma B. loved music and she talked about nights out on Biddle or Market Streets.

"Ya ever heard da *Maple Leaf Rag*?" Grandma B. asked one afternoon.

Rose shook her head, no.

"I suppose ya too young fo dat. Now dat's good music! Scott Joplin done wrote dat one, and I done saw him perform it at da Rosebud Café on Market. Man, dat was a hoppin' place. The young Tommy Turpin and Mr. Joplin would burn it up 'til late in'ta da night. We'd be havin' so much fun we'd lose track a time and stay up 'til two or three in da mornin'."

Rose had heard enough. She couldn't wait until the season was done.

There weren't many stops between Louisiana, Missouri, and St. Louis, but it still seemed like forever to Rose until they caught sight of the "Gateway to the West." Lilly Mae was more anxious than usual herself. She wanted to get home to New Orleans and show her family how well she could read.

The Capital had made it to St. Louis a couple times a season, only to leave again after taking on supplies and passengers for day trips back up to Alton or Silver Island. Just the sight of the huge city, especially framed by the magnificent metal arches of the Eads Bridge, had Rose's imagination going for days. Rose didn't get to set foot on the St. Louis shore until the twentieth of September. It was a day which set in motion things that would surprise even Rose.

~ ~ ~

The week before the end of the summer season, tempers were short all around. Rose didn't understand why it was still so hot and humid in September, until Lilly Mae pointed out that they had traveled down half the Mississippi, so it was bound to be hot way into the fall. Lilly Mae and Rose got into a few good fights about nothing much, mostly because they were tired and hot, and they wanted to be off the boat. But on Rose's last night on the Capitol, they were both in a good mood, and neither of them could sleep.

They were docked on the levee in St. Louis, between Eads Bridge and Poplar Bridge. Unlike usual, their window and door were wide open to capture any small bit of cool, night air. Unfortunately, that also let in the noise of the city, and this city didn't shut down at night like most of the towns they docked next to. The usual summer night sounds of frogs and crickets were drowned out by the sounds of the vehicles and horses which filled the night sky above St. Louis. The lights of the city were bright enough to illuminate the girls' room, and the temperature had dropped only five degrees since mid-afternoon. It didn't feel much different than it had during the day, and the heat of the city seemed to negate any coolness the river normally gave.

The girls laid in bed, stripped down to as little as they could and still be decent, moisture sitting on their still bodies as if they had walked a mile on a sunny day. There eyes were wide open, looking at the ceiling, with all kinds of thoughts racing through their heads. Lilly Mae was thinking of her family; she was picturing their faces as they hugged and greeted her upon her arrival home. She could see their looks of surprise as she took out one of her books and started to read. She couldn't help but smile.

Rose was thinking of all the wonders which lay ahead: Forest Park, the street cars that Grandma B. said they would take to get to her home, and the large buildings she saw from the boat. She was eager to get a good look at them up close. A city this size would be sure to have vast libraries, beautiful art museums, large theatres, and movie houses.... The possibilities were endless. The pier on the levee where the riverboats docked was a block away from the city. That block was empty at night, except for the railroad tracks which were elevated off the ground so horse carts and trucks could run underneath them unencumbered during the busy work day. Rose looked over toward Lilly Mae and noticed she was still awake. She sat up and dropped her bare feet to the floor.

"Let's go outside!" she whispered to Lilly Mae.

"It's late," Lilly Mae reminded her.

"I know, but it's too hot in here, and I can't sleep," she said, standing up. "Maybe it's a little cooler outside. Come on." She motioned Lilly Mae to follow.

Lilly Mae couldn't argue with cooler, but she wasn't going out there in just her tee shirt and undies like Rose. She slipped a dress on and followed out behind, down the partially lit hallway and onto the walkway on the side of the crew's cabins. They tried not to wake anyone up, since most everyone had their doors open as Rose and Lilly Mae had. Rose was leaning out over the rail; her smile seemed to illuminate her face even more than the lights of the city.

"Can't you just wait until tomorrow?" Rose said excitedly. "Look how big this city is; you can't even see where it begins or where it ends." She stretched her arms wide to illustrate her point.

Just past the gradually sloping levee and the elevated train tracks, there were four and five story buildings as a far as she could see, and deeper than her eyes could take her, but not her imagination.

"There must be thousands of people living in that city, and half of them still seem to be awake! Have you ever seen such a big city?"

Lilly Mae nodded her head. She had seen a city just as big; she lived in it, and it wasn't anything special to her. In fact, since she had been working the riverboat trade, she had come to enjoy the quiet, peace and green-brown solitude of river life. If her family didn't live in New Orleans, she wouldn't be in any hurry to go home.

"Oh, yeah, I forgot. You live in New Orleans," Rose remembered, "so this is no big deal to you."

Then Lilly Mae said something she never thought she would say to a white girl, something she had been contemplating for some time.

"Rose," she started with some hesitation, "would you like ta come down ta NaOrlins with me? Da captain won't mind if you hitch a ride down."

Rose's face lit up. "Really? You want me to come with you?" she said, as she grabbed Lilly Mae around the shoulders and squeezed as hard as she could. "Oh, that would be wonderful!"

Lilly Mae winced. Even though she had gotten to like this chatty white girl, she hadn't gotten used to the physical assaults of affection Rose doled out every so often. She wondered if all white girls touched each other this much.

"Girl, lighten up a bit; you're killin' me."

"Oh, I'm sorry."

Rose dropped her arms. She turned and looked back toward the city. This time her whole body smiled.

"New Orleans! I only dreamed I would make it down that far. My family won't believe that, for sure! Oh, now I'll never get to sleep!"

"Well, we oughda try. We got some cleanin' ta do for we get off dis here heap," Lilly Mae reminded her. "I's goin' ta bed," she said as she turned and headed inside.

"I suppose you're right, but it's not going to be easy," Rose whispered behind her. She stepped up quickly next to Lilly Mae and hooked their arms together.

"Imagine, New Orleans!" she started up in hushed tones. "You're going to have to tell me all about it. Can you see the ocean from there? Are there big parks like the one that Grandma B. talks about in St. Louis?"

As they laid back in their beds, Rose prattled on for quite some time, musing about what she would see and what she wanted to do when they got to New Orleans. Lilly Mae would add a "uh huh" here and a "yeah" there, but after a while she gave up responding. It didn't seem to matter to Rose. In fact, she didn't realize Lilly Mae had fallen asleep until she heard a snoring sound coming from her side of the room. Rose smiled, yawned, then rolled over to fall quickly to sleep, dreaming of big buildings and street cars.

~ ~ ~

The next morning Lilly Mae was serenaded out of her sleep to the melodious tune that Jeb was playing on the triangle, calling everyone to breakfast. It took Lilly Mae a bit to wake Rose up, but once Rose remembered what day it was, she was dressed and down to the kitchen before Lilly Mae had finished her hair. The mood in the kitchen was light, as everyone was ready for some time off, and the final paycheck which was coming for some. Grandma B. had even gotten to the kitchen a bit earlier than she had in the three weeks since she had her second spell. There were special cinnamon rolls on the counter, sausage in the frying pan, and pancakes on the griddle. The kitchen smelled grand. There was an unusual amount of conversation at the breakfast table, and this time it wasn't just Rose who was talking. Everyone seemed to have something to say: what they would do first when they got off the boat, what they were going to buy, who they were going to see.

When Lilly Mae brought out the pancakes, she had a separate plate with a cinnamon roll on it, which she sat down in front of Rose. It had a candle on it.

"Lilly Mae just tol' me last night ya done had your sweet sixteen birthday a couple weeks back. I didn't have time ta bake ya a cake, but I hope a sweet roll'll do," Grandma B. said with a smile.

"Lilly Mae, you weren't supposed to tell," Rose said looking at Lilly Mae, mildly cross.

Lilly Mae just shrugged her shoulders and grinned. Someone at the table started up the birthday song, and the whole room took up the tune; joy and well wishes reverberated off every wall. Rose's eyes welled up, and she worked hard to blink away the tears. She did miss her family so, but she had come to think of these people around this table as her family, and she was happy to be among them.

After breakfast was cleared, Rose checked with Captain Roy to make sure it was okay for her to ride the rest of the way to New

Orleans. He didn't mind, of course. In fact, he liked the idea of having a willing ear for the quiet trip south. Trips to the captain's office had become a regular affair for Rose, so she liked the idea of getting information about the other half of this grand river she called home. The rest of the trip was straight down to New Orleans with no excursions to take on, so the boat would only need a skeleton crew. Rose said her goodbyes to those who weren't staying on, and went to find Grandma B. to tell her about the change in plans. She was supposed to have stayed with Grandma B. a week, but she couldn't pass up an invitation to visit New Orleans. She hoped Grandma B. wouldn't mind.

The boat was staying in St. Louis for two days because that was where the company office was, and they needed to take on a new load of coal. The captain had administrative business to take care of before he could take the Capitol to warmer waters. Rose was still able to go with Grandma B. to visit her family, which seemed to ease Grandma B.'s disappointment at the change of plans. Exploring all of St. Louis would have to wait for another day. Lilly Mae was coming along too—Grandma B. made sure of that. Before they left the boat, however, Grandma B. summoned the two girls to her cabin.

When they walked into the room Grandma B. was sitting at her desk writing, but they hardly noticed her sitting there. Their eyes were immediately drawn to the wall above Grandma B.'s bed. They stood with their mouths as wide open as the first time they had seen it, but this time it was for a different reason entirely: the wall was bare. All that was left were dark shadows, nails, and pieces of tape where the pictures had hung surrounded by a faded, lighter hue.

Grandma B. finished what she was doing and turned to face the girls.

"Grandma B., why did you take all your pictures down?" Rose asked in amazement.

"I just didn't feels like I could leave'em here dis time. Don't ask me why, child. I dunno," she finished curtly, waving her hand in the air to push away any further questions.

"Now, the reason I done asked ya here is 'cause I wanted ta thank ya's for help'en me since I's been sick, specially dese last couple weeks."

"Oh, that's okay, Grandma B.," Rose answered for both girls, which didn't bother Lilly Mae. She was used to Rose answering for both of them. She still didn't feel comfortable conversing with Grandma B. as if she were a friend, as Rose seemed to be able to do. Back home she had to be careful what she said around black women Grandma B.'s age. She was more likely than not to be swatted "up-side the head" for no good reason, or no good reason Lilly Mae could think of, anyway. It didn't matter if you were family or not.

"I couldn't a made it da whole season wid'out your help," Grandma B. added.

"We didn't mind Grandma B., really," Rose replied, telling a bit of a white lie.

Of course, it was hard to keep going at times, with all the extra work and Grandma B. not feeling well most of the time. Rose was never sure she was doing the right thing by not telling the captain. At one point, about a week ago, she even started to walk up the pilot house steps to do just that, but changed her mind. Rose decided she had to honor the decision Grandma B.

was making for herself, even though she didn't agree with it. But what she had witnessed that day tore at her heart none-the-less.

~ ~ ~

The incident happened after they had just finished with an excursion out of Indian Cave and Jefferson Barracks—a beautiful wooded bluff south of St. Louis. It had been a particularly hot few days, and Grandma B. was more rosy-cheeked and sweaty than normal, so Rose kept a full glass of cold water next to her all morning long. Grandma B. couldn't make it past the noon meal. As she was heading up the steps to her cabin for a nap, Rose watched her slowly struggle with each step. When, without notice, one of her feet didn't quite make it up far enough and down she went, face first. Rose ran up behind her and reached for her waist to help her up. Grandma B. lay motionless. Rose's heart began to race.

"Oh God, I knew it! Grandma B., Grandma B., are you all right?"

Grandma B. eventually pushed herself away from the steps, groaning as she moved.

"Oh, I knew I should have said something, I knew it!" Rose said to herself, tears running down both her cheeks.

Grandma B. slowly turned herself around and sat gingerly on a step. She looked up at Rose's tear-streaked face and smiled. She reached her hand out to her cheek and wiped away a tear.

"I'll be all right, child. Just took a little tumble is all. Dese ol' legs ain't what day use ta be. Don't ya be worrin' your self none. I'll be fine in a minute or two."

"Don't you think you should tell the captain, Grandma? There's only one week left. I'm sure he'll let you stay on. Then we could get more help so you could rest," Rose pleaded with reddened eyes.

Grandma B. took Rose's hands softly in hers. As hard as Grandma B. could be at times, her softness could melt an iceberg.

"I know dis be hard on ya, child. I's sorry for dat. And I do appreciates all ya been doin' for me, I really do, but I gotta make it da whole season. See, I gets a bonus if'in I makes it da whole season, and I need dat money, child. I need dat money."

Rose looked down at the thin, brown, wrinkled hand which held hers as a thought ran through her head: *She's comforting me and she's the one that's really hurting.*

"I'll be okay. I just need ta rest a spell. If dis damn heat'ed break, I'd feel a sight better. Now, hep dis here old lady up da rest of da way. I think I done bruised my knee. My pride just flew out da winda, so I don't need ta be mindin' 'bout dat no mo."

Rose smiled, wiped her face with her apron, and took Grandma B.'s arm over her shoulder, gingerly helping her the remaining way to her cabin.

Rose didn't want to experience anything like that again, so she was happy they were leaving the boat and happy Grandma B. would finally get a good, long rest.

~ ~ ~

"Now, I ain't got nothin' of any worth ta give you girls for all dat ya done for me, so I wrote ya a little letter and put a little extra somethin' in da anvelope."

Grandma B. handed an envelope to each girl. Their names were written in somewhat uneven block letters on the front. Rose looked at the envelope, then back at Grandma B. For maybe the second time in her life, she didn't know what to say. She stood up, leaned over, and gave Grandma B. a kiss on the cheek, then sat back down, staring at the letter. Lilly Mae was touched by Grandma B.'s kindness, just as Rose was, and dropped all her apprehension to give Grandma B. a kiss on her other cheek.

"Now, ya all can look at'em later. It's high time we get off a dis here tub!" Grandma B. said with excitement.

She hadn't been home in six months and, for some reason she wasn't quite sure of, she was more anxious than normal to see her family. Maybe it was the disturbing dream she had had the night of that special dinner. In her dream she had fallen in the water and was franticly swimming toward the surface. As she swam upwards, she felt like her body was being pulled further down, the water pressing her chest, making it more difficult to breathe. In her dream she started to panic, gasping for air as she was jolted awake, sweat pouring off her face, her heart beating so hard she had to hold her chest to keep it from jumping out. Grandma B. knew dreams meant things, and what this one meant she didn't let herself know.

☙ 7 ❧

A new city brought new opportunities. Rose was always open to new opportunities, but was she ready for the consequences those new experiences would bring?

~ ~ ~

They stepped off the boat and onto a floating, covered pier which ran a good 300 ft along the levee. It had shorter sections of pier perpendicular to it, equally spaced along its length, which attached it to shore. There was another riverboat tied up to the pier, which was taking on passengers just like the Capitol had a few days ago. It took a little tussling with the crowd before Grandma B., Lilly Mae, and Rose made it off the pier and onto dry land. Rose had the strange urge to drop to her knees and kiss the ground, but she and Lilly Mae were each carrying one of Grandma B.'s suitcases, since Grandma B. had all she could do to walk among the crowds to make it to shore. They had the trek to the street car ahead of them, as well.

They walked under the elevated railroad tracks and stepped up to 4th Street, the first north-south street they came to. On the river side of 4th Street there was a lone stone building. Grandma B. said it was called the "Old Church". It was the largest church Rose had ever seen. It was made of light-colored stone and was at least three stories high, with large round pillars in the front, topped off by a tall pointed steeple. Rose found out later that it was over 100 years old. She would have loved to have a look inside, but Grandma B. looked tired already, so she didn't even ask.

Grandma B. expertly made her way across the busy street, with Lilly Mae close behind and Rose bringing up the rear. It was hard for Rose to concentrate on where they were going; there was too much to look at. The buildings closer to the levee looked in disrepair. Many of them were boarded up. Some were missing altogether, with just an empty, garbage-strewn lot in its place. Once they walked a few more blocks west to Broadway, the city started to improve in appearance.

On Broadway they turned and walked north two more blocks to Olive Street, stopping every block for Grandma B. to catch her breath. Once they reached Olive Street, they were surrounded by three and four story buildings and people of every persuasion going this way and that; white and colored men in suits and ties, women in dresses, and colored men in trucks or behind the occasional horse cart. Rose could see even bigger buildings further down the street. They had to be ten or fifteen stories high. Rose had never seen sky scrapers before or so many big buildings all huddled together. It all seemed larger than life.

Besides the cars and trucks everywhere, there were street cars making their way along tracks built right into the street. They were attached to wires which were suspended above the street, and they arched and snapped as the cars moved along the wire. Rose was mesmerized by it all. She was so preoccupied she didn't notice Grandma B. and Lilly Mae had stopped, and she ran right in to them.

"Oh, sorry 'bout that," Rose apologized.

"Pay attention girl. You ain't in Wisconsin no more! Keep your money in your front pocket and your eyes on da street," Grandma B. scolded.

Grandma B. checked her watch, then looked down the street.

"It's gonna be a small piece 'fore the car comes along. Put da suitcases down. I need to set a spell."

The girls did as they were told, and Grandma B. perched herself on the edge of the two suitcases.

"Keep your eye out, and let me know when ya sees it comin'," she added.

As they stood there waiting for the street car, Rose noticed something odd; she had the strange feeling that she was swaying.

"Lilly Mae, do you feel like you're moving?" Rose asked.

"Yeah, that always happens after ya been on the boat a long time. It'll stop after while."

"I wonder why I never felt this before?"

"'Cause ya probably never stood still long enough to feel it," Lilly May answered smugly.

Rose shook her head softly and grabbed a light pole to try and make the feeling go away sooner rather than later. She didn't like the way it stirred up her stomach.

After about fifteen minutes, the Olive Street car came into view.

"Here it comes, Grandma B.," Lilly Mae announced.

A group of people had gathered at the stop and were now shuffling toward the curb as the street car pulled up in front of them. Grandma B. rose slowly. Rose and Lilly Mae each grabbed a suitcase, as Grandma B. slowly made her way into the car.

"Well, long time no see, Grandma B.!" the colored man behind the controls said.

Grandma B. shook her head slowly, "Too long, Robert, too long."

Grandma B. put forty-five cents in a box at the top of the steps and explained she was paying for the two girls along with herself. The conductor smiled kindly at the girls as they lugged the suitcases up the steps behind Grandma B. They all found a seat and sat down.

"Lilly Mae, go get three transfers. I done forgot," Grandma B. ordered.

The street car seemed full already, but more people squeezed on at each stop along Olive Street, most having to stand, since all the seats were taken. They made the slow ride due west, stopping at most of the intersections to let folks on and off or for cross-traffic to move by. There was the same mix of people on the car that were on the street, with a few young children in matching school uniforms mixed in; some were even hanging out of the doorways. The windows all along the car were open, but the mix of sweaty bodies and women's perfume was making Rose feel a little claustrophobic. She turned her head and looked out the window for a bit more air and a better view.

Every street they passed seemed the same as the last; buildings and people were everywhere. Rose couldn't tell how tall the buildings were until the car got far enough down the road that she could look back and see the long, tall tunnel that stretched as far as she could see; the tall buildings looking like they would touch each other at the far end of the street. The further away they got, the closer the buildings became. Rose thought it was an interesting optical illusion. Eventually, they rode into an area where the street was wider and the buildings not as towering. But during their long trek down Olive Street, there wasn't a park or expanse of grass to be seen. All the buildings were close together, if not touching each other, with an occasional gas station or car lot along the way.

Finally, Grandma B. stood, and the girls rapidly followed suit. They teetered their way to a doorway on the wavering street car as it came to a slow stop. Grandma B. gingerly stepped down.

"You take care a yourself now, Grandma B., and say hi to Grace for me," the conductor said.

Grandma B. didn't say a thing; she just waved her hand above her head in acknowledgement, not even turning around.

They walked around the corner and stood kitty-corner to where they had gotten off. The girls put down the suitcases once again.

Rose noticed they were standing on Sarah Street. She thought that was a funny name for a street. They waited only a few minutes this time, and the street car showed up at the stop light across Olive Street. There were only a few people getting on this time. They found their seats and enjoyed a roomier ride up to Easton Avenue. When they got off this time, Grandma B. informed them they had to walk the rest of the way.

It was getting on to midday, and the day was heating up. The girls struggled a bit with Grandma B.'s suitcases, but Grandma B.

stopped every block or so to wipe her brow or catch her breath, so they had lots of opportunities to rest themselves. Rose took off her cap and stuffed her hair up underneath it. It had grown to her shoulders over the summer and was warm on her neck.

They turned onto St. Louis Avenue and finally stopped at a two-flat brick house which was painted red. Grandma B. didn't say a thing; she slowly walked up the sidewalk, grabbed hold of the rail on the small front porch, and pulled herself up the steps. The door on the right was closed. The one on the left was open. She pulled open the screen and stepped inside the open door without waiting for Rose or Lilly Mae to follow. She waddled straight ahead, down a long hall and into the kitchen at the back of the house. There she was greeted by a squeal of welcome and a hug from a young girl. Rose tentatively opened the screen door, and the two girls walked in and set the suitcases down. Rose took off her cap and stuffed it in her back pocket. A small boy, not much bigger than the girl they had seen, ran into the hall and up to Grandma B., giving her a big hug. Grandma B. was already sitting down at the kitchen table.

"You ain't gettin' too big to give your Grandma a kiss, is ya?" Grandma B. asked, pretending to be disappointed.

The little boy smiled and planted a big, wet kiss on Grandma B.'s cheek.

"Lordy, girls, what's da hold up? Come on in," she yelled down the hall.

At that, the two children turned and looked at the new-comers walking down the hallway toward them. Rose and Lilly Mae stood just inside the kitchen doorway, each not feeling comfortable enough to make it very far into the room.

"Della and Marcus, dis here be Rose and Lilly Mae," Grandma B. explained as she motioned first to Rose then to Lilly Mae.

"Hello," they said in unison.

"They're gonna stay with us a couple days."

The kids didn't say a thing, they just stared at the two strangers.

"Don't just stand der, take a load off," Grandma B. said, motioning to the other chairs around the table.

The girls moved slowly to the table and tentatively sat down, as the room seemed thick and hard to move in. The children's eyes were watching their every move.

"Now, ain't it polite ta offer our guests somethin' cold ta drink?" Grandma B. chided the children.

"Would you like some water, or we have iced tea?" asked Della in a polite tone. Rose estimated Della to be about seven.

"I'll have water, please," Rose replied.

"Me too," added Lilly Mae.

"Git your Grandma B. a tall iced tea, honey child, with lots a ice, ya hear."

"Yes, ma'am," was her respectful reply.

Rose noticed Grandma B. didn't flinch at the "ma'am" as she had when she had said it when they had first met. Maybe it was only something family could say.

Della took a pitcher of iced tea out of the refrigerator, set it on the counter, then pulled over a stool to reach up into the cupboard for the glasses. Rose noticed her difficulty and stood up quickly to help.

"Here, let me help you with that," she said, reaching above Della for the glasses.

Della looked up at the stranger and smiled.

"Thanks," Della said.

The two girls served up the drinks, then sat down to enjoy them. The warmth of the afternoon and the stillness of the air was heating the room and all of the inhabitants inside it.

"Where's Todd and your mama and daddy?" Grandma B. asked, after she drank half her tea straight down.

"Todd, he done went to the 'Y,' and Mama and Daddy are at the store. They got your letter and knew you was comin' home today."

Just then, a young, colored couple came into the house, each carrying a bag of groceries. They slowed up slightly when they caught sight of Rose and Lilly Mae sitting at the table with Grandma B.

"Oh Mama, you're home!" the young woman exclaimed as she set the bag on the table and gave Grandma B. a hug and kiss.

"Welcome home, Grandma," came a less enthusiastic greeting from the young man, who dutifully gave his mother-in-law a kiss on the cheek. Grace stood silently, looking curiously at her mother for a moment before she turned her attention to Rose and Lilly Mae.

"And who are *these* young ladies?" the woman asked in a polite, yet somewhat reserved tone.

"This here be Rose and Lilly Mae. Rose and Lilly Mae, this here be Darrell and Grace," Grandma B. said. "They be stayin' with us a few days."

"Nice to meet you," Rose said, standing and extending her hand to Grace and then to Darrell.

Lilly Mae stood slightly and nodded her head tentatively in greeting.

Grace and Darrell turned and stared at Grandma B.

"Well…, we didn't plan on extra visitors, Mama. You didn't tell us you were going to bring guests home," she said in a somewhat peeved tone.

"I don't need ta be tellin' ya everythin' dat happens in my own house, now do I?" came Grandma B.'s curt reply.

"Well, ya do if you want us to have enough food in the house!" Grace shot back.

She abruptly grabbed the groceries from the table and took them over to the counter where her husband was standing. She noisily began to empty the bags, not saying a word. She didn't have to. Rose could see the steam coming out of her ears. The air in the room had suddenly gotten thick again.

~ ~ ~

The girls both took a drink of their water and stared straight ahead. They all sat in silence until Grandma B. suggested the children take Rose and Lilly Mae out back and show them around. The girls immediately stood and followed the children out the back door. They didn't make it very far, however; once the children were out the back door they immediately sat down on the porch steps. If there was going to be adults arguing, they wanted to be in ear shot to hear what was said.

The backyard was quite small, only just wider than the house, closed in on each side by a wooden fence and an alley which separated Grandma B.'s backyard from the backyards of the houses just behind hers. The girls weren't sure what to do, so they just stood behind the children, each leaning on a porch post. They were all close enough to hear the conversation that transpired in the kitchen.

"We can't be keep'in no white girl here, Mama! What'll the neighbors say?" Grace started in. "And besides, we ain't got any extra beds. You know Todd's still livin' here. Where are they gonna sleep?"

"The children can sleep together, and Todd can sleep on the couch. And I don't give a tinkers damn 'bout what da neighbors say. Now, I don't want ta be hearin' no more 'bout dis. They be staying and dat be dat. There ain't no arguing gonna be happin' in dis here house."

After a long silence, they heard Grace speak up again.

"Well at any rate, I'm glad you're home, Mama," she said in a more reserved, surrendered voice. "Todd's been hold'en off gettin' a job, so he could watch the kids for us, and I done started my second year a nursing school, like I told ya in my letter. We were hopin' you could watch the kids for us when you got home."

"I don't know if I can watch dose kids, Grace. I done had two spells not too long ago, and I'm damn lucky I's even here; only by da grace a God, I tells ya. He done sent me dem two angels I done brought home."

"Spells? What do you mean spells?" Grace asked, sitting down next to her mother. "I thought you looked a little thin and over-tired." She grasped her mother's hand and looked into her eyes.

"It's da ol' Baas heart rearing its ugly head. Done cut me to da quick a couple a times. If it weren't for dem two girls, I would'da been home 'fore da season was over and probably in a pine box, I can tell you dat right now."

"Oh Mama, you should go ta Doc Anderson and get checked out."

"Don't need no doctor tellin' me what's wrong. All dey do is charge an arm and a leg and tells ya what ya already know. There ain't nothin' dey can do fo me, child. 'Sides, I still got some medicine a doctor up north done give me for when it gets bad enough. I just has ta take it easy for a while; get my strength back."

"Oh dear, Todd won't be too happy ta hear he can't go ta work yet, and he applied at the technical school for the second term. The boy's eighteen, Momma. He wants ta get on with his life."

"I can't help dat, child. Maybe in a month or so, after I done rested up a bit."

"It's that dumb boat, Mama. You should have quit that job years ago," Grace chided her.

"And what was I gonna live on den? Tell me dat," Grandma B. questioned.

"Well, they've got Social Security now, Mama. You should get off that boat, retire and get Social Security."

"They ain't gonna pay no old, negro woman ta sit on her ass and do nothin'," Grandma B. said with conviction, "An don't try and tell me any different!"

Grace could tell by the familiar tone, there was no talking to her mother at this point, so she didn't bother trying. There was a small silence, then the sound of a chair scraping across the floor.

"I got ta lay down a piece. Call me when dinner's ready, will ya?" Grandma B. said wearily.

"Sure Mama, you go lay down and rest," Grace replied. "We'll take care of things."

~ ~ ~

Once the kids realized there wasn't going to be any more arguing, they stepped off the porch and called for Rose and Lilly Mae to follow.

"Ya wanna see the neighborhood?" asked Della.

"Sure," Rose replied after a moment. She was still lost in thought about the conversation she just over-heard; especially the part where Grandma B. had said she was lucky to even be alive.

"Then come on," Della waved.

Della led the way, with Marcus skipping happily behind. At one point she slowed up and took his hand as they walked along. It made Rose think of John and Katie back home. They would have been about the same ages.

The first large building they came across was just a couple short blocks from their house.

"That there, that's the high school," Della explained.

The large two story building was stately looking, taking up at least two blocks and sitting up off the street, which made it look more impressive.

"This here's the church we go to," Della continued, after they had walked a few more blocks south. It was a moderate-sized red brick building which sat on the corner. The sign in front read:

Antioch Baptist Church
"Come and I shall give you rest. Matthew 11:28-30"

"What's that?" Rose asked, pointing to an enormous, six-story, white and red brick building under construction just east of the church.

"Oh, that's Holmer G. Hospital. That's the first hospital in St. Louis that's gonna be run by coloreds, just for coloreds."

Della said this in a way which gave Rose the impression she was repeating what she had heard from someone else.

"Ya wanna see our school? It's neat. I'm in kindergarden ya know," Marcus said, very proud of himself.

"Wow, kindergarden. I didn't know you were that old!" responded Rose.

Marcus shyly smiled at Rose and stood a little taller.

They walked back toward Grandma B.'s house, and just a block west of their house, they came to a three story brick building with the name Elleardsville written in cement above the entrance.

"This is Simmons school," Della explained. "Lots a kids go there."

The Ville looked like a nice place to live. The houses they saw were mostly brick, two-story, two-units like Grandma B.'s, placed very close together or right up next to each other. They had passed a small corner grocery on one corner and a liquor store on another. As they made their way around the neighborhood, Rose was suddenly keenly aware of the white path she made in the sea of black faces. The people she passed obviously weren't used to seeing a white person in their neighborhood; most kept eye contact with Rose longer than they normally would have. And the returned "Hellos" to Rose's greetings were either delayed or totally absent. It left her with an odd, uneasy feeling—an *I'm not sure I'm welcome* sort of feeling; something she had never felt before. Of course, Lilly Mae had no such angst.

When they made it back to the house, Della and Marcus were visibly tired, and all four of them were hot and sweaty. They slowly trudged up the steps, into the house and straight into the kitchen. Della stepped into the room first and said hello to a young man standing at the sink. It was her cousin Todd. He had a basketball under one arm and was drinking a glass of water with the other. He had brown shorts on and a white, sleeveless tee shirt which was streaked down the center, front and back, with sweat. His light brown, muscular arms gleamed and perspiration dotted his forehead. You could even see the perspiration on his scalp through his short, nappy hair.

Todd turned toward Della to return the greeting but was struck by what he saw. Marcus followed behind his sister, and behind him were Rose and Lilly Mae. His face was frozen in an awkward, gawking look when he caught sight of Rose; his mouth open to speak, but no words were coming out.

There stood the most beautiful girl he had ever seen. Her shoulder-length hair was an intriguing color—*rusty red-brick*, he thought. She stood tall, about four inches shy of his six feet two inch frame, filling out her dress in all the right places. But those eyes, those eyes were the most piercing color blue. He couldn't keep from staring at them.

He eventually noticed Lilly Mae behind her, but he didn't remember if he had seen her before or not. He knew he had never seen this white girl before. He would have remembered her.

As Rose stepped into the room, she noticed the young man looking in her direction. Her feet instantly melted into the floor, and her face froze at his intense stare. She could feel the color and heat come to her cheeks, and the sound of her quickening heart beat filled her ears. She instinctively looked away, but she couldn't keep her gaze away for long. *Is he still staring at me?* She wondered. One quick glance back up in his direction and her question was answered. She could feel his eyes following her as she and Lilly

Mae stepped around the table and stood behind the chairs. Of course, Lilly Mae had noticed the handsome, young man too, and she noticed that he wasn't looking at her.

A sweet, small voice broke the spell the teenagers were caught up in.

"Can I have some water too?" Marcus asked, looking up at his cousin.

"Oh, sure Marcus, sorry," he said as he awkwardly looked for a place to set down his basketball. "Here, hold this for me, would ya?" he said, handing the ball to the boy.

He reached up into the cupboard, got out a glass, filled it with water, and handed it to Marcus in exchange for the basketball. Then he turned around and faced the girls. Della had sat down at the table, so Rose and Lilly Mae followed suit.

"Are you going to introduce me to, to your friends, Della?" he asked, not really sure what to call the two strangers.

"This is Rose and Lilly Mae," she replied.

Todd reached out his hand but noticed it was a bit wet from the water glass, so he pulled it back, wiped it on his shorts then thrust it out again.

"Hello, I'm Todd. I'm Della and Marcus's cousin."

Rose and Lilly Mae both reached for his hand. Rose was closer, so she made contact first

"Hello, I'm Rose," she said, reflexively taking hold of his strong, firm grip.

His touch made her pink-up again, so she immediately let go and looked down into her lap for an instant before she remembered to introduce her usually quiet friend. "And…" Rose continued, turning toward Lilly Mae. But before Rose could finish, Lilly Mae spoke up for herself.

"I'm Lilly Mae," she said, grasping his hand and shaking it back as firm as he gave it.

There were a few seconds of silence which seemed like an eternity to Rose. This young man's eyes seemed to be boring right through her, heating her up even more.

Lilly Mae finally piped up after she realized her talkative friend had suddenly become mute.

"We've been workin' with your Gram'ma."

"Oh…, on the riverboat," he replied, nodding his head slowly in confirmation.

Of course he knew his grandmother worked on the riverboat, but he wasn't sure what else to say. There was another awkward silence.

"Where is Grandma B., anyway?" he finally asked, realizing she didn't appear to be around.

"She's restin'," supplied Della. "She had a couple spells, so she needs ta rest."

"Spells, whatta ya mean, spells?"

"I da know. She said somethin' 'bout her heart and that she needed ta rest," Della continued. "Said she couldn't look after us so you was gonna have to."

Rose could tell the news made Todd uneasy.

"Well, is she all right?" he asked as he pulled out a chair, turned it around, and sat down in it backwards, facing the table.

"She looks okay to me," was Della's reply.

Rose gathered up her courage to fill in the details.

"Your Grandmother had a couple heart attacks on the boat; one about two weeks ago and the first one three weeks before that."

Todd was looking intently at Rose as she spoke, his large, dark brown eyes fixed on hers.

"She's slowed down quite a bit, but she seems to be doing okay. I agree with your aunt, she probably should see a doctor. She really hasn't been the same since it happened, especially the last time."

"Yeah, she can't even make it all day without takin' a nap, and that's not like Grandma B.," Lilly Mae said, wanting to add in her two cents.

Todd sat back in his chair and stared off into nowhere, not saying a thing.

"And you get ta sleep on the davenport," Marcus pitched in, wanting to add something to the conversation.

Todd shook his head slightly, as if to wake himself out of a trance.

"What'd you say?" he asked, looking at Marcus.

"Grandma said Della and I gets to sleep together, and you gets to sleep on the davenport."

"Why's that?" he continued.

"'Cause Rose and Lilly Mae be staying with us for a few days," finished Della.

"Oh," Todd said, looking back at Rose a little surprised. "Well, that's all right. I don't mind," he said with sincerity.

"Where's Darrell and Grace?" he asked the children.

"The note here says they went back to the store for a few things," Della responded, picking up a piece of paper that sat in front of her.

"Well, I better go clean up before dinner," Todd said politely. Then he looked at Rose then Lilly Mae. "Nice to meet you both."

The girls both smiled and nodded their heads in agreement. After Todd left, Rose sank slightly into her chair. She was exhausted from just five minutes of conversation. This was a new phenomenon for a girl who could normally go on for hours without a break. *What was all this about*, she wondered?

~ ~ ~

The conversation at supper that evening was light, most of it coming from Darrell. Grace always seemed to have a somber face when Rose looked her way, and Todd was about as talkative as Lilly Mae. Darrell asked the girls about their families, their work on the riverboat, and where they lived. Rose's responses were short, and Lilly Mae couldn't make herself converse any more than Rose, even though she tried. When the conversation turned to St. Louis, Rose perked up.

"Either of you girls been to St. Louis before?" Darrell asked.

"No Sir," Rose replied.

Lilly Mae admitted she had been here on the riverboat, but she hadn't been any further than the levee.

"Todd, would you mind taking the girls 'round a little tamorrow?" asked Grandma B.

"Oh…um, sure."

He looked up hastily at Rose then went back to eating.

"A 'course, dat's after services. You girls can join us for services, can't ya? We got a mighty lot ta thank da good Lord for."

Rose did feel a wee bit guilty, she hadn't been to but one church service the whole summer, but she wasn't sure if it was okay for a Catholic girl to go to a Baptist church.

"Well, I'm not sure if I can. I mean, I was raised Catholic, and I'm not sure I can go to a Baptist church."

"Oh, honey child, dere's only one God dat done made dis here earth and all da poor souls dat lives upon it; folks just calls him by different names is all. He don't care if'in yous Baptist, Catholic, or a Jew. All he cares about is if'in we takes care a one another. Ya know, 'love one another as I done loved you'."

What Grandma B. said seemed to make sense to Rose. How could different Gods make the earth and all the humans on it? It just depended on where you grew up what you called the God that you prayed to. Lilly Mae, who was raised a Methodist, had to agree with Grandma B. She figured all the religions were basically the same; some just decided you couldn't eat meat on Friday, or you had to go to church on Saturday instead of Sunday. She never understood why there were all the different rules, and most of the rules didn't make any sense to her, anyway. That's why she didn't take to religion all that much. Especially since there seemed to be so many folks who claimed to be followers but who didn't do very God-like things, like cheating, and stealing, and lynching. Yeah, especially lynching.

"Well, then I think I probably can go. Is that okay with you, Lilly Mae?" asked Rose.

Lilly Mae agreed. She didn't want to hurt Grandma B.'s feelings either. And she figured everyone else would be going. She didn't want to be left home alone.

"But we didn't bring our dresses with us," continued Lilly Mae.

"Oh, we can see 'bout dat." Grandma B. said.

She turned toward Grace. "Maxine's girls are 'bout their size, don't ya think, Gracie?"

"I don't know 'bout that, Mama," Grace replied.

"Nonsense, dey're just da same size. You go over dere after supper and pick up a couple dresses for'em ta try. And don't forget ta get two pair a gloves," Grandma B. ordered.

Grace slumped, stone-faced into her chair, which made Rose uncomfortable. After overhearing the conversation in the kitchen, Rose knew Grace was none too happy to have her around.

~ ~ ~

That night Rose couldn't sleep. But it wasn't the thought of going to a Baptist church that was keeping her up. She actually thought it would be rather interesting to go, since she had never been in a Baptist church before. All kinds of other things were traveling through her head, thoughts of what she would see the next day on their tour of St. Louis, and particularly of who was going to be their guide.

Why did this young man make her feel so different? She just couldn't put her finger on it. She felt like she couldn't be herself when he was around, and that bothered her. She felt like there was some invisible but direct connection to him somehow; similar to what she felt when she was with Silus but different. And this connection touched a different part of her, a part which made her quiet and self-conscious. When he was in the room, her focus shifted; her attention was drawn to everything he did, or anything he said. She was uncomfortable with this unfamiliar feeling.

Then there was the conversation she had overheard from the kitchen. It kept playing back in her head—Grace not wanting a white girl to stay with them, but particularly the part where

Grandma B. admitted she was lucky to be alive. This convinced Rose even more that she should have told the captain about Grandma B.'s second spell, and now she felt guiltier than ever that she hadn't. That was reason enough to go to church. And there was the fact that Todd couldn't get a job or go on to school because he had to look after his cousins. Rose wasn't sure why he was living in his grandmother's house, but like her brother Michael, she could understand his disappointment with not being able to go to school.

"Lilly Mae, you asleep?" Rose whispered across the room.

"Huh," came the sleepy reply.

"Are you asleep?"

"I *was*. Whatcha want?"

"I need ta talk to you."

"Now?"

"Yes, now! Please!" Rose pleaded gently.

"Oh, all right," Lilly Mae gave in, somewhat disgusted.

"Let's go outside, so we don't wake up the kids," Rose finished.

They stepped out the front screen door into the cool night air—the first sign of the coming fall. They sat at the top of the steps. The street light on the corner was a distant night-light for them to see in their unfamiliar, darkened surroundings. There was a slight haze in the damp night, which gave the evening an eerie feel.

"Now, what's so damned important dat ya woke me out of a sound sleep?"

Rose hesitated. "What would you say if I decided not to go to New Orleans with you?" she finally said.

"What da ya mean?" asked Lilly Mae, still dazed from being half asleep.

"Well, I decided I'm going to stick around here for a while to help Grandma B. watch her grandkids."

Lilly Mae just looked at her in silence, brow furrowed in confusion.

Rose continued, "I figured I could see New Orleans anytime, and Grandma B.'s not feeling up to watching her grandkids, so I thought I should stay and help her out." She hesitated a moment, looking tentatively into Lilly Mae's face. "Are you mad at me?"

Lilly Mae didn't say anything at first; she just looked out into the still and hazy night. She was fully awake now, but she didn't know what to say about what she had just heard. Why didn't Rose want to go with her? She had let down her guard and let Rose closer to her than anyone she had known before, and now Rose was throwing her offer down at her feet. *Why is she doing this?*

"I guess that's up to you, Rose," was all she could think to say, an obviously disappointed tone in her voice.

"It's not that I don't wanna go. You know I do. I just feel like I should stay and help them out, at least until Grandma B.'s feeling better," Rose explained. "And it's not fair to Todd to have to put off work and school when I'm not doing anything."

Lilly Mae suddenly sat up straight and looked directly at Rose.

"Oh, that's it," Lilly Mae replied, indignation written all over her face. "You're stayin' 'cause a Todd!"

"No, that's not it! Well, maybe a little, but that's not the main reason. I don't even know him," she said, slightly confused and upset with the poor way she was attempting to explain her reasoning.

She wasn't even totally sure herself why she was doing this, and what she was trying to say didn't seem to be coming across very well.

"That's right, ya don't even know'em" Lilly Mae said, looking away. "And he's black!" she added curtly.

"What's that got to do with it?" Rose replied, not sure of what Lilly Mae was getting at.

Rose paused a few seconds, looking out into the street. She gathered her thoughts and looked back at Lilly Mae.

"Look, all I know is that Grandma B. can't do what they want her to do, and I can help. I'm really sorry, Lilly Mae," Rose finished.

Lilly Mae didn't look at Rose; she just sat there staring down at the ground in front of her. Then without saying a thing, she stood and turned to go inside.

"Lilly Mae, don't go away mad! Come on!" Rose pleaded to no avail.

The screen door slapped shut behind her.

Now Rose was really confused. She covered her face with her hands, then ran her fingers back through her hair.

"What have I done?" she said softly to herself.

❧ 8 ❧

Friendships are fragile things. One day you're thick as thieves, the next you can't even speak to each other for fear of making the rift that's come between you even wider.

Sometimes relationships need a little space, a small stretch of time to mull over all those experience you've had together—good and bad—that you've made it through already. There is a history here, a knowing without saying, an admiration and respect, and a past which gives the benefit of the doubt that what ever was said or what ever was done to cause the rift in the first place, would eventually be understood and ultimately forgiven.

Rose hoped in her heart she had such a history with Lilly Mae.

~ ~ ~

The next morning, the girls got ready for church in silence. Rose wanted to say something to Lilly Mae in the worst way; she wanted to tell her that just because she wasn't going with her to New Orleans did not mean she cared for her any less; she wanted to tell her she was the first real girlfriend she's ever had, and she wouldn't trade her friendship for all the tea in China, but she couldn't. She had learned over the summer, it was best to let Lilly Mae stew a while about things which were upsetting her before broaching the subject. So that was what she did.

After they got dressed, they headed for the kitchen and a quick breakfast, then out the door to church. It was just a short walk to the Antioch Church the girls had seen the day before. It seemed like half the neighborhood was walking to church with them; all greeting each other with pleasantries such as, "Glorious morn'in the Lord done give us," or "Don't you look fine this morning Deaconess Baas."

Many folks were particularly pleased to see Grandma B., and they stopped and greeted her specifically. Rose didn't know what a deaconess was, but she assumed it was important for all the attention Grandma B. was getting.

Grandma B. was obviously in her element, knowing just what to do—smiling and deflecting compliments about her new hat, which she had picked up at their stop in Rock Island; gingerly giving hugs to the women who gushed over seeing her again after, "…such a long time." She seemed to know everyone they met.

There were also questions about the two young strangers. Rose got a few odd looks, but most people were polite and greeted both girls warmly. Grandma B. seemed pleased she could show off some of her kitchen help, to remind folks of the important job she had all summer. But Grandma B. wasn't haughty or rude; she only had kind words to say about Rose and Lilly Mae.

They finally made it to the front step and into church. The walk to church had taken almost a half-hour, when it only should have taken ten minutes. Rose realized then why they left the house so early. Inside the church there was the loud buzz of muted voices talking, and the hand fans were working hard already, trying to move air around the colorful hats and starched white shirts and ties.

Grandma B. walked out from underneath the balcony, which ran along three-quarters of the room, and straight up the center aisle to the second row, which was still open despite every seat around it being filled. Grandma B. continued to greet folks with a head nod or a small hand wave as she motioned Lilly Mae, Rose, and the rest of her family into the pew before her. Once everyone was in, she sat down quietly on the end. It reminded Rose of how a mother hen gathers her chicks together, then stands wary yet content once her chicks are where she wanted them to be.

Before long, the service started. A man in a white robe stepped out from a side door in the front of the church. He was followed by another man in a suit and tie, a woman, then a whole group of people in white robes who lined up in two rows along the front wall of the church, right underneath a row of gold organ pipes. Rose was surprised to see Todd's face among them. She hadn't even noticed his absence in the pew. The woman sat at the organ, and the man in the suit sat next to the man who Rose assumed must be the priest. They sat in the center of a small stage, right in front of the choir. Rose would find out later, when Grandma B. introduced him after the service, the man she thought was the priest was called "Reverend." She was glad she had kept her ignorance to herself. The congregation all stood as they came in, grabbing a hymnal and automatically opening it up to the hymn number displayed on the board to the right of the choir. Rose found a hymnal too and opened it up, getting ready to sing, but she would never be ready for the type of singing which was about to break forth unto the heavens.

~ ~ ~

The organ started to play softly, the choir humming along, stepping to one side then the other along with the music. The congregation instantly picked up the rhythm and started to hum. Then the singing, Alleluia, the singing! A young, full-figured, dark brown woman in the choir stepped forward, opened her mouth and started to spread sweet jelly and jam all over the congregation without reserve. The choir lapped up her same sweet words and shared them again to add an exquisite mix of flavors to the words she was spreading across the room. She stirred the words softly, mixing her pallet and tantalizing the congregation with their richness and depth. Gradually the froth and shear volume of the infusion intoxicated everyone in the room. The glorious harmonies and inspiring words shared with such power and conviction that if you weren't converted to Christianity, wanting to praise the Lord right there on the spot, there must be something wrong with you. The music pulled you out of yourself and up into the high ceiling to be mingled with all the other souls there, praising God and giving him glory. The song finally crescendoed with the soloist slowly, skillfully adding her last ingredients, while "Amen Sister!" and "Praise the Lord!" floated out here and there from the congregation to give it that last bit of spice.

Most folks by that time had their arms waving above their heads, as if to keep hold of their spirits as they soared in the room above them. Rose's sturdy German soul wasn't able to leave the ground, but her young Irish spirit couldn't stop clapping and singing along with everyone else, pulling in the warm, sweet taste and filling her soul.

Once the song had ended, everyone sat back down; the women reaching for their fans to begin their perpetual waving. Besides stirring the soul, the song had stirred up the heat and the perspiration. The woman sitting next to Rose gave her a fan to cool herself. Rose thanked her with a smile and a nod of her head.

On one side of the fan was an advertisement—"*Ross and Milner Funeral Services*"—the other had a scripture reading— "Wherever two or more are gathered, there I am also, Matthew 18:20."

Rose had never really believed that one. In fact, she thought God was with her more often when she was alone than when she was with other people, especially when she was outside hanging out with her dog Max.

That was just one of many things Rose didn't understand about the Bible, despite being in Sunday school since she was old enough to remember. Later, she would develop a different understanding about that scripture reading and other aspects of her burgeoning spirituality from a person whom she would least expect, but for now, she was happy with the comfort it brought in the form of cool air moving across her warm neck.

~ ~ ~

Rose thought the service, in general, was similar to the service she was accustomed to at St. Mary's back home. But unlike the Catholic folks back home, the people here did everything with such conviviality and fervor. Besides the singing keeping you on your toes, the man in the suit reading the bible verses made you sit up and listen. And then there was the sermon; the Reverend made sure you knew every detail of the scripture reading and just what you were expected to do about it.

The whole sermon seemed choreographed; the organist played softly behind him as he spoke, giving his words added weight and lift all at the same time. The Reverend spoke of storms, all kind of storms: storms of a personal kind, storms of a financial kind, storms of an occupational kind, and last but not least, storms of a spiritual kind.

And if you were one of the few who thought you were riding high, never really experiencing any of these tumults first-hand, just wait, he assured you, they were coming. It was just a matter of time.

But he didn't leave you there drowning in your sorrow. He masterfully, and with unwavering conviction, rescued you from their cold, shadowy midst, out of the depths of their sinking and, at times, all consuming power. The life raft was manned by the One—which, he assured, is always there. The only One—he reminded—you can rely on without fail. And the One—you could tell—he knew on a personal level.

He wrote his prose with deftness on each and every heart in that sanctuary. He gave each person, including Rose, the feeling that he was speaking specifically to them. Rose tried to blink away the water which was slowing filling in her eyes as he spoke, but a tear escaped and ran down the side of her cheek. Rose quickly wiped it away with her hand, stealthily glancing around in hopes that no one had noticed. But someone had.

The woman next to Rose who had handed her the fan, now handed her a Kleenex. Rose self-consciously accepted it but was comforted when she noticed the woman had a Kleenex of her own. At that moment, Rose felt the solidarity of womanhood; the shared, centuries-old connection which says without words "We have to stick together, you and I." This was added to the comfort and shared healing which tears bring.

She remembered this same cathartic feeling with Lilly Mae on the sands of the Mississippi those many months ago. The familiarity of the feeling stirred up her own private storm, which she thought had died away those many weeks ago, and the tears and ache began again with uncomfortable familiarity.

The Reverend, however, wasn't through creating his own storm. His voice grew louder and he spoke so rapidly Rose was only able catch a word here and an exclamation point there.

It didn't seem to matter, though. She was swept up in the winds of salvation, and a small *Praise the Lord* crept up inside of her, wanting to come out. The others in the room had no such consternation; they were freely calling out their affirmations of "Amen", "Praise the Lord," and "Mmm Hmm," as the Reverend slowly brought the storms to bay.

The room automatically quieted and heads bowed as he ended his message with a prayer.

"...and we want to thank you Lord, for all that you give us each day; for bringin' us through the storms and lighting our way."

A resounding "Amen!" came from the congregation.

"We want to give you special thanks for bringing our Sister, Eleanor, back to us after a long journey away."

"Thank you Jesus!"

Rose wondered if he was speaking of Grandma B., as Grandma B. sat up a little straighter in the pew and nodded her head slightly.

"We ask your healing, dear Lord, for our brother, Thomas, who is still in the hospital, and for the family of our brother, William,"

A woman a few pews back lifted her arms up and wailed softly, flopping her arms back down as she cried into her handkerchief and was comforted by those sitting around her.

"...who was taken from us after such a short time in your service. For these things and the many other things that we hold in our hearts that only you can know and only you can heal, we praise your name dear Lord, Amen."

How did he know that I needed healing? Rose thought. How did he know her heart ached with guilt—guilt for not helping the one woman who helped her when she needed help the most?

She remembered Father Kelly telling their Sunday school class, if you ever did anything wrong, you needn't be afraid to ask for forgiveness. God was always willing to forgive if we were truly sorry for what we did. Back then, Rose usually had some minor things to be sorry for: hitting her sister or being short with her Mother, but this feeling today was on a whole different level of sorrow. Rose felt that here, in this church, on this Sunday, that God would forgive her for not telling Captain Roy about Grandma B.'s second attack. Her heart was lifted slightly of its burden as she closed her eyes and bowed her head.

But there was something else, something more earthly than celestial which kept this burden tethered in place. Could she forgive herself? It would be many years and many experiences later when she would discover she didn't even need to ask for God's forgiveness; she would always have that. It would be the art of forgiving herself which would come more slowly with time.

Rose had another prayer that she sent out to the very present God she felt inside the church that day; she prayed she could find a way to let Lilly Mae know how much she cared for her. She didn't want her to go home feeling bad. And she really didn't want to lose Lilly Mae as a friend. She opened her eyes, gazed down the pew, first toward Lilly Mae, then at Grandma B., then closed her eyes again and sighed, alone with her God.

~ ~ ~

Amazingly, on the way home there were still people who hadn't seen Grandma B., so it took them just as long to make it home as it had to get there. Rose was a bit anxious; she wanted to get home and start their tour of the city. As they made their way back, Rose tested the waters with Lilly Mae, asking a few simple questions about the church service. Lilly Mae's answers gave Rose a little hope; they were polite, though to the point. It was a start.

As soon as they changed out of their dresses, they met their tour guide on the front porch.

"Anything in particular you wanna see?" Todd asked, appearing a little more interested in the idea than the night before.

Rose didn't say anything at first. She looked at Lilly Mae, hoping she would make a suggestion. When she didn't, Rose came up with one herself.

"I'd like to see Forest Park, and maybe Market Street. Grandma B. told us about those places."

"Well, Market Street's a little rough, but I could show you Grand Boulevard. There's a few things to see there. We could go that way on the way to the park."

"That sounds great," Rose beamed.

She looked at Lilly Mae, then lost a little of her glow; Lilly Mae was looking down at the ground, a blank expression on her face as if she wasn't paying attention.

"Okay then, let's go!" Todd said encouragingly.

They walked the nine short blocks south to Easton Avenue, the main shopping district in the Ville, with Todd pointing out some of the more interesting buildings in the neighborhood on the way. Then four blocks east, they hopped on a street car on Grand Boulevard. They had been riding it just a couple of blocks when Rose insisted they get out and walk. They were getting into an area of shops and interesting buildings and Rose wanted to take a closer look. They walked by bakeries which smelled divine. Rose had to stop in at least one to pick up a sample of something sweet, knowing Lilly Mae had a sweet tooth too. Then there were the shops—you could buy anything from clothes to china figurines, jewelry, or even tobacco. The sights and smells even brought Lilly Mae out of her funk.

Eventually, they came to the entertainment halls and night clubs. There were neon signs in the shape of instruments, with names which, during the day, only hinted at the sights and sounds that would appear when the sun went down. What impressed Rose the most were the theatres: the St. Louis, the Shubert-Rialto and most impressive of all, the Fox. It had shiny, copper-encased glass doors across the front and a large, white stone façade at least three stories high above.

As Rose pulled her nose away from the glass door of the Fox, she noticed the billboard for the current show. She couldn't believe what she saw. She pulled Lilly Mae away from the door to look.

"Lilly Mae, look at this! They're playing *The Alibi*!" Rose said excitedly.

"So?" said Lilly Mae.

"So! Read the fine print."

An adaptation of the Agatha Christie book "The Murder of Roger Ackroyd."

"Hey, that's the book we read!" Lilly Mae brightened. She couldn't read the word *adaptation*, but she did recognize the book title.

"Yah! Isn't that neat? We need to see that!" Rose declared.

"Yeah, that'd be great," Lilly Mae admitted in a somewhat dejected tone. "But I'm leavin' tomorrow."

"So…let's see it tonight!" Rose beamed, immediately turning toward Todd who wasn't sure why they were both so excited. "You don't think that Grandma B. would mind, do you?"

"I don't think so, though you know you can't sit together. It's a segregated theatre," Todd explained.

"Oh damn! I'm not doing that again!" Rose swore.

She covered her mouth the moment she realized she had said that out loud. Todd raised his eye brows, and Lilly Mae turned and looked in surprise at her friend.

"Well, little miss goodie-two-shoes can swear too!" she teased.

A smirk appeared on Rose's face.

"Oh, hush up," Rose teased back.

They all stood there looking at the billboard for a few moments when Rose's expression brightened once more.

"Todd, you said one of your Aunts had gone to the Poro Beauty College that you showed us?"

"Yeah, my Aunt Tilley, why?"

"Does she do makeup and stuff?" Rose asked.

"I suppose so. I don't really pay that much attention to tell you the truth."

Rose turned toward Lilly Mae.

"Lilly Mae, what would you think about changing color?"

"What you talkin' 'bout, Girl?" Lilly Mae stared with consternation at Rose. "Have you flipped your lid?"

"No, no, no, just listen. What if we asked Todd's Aunt Tilley to make you up white, then we could both sit and watch the play together!" Rose explained, beaming.

"Are you crazy? It'd never work," Lilly Mae replied.

But as she thought about it, she had to admit she *would* like to see the play, and it would be even better if she could sit with Rose in the white section on the main floor of the theatre, instead of the balcony or way in the back.

"Even if she could make me up white, I never did see a white girl with brown, nappy hair!" she added, pulling out a curl and letting it spring back in place.

Todd snickered at the thought.

Rose slapped him playfully. "Cut it out. You're no help." The group was silent again until Rose piped up once more.

"I knew this old lady at our church that all the kids talked about behind her back. She always wore a wig to church. It looked funny because it was really nice hair on a really old lady; it just didn't fit, but it sure looked real. I'm sure Todd's aunt could get us a wig for you to wear."

Lilly Mae was silent for a moment.

"Aw, come on Lilly Mae. It would be my treat, for disappointing you by not going with you," Rose pleaded. "Wouldn't it be great to see the book acted out right in front of your eyes, all the costumes and the actors? Just imagine it!"

"Whatta ya mean, 'not going with you'? Where you goin'?" Todd asked Rose. He thought the plan was for Rose and Lilly Mae to leave the next day for New Orleans.

Lilly Mae looked down at the ground.

Rose explained, "I'm planning on staying here to watch the kids for Grandma B. That is, if it's okay with Grace and Darrell, of course. I haven't mentioned it to anyone yet, except Lilly Mae."

"Oh!" was all Todd said, registering what that meant for him as well as for his grandmother.

After a moment, he spoke again.

"We could probably get a wig from the 'Y'. They've used wigs in the circus they have every year."

"Circus? They have a circus, like with animals and stuff?" questioned Rose.

"No, they just call it a circus. It's kind of like a review, you know, like a vaudeville show with lots of different costumes and acts. It's pretty good really."

"That'd be great; could we go by there now and see if they have one?" Rose asked impatiently.

"Sure, it's not too far from here. We can go after dinner. There's a lunch counter in Liggett's on the corner; we can eat there. Is that okay with you?" he asked, looking at both of the girls.

"Liggett's? What's Liggett's?" Lilly Mae asked, always looking out for her stomach.

"It's a drug store. They've got all kinds of stuff to eat: sandwiches, soup, burgers, that short of thing," Todd explained.

"Sounds good to me!" Rose chimed in.

"Okay," Lilly Mae agreed.

Rose grabbed Lilly Mae's arm, and down the street they went; Rose talked a mile a minute about the Agatha Christie book and how it might look acted out in play form. Rose wasn't consciously trying, but she was getting Lilly Mae excited about the whole idea, though in Lilly Mae's mind, the thought of putting on white face hung obtrusively in the way of a good time.

They stepped into the drug store. The lunch counter and accompanying chrome-based stools ran along the back, left side of the store with booths neatly lined up just opposite. Todd walked to the back of the restaurant where the other coloreds were sitting. Lilly Mae followed. Rose halted momentarily when she realized she was the only white person in this section. She guessed coloreds couldn't sit with the whites, but it didn't say anything about whites not being able to sit with the coloreds, so she sat down in the booth next to Lilly Mae. She wasn't so sure of her assumption, however, after the white waitress gave her that *Are you crazy?* look when she came up to take their order.

After lunch, the kids walked down a couple blocks south to Lindell and picked up another street car for the six blocks east to the YMCA.

When they walked into the lobby, Rose got that "black speck in a glass of white milk" feeling again; there wasn't a white face to be seen. Todd left the girls there and went to see if he could find a wig. First he came back with a Lana Turner hairdo. Both girls shook their heads and sent him back to look for something with more curl. Next into the room was Claudette Colbert. The girls agreed it was too short and too blond, so back he went again. The third time was the charm; he had found the dark flowing locks of Dorothy Lamour, and he was wearing it on his head. That suited the girls just fine, and they doubled over with laughter at the sight.

Next they made an appointment at Miss Tilley's House of Hair. Todd called his aunt on a pay phone in the lobby of the "Y" to make the appointment. He didn't tell her what it was he exactly needed her to do, but he explained it was for a show tonight, and it was very important. Normally, she wasn't open on Sunday, but she said she would make an exception since Todd was her favorite nephew.

The appointment wasn't until four, so they had some time to take in a few more sights. They headed back up Lindell to Forest Park.

The park was every bit as wonderful as Grandma B. had described, at least the parts they could see. There wasn't a way to get around the large park except on foot, so they didn't make it very far. Rose figured she'd have time later to come back and check things out in detail. It would be a great place to bring the kids, she thought.

~ ~ ~

Four o'clock rolled around in no time, and Rose made sure they were at the shop right on time. The show started at seven, and they had to get dressed and eat dinner yet, so they didn't have a lot of time to spare. The shop was about three miles west of the park, on Market Street. The place was empty except for Todd's Aunt, a large, short woman with dark brown skin. She was standing at a mirror arranging a supply of rollers. When she saw who had stepped through the door, she called out to her nephew.

"Todd, you handsome thing you, come over here and give your auntie some suga'."

Todd hesitated, glancing at Rose before he walked over to his aunt to be enveloped in her all encompassing arms and full chest.

"So who are *these* young ladies?" the tone of her voice implying there might be some special attachment Todd had to the girls, or at least to one of them.

"This is Rose and Lilly Mae," he said, pointing to the girls. "They helped Grandma B. out on the boat this summer."

"Oh, these are the angels that Grandma B. done told me 'bout."

At that, she walked around her chair, came up to Lilly Mae, then Rose, and gave each girl a hug just as big as the one she had doled out to Todd.

"Grandma B. done tol' us what you did for her, and we greatly appreciate it." *Wow, news travels fast*, Rose thought. Aunt Tilley walked behind Lilly Mae and started playing with her hair.

"So what can I do for ya?"

Rose spoke up. "Well, what we actually need is for you to make Lilly Mae look like she's white."

Aunt Tilley turned sharply to Rose with a queer expression on her face.

"Now why would you be want'en to change that beautiful, sweet, honey brown color the Lord done give this child?"

"Well, we want to go to the show at the Fox theatre tonight, and we can't sit together on the main floor unless Lilly Mae is white," Rose explained.

"Well, bless my soul," Tilley exclaimed putting her hands on her hips. "I never done thought a doin' that before. They'd never take me for no white woman, anyway. They'd take one look at my full, womanly figure and know there was ebony underneath that ivory, for sure." She turned sideways to show off her ample figure, laughing a hearty, full laugh which filled the room and spread to everyone in it.

"Come on over here, child," she said, motioning Lilly Mae to sit in the chair in front of the mirror.

"Well, your color's soft enough that this shouldn't be a problem," she continued as she pulled back Lilly Mae's hair away from her face. "But this here wool rug won't fool a soul."

"Oh, we thought of that already," Rose added, pulling the wig out of the bag she was carrying.

"Oh, now ain't that a nice 'do," Aunt Tilley said, running her fingers through the silky strands. "That'll do, that'll do just fine."

She pulled out a wooden head from a drawer and placed the wig on top of it, then she turned back to Lilly Mae.

"First we'll have to put this in corn-rows, then we can start on the face. What time's your show tonight?" Aunt Tilley asked.

"Seven," Lilly Mae answered.

"Well, then I better call for reinforcements. And we gotta doll you up too, sweet thing."

Aunt Tilley stepped up behind Rose and started running her fingers through her hair.

"Oh, I love the feel of a white woman's hair, 'specially the young ones. They ain't baked and dyed the hell out of it yet. And this is such a pretty color too. Is this your natural color, child?"

"Oh, I don't need my hair done," Rose replied, a little anxious with this stranger tussling her hair about.

But to Rose's surprise, behind her statement of refusal was a small glimmer of hope that Todd's aunt would do her hair along with Lilly Mae's.

"I can't do one without the other, it just ain't happenin'. You'd look like a mismatched pair."

Rose tried to hold down her excitement. This was supposed to be for Lilly Mae, she reminded herself. She had never had her hair done before, no matter how many times Gertie had asked; she never had a reason to, or the desire. But the thought excited her now without the reasoning for why. She looked at Todd in the mirror; she was beaming from the inside out.

Aunt Tilley put down the phone and turned toward the group. "Reinforcements are on the way!" she said with a smile.

And she wasn't kidding. It wasn't ten minutes before two ladies showed up, soon followed by two more. They quickly got their assignments and got to work on the two excited, young women. Todd walked up to his aunt and asked where she kept *The Crisis*. She pointed to the top drawer of her desk, explaining that politics made people ugly, and she wasn't in the "ugly business," so she kept it out of sight. Todd found where it was hidden and retreated to a chair opposite the girls. Rose wondered what *The Crisis* was all about, since it seemed to capture all of Todd's attention.

Rose sat and looked at herself in the mirror with all the colored ladies around her, each one taking turns feeling her hair, commenting on the color and arguing about what needed to be done, pulling Rose's hair and subsequently her head, this way and that in the process.

Aunt Tilley was a quarter of the way done with Lilly Mae's corn-rows—which Rose found out was a way to braid her hair so it held tight to her scalp in neat, even rows—when she ordered someone to take over on Lilly Mae so she could make the final decision on what to do with Rose. Rose and Lilly Mae looked at each other and smiled. Rose could tell Lilly Mae was enjoying herself, and that made her feel even better. Rose felt special too, being primped over by so many people, and she loved to listen to these women talk.

Once the decision was made on what to do with Rose, Aunt Tilley went back to work on Lilly Mae with two of the women. She handed Rose off to a woman named Pearl. Pearl was younger than Aunt Tilley and just the opposite on the color wheel; she looked almost white. She had an obvious sense of style; her hair was cut very short, curled under at the ends and on the bangs, dyed a blond-red color and straight as any white woman's. She wore dangly clip earrings, which waved around as she moved her head, and she sported the latest fashion—a sleek crepe three-quarter length skirt, silk short-sleeved blouse, which did nothing to hide the fullness of her breasts, and brown sandal shoes with a moderately wide, two-inch heel. In addition to all this, she was obviously skilled at what she was doing; she could talk, give orders to her assistant, and do Rose's hair all without skipping a beat.

And the things these women talked about—Rose could not believe it. They particularly liked to talk about men; how so-and-so's husband was "a real looker," or "a good for nothin' " who had lost their job recently, or so-and-so's husband "was takin' her to Chicago for Christmas!" The general consensus was, we all would be better off without'em—until it came time to close the bedroom door, that is. "Yes, ma'am, they sure are good for somethin' then."

The color in Rose's face came out at the suggestion, and her ears started to burn. She looked into the mirror and was glad Todd hadn't looked up from his paper.

And if that wasn't bed enough, the discussion turned to women's issues. One short, stocky woman named Bess commented that she was glad when her "monthly friend" would come, "so it'id keep the old goat from pawin' at me for at least a week and longer, if I could convince'im it wasn't over yet." Another told of how she had hot flashes so bad, she had to get up and change her night gown in the middle of the night. Then the remedies started to fly. Everyone had their own sure-fire way to help, handed down from someone's grandmother or old dead aunt.

Rose couldn't believe what these women were saying, especially considering there was a man in the room. They all acted like he wasn't even there, and luckily for Rose, Todd didn't seem to pay any particular attention. Rose had never been in a beauty salon before, but she had been in a kitchen full of women at family gatherings back home or at church dinners, and those women never talked about anything like these women did. She looked at Lilly Mae in amazement, but Lilly Mae sat there like she had heard it all before. And she had, of course; when she was young, her mother had dragged her to the local beauty shop every other week or so to get her hair done in braids, which stuck straight up all over her head, and in corn-rows when she got older.

Both girls' hair was done in record time, so the entourage turned to their faces. It took a few more of the women to pow-wow around Lilly Mae and her white-face project, so Rose was left with Pearl and one other woman, Sal. Rose thought both these women's make-up looked wonderful, so she had high hopes for how nice she might look when they were through. Gerty was not allowed to wear makeup, other than a little mascara for Sunday service, so Rose felt a little like she was getting away with something special. The thought made her both excited and nervous.

As they were doing Rose's face, she couldn't turn her head to check out what Lilly Mae was looking like. When Pearl finally stepped away and Rose saw herself in the mirror, she couldn't believe what she saw. She looked beautiful; just like the models in Gerty's fashion magazines! Rose changed her focus and looked back at where Todd was sitting, and their eyes met. He had that same open-mouthed stare that he had in the kitchen the first day they met. Rose glanced quickly at Lilly Mae to make sure she wasn't looking. They were still finishing up on her face, so luckily she was occupied.

Rose stood up stiffly; unaccustomed to the new, artificial feeling of her made up face and head, afraid and sure she would mess it up by making a wrong move. She stood behind Lilly Mae, who couldn't see herself yet because of the large figure of Aunt Tilley standing in front of her still working on her face.

Once they had finished Lilly Mae, Aunt Tilley took the wig from the mannequin head and gingerly placed it onto Lilly Mae's. A few choice hair pins, and she was set. She swung her around for the whole room to see.

"Meet the new Lilly Mae. Or should we call you Lilly White?" Aunt Tilley announced with amusement.

The room was abuzz with excitement. It was amazing! She really did look white. They had put the makeup all the way down her neck, the front of her chest, and even on her ears, so you couldn't see a brown spot anywhere. Lilly Mae stood up as stiffly as Rose had. She was no more accustomed to all this than Rose, plus she had on an artificial head of hair. Lilly Mae looked at Todd who was shaking his head, astonished at the transformation.

Lilly Mae walked over to the mirror in front of the chair to get a closer look at herself. She couldn't believe it either; she really did look like a white girl. Even though she didn't like the idea, she had to admit she didn't look too bad.

"A pair a white gloves, and you could fool your own grandmother," Pearl joked, and everyone laughed.

On the street car back to Grandma B.'s house, Lilly Mae insisted they sit in the back. Todd sat opposite both girls. He couldn't keep his eyes off them; Rose, for her enhanced beauty and Lilly Mae, for her white skin and wig. Both girls kept their gaze in other places, feeling his stare none-the-less.

Grandma B. nearly fell over in her chair at the sight of Lilly Mae. She knew it had to be some scheme Rose had cooked up. Rose was still a bit upset that Aunt Tilley wouldn't take any money for all the work she had done for them, but Grandma B. assured her that working in the salon was what her daughter lived for. Rose decided she was going to pay her back somehow; if it wasn't with money, it would be with something else.

The girls looked even better once they had put on their dresses. Lilly Mae had to borrow a long-sleeved shirt from Grace and a pair of gloves from Grandma B. to complete the disguise, but once fully dressed, there was no question that two white girls were going to the theatre.

Todd volunteered to escort them to the cable car. The walk was a quiet one. Rose didn't feel quite herself with all the hair spray and make-up. It made her oddly reticent to speak. She forced out a few questions about the book to Lilly Mae, but Lilly Mae's responses were short and to the point. She was having second thoughts about being a white girl; not sure they could pull-off the ruse. She was glad this night was a little cooler than it had been lately, so her makeup wouldn't run from the added heat the long sleeves and stockings were creating. And ever since they had put the makeup on her, she had this unquenchable urge to scratch her nose. The best she could do was to twitch it like a rabbit.

Todd was just as unsure of what to say. He still wasn't used to their new personas.

They all stood in silence as the street car pulled up to their stop.

"Have a good time at the show!" Todd told them as they headed for the car.

"We will!" Rose replied.

"Thanks," Lilly Mae finished.

They stepped on and waved to Todd as the car pulled away. Todd smiled and waved back.

~ ~ ~

The glassed-in ticket booth stood in the center of a long row of glass doors, each of which sported in its center a pair of copper, metal animals which were half bird and half lion. They looked more mysterious at night than they had earlier that day, as if they were guarding a secret that lay within. Rose purchased their tickets, and they stepped up to the door of the theatre. A young white man in a stiff, dark maroon uniform opened the door. Both girls flinched at the courtesy. Lilly Mae immediately looked down at the ground and walked in close behind Rose. Once in, she turned to look back out at the doorman. He hadn't even noticed her. When she turned around, she nearly walked right into Rose, and she soon discovered why; what lay behind the second set of open glass doors was a scene neither of them could have ever imagined.

They slowly made their way forward, not knowing where to look first. Straight in front of them, across the expansive lobby, was a wide carpeted staircase guarded by two gold lions. Their jeweled eyes flashed as if to warn any intruder that might dare to venture into their realm. Rose-colored, marble pillars at least three feet in diameter flanked the front and the sides of the room and held up ornate, gilded steps five stories above them, which descended upward to a brilliant blue ceiling with an embellished illustration of a sun at its center. Gold was the dominant decorative theme in the room, except for the carpet, which matched the rose of the pillars and depicted an elephant riding waves of orange and gray. When they made their way up the flight of stairs, passed the lions, they turned to see an immense tapestry that hung above the doors they had just walked through. Woven in glorious color was what looked like a Persian prince sitting cross-legged on an opulent carpet. It was all magnificent.

People were grudgingly making their way past the gawking pair when Lilly Mae finally came to her senses and pushed Rose ahead. She was eager to get to their seats and out of view. She knew once she was out of the bright lights of the lobby, she would feel more at ease. She was surprised how little the people looked at her. *Surely*, she thought, *they can see through all this stuff.* No one seemed interested. The only odd look she received was from an elderly, colored woman as they parted ways on the staircase; Lilly Mae, heading for the whites-only mezzanine, the old woman, heading up the long flight of oblong spiral steps to the upper balcony. It was probably the look of guilt that she had seen underneath Lilly Mae's powdery mask, not the brown of her skin.

As they stepped into the auditorium, they were again transfixed by the spectacle laid out before them; the rose-colored pillars were here as well, running along both sides of the large room. The red and gold curtained stage was topped with what looked like a gold crown, crested in the center with the gold head of an elephant.

The girls made their way passed a winged lion, which capped the end of the rail and held in row upon row of red velvet seats stretching up and to their left, with a smaller expanse of seats to their right; the latter being where they were to sit for the evening. Rose had wanted seats down on the main level, but they were too expensive; the mezzanine was the next best thing. Ultimately, Rose didn't really care where they sat, as long as they were together. Once in their seats, their gaze was drawn to the ceiling above their heads. It was round and shaped like draped cloth, open in the center with the same sky-blue color and sun design as in the lobby. From this sun, a large, round sphere covered with multi-colored lights was suspended. The design conjured up an image in Rose's mind of a rich Persians King's tent, filled with dancing girls scantly clad in layers of chiffon, with metal spangles and jewels around their ankles, wrists, and necks. At this point she didn't care what she saw; being inside this theatre was well worth the price of admission.

Soon the lights went down, and Lilly Mae was finally able to relax. Rose grasped Lilly Mae's hand and squeezed, sitting back in her seat as the curtain parted, and the world of Roger Ackroyd appeared before them.

The play enveloped them both, voyeurs in a world they already knew; anticipating the next step, the next move. Both were shocked when the curtains went down and the lights went up before the play was even finished. Rose checked the program —intermission. They made their way to the bathroom. Rose was excited to see what it looked like. She always thought the best place to tell if an establishment was really classy was in the bathroom, and this would give her the opportunity to examine a little closer what some of the women were wearing.

She wasn't disappointed. As Lilly Mae was adjusting her stockings in the toilet stall, assuring they wouldn't fall down and reveal her true identity, Rose took in every detail of the bathroom, including the women inside it. She repeated what she'd seen to Lilly Mae, as they made their way back to their seats, as if Lilly Mae hadn't been in the same room with her; the highlight being the stained glass in the ceiling of the sitting room. It depicted a lady lounging in a chair with a cigarette in her hand, showing her leg from her knee down. It was scandalous. But not as scandalous as the real lady in a lilac-blue, silk crepe evening dress; it had a slit in the back which went all the way down to her waist. Rose didn't get to see the front of the gown, but she wondered what the woman used to hold up her breasts.

Knowing the ending of the play didn't dampen the excitement the girls felt as the play came to its climax. With Rose perched on the edge of her seat, Lilly Mae was sure Rose was going to call out the name of the murderer right before it was revealed, so she pulled Rose gently back in her seat. Rose smiled and grabbed Lilly Mae's hand, lifting her shoulders toward her ears as if to increase the power of her excitement.

When the lights went up, and they slowly shuffled out with the others, Lilly Mae held gently on to the back of Rose's arm so as not to get separated in the crowd.

"Rose, thanks for takin' me to da play, gettin' me all dolled up and everything," she said softly. "I wasn't sure it'a worked, but it did. And da play was great! I'm sorry you can't come with me ta NaOrlins, but you're welcome ta visit anytime."

Rose stopped amid all the shuffling bodies and gave Lilly Mae her now signature bear hug. Lilly Mae was comforted by the old, crushing feeling.

Rose was smiling as she let go of Lilly Mae, but that soon turned to surprise. Rose looked at down at the shoulder of her own dress. Lilly Mae looked, too, not sure what was capturing Rose's attention.

"Keep your chin down Lilly Mae," Rose whispered, pointing to her own chin, eyes wide with explanation. "The colored girl I came to town with just showed up!"

It took a few seconds, but Lilly Mae caught on to what Rose was trying to tell her and immediately put her hand to her chin, dropping it down toward her chest

"Let's get outta here, quick!" Lilly Mae ordered.

Rose wound her way skillfully through the crowd and out onto the street, with Lilly Mae holding tight to the back of Rose's dress. They didn't even think about getting a street car, they just started walking rapidly down Grand Boulevard. Once they were far enough away from the theatre, they both started to laugh, holding on to each other, happy and relieved their masquerade had worked, and comforted in their renewed friendship—all animosity forgotten. They talked about their night out the whole way home, which, surprisingly, seemed to only take minutes. Once home, Grandma B. had to yell at them twice "to keep it down," but the giggles refused to be squelched as they removed their makeup, each girl trying to look more hideous than the other as they smeared it all over their faces.

They fell into bed exhausted and instantly to sleep, the smiles hidden within their dreams, only to pop right back onto their faces upon waking the next morning.

~ ~ ~

The events of the previous evening were recounted to all at the breakfast table the next morning. In addition to the news that Rose would be staying to watch the children, there was much to share with the family that morning. Rose's news was an unexpected surprise to Grace. She looked at Rose with a furrowed brow, sure she was up to something. It didn't surprise Grandma B., however.

The children didn't seem to mind the idea, which pleased Rose almost as much as the look on Grandma B.'s face. But Grandma B. didn't understand why Rose was giving up her chance to visit New Orleans; she knew how much Rose liked to travel. Once she agreed to the idea of Rose staying on to help, she had one stipulation for the girl.

"Now Rose, if you be stayin' you might as well be goin' ta school. Smart girl like you needs ta go ta school," Grandma B. scolded.

"Oh, I've got plenty of time for school, Grandma B. I can do that any time."

"Now, you listen here. It be hard enough for women ta make it in dis here world. You can't be relyin' on no man ta look after ya; you gots to rely on ya'self. When ya don't know things, dat's when folks takes advantage. I didn't let dat happen ta any a my girls, and I ain't lettin' dat happen ta you. I know your mama and daddy don't think no different. Don't try and tell me dey do!"

Rose looked down at the ground in defeat; she couldn't think of a reply to all that. The truth is hard to argue.

"All right den. Come tamorrow mornin' you and I be going ta sign ya up for school. You can walk da kids ta school on your way and pick'em up on your way home. Den in da evenin', ya can help me get supper on. I ain't taught ya all I know for nothin'," Grandma B. said, slipping on her tough façade.

Rose saw right through it, though, and gave her a big hug.

The rest of the day was a bit morose for Rose. She had to say goodbye to her best friend, and there was a wee small part of her that wished Lilly Mae would try and talk her into going with her. She would love to see New Orleans.

Todd volunteered to accompany the girls to the levee, where the Capital was waiting for its trip south. He wanted to apply for a job downtown anyway, so he figured it was on his way.

Rose made the group stop on the way at a bookstore, so she could buy Lilly Mae a going-away present. She picked out another Agatha Christie novel, since the first one brought them such luck. She made sure she wrote something inside the cover before the clerk wrapped it up.

The goodbye was tearful for both girls; each feeling uneasy with how their obvious closeness was making them feel, but comforted by the fact that it was a shared feeling. Lilly Mae waved to Rose and Todd as she stood at the rail of the riverboat, clutching her wrapped book to her chest.

"I wrote something in the cover," Rose called out as the paddles churned up the water and pushed the boat slowly out onto the brown, watery highway.

"Come and visit!" Lilly Mae yelled back.

She didn't turn and walk inside until Rose and Todd were just specks on the river's edge. Once in her cabin, she threw her things on Rose's empty bed. The small room seemed so large, and strange, and quiet without Rose, who would normally be talking a mile a minute about all the things they had seen and done on their short visit to St. Louis.

Lilly Mae plopped herself on the side of her bed. She looked at the wrapped book and opened it slowly. Lilly Mae smiled when she saw who the author was. She opened the cover and read the inscription.

To my BEST *friend,*
I will miss you dearly, Lilly Mae, and hope to see you soon. Think of me often, as I will be thinking of you. Keep reading!
                    With Sincerity and the Deepest Affection,
                                Rose Marie Krantz
                                September 17th, 1936

Lilly Mae smiled, sat herself at the head of her bed, and began to read.

ക 9 ൟ

The old adage goes: when one door closes, another one opens. It's just not necessarily the door we might think.

~ ~ ~

Todd and Rose headed up to Washington Avenue, the garment district, where Todd slipped into the Brown Shoes building to apply for a job. Rose preferred to stay outside to look at all the buildings and the people who were milling about. It also allowed her to settle the butterflies in her stomach. They seemed to have returned now that she was alone with Todd.

She sat down the bulging bundle of her things which she had taken off the boat. It had gotten heavier and larger than when she had started this adventure, just three short months ago. It felt like a lifetime.

There were more trucks and horse carts on this street, compared to Olive, loading and unloading boxes of shoes, bundles of clothes…, but just as many high-rise brick and stone buildings to gaze up at. They were all eight-plus stories high and went on for blocks. All of it fascinated Rose, so she hardly felt any time had passed when Todd stepped back outside.

"So'd ya get the job?" Rose inquired, looking at him hopefully.

"I just filled out an application. They'll let me know in a couple of days," Todd said, with an odd look on his face. "Haven't you ever applied for a job before?"

"Only the one for the Capitol, and I did that over the phone."

"That's your first job?" Todd said, surprised. He had started work when he was ten, selling papers.

"Oh, I worked all right, on our farm—stacking wood, cleaning the barn, feeding and looking after the pigs and horses, taking care of the chickens. I didn't get paid much, only a quarter of what we made selling eggs, but it didn't really matter. There isn't much to do where I live," Rose said with a slightly disgusted tone, trying to point out how much more interesting life in St. Louis was verses on a farm in Wisconsin.

"It sounds like hard work," Todd replied, a bit ashamed he thought Rose had had it easy.

"It is! And smelly at times. But you get used to it," Rose said nonchalantly. "Hey, I was meaning to ask you what that paper was that you were reading so intently in your aunt's beauty shop."

Rose had seen a few copies of this same paper sitting around Grandma B.'s house but hadn't had time to look at them yet.

"*The Crisis?*"

"Yah, that's it," she said. "Is that the local paper?"

"In my neighborhood it is. Actually, it's a paper put out by the NAACP, in New York."

"NAACP, what's that?"

"National Association for the Advancement of Colored People," Todd explained. "It's an organization to help colored people organize for better rights."

"Sounds like a good idea. It seems silly that you can't even sit in the same movie together," Rose said with indignation.

"It's a lot more than just movie theatres, Rose," Todd explained gently. "There's still states that make registering to vote so difficult and so intimidating that most blacks don't even try."

Rose was stunned to silence. She didn't remember learning anything like that from Miss Turner.

"It's also about the right to the same job opportunities as whites, the right to live wherever you want, the right to go to school where you want, and get a decent education…"

"You mean you can't go to school wherever you want?" Rose asked, surprised.

"Nope. I would love to go to the University of Missouri, but I can't 'cause I'm colored," he said, looking down at the sidewalk as they started walking toward the corner. "I'm probably going to go to Tuskegee instead—that's an all-black school in Alabama, but I can't afford it yet. That's why I'm going to technical school next term, so I can get a better job than the one I applied for at the shoe company, to earn more money for college."

Rose thought this might be a good time to find out a little more about why he lived with his grandmother.

"Your parents can't help you go to school?" she asked tentatively.

"No, my dad died in a beer plant accident at Anheuser, and my mom couldn't handle it after that, so she took off," he said quietly.

"Oh," was all Rose could think to say.

Maybe her life on the farm with her mother, father, and eight siblings wasn't so bad. At least she had parents to go home to. She kept quiet the rest of the way back to Grandma B.'s.

~ ~ ~

"Well, 'bout time you got back," Grandma B. barked. "We got'ta set ya up for school. Don't bother sittin' down, we'll just head right out. Why don't ya help Grace with dinner, Todd. We'll eat when we get back."

Rose and Grandma B. walked to catch a street car, which took them the ten or twelve blocks to get to the school. Grandma B. didn't look as tired as she had on the boat, but her rested appearance didn't quicken her pace any. Rose didn't mind; she enjoyed checking out more of the neighborhood. It seemed that every home in the Ville was made out of brick.

After they stepped off the street car and came closer to the school, Rose suddenly realized they weren't seeing any more brown faces; everyone here was white. The houses were the same, mostly two- and three-story brick homes as in Grandma B.'s neighborhood, but instead of two doors in the front of the building, there was only one.

They faced the large, three-story, red and white brick building, with Soldan written above the entrance doors in white cement. The school looked like it was plucked out of a city in England, with its castle-like architectural style. It was huge—encompassing the whole block—with the athletic field taking up the block across the street.

"Now, when we gets inside, ya follow my lead," Grandma B. whispered to Rose as they mounted the second set of steps.

What does she mean by that? Rose thought. They stepped inside the building and went up another flight of steps facing the open doors to what was obviously the auditorium; Rose could see the seats which sloped down to a curtained stage. Rose hadn't been too excited about going to school up to this point, but the prospect of using that stage planted a seed of anticipation in her mind.

Just then a bell rang. Young, uniformed white girls and boys seemed to come out of nowhere. The high ceilinged hall echoed with the sounds of their many voices and shuffling feet. Most of the girls gave Rose, standing in her slacks and tee shirt, a queer glance as they moved past. They didn't seem to take notice of Grandma B.

Grandma B. spied a door which had "office" written on it. She pulled on Rose's arm, jerking her out of her preoccupation with the students and toward the door.

"I'm lookin' ta register dis here girl in school," Grandma B. said to the neatly manicured lady sitting behind the desk.

"And you are…?" the lady replied somewhat indignantly.

"I'm Miss Tilley Moore," Grandma B. said, in a southern drawl Rose had never heard before. "I look after dis here child for her parents."

Rose jerked her head around, looking at Grandma B. in amazement.

What did she just say?

"And where are your parents?" the women asked, turning to Rose.

"They be on a boat ta Europe," Grandma B. quickly answered. "We just moved here from Louisiana, and her daddy got called away fo' business," Grandma B. paused. "He's in da oil business, ya know. Well, anyway, I's taken care a dis here child since she was an infant. Taken care a her like she was my own."

"Yes, yes, that's all fine but…," the women said, trying to cut Grandma B. off, but Grandma B. would have none of it; she was having too much fun.

"We done set up a house on Treadway Boulevard, and I done come ta get dis child inta school. The Mr. and Mrs. want only da best, only da best," Grandma B. concluded, smiling at the young woman, then at Rose.

The young lady looked Rose up and down.

"Oh, is that so?" she replied, not sure Rose's clothes matched the story Grandma B. was weaving.

Rose couldn't stop staring at Grandma B. *What a yarn she's telling. And that southern drawl!,* she thought. She was seeing a side of Grandma B. she didn't even know existed.

"Well, I suppose we can set you up. Will you be starting with us as a sophomore?" the women asked Rose.

"No a freshman," Grandma B. answered again for Rose. "We spent all last year in da Orient, so she done lost a year."

The women looked upset with Grandma B. for continuing to answer for Rose.

"Well, we'll need these forms filled out," she said, pulling some papers out of a file and handing them to Rose. "And the school fees are twenty dollars. You can sit down over there."

She pointed to a row of chairs against the wall across from her desk.

Grandma B. took the papers from Rose, and the two sat down across from the young lady.

"What are you doing Grandma B.?!" Rose whispered through clinched teeth, so the women couldn't tell what she was saying.

"Never you mind, child. Dis be da best white public school 'round here, so ya might as well go here."

"My parents are in Europe?" Rose questioned excitedly.

"Pretty good, huh? Just thought dat all up on da spur a da moment," Grandma B. said, quite proud of herself. "When I said we lived on Treadwell, dat clinched it, though."

They finished filling out the paper work, handed the young lady the twenty dollars, and started for home. Rose tried to get Grandma B. to let her pay her back for the school fees, but she wouldn't have it. Later Rose made sure Todd took her to the place where she needed to buy her school uniform instead of Grandma B., so she could pay for that herself. After a week in school, Rose decided she also needed another pair of shoes. She was tired of trying to hide her old shoes when ever she sat down. They weren't quite like what the other girls were wearing, and the shoe polish Rose had used to try and clean them up didn't hide their worn appearance by much.

~ ~ ~

The first few weeks of school were busy for Rose; she had a lot of assignments to do to catch up with the rest of the class. Todd helped her some in the afternoons before he had to go to work at the shoe factory. Rose was impressed by how much he knew. She knew he like to read—his face was always in a book or the newspaper.

She was getting a little worried though; she hadn't really made any friends, despite her small attempts during dinner. All the girls seemed to move in tight groups, not letting strangers talk to them much. She didn't have time before or after school to make friends either; she got to class just on time after dropping Della and Marcus off at Simmons school and had to run right out after the last bell to pick them up again. This also meant she didn't have time to participate in any of the after school clubs or sports. Rose didn't mind too much though; school was better than she expected. She was learning a lot already. She also realized this was a tough school, full of mostly very smart kids—a far cry from the one-room school-house she was use to. She wasn't at the top of her class anymore.

Rose's first chance to make a friend came unexpectedly on a school field trip. It was biology class. They were studying water plants, so their teacher, Miss Krum, took them out of school for the afternoon for a trip to Forest Park. The park was just a few blocks from the school, so it was a great place for a little hands-on experience.

Once there, a girl in one of the more popular groups at school got into some trouble.

"Um…, did you know you're standing in poison ivy?" Rose asked the girl who had wandered over to the edge of a pond they were studying.

"Oh, my God!" she yelled out as she pulled up her three quarter length skirt to look down at her feet, high stepping out of the plants as fast as she could. A few minutes later the itching started.

"Why do my hands itch?" the girl asked to no one in particular.

"You must have touched your shoes or maybe the hem of you skirt," supplied Rose. "It's the oil on the plant that makes people itch."

"Well, if you're so smart," the girl said with indignation, then fear, "how do I stop it?"

Rose didn't say anything. She looked around the edge of the pond and spotted a leggy looking plant with small, orange flowers. She pulled some out of the ground, broke the stem in a couple of places and started walking toward the itching girl.

"Hold out your hand," Rose ordered her.

"What are you doing?" she questioned Rose.

"Do you want the itching to stop or not?" Rose asked very matter-a-factly.

The girl held out her hand, somewhat reluctantly, to allow Rose to spread the gooey sap of the plant all over the red spots, which were just starting to appear on her palm. No sooner had Rose thrown the stems of the plant away, than the itching had stopped.

"Hey, how'd you do that?" the girl asked Rose.

"It's jewel weed. My dad taught me that after I got in a patch of nettles when we were fishing."

"Well, thanks," the girl said, rather sheepishly. "My name is Monica, Monica Greenwall. What's yours?" she said, sticking out her other hand toward Rose.

"I'm Rose, Rose Krantz," she said, shaking her hand.

"I've noticed you in math class. You're pretty smart, aren't you?" Monica replied.

"I don't know about that," Rose said, looking down at the ground.

"Do you want to join our study group?" Monica continued. "We're meeting at my house this Saturday to study for the big test old lady Meyers is giving us next week, and we could use a math brain like you."

Rose knew Monica ran with a particularly popular group at school. She wasn't sure she would fit in, but she hadn't gotten any other offers so far, so Rose thought she might as well accept.

"Okay…, sure, but I'll have to check with Grand…" she cut herself off. "I'll have to check with my nanny to see if I can come."

"Your nanny?" Monica asked, raising her eyebrows.

"Oh, my parents are in Europe, so my nanny is looking after me while they're gone," Rose said, embarrassed by the lie.

"Well, let me know tomorrow, okay?" she chirped. "And thanks for the stuff for my hand. What'd you call it?"

"Jewel weed."

"Yeah, jewel weed," Monica repeated,

"And you better change your clothes right away when you get home," Rose recommended.

"Oh. Sure. Thanks!" Monica said cheerfully as if nothing had just happened.

Then Monica turned and walked away with the rest of her friends.

~ ~ ~

Grandma B. didn't mind, of course, if Rose went to Monica's home. She was glad Rose was finally making some white friends. She thought everyone should have friends "of their own kind" to talk to (not that Grandma B thought whites and coloreds shouldn't mix socially; she just knew it was safer not to).

It took Rose a little time to find where Monica lived. She was walking in a neighborhood where most of the streets had high fences and elaborate entrances. One entrance had a red brick building, which looked like it was taken right off the front of a castle; it had three pointed peaks and a clock in the center. Another one was made of white stone and had a beautiful sculpture of a lady in the center. The houses beyond these gates were bigger than anything Rose had ever seen before, some with palatial, manicured lawns. Once she finally found Hortense Place, she was glad the entrance to the street wasn't quite as ostentatious and the houses not quite as large as the streets she had just passed. Hortense had two large, black metal gates which stood open attached to two brick pillars with round concrete orbs balanced on top.

Standing in front of Monica's house, Rose was a little nervous about going inside. She didn't know Monica, and she had never hung around with someone who lived this sort of life style. It was a far cry from the farm house she grew up in and the two-flat building which Grandma B. lived in. Monica's house was a three-story colonial with gray bricks and black shutters—the third story being three windowed dormers across the front. There was a shiny black car in the driveway, which ran up the side of the house, and a detached, two car garage in the back. Rose walked slowly up to the double front doors and rang the bell.

After a few moments an older, colored woman opened the door just as Monica was bounding down the steps behind her. The colored woman stepped out of Monica's way as she ran up to Rose, neither person acknowledging the other.

"Hey, you made it. Great!" Monica exclaimed. Monica had a high pitched, cheerful way of talking when she was happy or excited. Rose wasn't sure what to think of that, so she just ignored it.

"We're in my room. Come on up," she motioned to Rose, then hesitated. "Oh. I should probably introduce you to my parents though. They want to meet the girl who *saved* their daughter," she said sarcastically. "They're out on the patio."

Monica took Rose to the back of the house, through a finely decorated living room, a large, immaculate kitchen, and out onto a red brick patio, which was flooded in sunlight and surrounded by flowers in full bloom.

"Mom, Dad, this is Rose," said Monica.

Both parents were reading; Monica's father, a stack of papers with a pencil in hand, her mother, a book. They looked up as Monica spoke, her father getting to his feet.

"Well, this is the botanist we have heard so much about," said the handsome, gray-templed man, extending his hand to Rose.

"Excuse me?" Rose said, not exactly sure what a botanist was and why he was giving her that title.

"You helped our Monny with her poison ivy!" he replied, enthusiastically.

"Yes," the mother added, sitting on the edge of her white wicker chair. "We were so grateful you knew what to do! Luella had to wear garden gloves to help Monny out of her clothes."

"*Monica,* mother—please!" Monica said indignantly.

Her mother rolled her eyes at her daughter in mild irritation.

"At any rate, we're glad to meet you," she continued, holding out her limp-looking hand for Rose to shake.

"Monny—Monica says you're quite the math wiz too," her father said, correcting himself. "Maybe you could help me with my books sometime." He shook his head and pointing to the papers sitting all around him. "I had to fire my bookkeeper this week because she couldn't add two and two!"

"My dad's a doctor," Monica explained. "He has his own medical clinic.

"Where are you from my dear?" Monica's mother asked.

"I'm..., I'm from Louisiana," Rose said, not forgetting this time where Grandma B. had said they had come from.

"But you don't have that nice southern accent," Monica's father questioned.

"Oh, that's because...um...that's because I was born in Louisiana but grew up in...in Chicago," Rose lied, trying to think of a big city an oil executive might live in that would give her a mid-western accent.

"Oh," said Monica's father. "That would explain it."

"What does your father do?" Monica's mother asked.

"Enough of the fifth degree," Monica interrupted, to Rose's relief. "We're gonna go study for our math test. Come on, Rose," Monica motioned for Rose to follow her back into the house.

"It was very nice to meet you," Rose said as she started after Monica. "If you really want some help with your books Mr. Greenwall, let me know. I have most weekends free."

"I might take you up on that!" Monica's father replied, perking up a bit.

"Nice to meet you too, Rose," Monica's mother called after her. She turned toward her husband after Rose was out of sight. "Seems like a nice girl. A little nervous perhaps, but nice," she said.

He nodded his head in agreement and turned back to his papers.

~ ~ ~

Rose had made some brownie points with the girls in Monica's clique that Saturday; almost all of them did very well on their math test that next week, and right or wrong, they attributed their success to Rose. From that time on, Rose was included at their dinner table and was always invited to their study groups. Though Rose thought the girls seemed rather preoccupied with boys and the latest fashion, most of them took their studies fairly seriously. Probably because Soldan was one of the more prestigious public schools in the area, and if you went to Soldan, your parents expected you to do well.

Monica's father did ask for Rose's help straightening out his books the next few weekends. Rose didn't mind; he made her accept some money for her efforts, so it kept her in spending money. Rose did such a good job on the books that Monica's father hired her to help in his office on a regular basis, filing, stuffing envelopes and other administrative tasks the regular office staff couldn't get around to during the week. This ensured Rose made it to Monica's almost every Saturday, and they treated her like she was a part of their family. Rose quite enjoyed being a part of a loving family again. Grandma B.'s family was very loving too, of course, but Grace's quiet animosity toward Rose always made her feel a slight tension when she was there, so she never felt quite at home.

Being with Monica's family also made Rose feel homesick. Rose had continued to write to her family, to let them know what she was doing and that she was fine, but she never included a return address. She didn't want them to find her and drag her home. But late at night, lying in bed, she missed knowing how they were doing. Was Michael still able to go to school? Was the new baby a boy or a girl? She didn't even know. These questions crept into her heart late at night when all was quiet and still.

Monica's family was small; she had a brother who was two years younger, but that was it. It seemed strange to Rose to have such a big house with a cook, a maid, and a grounds keeper all to help with such a small family. Rose tried not to talk to Monica or anyone else about her family. She didn't want to lie if she could help it, and she didn't want anyone to find out she really lived in the Ville, not on an upscale street like Monica and most of the other girls in her group. If someone found out and told the school, Rose felt sure they wouldn't let her continue to go to school there. She was enjoying being back at school, and she didn't want to take the chance. She also didn't think her new friends would understand her living arrangement. Most of her girl friends had servants who were colored, and they wouldn't be caught dead having a colored person as a friend, let alone live in their home.

Rose had to be especially careful around Alyssa; she was the unofficial ring-leader of their group. She lived on Washington Terrace, the street with the castle-like entrance. Alyssa didn't seem to believe what Rose was telling her about her make-believe parents and her make-believe house. And, for some reason which Rose could never figure out, she didn't like having Rose in their group. She only went along with the idea because Monica liked Rose so well. Rose knew if she made one wrong move or said the wrong thing, Alyssa would find her out.

~ ~ ~

When Rose wasn't working in the Greenwall medical office, and Todd wasn't working a weekend shift at Brown's, Todd was Rose's guide to St. Louis. He enjoyed the enthusiasm and excitement she had at every new destination they went to. He made a private game of it. Each time they went out, he would try and find something more interesting, more exciting for Rose than the time before; getting to know Rose better with each subsequent adventure. He had never spent any time with a white girl before, and he was pleasantly surprised at how much they had in common and how much he enjoyed her company.

He showed Rose the inside of the old church, which she had seen the first day she arrived in St. Louis. He showed her the downtown public library, with its high ceilings of sculpted wood, its marble entrance way, and colorful stained glass windows that illuminated the steps leading up to the second floor. It was the most beautiful library Rose had ever seen and became one of their favorite spots to study, especially after Todd started technical school after the winter break.

The Missouri Botanical Garden was also a hit, but by the time they had made it there it was late October, and most of the plants were past their peak. So one day Todd decided to surprise Rose by taking her to the Jewel Box. It had just opened in Forest Park, and he wanted to show it to her before she discovered it herself. They usually took Della and Marcus along on their excursions, but today Todd made sure they were alone. Saturday was meeting day for the NAACP, and Grace and Darrell were active members, so Todd asked Grandma B. if she could watch the kids for them.

"Ya know, child, what you doin' with dat girl ain't right."

Todd looked at his grandmother in surprise. He didn't think anyone was paying that much attention.

"I ain't doin' nothin' wrong!" he insisted.

"It ain't what your doin', it's who your doin' it with."

Todd looked at her in silence then looked down at the ground.

"It's gonna lead ta no good, you mark my words," she said, trying to be more forceful with her warning. But it fell on deaf ears.

Grandma B. reluctantly agreed to watch the children that afternoon.

~ ~ ~

"Where are you taking me this time?" asked Rose.

"You'll see," Todd replied with a wry smile on his face.

Rose knew it was no use trying to wrangle any other information out of him. She had tried before, and Todd was always resolutely mute. Rose had gotten over that slightly uncomfortable feeling she initially had around Todd, and he had stopped staring at her so much. Though every once in a while, Rose would have an odd feeling someone was looking at her, only to find it was Todd. It embarrassed her, though she liked it all the same.

The looks Rose couldn't get used to were the stares they both got from the white and colored people they met when they were out together; the *What do you think you are doing?* sort of looks. Rose had mostly learned to ignore it, but it bothered her none-the-less. She and Lilly Mae received those looks at times, but not half as much as when she and Todd were together.

Once she even had a kindly looking, old white lady who was sitting next to her on the street car ask her: "You're not with that darkie are you?" When Rose had answered in the affirmative she shot back, "What's wrong with you child? They'll mug you so much as look at you."

Rose got up and motioned Todd to move to the back of the car.

Their relationship grew steadily, though somewhat tentatively on both parts. There was an ease they had when being together which was unmistakable to both parties, and they quickly fell in with each other.

It was a cold, crisp, early December day when Todd took her to the Jewel Box. An unusually early frost still covered the ground and sparkled on each blade of grass like a Christmas globe in the clear, bright sun. Rose pulled the collar of her jacket up past her ears. Grandma B. had shown her a great second-hand store where she had picked up her winter gear at a very reasonable price, but they didn't quite have her size jacket, so the one she purchased was a bit big. She had taken to keeping her hair in a pony-tail lately, which she liked because it kept her hair out of her face, but at this moment she was wishing it was down, covering her ears and the goose bumps on her neck.

When they stepped off the street car at Forest Park, Rose was still not sure what Todd had up his sleeve. She thought they had seen everything in the park already: the grand Muni outdoor theatre, the golf course (which they had even played, but only from seven to twelve on Saturday, because they didn't let Negroes on the course at any other time), the zoo with the aviary, which was a gift from the Smithsonian Institute during the 1904 Worlds Fair, the art museum, and the lakes, with miles of rolling green and forested park in between. It was a little odd, Rose thought, because Della and Marcus usually came along on their excursions, but today Todd told her they would be alone.

The oddity of being alone with Todd, and under such mysterious circumstances, stirred idle emotions within Rose. It was the old, slightly unsettled feeling she had her first week in St. Louis, but this time it was punctuated with a spark of desire.

"Now you have to put this on," Todd said, placing one of his handkerchiefs around her eyes before she had a chance to protest.

"Why do I have to wear this?" Rose asked, tingling mildly from Todd's touch and the closeness of his body to hers.

"Because I can't wrap it; it's too big," Todd answered in a joking tone. "And I want it to be a surprise! Think of it as an early Christmas present."

He smiled broadly, sure Rose was going to love the gift.

Once blindfolded, Todd put her arm around his and led her slowly along, telling her when to step up, when to turn right or left. It was a different sensation, Rose discovered, being blind and being led by someone. At first she didn't like her lack of control, anxious with her inability to see what was around her, what could be coming at her—a remnant of that night on the riverboat. She took a deep breath to calm herself. Once she was able to settle her anxiety, her mind was pulled in another direction, this time toward Todd.

The first thing she noticed was the firmness of his arm. The hours he spent at the YMCA lifting weights, playing basketball with his friends, or swimming could be felt even through his coat. Then there was his smell. She had never really noticed it before, but there was a faint piney smell about him. She thought it was coming from the direction of his head. *Maybe it was one of Madame Poro's hair care products that Aunt Tilley sold,* Rose thought.

Lastly there was the voice; it was like the mellow tone of a pipe organ, reverberating through her, heightening her senses so every word made her pang for more. Rose thought his voice matched perfectly with the nutmeg color of his skin and the soft look of his blemish-free face, both of which she could see quite clearly, despite the blindfold that covered her eyes. It also reinforced her feeling of ease. There was rarely a wrinkle of care when she heard this voice, and it was thrilling to be hearing it now, as she blindly held on to his eighteen-year-old arm.

She was still working through these sensations when the cold wind picked up and swirled around them, giving Rose the clue that their environment had just changed. They both stood still.

"Stand here a minute," Todd said with excitement in his voice.

He unlatched Rose from his arm, grasping her hand he stretched out for the door which stood in front of them.

Rose felt the swish of the door opening. A waft of warm, moist air filled her nostrils and caressed her face. She couldn't imagine where he was taking her. Todd grasped her arm around his once more and cautiously led her in to the warmth.

He let go of her arm fully once they were through the door, and stepped behind her, working on the knot of her blindfold.

"You ready?" he asked with even more excitement, still holding the handkerchief in place.

New smells were hitting Rose from all directions, but she was too excited to try and figure out what they were.

"Quit teasing. Let me see!"

He let the handkerchief fall. The bright light of the early morning sun blinded her eyes momentarily. She blinked and refocused, finally seeing the beauty that lay before her. It was a conservatory, bigger than anything she had ever seen before. Just past the entrance were two small palms which stood on each side of a path of fine stones, and beyond that, a vast tropical garden: flowers, vines, and even a meandering, babbling brook winding its way amongst the vegetation.

"It's beautiful, Todd!" Rose said in amazement. "You've outdone yourself this time," she congratulated him, then grabbed his hand without thinking and pulled him into the dripping greenery. His face glowed as he followed Rose, both from the vicarious satisfaction of exciting her even more than the trip to the library and from the warmth and smoothness of her touch.

Rose's eyes darted this way and that, pointing out the redness of this particular flower, or the shape of that odd looking plant, stopping on occasion to inhale deeply and fill her body and soul with a particularly sweet smell or odd odor which might have caught her attention. As per his usual, Todd hardly said a word; he too was impressed by all the beauty and greenery which surrounded him, in addition to the beauty that was towing him along. Todd enjoyed how acutely Rose discovered new things. She always revealed new things for him at places he'd seen and been to many times before. It transformed his mundane world into something much brighter, more hopeful. It was addicting.

But he knew, as he gazed at the radiant face and auburn locks that held sway over his better judgment, that he was getting too close.

At first it was Rose's beauty which caught his eye—her hair, her eyes, the perfect shape of her hips. But the more he got to know her, these outwardly things became icing on the cake; a cake which was very smart and funny and warm and white!

It just wasn't done. He knew *that* too. The fact that Rose didn't seem to care that he was black and she was white made it that much easier to get close to her. And now, after today, he knew she felt something for him as well, but she was too young, too naïve to know better. He wasn't. He had to watch himself, though it was becoming increasingly difficult the more time he spent with her.

"Hey, what's the matter?" Rose asked with a concerned look. She had noticed his change in disposition.

"Oh, nothing," he said, trying to lighten his mood. "But we probably should go soon."

He had purposely brought Rose to the conservatory just after it opened so there would be fewer people to point and whisper and stare. He wanted this to be a pleasant experience for both of them.

"Oh, just a little longer," she squeaked in excitement, running off to another part of the indoor rain forest. Rose looked back to see if Todd was following when she was stopped dead in her tracks. She stood staring in disbelief. Standing fifty feet away from her, separated only by vines and leaves, was the bane of her existence.

~ ~ ~

Rose's heart dropped to the floor, and her feet cemented in place as she stood slack-jawed at the sight; it was Alyssa Morgan standing in the doorway of the atrium taking off her coat. Heat ascended to Rose's face, and her heartbeat sounded so loud in her ears, it took her attention away from the hard knot that had instantly taken the place of her stomach. Rose unglued her feet and quickly ran back to find Todd.

"Maybe we *should* go," she said to him nervously, glancing in the direction of the front doors.

Todd was surprised at the change of heart but stood and started to walk in the direction they had come.

"Do they have a back door?" Rose asked quickly. "I want to see that too." She grabbed his hand and unintentionally jerked him in the other direction. When they reached the back door, she hastily threw on her coat and stepped out into the stinging cold wind; a wind she hardly noticed from the heat Rose's body was creating.

Rose was unusually quiet on the way home. Todd wanted to try and keep Rose at arms length, but he didn't want her to be upset with him, and something had upset her back there. He assumed it had been him.

Rose was disappointed. She had loved being with Todd; the excitement of him standing close, holding his hand and being alone, away from the staring eyes of people who obviously thought they shouldn't be together. Grace obviously didn't like it. On top of her not trusting Rose, she always gave Rose a look of disapproval whenever she and Todd went out on their weekend excursions. It didn't seem to matter that her children were going along with them. Even Grandma B. had suggested to Rose that maybe they were spending too much time together. She kept asking Rose if she had met any handsome boys at school yet.

"Is there something wrong, Rose?" Todd asked tentatively, looking into her stone cold, flushed face as she stared off into nowhere.

"No-no, Todd, of course not. It was the best place yet!" Rose said, forcing a smile but being very sincere.

"Okay," Todd said, trying to believe her, but he was not quite sure if he did.

They both sat in an uncomfortable silence, lost in their own thoughts the rest of the way home.

When they stepped off the street car, the brisk December air swirled around them, waking them both momentarily out of their forlorn moods.

"Todd, can I ask you a question?" Rose said as they started to walk toward home.

"Sure," he said, brightening at the chance to talk again but a little anxious about what Rose might ask.

"How come Grace seems to dislike me so much?"

"Oh...," he said, relieved that it wasn't a particularly uncomfortable question about the two of them. "Well, that's just Grace. She doesn't trust anyone, especially anyone who's white. She had met this white woman in an office that she was working in before she started nursing school. She thought she was a friend. That was until she lost her job on account of this women lying to their boss. He told him that Grace had stolen somethin' from the company. See, she wanted Grace's job 'cause it paid better than hers. She didn't think a negro woman should be paid more than a white one, even though she was the cleaning help and Grace was a file clerk."

"No wonder she doesn't like white people," Rose said, nodding her head in understanding. "But there's this girl at school, she doesn't like me either. I've tired to be nice to her; save her a good seat at dinner, help her with her homework, but she's always out to get me. I'm not sure what to do."

Todd stopped and looked straight at Rose.

"You know what your problem is, Rose?" he started. "You care too much about what other people think. You can't be everyone's friend, and not everyone you meet is going to like you."

He picked up her hand as he finished, softening the expression on his face. "You're a nice girl, Rose. You're smart and fun to be with, and you care about other people." Rose's face beamed as he spoke. "So don't worry what other people think. If they can't see those things, then they're probably not worth being friends with anyway."

The two stared at each other in silence before Rose dropped her gaze, a slight blush on her face. Todd realized what he was doing and let go of her hand. They turned and continued walking back toward home.

"I guess you're right, Todd," Rose said, realizing she did care even what strangers thought about her. "How'd you get so smart?" she asked, half teasing, half being sincere.

"Oh, just born that way I guess," he said with rakish grin. "Actually, Grandma B. helped me figure that out a long time ago. When you're colored, you have to learn that lesson at an early age, or you won't amount to nothin'."

Rose had a smile on her face and a slight bounce in her step the rest of the way home. Did Todd really think all those nice things about her? She knew he cared for her, at least a little, but hearing him say those nice things made her troubled thoughts of Grace and Alyssa float easily away in the cold December breeze.

The day had turned out well after all.

~ ~ ~

Just before the Christmas holiday, it was a Soldan tradition to have a winter dance. Rose and the other girls in her clique were excited about the prospect of their first high school dance. Rose had elicited the help of Aunt Tilley and Tilley's friend Pearl to help her pick out a dress at the second-hand store. There was quite a lot of bickering between the two about what a sixteen-year-old should wear—Rose, preferring to take Pearl's side of things since she tended to pick garments which were a little more risqué and in style. Tilley's taste went for more coverage and less curve. They all finally agreed on a gray-blue, knit dress with long sleeves and a high, tie-collar to fit Aunt Tilley's taste, and a sleek fit and smart belt to satisfy Pearl's. Rose hoped it was nice enough to fool her classmates that it wasn't new, particularly Alyssa. They both volunteered to do up her hair and face, but she only agreed after they promised she could pay them something.

The dance was being held in the school gym. A group of girls, including Rose and Monica, spent the morning decorating it in a starry-night theme—shiny, silver painted, paper stars and crescent moons hung from wire which had been strung across the gym, with the same moons and stars taped to the shiny tile walls. But it didn't really sparkle until that evening when the lights were low, and the hard edges were smoothed by the flickering candles at each table and around the punch bowl.

The school had hired a colored band to play at the dance. Rose felt a little uncomfortable as they were setting up in front of the large crowd of white boys and girls. They didn't seem to take any notice that they were the only colored people in the building.

"You look great, Rose," Monica chirped as they huddled together waiting for the rest of their group to arrive. "Your hair and your makeup look really nice. Who did it?"

"Aunt...," Rose stopped herself. "A friend of my aunt has a beauty shop in St. Louis."

Rose smiled to herself. The thought of Monica having her hair done in a colored woman's salon was amusing. Rose figured that fact alone would put curls in Monica's hair, even without the use of a hot iron.

"You look nice too, Monica," Rose said sincerely.

Monica held out the flared bottom of her rose-colored skirt, letting the soft crepe fabric flow like water as she waved it back and forth for effect. The taffeta bodice had a short V-neckline ending in a fabric rose, with silk ribbon wrapping down and around her waist to the back. The whole thing shimmered as she turned this way then that, a prickle of envy crossing Rose's mind.

"Thanks," she said. "My mom took me to Famous Barr to get it. It cost twenty five dollars!"

That was one thing Rose liked about Monica; even though she was well-off, she didn't act like it. She never threw her family's wealth in Rose's face as some of the girls in their group did, particularly Alyssa. As the two girls were talking, Alyssa strode up to them in a dark maroon, velvet number, with two of the other girls in their group trailing close behind.

"You look great, Alyssa!" Monica said sincerely.

"Yeah, thanks," she said, raising her head in the air, not returning the compliment. She gave a sideways glance at Rose and turned herself away, disapprovingly.

"Anybody here yet?" she asked, directing her question more at Monica than at Rose, as she gazed around the room full of well-dressed boys and girls.

"Well, Matthew's here if that's who you're looking for," Monica said. "He's over in the corner, by the bathrooms."

Alyssa turned and strode over to where a gang of uncomfortable looking boys in suits and bow ties were standing, the rest of the girls following behind.

"Hey, Matt," Alyssa said, trying to be casual but standing in such a way to best showed off her ensemble.

"Hey, Alyssa," he said, looking briefly up from the middle of the group of boys.

Matthew Colombo was one of the more popular boys in Rose's class and one of the tallest. He had grown before most of the other boys and even had some facial hair, which he was particularly proud of, even though it was blond, and you could hardly see it. Rose had to admit, he was very handsome with his curly blond hair, broad shoulders, and trim figure. Rose could tell, like Todd, he must get a lot of exercise. She remembered Alyssa saying she had gone to watch him in a polo match a couple months ago. Alyssa liked Matt, and he seemed to reciprocate the feeling, but Rose thought more out of convenience than true friendship or affection.

Rose noticed when he looked up to say hello to Alyssa, he soon turned his gaze toward her. One of the other boys, Matt's friend, Ryan Bryce, was looking at Rose too. He whispered something into Matthew's ear. Matthew smiled and nodded his head in agreement, not taking his eyes off Rose. Alyssa also noticed, and she glanced at Rose with a sneer.

Just then the music started, and the uncomfortable moment was diverted as everyone's attention turned toward the band.

"So, you gonna ask me to dance, Matt?" Alyssa asked, being more forward than any of the other girls dared.

"Oh…sure," he said, and he held out his arm, leading her out onto the empty dance floor.

After they were alone in the middle of the gym for a minute or two, other couples started to slowly fill in around them. The boy Monica liked, Richard Gallager, asked her to dance, and a few of the other girls in their group were led out onto the floor—broad, shy smiles across their sheepish faces. Rose was standing next to one of the other girls when she was surprised by a tap on her shoulder; it was Ryan Bryce.

"You wanna dance?" he asked timidly.

"Sure!" she said.

As they stiffly moved around the dance floor at arms length, both Ryan and Rose watched carefully around them so as to avoid any collisions with others in the room. Rose stared at Ryan a moment, thinking about what she was doing. This was her first high school dance with a boy, and he wasn't a half-bad dancer, at that. Rose had never paid much attention to the boys at school. She was too busy with her school work or with her friends. Besides, she wasn't particularly interested in any of the boys she had met at school. Ryan Bryce was an okay looking boy. He hung around with Matt and his gang, but he had never said anything to Rose until tonight. And Rose noticed there was no electricity in his touch as there was in Todd's.

After a few turns around the gym floor, Ryan eventually spoke up.

"Um…, You look nice, Rose."

"Thanks, Ryan. You look nice too."

Then there was silence. That was the extent of their conversation. There didn't seem to be too much else to say, but neither one seemed to mind. They just kept moving around the floor cautiously until the song was done.

"Thanks," he said as they stepped apart.

"Sure," came Rose's reply.

The girls and boys retreated to their respective troupes, and the awkward drama was repeated many times over throughout the evening. At one point, even Matt Colombo asked Rose to dance. She was so nervous she couldn't get herself to say even two words to him; nervous because he was one of the most popular boys in her class, and nervous because she knew Alyssa wouldn't be happy seeing them dancing together.

Rose was asked to dance by a few other boys that evening, but she was relieved when the night was over, and she could relax and breathe normally. Trying to make polite conversation was harder than she thought it would be, and being all dressed up with makeup and a stiff hair style was making her tired. It all felt so unnatural and heavy, but she was still glad she had come to the dance none-the-less. That is, until she ran into Alyssa Morgan coming out of the girl's bathroom.

"Well, if it isn't Miss Krantz," she said in the snottiest tone she could conjure up. "You know, I saw your dress in the store, and I was thinking of getting it myself," she continued, surprising Rose with a compliment. "No, come to think of it, that was last year."

She laughed half-heartedly. The other girls who surrounded her giggled along with her. Then Alyssa leaned in close with a less jovial look on her face.

"Listen Rose, I don't know what you're up to, pretending to be someone you're not, but don't even think about Matthew Colombo. He's way out of your league."

At that, she turned and stomped away, leaving Rose wide-eyed and bewildered.

On the way home on the street car, Rose couldn't stop thinking about what Alyssa had said. She had tried to ignore her, as Todd had suggested. She was polite to her, but she had stopped going out of her way to be a friend. It wasn't her fault Matt had asked her to dance. Why did Alyssa seem to hate her so much?

These thoughts went around and around in Rose's head that night, reluctantly subsiding long enough to allow her to fall asleep.

She woke the next morning only to have the same recording play repeatedly in her mind. She had to stop it, and she knew who to go to for help.

~ ~ ~

Rose held back in the kitchen after the breakfast dishes were cleaned up and everyone else had gone to get ready for church, everyone except Grandma B.

"Grandma, I need your help," Rose piped up.

"I was wonderin' when ya was gonna say somethin'. You done chewed those eggs so long I'd thought it was your last meal on dis here earth. What's da matta, child?"

"Well, there's this really rich girl at school, her name is Alyssa, and for some reason she's out to get me!"

"Out to get'cha! What'cha mean? Is she trying ta pick a fight wich you?" Grandma B. asked, getting a little riled.

"Not a fist fight, if that's what you mean. No, she just doesn't like me. She seems to know I'm not really from a rich family, and she's just waiting for me to say something or do something to prove it."

"Yeah, dats my fault I'm afraid. I shoudn'ta started dat der lie in da first place," Grandma B. admitted. "Lyin' always comes ta no good. But I didn't know how else ta get ya inta dat school. You too smart ta go ta does other public schools. I's sorry child." She shook her head, disappointed with herself. "Da only thing I can tell ya is ya has ta try and not take what dis here girl says and does ta heart."

Grandma B. sat down at the table. Rose sat down across from her.

"Ya don't know where she's comin' from—what her family's like, how she done been brought up. Der's lots a things dat can make a person say and do nasty things ta others."

Rose looked at Grandma B. intently, not wanting to miss a thing.

"Believe it or not, it really ain't about you. She's just afraid a somethin'. Pro'bly afraid you'll find out she's not who she pretends ta be; afraid maybe you'll find out she's just like da rest a us."

Rose's eyes opened in amazement at these words. *Alyssa Morgan, afraid!* Rose didn't think Alyssa would have been afraid of anything. But maybe Grandma B. was right; maybe there was something she was trying to hide. If Alyssa put her attention on Rose, then no one would bother thinking about her.

As Rose lay in bed that evening looking up at the darkened ceiling, which by now she knew by every crack and crevice, she was amused and surprised at all the things she had learned since she had met Alyssa Morgan. She tried not to worry now if someone didn't seem to like her. There were plenty of people she met whom she got along with just fine, so it wasn't such a big deal when she met people who didn't seem to like her. Now, with the help of Grandma B. and Todd, she had come to the realization that people like Alyssa and Grace do things and say things because of their own experiences, their own lives, their own fears. Maybe the nasty remarks they shot her way, or the ill will they seemed to feel toward her was their way of making themselves feel better—letting off steam from something which had nothing what-so-ever to do with her. This was quite an expanding idea Grandma B. had given Rose.

No one but Lilly Mae and Grandma B. knew why she jumped two feet whenever someone came up behind her and touched her unexpectedly. Rose realized everyone had their own experiences and secrets which made them act they way they did. As she lay there thinking all these deep thoughts, she had the strange urge to thank Alyssa for what she had unknowingly taught her. She wondered if she would ever get the chance. She shook her head gently. She rather doubted it.

~ ~ ~

Soon Christmas was upon them. It was hard for any of the students at Soldan to keep their minds on final exams, including Rose. There were too many distractions: the streets were bustling as people rushed in and out of stores, gaily decorated for the season, there were up-coming trips to visit extended family, and two weeks of vacation without school work. That was the most common daydream at school.

Monica's house was also full of Christmas colors—ribbons, holly, swags and garlands of pine and the biggest tree Rose had ever seen. Mrs. Greenwall was particularly proud of the tree. It was covered with glass ornaments from all around the world. Grandma B. hadn't gotten a tree yet. She said Santa brought it on Christmas Eve, but Todd told Rose they waited until the day before Christmas because that was when the trees at the tree lots went on sale.

Rose stood looking at the tree at Monica's the weekend before exams, when the room contracted around her, and she found herself standing in the midst of her family as they were hanging ornaments on their tree.

The tradition at the Krantz home was to go out on their property and find a pine tree that was the biggest they could find, yet small enough to fit in their living room. The whole family would bundle up to go out in the cold, clear, and usually white December weather to help choose the perfect tree. Once they got it home, Rose's father would put it in his homemade stand and tie it to the stair railing in the living room so it wouldn't fall. The trees that grew around their farm were usually a bit scrawny, but once they got it home, the transformation began. The family would decorated it with shiny, string-covered balls of white and gold, little angels, which had real feathers for skirts and painted porcelain heads, strands of popcorn and cranberries which took hours to make, and every homemade ornament each Krantz child had ever made in school or in Sunday school. It was quite a sight and always an experience Rose thoroughly enjoyed.

They would tune the radio to a station playing Christmas songs and sing carols as they decorated the tree, eating snacks and sweets their mother had substituted for supper on this special night. The wood stove kept them all toasty warm as the frost built up on the windows and made the outside look even more like a winter wonderland.

"The tree is lovely, isn't it dear?" said Mrs. Greenwall, pulling Rose back into the room.

"Oh, yes it is beautiful," replied Rose, blinking away the water which had filled her eyes.

"Are you all right?

"Yes. I'm fine."

"Rose, I'd like you to give this to your parents. It's an invitation to our New Years Eve gathering—just cocktails and hors d'oeuvres with our friends, nothing fancy," she said, giving Rose a large envelope. "I thought it would be a nice way to finally meet your parents. You're welcome to come along, of course. Monny would love to have someone to kibitz with."

Rose stood gawking at Mrs. Greenwall, not sure what to say.

"And about next Friday, we'd like to pick you up at six if that's okay," she continued.

"Friday?" Rose questioned, still dazed by the New Years invitation.

"*The Nutcracker*, dear?"

"Oh, yah." Rose did remember.

She was very excited to see her first ballet, but they couldn't pick her up. That wouldn't work at all. What could she do?

"I..., um, wanted to talk to you about that, Mrs. Greenwall. Since I only have one exam that day, my Mom was going to take me Christmas shopping, so she wondered if she could just drop me off at the Kiel."

"Oh that would be fine, dear. Then we'll get to meet her briefly. That would be nice. If you're there about twenty minutes before seven, then we'll have time to get to our seats and get settled. It will be very crowded, I'm sure. It is every year."

Rose sighed and smiled at Mrs. Greenwall demurely, another lie sitting uncomfortably between them.

~ ~ ~

Rose stood among the crowd outside the Kiel auditorium and opera house. She wore the same dress she had worn to the school Christmas dance, dressed up a little, thanks to Grandma B., with a satin ribbon around her waist in place of the belt and a smaller one around her neck and a pearlized piece of cosmetic jewelry to give it a little splash. Aunt Tilley did her usual magic on her hair, and it was all topped off with a short dress-coat donated by Pearl.

"My, don't you look lovely, Rose," Mrs. Greenwall commented to Rose as she and Monica stepped up to Rose on the sidewalk.

"Where's your mother, dear?

"Oh...."

Rose hesitated. In all the excitement she had forgotten her mother was supposed to be here dropping her off.

"Yes..., um. My brother wasn't feeling well this morning, so she wanted to get right home to check on him."

Rose blinked anxiously and wide-eyed at Mrs. Greenwall, who seemed less inclined to accept her explanation than previously.

"She sends her apologies."

Just then, Mr. Greenwall and his son stepped up to the group after parking their car. "Shall we go in, ladies and gentleman?" he asked, saving Rose from any further explanations.

Mrs. Greenwall gave Rose one last questioning look then took her husband's arm. Monica's brother and the girls followed them into the theatre.

~ ~ ~

The Christmas season was turning out to be very busy. Rose didn't have much time to think about home; she was studying hard for exams; and at Grandma B. and Todd's urging, she had joined the Antioch Baptist church choir, in addition to all the Christmas shopping she still had to do. She knew what she was going to get for most everyone: doll clothes for Della, a new truck for Marcus, white church gloves for Grandma B. (turned out she *was* the white glove type), a pocket knife for Darrell, a head scarf for Grace, a book for Monica, and for Todd, a year's subscription to *The Crisis*. But she was most excited about what she was going to send back home.

The holiday season was making her quite homesick, so she decided she was going to send her family a gift in the mail. It was a music box she had found at Schwardtmanns—an amazing toy store Todd took her to on Washington Avenue. The outside of the music box was dark mahogany, and when you opened it, it played *Let it Snow* as small figure skaters danced in circles on a sheet of ice, reflected in a frosted mirror tucked under the cover. She only wished she could see their faces as they opened it. Now she just had to find time to mail it. The Saturday before Christmas would have to do.

~ ~ ~

It was midnight, Christmas night, and Rose lay in bed exhausted but unable to sleep. So much had gone on in just a few days that she couldn't get her mind to settle down. The Christmas Eve service was wonderful. The Baptist church, like St. Mary's, was decorated in ribbons, pine bows and candles. The choir really moved this night, with some of Rose's favorite Christmas carols, but she was particularly proud of Todd and his solo of *Go tell it on the Mountain*. He did a wonderful job. The Reverend Cook's sermon about the salvation which was brought to all people this night—black, white, yellow or brown—in the form of a baby boy, moved Rose to tears. The live nativity scene, which greeted everyone as they left the church, was particularly interesting to Rose. She had never seen an all-colored nativity. The only colored character in St. Mary's ceramic nativity was one of the three kings.

Everyone had liked their Christmas presents; even Grace's cold shoulder seemed to melt slightly when she realized Rose had given her a gift. Grace hadn't gotten anything for Rose, but Rose hadn't really expected anything either. The expression on Grace's face was enough of a gift for Rose; it was a glimmer of hope that maybe, one day, they could be friends, or at least not be adversaries. Todd had liked his gift, and he had given Rose a beautifully bound edition of *The Complete Works of Williams Shakespeare*, with a promise that they would see one of his plays at the Muni this coming summer. Rose wasn't sure where she was going to be this summer, but she didn't say anything about that to Todd.

Another wonderful event for Rose that Christmas was *The Nutcracker!* If Rose thought folks were dressed up when they went to see *The Alibi,* she was mistaken. The women and men who were at *The Nutcracker* were dressed to the nines; the ladies were in sleek, long, flowing gowns of silk, satin or that wonderful new fabric: rayon. Many of them wore fur stoles and lots of spangly jewels. The men wore handsome, black tuxedos and black bow ties. The performance was magical; the music, costumes and dancers easily transported Rose to the magical world of soldiers and sugar plum fairies.

Rose also felt pretty good about her exams. She had never had a week of just exams before, but not having classes during her exam week gave her extra time to study, so she thought she did pretty well, overall.

As Rose lay in bed, sleep started to over take her. She shut her eyes, squeezing out a tear as she envisioned the faces of her family circled around the present she had sent, listening to *Let it Snow.*

The rest of Christmas break went by quickly for Rose. She made it through most of her book of Shakespeare since, unlike at home, she didn't have any snow to play in during her time off. Rose's heart was lifted when she woke one morning a couple days after Christmas to a snow-covered landscape, but the thrill didn't last long when it melted by that afternoon. Rose was determined after that, when she finally settled down, she would live where it snowed in winter, and it stayed.

Rose had escaped the Greenwall's New Years Eve party fairly easily. She had decided upon a rather simple excuse of a prior engagement for her parents to miss the party, but when Mrs. Greenwall wanted to talk to her mother about it, Rose had to think of something quick. She told her that they had left town just the night before. Mrs. Greenwall's reaction made Rose feel like she didn't know how much longer she was going to believe her stories of mostly absent parents. Juggling the lies was starting to wear on Rose. She wasn't sure if she could keep up the façade.

❧ 10 ❧

There is a history in America's melting-pot of a people which has evolved more slowly, more insidiously than most because, frankly, it is easy to single these people out. They can't blend in as readily as the Italians, the Germans, the Irish, or the Poles. And for some, there always has to be someone "beneath;" someone they stand above. How else do you know that you've "made it"?

They were brought over by boat, in abhorrent conditions, and those that made the trip were enslaved to a life of drudgery and hardship. A generation grew up in this and knew no different. Emancipation came and went as the *haves* slowly discovered how to restrict new-found freedoms; so the carrot of opportunity dangled, while the stick of repression hovered always at the ready.

But still it was there, and people pushed and crawled and stole their way along—Booker T. Washington, Ida B. Wells, Annie Malone, W.E.B. DuBois, and James Turner to name a few. So now there was more that was separate-but-equal; a *feeling* in that community that what *they* had, *we* had; what *they* could achieve, *we* could achieve. But it was all quite separate; not part of the larger society, just subservient to it. So for this generation, some things had changed and some things had not. Grandma B. knew this; Todd and Rose would soon find out.

~ ~ ~

The spring semester trudged along slowly. January and February were fairly gray months; mostly overcast with rain, freezing rain, or very wet snow which never stayed, dampening most everyone's spirits. To make matters worse, there were a few close calls with Alyssa and the girls. Alyssa had come up with the brilliant idea of moving the study group each week, so that each time they met it was at a different girl's home. When it was Rose's turn to host the group, Rose called and told them she was sick and couldn't meet. On Rose's next turn, she spent a whole weekend's worth of pay treating the girls at the soda shop instead of going to her house. All the girls seemed pleased with the switch, except Alyssa.

Then there was Grandma B. Despite the fact that she sat most of the time, giving orders to everyone around her, she didn't seem to be getting any better. She hadn't had any more spells, or at least not that Rose could tell. What Rose didn't know was that Grandma B.'s drowning dream had started up again, but since she was no longer on the river, Grandma B. pushed it away as inconsequential.

The thing that kept Rose going during the dreary winter months was the young man that she couldn't stop thinking about. His deep eyes and calm demeanor were magnets for Rose's troubled heart. He continued to show her the special places of St. Louis: city hall, which looked like a European villa, and Union Station, whose grand hall, with its blue-green stone floor and beautiful stained glass, turned out to be one of Rose's favorite places in the city. She loved to watch the passengers coming and going from the trains. With their tearful goodbyes and emotional hellos, she could be a voyeur into the lives of these strangers, imagining their different lives; the places they lived, the people they loved, and the adventures they would soon encounter.

Strolls with Todd along the sparcely populated Eads Bridge came in a close second; here she could talk with Todd, and they could even hold hands on occasion, without a lot of people staring at them. It also brought Rose back to the river and the possibilities for adventure; the fresh breeze off the water hinted of spring, and the sight of the occasional riverboat called to Rose as sure as if Lilly Mae were talking to her, telling her, "Come visit. It'll be fun!" New Orleans *would* be a great adventure, but her heart was split. There, standing beside her, was a most gentle, nurturing, and intelligent young man; a young man who obviously cared for her and who she cared for as well.

Tower Grove and Fairground Parks were also good places to get lost in. But, strangely enough, the huge, rolling, wooded Bellefontaine Cemetery was a place Rose enjoyed even more. She often went there alone just to think and walk among the monuments, headstones and trees. And when she was tired of thinking, she would look at the names and dates on the headstones and be transported to another time and place so many years ago. There was something quieting about the place that comforted Rose.

Rose and Todd would also make an occasional early morning trip back to the Jewel Box to lift their spirits on particularly dreary winter days. Of course, this place meant something special to Rose. It was where she had learned for sure that Todd had special feelings for her.

When April came around, they decided to bring Grandma B. to the Easter display, which transformed the tropical rainforest to an aromatic, spring garden with tulips, hyacinths, and daffodils lining the walkways. It took them quite a while to get there, since Grandma B. seemed to slow with each successive month, but the look on her face when they stepped through the doors made it all worth while. Grandma B. talked about it for weeks afterwards.

May didn't come soon enough for Rose. That was the month of Todd's birthday, and she wanted to give him something special.

~ ~ ~

"So what's so important that we had to come here for?" Todd asked as they sat in the swings of the Simmons Grade School playground.

"Well, I wasn't sure Grandma B. would approve of my birthday present for you, so I thought I should give it to you before the party," Rose explained. "Here, open it."

She shoved a small, thin, brown paper package into his hands.

"You didn't need to get me anything, Rose," Todd said sincerely.

Rose rolled her eyes and shook her head softly, giving him that, *of course I did, silly,* look. "Just open it!"

Wrapped in the brown paper was a book: *From Here to Eternity.*

"Open it up!" Rose said excitedly.

When Todd opened up the cover, two small, narrow pieces of paper fell to the ground. He picked them up, and as he read what was printed on them, a large grin spread across his face.

"How'd you get these?" he questioned as he gazed down in amazement at the two tickets with "Louis Armstrong" written across them. "My friends told me they were all sold out."

"I've got my connections," she said smiling back at him. "I thought you and Nathan would like to go."

"These are great, Rose. Thanks!"

He looked up at her and smiled. Then he hesitated a moment. Slowly he reached across for the chain of her swing and pulled her close. Rose could feel her heart suddenly start to race and the heat rise around her face as they stared into each others eyes for what seemed like minutes. The pupils in his dark brown eyes were wide open. The large black orbs, like black holes, were sucking up everything close by, starting with Rose's heart, which was now a large lump in her throat and was pounding in her ears.

Todd moved closer still, narrowing the small gap between them. He kissed Rose softly on the lips, lingering only a moment. A tingle ran though Rose's body. Her face and ears burned from the rush of blood to her head, a heat, that she thought for sure Todd could feel, radiated from her cheeks. Rose could also see the blush in Todd's cheeks, as he looked down at the ground with boyish embarrassment. But for Rose, there was more than just a change in color; that small, tender kiss left an indelible mark on Rose's heart. It was her first.

"And I like the book too, Rose," he said, looking back up at her and smiling.

~ ~ ~

The night of the concert was soon upon them. Grace and Darrell were going to the concert as well, so there was much excitement at the dinner table that evening. (That is how Rose got the tickets; Darrell had picked them up for her.) Grandma B. was more excited that Billie Holiday was opening for the famous Mr. Armstrong. She had heard the up-and-coming singer on the radio and would have loved to have seen her in person. She knew, however, that going to clubs was a young person's game, and she contented herself with playing the grandmother, spoiling her grandchildren with a special treat of popcorn in front of the radio as they listened to their favorite—*Buck Rogers*.

Rose and Todd stood on the front porch waiting for Nathan, who was late. They had just said goodbye to Grace and Darrell. They didn't want to wait any longer for Todd's friend. Todd had told them he would meet them at the club.

"Where's Nathan?" asked Rose, after they had waited about five minutes more.

Todd turned and looked down the street. He wanted to make sure Grace and Darrell were well out of sight.

"Well, Nathan's not coming. To tell you the truth, I didn't even ask him," he paused, grasping her hand and looking into her eyes. "I want you to go with me, Rose."

Rose looked at him in surprise. She knew the club he was going to was a black club, so she didn't understand how she would be able to go. "Are you sure it will be okay? I mean, it's a Negro club, isn't it?"

"Yeah," he said confidently. "But there'll be so many people there, they'll hardly notice you."

"Okay. If you think it's all right," Rose said hesitantly. She was not sure he was right, but she wanted to believe him all the same. "I'll go tell Grandma B."

"Oh, you better not. She won't like it. Why don't you tell her you're going over to Monica's?"

"I suppose you're right," she agreed reluctantly. "Give me a minute. I'm going to change into something a little nicer," she said, looking at Todd in his white shirt and tie.

When Rose stepped back out onto the porch, Todd was waiting for her with a wide grin across his face. Rose's apprehension melted the minute he took her hand.

As they walked up the street toward the club, they saw the swell of colored people dressed as if they were going to church, but the neon light reflecting *Rosebud* in their eyes gave away their true destination.

Todd unconsciously gripped Rose's hand tightly as they stepped up into line. As they stood waiting to get inside, a few the men and women who stood around them stared at Rose. They all could hear the raspy, siren sounds of Billie Holiday wafting out of the door as it opened periodically to let people in. The people standing in front of them were craning their necks and pushing forward with a bit of intention, eager to get inside before they missed too much.

This was their chance; this was their chance to let go, to leave the anxiety and fear of their every day lives behind them; the lack of job security, the lack of educational opportunity, the tentativeness of their place in society. It all melted away. Here they didn't have to apologize for who they were. Here they could feel the potential of what they really could be. Music was a way out, if only for a time—a kind of nourishment, a way to feel alive, to feel the sensuousness and ease their bodies could move in. And music fueled their souls. Jazz, blues, and old ragtime flamed the fire within and burned up the constrictions of yesterday, allowing them to breathe freely, feeling only the here and now.

Finally, it was Todd and Rose's turn to go in. Todd handed the doorman the tickets and started to walk inside. When the doorman looked up and noticed Rose, he stepped in front of her, blocking the doorway and shoving her ticket back into her hand.

"You can't come in here," he said in a low, gruff voice.

Todd stepped back out the door as people started to press impatiently into them from behind.

"What'd ya mean she can't come in? She's got a ticket, ain't she!" Todd said, impatience in his voice.

"She's white, ain't she?" the man shot back.

"Listen, she's with me," Todd said in a more conciliatory tone.

"Well, then you're outta here too," the doorman said grabbing both their arms and turning them away.

"But she's practically black," Todd continued, trying to keep things on the light side. "She worked all summer in the kitchen of a riverboat with a bunch of Negroes, and she's living with my grandma in the Ville."

"Well, ain't that nice," he said sarcastically, though Rose could tell he was losing his patience, and so were the people waiting in line behind them. Todd and Rose felt pressure from the bodies as they started to push with more force toward the door, with calls of, "Get the whitie outta here!," and, "Yeah, get her outta here!" coming from somewhere in the crowd. Rose tugged on Todd's arm, her eyes pleading with him for them to leave.

"No, Rose!" he said to her forcefully, his face tightening with resolve.

Rose had never seen him this way before, and it added to her anxiety. She could feel the tension building all around her.

"We've got every right to be here," Todd continued, then he turned toward the doorman again, who waved to a large, black man from inside. The bouncer stepped outside the door and stood right next to Todd, towering over him both in height and width. Rose stepped back instinctively.

"All right, man, time ta go," he said as he took Todd by the arm and led him out of the line.

But Todd wouldn't have it; he wrenched himself free, elbowing the bouncer in the chest, making him take a step backward. This made the man's eyes widen and his chest swell as Todd turned to face him. Rose tried to step between them only to be pushed hard, backwards into the door by the bouncer, hitting her head on its metal frame. She staggered, dropped back against the front window and slid slowly to the ground, legs and shoes that surrounded her blurring and eventually going dark.

The commotion outside, and the loud thud of something hitting the glass, made Grace turn around and look. Grace and Darrell had stayed close to the entrance to wait for Todd and his friend. There were a couple people huddled over what looked like a person, a streak of something dark smearing the glass above the person's head. When she looked up and she saw her nephew, bloody and flailing, arms held behind his back by a large man, she ran to the door in surprise.

"Le'me out! Le'me out!" Grace yelled at the doorman, pushing people aside as they watched the free show just outside.

She ran up to Todd, who didn't even seem to notice she was there. He was staring with a combination of rage and bewilderment over her shoulder, trying to break free of his captor. He was also yelling something she couldn't quite make out, as he fought hard for his freedom.

"Let go of him!" Grace yelled, slugging the large man in the arm. The bouncer looked down at her as someone would look at a fly that was annoying them. "What's the matter wich you," she yelled and pounded on him again. "Why don't you let'im go?"

Todd finally realized that Grace was standing next to him, and he stopped fighting. By this time, Darrell had caught up with Grace.

"She's hurt! Make him let go! She's hurt!" Todd yelled, struggling again to get free.

"Who's hurt, Todd, who?" Darrell asked.

"Rose!" he yelled.

And at that, both Darrell and Grace turned around and looked in the direction of Todd's pleading gaze to see Rose's limp body leaning against the door, with what Grace now recognized was blood streaking the glass above her head. A couple of people stood around her; one person was squatting down looking at her face. He looked up and said in a sullen tone, "I think she's dead."

~ ~ ~

Everyone froze in place, as if those words had thrust a lost but required reverence upon them of a soul that had passed, in this case, without their knowledge. There were many thoughts

229

floating inconspicuously in the silence: thoughts of anxiety from the strangers standing around Rose, not wanting to be part of this now-gruesome scene on their one night out; thoughts of fear from the doorman and bouncer, both of whom knew having a dead white girl in front of their club would be very hard to explain to the police; thoughts of bewilderment from Grace and Darrell, wondering why Rose was here at all and how this had happened in the first place. And Todd, well, Todd only had one thought, and it was quite simple, he repeated it over and over in his head. *Oh my God, what have I done?*

Finally, realizing the bouncer had loosened his grip, Todd broke free, pushing past Grace and Darrell who were still cemented in their place, gazing down at the dead white girl they hardly knew. Todd pushed away the people standing over Rose, knelt down next to her, and pulled her into his arms. Rose's body laid limp. Blood still seeped steadily from her head, bright red onto the sleeve of his very white shirt, staining his skin and his soul with the bitter, wet reality of another loss, another love that was denied him. But this time he knew—this was his own doing.

"My God, what have I done?" he finally called out loud in anguish, while tears streamed down his face and onto Rose as he rocked her gently back and forth.

When he looked up, Grace and Darrell were kneeling over them. Grace was examining Rose; she had her fingers on her wrist and a hand on her chest. She looked up at Todd, eyes wide in surprise.

"Todd, she's not dead!" She tilted Rose's head back and pulled up one of her eyelids. "She's unconscious; she got knocked out, but she's not dead!" Grace reached her hand around the back of

Rose's head, then pulled it out again, her fingers wet and brightly stained. "She's bleedin' pretty good, though. We need to get her to the hospital," Grace said, looking over at her husband. "Darrell, you take Rose, and I'll get a taxi," she ordered, standing up next to them. Todd immediately stood with Rose still in his arms, but he wouldn't let her go when Darrell reached out to take her from him.

"Let go of her, Todd! She needs a doctor!" Grace ordered, tugging on his arm.

"I'll take her!" he said, walking toward the road.

Darrell pushed people out of the way. He waved down a service car as Grace tried to reason with him.

"Todd, you need to let us take her. They're not gonna let you in the hospital anyway, you're not her kin. Besides, the police might start askin' questions if you show up all beat-up and bloody, carrying an unconscious white girl." Todd stopped in place at the reality of Grace's words. Grace's tone softened as did the grip on his arm. "Now let Darrell have her, Todd. We'll take care a her, I promise. Go home and clean yourself up. I'll call ya once I have a talk with the doctor." She smiled softly at him. Todd reluctantly placed Rose gently in Darrell's arms.

Rose stirred and moaned. The lovely pine-smelling dream had changed, replaced by a searing, pounding weight in her head. There was motion and soft voices, which she couldn't quite make out through the oppressive hammer that was hitting the back of her head.

She moved! Todd brightened. *I heard her make a noise! Praise God! Oh please God, make her all right!* Todd reached out impotently toward the taxi.

"Saint Mary's, and hurry!" was all he heard as the door slammed shut, and the red tail lights rushed out of sight. He stood there, face streaked with tears, nose puffing from the bouncer's blow, his blood and Rose's mingled and indistinguishable, bright red all over his shirt. He was a beaten man. He turned and ran away from the crowd—away from the stares, away from the pain of what they denied him—his people. They were no different than the whites who pointed and whispered, who said with their eyes what he didn't want to believe. He ran into the darkness, hoping to be swallowed by the blackness, so he wouldn't have to think, wouldn't have to dream anymore of what could never be. He ran until he could run no more.

~ ~ ~

"Who's there?" came a suspicious voice from the front room, as the kitchen door squeaked shut. He couldn't let his grandmother see him like this. He took a deep breath to try and calm himself and responded in as normal a tone as he could so as not to let on that something had happened.

"Just Todd, Gram'ma. Um...I...I forgot my wallet," he said. Without hesitating he tore off his shirt, crumpled it up in a ball, and threw it in the garbage can. He went to his room for a clean one, then into the bathroom to wash up.

Leaning on the sink, he looked at the sorrowful reflection in the mirror, as the water drowned out the giggles and laughter coming from the other room. He didn't see the blood, the swollen nose, or the bloodshot eyes. All he could see was a fool. How could he have been so stupid? Why did he think these people would be any different? He hadn't let himself acknowledge the fact that he knew they wouldn't be. They had gotten plenty of stares and whispers from colored people when they were out together around town. He knew he was viewed as a troublemaker; stirring up trouble of the most obvious kind. The only context which they knew that a black man and a white girl could be associated together was through the accusation of rape. He knew their relationship was the most threatening to both sides, but he had just wanted this so badly he pretended it would be so, and he had almost killed Rose because of it. He hung his head in shame. He couldn't look at this man any longer. He was an idiot, and he knew it.

"You okay, child?" came a soft voice outside the bathroom door.

"Yeah, I'm fine Gram'ma," he called back out to her, burying his face in the water, washing the blood, and tears, and pity down the drain. He slipped on the clean shirt, then slowly turned the knob on the bathroom door. Luckily, Grandma B. had returned to the living room with the children. As he stepped back into the kitchen, he was startled by the ring of the phone.

"I'll get it!" he yelled out to her, his heart racing for fear Grandma B. would come into the kitchen and see his swollen face and equally afraid of what he might hear on the other end of the line.

"Todd, is that you?" asked the familiar voice on the line.

"Yeah, it's me," he softly, "W-w-what's…, how's…, is Rose okay?" he finally got out. There was a small silence. *Why isn't she talking? Why isn't she telling me what's going on? Oh my God, she did die!*

"Wait a minute. The doctor just came outta her room," Grace said finally. There were muffled voices in the background.

What was he saying? Is she okay? Say something, Grace! Say something!

"Todd, you still there?"

"What'd he say, Grace? What's happening?" he asked more anxious than ever.

"Dr. Miller said she hit her head pretty hard. She has to be monitored for a while…."

"But is she going to be okay? Is she all right?" Todd cut in.

"Calm down, Todd. I'm trying to tell ya. Dr. Miller said that because she was knocked out, she needs to be watched for a while to make sure she doesn't have a concussion."

"But is she okay, Grace? Is she gonna to be okay?" he asked again.

"She's fully awake now and seems to be doing fine, considering what she's been through," Grace finally said. Todd sat down hard on a kitchen chair, tears forming in his eyes again. "He had to put a few stitches in her head to stop the bleeding, but he said that it was just a superficial wound."

Grace paused a moment, expecting a response, but when she didn't get one she continued, "He wants to keep her here for a few days and make sure she's okay."

Todd sat up straight. "I'm coming down," he said resolutely.

"Don't bother. They won't let you see her. They want her to rest; she's lost some blood, and she's been put through a lot. They don't want anyone to see her right now," Grace said with conviction.

"But I've got to see her. I've got to tell her…." He stopped for a moment. "I've got to make her understand…." He hesitated, looking for the right words.

"She understands. She understands what a damn fool you were, trying to bring her to a place like that. What'd you think you were gonna do—waltz right through that door like you was Homer Phillips or somethin'?" Grace snapped at him.

"But..., but I...."

"But nothin'. You coulda' got yourself hurt, and Rose could'a been worse off than she already is now. What the *hell* where you thinkin', boy?"

There was another long silence.

"Well, I gotta go," Grace finally said. "I'm gonna sit with her a while, but I'll send Darrell home."

There was another period of silence.

"Are you there, Todd?"

"Yeah, I'm here," he said, his voice devoid of all emotion now.

"Tell Grandma I'll be home late."

There was more silence.

"I'll make sure she's okay before I leave," she said in a more consoling voice.

Todd hung up the phone without saying goodbye. Grandma B. didn't hear Todd's voice any longer, so she stood up and headed for the kitchen.

"Who was that?" Grandma B. asked, as she stepped in to an empty room. One of the kitchen chairs was pulled out from the table and the back door was still open. She walked over to the door and closed it. On her way back to the living room, she noticed something odd in the waste basket. She bent over and slowly pulled it out of the trash. Covering her mouth with her hand, she staggered over to the chair and sat down hard, gazing wide eyed at the blood-stained shirt, beads of sweat slowly forming on her forehead.

~ ~ ~

Grandma B. was woken out of a fitful sleep by the sound of a chair being scraped across the kitchen floor. She got out of bed, put on her robe, and went to see what she already knew she would find. She fingered the bottle of pills still in her robe pocket. Sitting at the table, head resting on folded arms, was Todd, motionless and mute. She made her way over to him and touched him on the shoulder. He sat up with a start, staring at her with his beaten, dreary face.

Suddenly, she was back in a small shack just off of Market Street, years ago, when she was a young woman, not married but a couple of months. It was then that she had been woken in the middle of the night with that sour, fermented smell hovering over her, groping for her in the black of night. It made her hesitate a moment, but when the swollen, baby brown face came back into focus, she remembered where she was. She slowly sat down, not saying a word. Todd dropped his head back down, holding it just inches from the table top. He would speak when he was ready. Grandma B. knew it took time to let out the poison, and she had nothing but time.

"I almost got Rose killed, Gram'ma," Todd finally said in a slurred, gravely voice. "I wanted to take her out to celebrate my birthday, and I almost got her killed. It's all my fault." He buried the heels of his hands into his eyes.

There was another silence.

"I know what happened, child," Grandma B. said softly. "Darrell done told me all about it."

Todd looked up at her. His unfocused, droopy eyes giving away for sure what Grandma B. already knew from his smell—he was drunk. One of his elbows slid unexpectedly off the table, and he just caught his face from hitting the table top. He sat there staring forlorn at Grandma B. But he couldn't look at her for long—he was too ashamed. He rested both arms back on the table and turned his gaze straight ahead.

"I just wanted to have good time…, for my birthday. I thought that with all those people 'round we'd just…, just get lost in the crowd."

He looked back at Grandma B. with pleading, red eyes.

"I love her Gram'ma! I didn't mean for her to get hurt!" he said, tears welling once more. "I just wanted someone of my own to love, someone I could care for that was my own."

Grandma B. looked at him lovingly, feeling his pain; knowing he had lost his father at the tender age of six with his mother leaving him soon thereafter; knowing what that did to a young boy who still needed that close, binding love. The kind of love that you know is yours without asking. The kind of love that ties you so close to the other that when it is taken away it leaves a hole which is never filled; that can come up months and years later and swallow you unexpectedly, like the loss was just yesterday. She ached for the crumpled child sitting beside her—the child who was trying to be a man. She had tried to fill in as best she could, but she knew a mother's love is like no other; hers came in a poor second.

She stood up next to the boy. He turned and buried his face in her waist, dampening her robe, and shaking her gently as she easily pulled out his anguish and let it fall, wet and beaten, to the floor. Her wrinkled face and mesh-covered heart were testaments to her skill of taking away pain without pulling it inside. When the shaking had stopped, Grandma B. pulled a chair up next to him so she could touch him as she spoke.

"Da world ain't ready for ya ta love Rose, child. Der's things dat no matta how much we wants'em, dey ain't gonna happen, least not in our lifetime. Grace and Darrell can go ta as many meetin's as dey like, but until most of da folks in dis here world do what da good Lord done told'em, it just ain't gonna happen."

She reached up and put Todd's wet and weary face in both her hands.

"Da Lord don't give ya nothin' ya can't handle. Ya gonna be all right, and Rosie's gonna be all right too. Now let's go ta bed."

She helped Todd to his feet.

"Da sun'ill be up soon, and ya don't want ta be awake ta see dat dis mornin'. I guarantee it!" she said with a slight smile, a smile which hinted that maybe she had been there before herself, once or twice.

Todd mechanically stood and shuffled toward his bedroom, Grandma B. leading him from behind until he was gently tucked into bed, clothes and all. He was out as soon as his head hit the pillow.

~ ~ ~

Rose stayed in the hospital a couple of days, and when she came home, Grandma B. insisted she stay out of school the rest of the week to recover. Rose wished she was at school, though; she wanted to stop thinking about what had happened and how it had changed her relationship with Todd. When he came home from school or work, the only thing she could get out of him was, "Hello." If she tried to strike up a conversation, he would answer her question as concisely as he could, then immediately leave the room. After four days of this, Rose finally broke down. Grandma B. heard her crying through the closed bedroom door. She knocked quietly.

"Can I come in?"

Rose quickly wiped her eyes with her handkerchief and blew her nose.

"Sure, Grandma B.," she said as normally as she could.

Grandma B. made her way over to the side of the bed and sat down slowly.

"What's a matter, child?" she asked softly, as she reached out and rested her hand on Rose's knee. Then it came; it was as if Grandma B. had unplugged the dike in Rose's heart just with the touch of her hand; all the frustration, fear, anxiety, and sadness came spilling out. Rose leaned forward and cried on Grandma B.'s shoulder, as she had that moon-lit night so long ago, her body shaking and soaking Grandma B.'s house dress almost clean through. When the crying slowed and Rose came up for air, Grandma B. handed her her handkerchief and waited for Rose to speak.

"Todd hates me, Grandma B. He's upset with me for what happened the other night. I got in the way and ruined our evening, and now he won't talk to me," she said as the tears welled up in her eyes.

"Honey child, ya got it all wrong. He don't hate you. He ain't talkin' ta ya 'cause he's afraid."

"Afraid? Afraid of what?"

"Afraid he'll get close ta ya ag'in. He feels it was his fault, ya gettin' hurt, and he's afraid if he talks ta ya, he'll admit he still likes ya. And he doesn't want ta hurt ya anymore. Clamin' up's his way a doin' dat."

"Well, why doesn't he just tell me, instead of trying to avoid me all the time, making me feel like I did somethin' wrong!"

"Child, dat's a man for ya. They have da best a intentions sometimes, but dey think if dey talk about somethin' it'll make it worse. Dey think if dey just don't say anything, it'll go away. It don't get no better when dey're older, neither."

"Well, I'm not going away!"

"No ya ain't!" Grandma B. agreed, tapping her on the knee. "So you just tell 'im straight out. Best way ta start is ta tell 'em how ya feel, how what he's doin' by not talkin' is makin' ya feel. Dat oughta be good enough ta crack da ice."

"Thanks, Grandma B.! I'll do it tonight, right after dinner," she said, reaching forward and giving Grandma B. one of her signature bear-hugs.

"Lord, child, I'm gonna need dem lungs yet!"

"Oh, sorry," Rose apologized, letting her go.

That evening, while they were all cleaning off the table, Rose told Todd she needed to talk with him after they were done. Grandma B. excused them both from helping in the kitchen, and they stepped out the back door, Grandma B. shooing the kids away from the screen.

Rose stepped off the porch and turned to face Todd.

"I need to talk to you," Rose said as firmly as she could to keep her courage up.

"Okay," was all he said, and he sat down on the steps looking out but avoiding Rose's eyes.

"Ever since I came home you've hardly said two words to me." Rose looked down at the ground. "I'm sorry I got us into trouble that night. If I hadn't gotten in the way, then…."

"Rose, you can stop right there," Todd interrupted. "It wasn't your fault. Don't you ever think that." He looked her straight in the eye. "It was my fault. I shouldn't have taken you there in the first place."

"Well, we probably both knew it wasn't such a good idea, but why the silent treatment? I feel like I've done something wrong."

"It's not you Rose," he said.

He looked down at the ground, as if there, somewhere, were words written in the earth by another thwarted lover. Words which would help him explain the way it was; the way it had to be. But she wasn't a Negro. She didn't know the way things were—to see all these things around you that you couldn't have. She didn't know what it was like to always be watching, always looking out for that next disappointment, that next door that would be closed in your face. Constantly trying to be one step ahead, so you could push ahead, always ahead, never looking back. It took a lot out of you, but the alternative wasn't living—it was just existing. Todd had seen many Negroes who lived that kind of life: living day to day; paying rent higher than any white person would in some tenement or shack no white person would step foot in; working at some service job cleaning floors or hauling goods; not being able to give your kids better than what you had. He had seen it, all right, and he wanted better. He was trying to look ahead. He didn't want to look back on the hurt; back on a love he could never have and should never have contemplated in the first place.

But Rose…, Rose was too sweet to hurt, too naïve, and too white to understand all that. But how to tell her? How could he let her down easy without hurting her more than he already had? All this coursed through his mind in the seconds he futilely searched the ground for the right words to say.

"I do like you Rose." *More than you will ever know*. His eyes now fixed upon her. "But it just isn't going to work. I'm sorry."

They stared at each other in silence, both knowing what Todd had said was the truth. Todd stood and slowly went inside.

~ ~ ~

The kids at school wondered why Rose had been gone a whole week; the scar on her head convinced them of her fictitious fall off a swing at the park and her need to convalesce.

After Todd and Rose's conversation that night, things lightened up a bit around the Baas home. Even though Todd wouldn't invite Rose to study with him or sit with him on the porch and talk for hours on end like they use to, he at least stopped avoiding her. Rose took consolation in being able to sit in the same room with him and read, or laugh along side him listening to Edgar Bergan and Charlie McCarthy on the radio.

At school Rose purposefully tried to get Ryan Beeper to talk to her more than the usual, "Hi, Rose," he gave her in the lunch room or when passing in the hall. She thought it might help distract her; get her mind off of Todd. But as much as she tried, Ryan's conversations about what he did at basketball practice or how hard the mid-term exams had been, couldn't keep Rose's interest.

Didn't these boys do anything outside of sports and school? Didn't they care that the Hindenburg just burned up in New York City, killing twenty –three people? Or that Americans were dying at this very moment in Spain? she wondered in frustration.

If Rose was truly honest with herself though, she would have realized she hadn't been interested in the world outside her own life until just recently, until she had met Todd. Through him she had come to see how the things that happened around the world, or at least in the United States, affected her and the people around her. It was a change she wasn't even aware of.

Since the boys didn't keep much of her attention, she buried herself in her school work and her weekend job at Dr. Greenwall's medical clinic. Rose even volunteered to help with patients on Saturdays, when Monica's dad would see those small emergency cuts, unrelenting pains, and sudden illnesses which just couldn't wait until Monday. She found she enjoyed working with patients much more than her usual paperwork tasks. It always gave her a good feeling when she could hold someone's hand to help them stay calm, or help Dr. Greenwall with a particularly difficult patient. She also discovered an aptitude for being a medical assistant; she wasn't squeamish when she would assist him while he sutured cuts, and she had a level head when there was a true medical emergency to deal with. But most importantly to Rose was, while she was helping others, her spirits were given an added lift, something which had been missing of late.

Monica's dad recognized Rose's skills, so he made her his official Saturday morning assistant and gave her a raise on top of that. She would work at the clinic every Saturday morning, then it was back to the Greenwall home for dinner, and usually a study session with Monica in the afternoon. Or if Monica could con Rose into it, a game of tennis or a bike ride in the park.

Rose noticed that spring came earlier in St. Louis than it did in southwest Wisconsin, and she basked in the warm afternoon sun whenever she could. It felt good to heat herself up like a snake in the early morning sun—baking her cares and woes until they shrived up into nothing; at least for an hour or so.

The end of the school year was upon Rose before she knew it. Ryan had asked her to the spring dance, which was scheduled for two weeks before exams. Rose hadn't said no, but she hadn't said yes, either. She wasn't in the mood to go with a boy to the dance, but she knew most of her friends were going – the boys feeling a bit braver, knowing they wouldn't see most of these girls all summer. Grandma B. clinched her decision when she surprised her with the cutest sailor pants-suit, which she had made for Rose to wear to the dance. It was all white linen with a navy blue tie around the V-neck, matching the navy blue braid which went around the edge of the large, square-backed collar and short sleeves. It had a high waist and wide legs, and was topped off with a smart belt around the middle. Rose didn't have the heart to disappoint Grandma B., so she agreed to go with Ryan.

"Now ya have fun, ya hear!" Grandma B. called out from the front porch, as Rose left for the party. "She do look smart in dat suit, if I do say so ma'self," Grandma B. said to herself as she watched Rose walk down the street and out of sight.

As Grandma B. watched her walk away, she reflected on how much Rose had grown in the nine months that she had been living with them. She was one of the family now; it wasn't strange anymore to put the seventh plate on the table. And Grandma B.'s pride for Rose was no different than for any of her other children or grandchildren when Rose did well in school or sang in the church choir. The ladies in the McKinney Mutual Aid Society at church stopped asking how long Rose was going to stay and started asking if she was going to help with the community Sunday school program over the summer.

Rose was also noticing the changes. As she walked down the now familiar streets, she didn't get the odd stares anymore. In fact, she knew, or at least recognized and said, "Hi," to, most of the people she met along the way. Her white skin had darkened a shade or two in their eyes, and Rose felt a little darker herself. Now, she only noticed her paleness when she went into a black establishment somewhere other than the Ville. Then she'd get that strange, "Can I help you?" *I think you stepped inside the wrong store,* response. But Rose took it in stride. She was used to it now.

The warmer winds were blowing thoughts of Lilly Mae and the river through Rose. Even Grandma B. talked about getting back on the boat, despite Grace's pleas to the contrary. She didn't talk about it with her usual conviction though, so Rose wasn't convinced she was going to go through with it. Rose thought it was probably best if she didn't for her own sake. If Grandma B. decided not to go back, Rose wasn't sure what she was going to do. She hadn't seen her family in almost a year, so she thought about going home to see them. She had kept up the letters, so they knew she was safe, but she had no idea how any of them were.

On the other hand, Lilly Mae had invited her to New Orleans. Perhaps with the money she had made in the clinic, she could take a trip down to see Lilly Mae for a month or so, then head back home for school in the fall. But how was she going to find Lilly Mae? Rose had no idea. These two very separate directions tugged at her, each trying to make her decide in their favor; the comfort and warmth of her family, or the adventure and unknown of an exotic city; the smiles and affection of her parents and siblings, or the faces and lives of the many different people she was sure to meet in the Crescent City. And then there was Todd....

Rose stepped lightly off the street car and headed for school, leaving her quandary behind and attending to her present mild anxiety; looking for any familiar girl friend she could hook up with before she had to sit with Ryan Beeper.

ಸ 11 ಅ

It's kind of funny, how days that change our lives in significant ways seem like every other day when we first get up in the morning. We get out of the same bed we've gotten out of a thousand times before, not knowing, not thinking things might be significantly different when we go back to that same bed just fifteen or so hours later. We put on our same clothes, eat our same breakfast, and head out for our day like any other day, oblivious to the potential for change—for the better, or for the worse.

~ ~ ~

Grandma B. knew. Grandma B. had a feeling in her bones that something was going to be different this day; she just didn't know what. When she sent Rose on her way to meet the white boy at the school dance, she felt like she had put something in motion; she felt like something was going to happen that she couldn't stop. Along side of her pride for Rose, there was a nervousness as she watched her walk down the street.

When Rose turned the corner, Grandma B. was about to step inside when Della ran down the sidewalk all in a state.

"Gram'ma, Gram'ma…, is Mama or Daddy home? Marcus done hurt hisself…on the monkey bars…, he's bleeding!" she said with difficulty, all out of breath.

"No, child, dey ain't here," she said in haste, urging the child back down the porch steps. "I'll come…, I'll come."

Grandma B. moved faster than she had in many months. If one of her babies was hurt, then she needed to get to him quickly. When they got up to the school playground, Marcus was sitting against the monkey bars holding his arm, blood weeping through his fingers; dark, wet streaks down his cheeks. His crying started anew when he caught sight of Grandma B. and his sister. Grandma B. knelt down next to him, wiping the beads of sweat from her brow, trying to catch her breath. She examined his wound and decided he was going to live, even though Marcus thought differently.

"We'll take ya home and clean ya up so you's good as new," Grandma B. assured him, holding him tight as they slowly walked back home. "I didn't have six kids for nothing'. Your Gram'ma's da best at mending elbows—da very best! Did I ever tells ya 'bout da time your Uncle Matthew fell off dese here same monkey bars… .'" Grandma B. continued, applying her sweet verbal balm, as only Grandma B. could, soothing Marcus's cut even before she had put on a single band-aide.

Grandma B. sat in the kitchen after she had cleaned and bandaged Marcus' elbow and put the children in front of the radio. That familiar tightness in her chest hadn't subsided as she sat in the kitchen like she hoped it would, and her breathing was different.

Why can't I catch my breath? I's been sittin' here five minutes now. It should be better. She decided she should go get one of the last of the pills she had gotten on the riverboat those many months ago. They had surely come in handy since she had been home. When she stood up to head to her bedroom, her heart made a strange jump in her chest. The feeling startled her so much that she staggered backward and tried to sit back down, but she missed the chair and landed hard on the floor, then tipped onto her back.

Grandma B.'s eyes widened with surprise. Suddenly, she had an extremely uncomfortable feeling, a feeling like she was drowning. Grandma's drowning dream hit her full force. There wasn't a drop of water in sight, but she knew she was drowning all the same. She tried to call for the children, but they couldn't hear her from underwater; all that came out was a whisper and a gurgle, which couldn't be heard over the sounds of Buck Rogers and company. Grandma B. floundered in her private pool of water, knowing if she didn't sit herself upright she was going to drown. Just as she was making her last attempt to swim up for air, a pair of angel hands came up from behind and easily lifted her to the top of the water.

"Gram'ma…, Gram'ma, what's the matter?" Todd questioned her anxiously. "Whattcha doin' on the floor?" But Grandma B. had to gasp for air; there was no time for talk, no time for explanations just yet. Air was the important thing, and it was coming in now; it was being pulled in. Todd had saved her from drowning.

~ ~ ~

Everyone stood around her bed staring at her with questioning looks—Grace and Darrell on her right, Della, Marcus, and Todd on her left. But there was one missing. Grandma B. wanted her Rose, so Todd was sent out to get her. Grandma B. hated to take her from her party—a party she was going to with a white boy. It was important for her to forget, to move on to someone new. She had to go, Grandma B. made sure of that. But Grandma B. needed her now.

Todd stood outside the front doors of the school, not sure how to find the gym, and apprehensive about who might try and stop him in this all-white school. It was after hours. He obviously didn't belong there, but it didn't matter. Grandma B. had asked for Rose, and he was going to find her.

He made his way around the empty halls, heading for the music which echoed faintly in front of him. As he stepped through the gym doors, a teacher noticed his presence and went over to investigate.

"May I help you, young man?" came the very familiar—*you're in the wrong place, boy*—tone.

"I'm looking for Rose, Rose Krantz. Can you help me find her, please? It's a family emergency."

"Oh, well...," *I see, you're the help, sent to find your employer's child. That makes sense.* "Please wait here. I'll see if I can find her."

Todd scanned the room as the woman headed into the crowded gym, heads turning toward Todd as she made her way among the children, asking for Rose. Then he spotted her. She was turning around to look at who everyone was whispering and pointing at. Rose's throat tightened, and a knot instantly formed in her stomach. *Todd! Why is he here? What's going on?*

She met him halfway across the gym floor, her friends trailing behind, asking her all kinds of questions she didn't really hear.

"What's the matter, Todd? Why are you here?" Rose asked in a subdued voice, trying to keep their conversation as private as she could in a gym full of staring students.

"It's Grandma B.; she's very sick. She's asking for you. We need to go," he said, grasping her hand and leading her toward the door.

"Wait a minute," Rose said, pulling her hand away. "Tell me what's going on."

"Yes, I'd like to know what's going on as well!" came another voice behind them. Rose turned around to stand face to face with Alyssa Morgan, her eyes narrow, hands on her hips. "Who is this *boy*, and what does he want with *you*, Rose?"

Rose hesitated. The ruse was over. Staring at Alyssa, Rose knew the next time she opened her mouth to speak she would no longer be Rose—the quiet, nice, smart girl from down the street, but Rose—the white girl who lives with Negroes. She knew she would no longer be welcome at the lunch table or be asked to join their study groups. She wasn't even sure she would still be allowed to go to school here any longer. She had lied to them. She had lied to them all. Then she saw Monica stepping up timidly behind Alyssa.

"This is Todd," Rose said slowly.

"And *who* is Todd?" Alyssa continued, pressing her for the answer she knew Rose did not want to give.

Rose looked past Alyssa. She didn't need to tell Alyssa anything, but Monica—Monica deserved an answer.

"I live with Todd and his family in the Ville," she said without hesitation.

There was a general gasp from the children and adults standing around them, and the air suddenly changed; Rose felt as if there was more space around her, and the room had somehow gotten colder.

"I knew it! I knew you were a phony!" Alyssa crowed in righteous indignation. "Didn't I tell you she was a phony!" her voice loud enough for anyone and everyone to hear.

Rose was still looking at Monica. The shocked look on her face hurt more than anything Alyssa could say.

"I'm sorry, Monica. I wanted to tell you so many times, but I-I couldn't."

"You lied to me," Monica said, hurt flowing out of every syllable. "I thought you were my friend." The hurt turned instantly to anger. Her eyes narrowed, "Friends don't lie to each other."

Rose hung her head in shame, the truth covering her like a heavy blanket, making it difficult for her to respond or even move.

"We need to go," Todd said finally, breaking the deafening silence.

At that, Monica turned and walked away. Rose turned and followed Todd out. She could still hear Alyssa ranting in the background.

There was silence in the taxi as it started for the Ville. Rose didn't know what to say and neither did Todd. She could tell there was something wrong. Todd acted unusually distant, almost cold. Rose knew she deserved no less, but she wasn't quite up to explaining herself to him just now. She wasn't sure what to say. She wasn't sure of anything. Then a light popped on in Rose's head— Grandma B. was very ill! She needed to know what was going on. Todd quietly filled her in on what had happened, explaining that Doctor Anderson was busy delivering a baby, so they were all just waiting for him to stop by the house when he was done.

"Wait a minute. Stop the car," Rose told the driver. "Stop the car!" she said more insistently. "Please go to Hortense Place, right away!"

"What are you doing, Rose?" Todd asked.

"Doctor Greenwall! He'd be willing to help, I'm sure of it!" she said with excitement.

"But he's a white-folk's doctor, Rose. He won't come to the Ville!"

"Yes, he will. I'm sure he will. Just leave it up to me," Rose said confidently. "Here..., here it is. Stop here, please!"

Rose got out of the car and shut the door behind her. "I have to do this myself Todd, sorry. It'll work better this way. I'll meet you at home," she called out as she turned and ran up to the front doors.

Luella answered the door and showed Rose to the library where Mr. Greenwall was sitting alone, reading.

"Rose, what in the devil are you doing here? Is something wrong? Is Monica with you?" he asked, sure of some problem by the color in her cheeks and the rapidness of her breath.

"I'm sorry to bother you Mr. Greenwall. Monica's fine. She's still at the party," she said with a pang of guilt. "It's my grandmother. She's very ill, and her doctor is delivering a baby and can't come, so I thought maybe..., maybe you could come and take a look at her."

"Well, of course my dear. Let me get my bag, and we'll head right out," he assured her, as he walked over to the chair where his large, black bag always sat ready to go. "Luella!" he yelled down the hall, "Tell the Misses I was called out on an emergency. I'll be back soon."

They got into the large, black car. Rose slipping easily into the front seat on the soft leather upholstery.

"Where does your grandmother live?" Mr. Greenwall asked.

"Um…, I'll show you. I don't know the names of the streets very well," Rose lied, not wanting to give away their destination just yet. "Just head for Taylor. I'll direct you from there."

As they were heading north on Taylor Street, Doctor Greenwall hesitated at Rose's request to turn west onto Easton, the colored shopping district. But the request to turn north onto Whittier, in the middle of the Ville, made him pull the car over and stop.

"Now, are you going to tell me what's going on here, young lady?"

Rose paused, not sure where to begin. "I'm sorry Mr. Greenwall. I planned on telling you before we went in, but I wanted to get you there first. Grandma B. is very ill."

"Well, I'm not going anywhere until you explain to me what is going on."

"Well, I don't really live on Treadway. I live here in the Ville with a Negro family." Doctor Greenwall sat upright in his seat. "I ran away from home last July and took a job on a riverboat called the Capitol. I worked in the kitchen with Grandma B., I mean Mrs. Baas. She prefers to be called Grandma B. Anyway, I owe her a lot; she taught me how to cook, she watched out for me, and she helped one night…, when a young man came into my cabin…." Rose hesitated, looking down in her lap. "He was a bad man Mr. Greenwall. He held me down and he…."

Rose couldn't get herself to say it out loud; to say what actually happened that night. She had never said anything to anyone about it after it had happened, and it was as if saying it out loud would give it more credence—make it more real than she wanted it to be. And she was ashamed, even though Grandma B. said she shouldn't be. She couldn't help how she felt.

"He touched me…, he almost…well, Grandma B. stopped him from doing something even worse."

Rose was silent for a moment. She blinked quickly to keep the tears from falling.

"Anyway, she had a spell, actually a couple spells on the boat after that. The doctor said it was her heart, and the second time it happened she wouldn't let us go for help. She was afraid of losing her job. So I didn't say anything," Rose admitted, looking down at her hands again. "And now she's probably had another one, but this time she can't get out of bed! I'm really afraid for her, Mr. Greenwall. I don't want her to die!"

"Well, that's quite a story, Rose," he said quietly. "But I'm not really the right person to see this Mrs. Baas, I'm afraid."

"You're a doctor, aren't you?" Rose pleaded.

"Well, of course, but it's best if her own physician sees her. He knows her history; all the different things she's had over the years. And she's…, well…, she'd feel better with her own…," he hesitated, groping for the right words to use, "…her own kind of doctor. It's just best, Rose. I'm sorry."

"Mr. Greenwall, you have to help. If we wait for Doctor Anderson it might be too late!"

"I'm sorry, Rose," he said, putting the car in gear, looking to his left to make sure it was clear for him to turn around.

Rose grasped his arm, and he stopped the car.

"Mr. Greenwall, can I ask you a question?" Rose said, not stopping for a reply. "When you went to medical school, did they have different anatomy books for white folks and black?

"Of course not."

"When you look deep into a cut or listen to someone's heart, can you tell if that person is white or black?" Rose asked, again, not waiting for an answer. "You're a compassionate man, Mr. Greenwall, and a good doctor. I see it every Saturday when you help those little kids and those older folks feel better, even when sometimes there isn't really much wrong with them at all."

Doctor Greenwall remained silent, looking straight out of the windshield ahead of him.

"I've lived with these people more than nine months now, and they're no different than you or me. They have the same dreams and the same wants and the same bodies that fail them. I know I can't make you help Grandma B., Mr. Greenwall, but I beg of you, as a doctor, she needs your help. I know you can find it in your heart to help her!"

Doctor Greenwall kept his eyes straight ahead, not saying a word. Rose stared at him, praying a silent prayer of hope.

~ ~ ~

Doctor Greenwall reached up for the stick shift and put the car back in gear. They started to move forward, and to Rose's amazement, he didn't move the steering wheel to turn the car around; he kept going straight ahead. Rose's heart leapt, and a tear of joy escaped down the side of her face, but she didn't say a word about his change of heart, she just directed him the rest of the way to Grandma B.'s home.

The living room was packed as the good doctor stepped in through the front door, behind Rose. All heads turned and the room hushed at the sight of his very white face. Rose recognized Aunt Tilley on the davenport, handkerchief in hand, eyes puffy, talking to her sisters.

"She's just through here," Rose instructed, leading the doctor to Grandma B.'s room.

When she opened the door, Grace and Todd turned to see who was entering. A questioning look swept across their faces when they caught sight of the man who followed Rose into the room. Grace stood up out of her chair, which sat next to Grandma B.'s bed, and went to meet them at the door.

"This is Doctor Greenwall, Grace," Rose explained. "He's come to look at Grandma B."

"Nice to meet you, doctor," Grace said slowly. She held out her hand to shake his, still surprised at their unexpected guest.

"Well, how's the patient?" the doctor said, walking up to Grandma B.'s bedside.

"Well, her respiration rate is a little fast and shallow. I don't have a stethoscope, but from what I can hear, I think she's got some ralls goin' on, which would make sense since she has trouble breathing if she tries to lie down. Her pulse is ninety-five and irregular, but her temperature's normal," Grace continued as if she were spouting off vital signs of a mock patient to her nursing instructor.

The doctor stood staring at Grace, surprised at getting an answer to what he thought was a rhetorical question. Grace noticed his surprise and let him in on the fact that she was in her second year of nursing school at St. Mary's.

"Perhaps we should have some privacy then," he said, turning toward Grandma B., expecting his new assistant to continue her role and clear the room for him to examine his new patient.

Grandma B. was sitting propped in bed, eyes just slits, but her ears open all the way.

"Mrs. Baas," the doctor spoke loudly and slowly, bending down to Grandma B.'s level. "My name is Doctor Greenwall. I'm the doctor Rose has been working for."

Grandma B. opened her eyes slowly. They were clear and bright, not clouded as they might have been if she really had been sleeping.

"Ya'll don't have ta yell," she retorted. "It's my heart dat's da problem. My ears is just fine."

Doctor Greenwall turned and smiled at Rose as she stood in the doorway, knowing now what he was in for.

Grace closed the door, and Todd and Rose headed out into the living room. Everyone looked up as they entered the room, questioning looks over all their faces. Rose hesitated a moment, looked at Todd, and kept on walking right out onto the front porch. She couldn't handle all the questions, and she could tell by the look on Todd's face, he would take care of it. A few minutes later she heard the screen creak open slowly. She knew he was standing behind her, as she sat on the top stoop looking out on to the street.

"I'm sorry, Todd," she started, turning around to face him. "I should have told them who I really was and where I really lived, but Grandma B. said I lived in this rich neighborhood over by the school, like all the other kids, so I didn't think I could tell them the truth. I thought they would kick me out of school if they found out," Rose rambled on. "And Mr. Greenwall, well, I didn't think he'd let me work in the clinic if he knew, or let me be friends with Monica...." She dropped her head in shame. "I should have told Monica."

"Yeah, you should have told Monica," Todd agreed, not in an accusatory tone but in a tone that let Rose know he really did understand. He didn't agree with what she had done, but he understood, in part, why she did it.

"I'm not sure if she is ever going to speak to me again. I wouldn't blame her if she didn't."

They both sat in silence. Then Rose brought up the other pressing issue which was on both their minds this evening.

"Do you think Grandma B.'s gonna be okay?"

"I da'know," Todd replied. "Rose…, I…," but before he could finish his sentence, before he could thank her for bringing the doctor to look at Grandma B., they were both drawn to the commotion going on in the front room. They turned and saw Grace leading Doctor Greenwall to the front door.

"Thank you, doctor," Grace said. "We really appreciate ya coming out here."

"It's not a problem," he said. He looked outside the screen door and saw Rose on the other side. "It's what I do." He smiled a knowing smile at Rose. "And when Homer Phillips Hospital opens, they're going to be lucky to have a good nurse like you on their staff," he said, turning back to Grace. "Your mother is in good hands."

Grace smiled and softened at the kind words.

"Thank you, doctor," she said, a bit embarrassed by the compliments.

Doctor Greenwall stepped out onto the porch.

"I'll see you next Saturday, Rose?"

"Oh…, sure," Rose said, surprised at the proposition. "Eight o'clock as usual!"

"Eight o'clock it is."

Then he stepped off the porch, put his black bag in the front seat of his car and drove away.

~ ~ ~

The questions were flying when Rose and Todd stepped back into the living room. Everyone wanted to know what the doctor had said.

"Well, he said that she's accumulated fluid in her lungs. That's why she can't lay down. And her heart..., her heart is failing. It's not pumping like it should, so that's why she's accumulating the fluid and her legs are edematous," Grace explained.

Then Aunt Tilley spoke up, asking the question that was on everyone's mind. "So what's that mean in English, Grace? Is she gonna get better? Is there anything they can do for her?"

Grace didn't answer. She didn't need to. The tears welling in her eyes; and the heavy burden which was weighing down her shoulders and keeping her tongue mute told everyone what she didn't want to say. Tilley stood and went over to her, wrapped her arms around her and held her tight as they wept softly and silently together.

Their release of emotion, their acknowledgement of her unanswered question, allowed the others in the room to release the anxiety they had all been keeping close to the surface. They were finally able to acknowledge what they all had feared most: the matriarch of their family was going to leave them. The women who was a part of each of their lives was going to die. She had touched all of them, particularly through her tough love, which softened instantly at any cry for help or from a grandchild's smile. It was a love that followed them and supported them in whatever they did and wherever they went. The rock of their family foundation was cracking before their eyes and would soon be nothing but dust. The pain in the room was palpable. The men did not escape it any more than the women. Todd leaned against the wall, looking for something solid to help support the words which no one wanted or needed to say. For Todd, Grandma B. had been more of a mother to him than his own mother had ever been. Without a father, he didn't know where to turn.

Of course, Rose was not immune to their sorrow. These were people she had come to know as family. In addition, her own burden of guilt was rearing its ugly head, to remind her of the *should haves* and *could haves* of days gone by. She had come to love Grandma B. as much as her own grandmothers, and she wasn't ready to let her go. She turned toward Todd who was staring off into nowhere. Rose reached for him and held him close, dropping her head on his shoulder, tears flowing freely.

Rose had been there only a moment when she felt Todd stiffen beneath her. She lifted her head, her eyes searching for an explanation. Todd looked her straight in the eye and held her by her shoulders away from him. The sadness which still enveloped him was masked lightly by a look Rose could not mistake. He spoke to her as gently as he could with those deep, brown eyes. He told her he could not help her. He was sorry, but he could not be the one to help her through this. It was just too hard. He couldn't let himself get close again. He wanted to, but he couldn't.

He said all this without saying a word—the firmness of his grip, the look in his eyes, the pity that swept momentarily across his face—Rose could read it all without a word being said. Rose grew up a little more in that moment. She moved one more step closer to womanhood; one step closer to the realization of a truth which had to be acknowledged, had to be dealt with for someone else's sake, and ultimately, for your own. The realization of having to pick up a burden and carry it, even if you don't know all the reasons why; but knowing it's what must be done all the same. Where contemplation and questioning must be left for later; now there must be a response and, preferably, a mature one.

Rose stepped away, acknowledging what he had conveyed to her by the look in her eyes and the eventual drop of her head. Todd sighed in relief at the gesture, then took back his sadness. He dropped his eyes to the ground and walked out the front door.

Rose stood at the screen door looking out at the tall, strong, familiar silhouette standing on the curb. He looked back briefly, turned away again, and quickly crossed the street. Now she knew Todd was gone from her forever, and soon Grandma B. would leave her as well. There was an emptiness in her heart, a hunger, which started to grow that night, and she would know for some time to come.

~ ~ ~

The funeral was that next Thursday. Grandma B. never got out of her bed again but slowly, day by day, she moved closer to her promised land. They found her one morning, lieing down flat in bed with a soft, peaceful look on her face. Rose thought she even saw a small smile.

Rose stood with the grandchildren in the back of the church, watching the succession of friends and congregation members—a sea of black dresses and hats, of suits and ties—filing past the line of Grandma's very large family. They would shake each family member's hand, acknowledging their sorrows, and helping them ease the pain of their loss with the familiarity of tradition and the community of sympathetic souls.

Rose's eyes had dried up by this time. She had cried so many times in this last week she could hardly keep herself in handkerchiefs. The emptiness was now a familiar mantle she wore, both outside and in. The scene which took place in front of her was almost hard to register as real. It was just a play, a production played out in front of her, but not really making its way inside. Rose didn't feel like there was an inside, just the mechanical doing of the everyday. She made it her mission at the funeral to take care of Marcus, Della, and the other grandchildren. It was one of the few things she could accomplish—trying to keep them out of trouble and occupied while the long line made its way past the family and the closed casket which held the body of Grandma B.

When the service started and everyone had sat down in their place, a quiet came over the room so profound, Rose was effortlessly transported back to Grandma B.'s bedroom the day before she died.

Rose hadn't gone to school the few days before Grandma B.'s passing. She wanted to stay by her side as long as she could, besides not even being sure if the school board was going to let her back in to school after what had happened at the dance. That seemed so long ago and so unimportant.

"Rose, go over ta da dresser, and open dat der top drawer," Grandma B. asked, turning her head towards the dresser, but not lifting her head off the pillow. Rose did as she was told. "In der's my starch box. Pulls it out for me."

Rose took it out tenderly, as if it were made of glass.

"Bring it on over here," Grandma B. motioned to her. "Pull up a chair now. I want ya ta open it up."

Rose gingerly pried off the metal lid. Inside were all different types of objects: a glittering rock, which looked almost like gold; a beautiful purple button, covered with small, iridescent purple jewels; a slightly crimpled feather of brown and gold stripes, topped with a dark brown plume; a rock which was as black as night; a round piece of green glass, smooth around every edge; and glued to the inside lid were magazine clippings of a snow-capped mountain, a Japanese temple, the Eiffel Tower, and more. Rose had no idea Grandma B. would have kept such an array of things.

"What's all this, Grandma?" Rose asked.

"Just some things I picked up along da river. And dat der," she said, pointing to the inside cover. "Dose be places I wanted ta see but never did get to."

Rose and Grandma B. sat for almost an hour talking about each item in the box, where Grandma B. had found it, and why she liked it so much. When they were done, Grandma B. closed the box and pushed it toward Rose.

"I want ya ta have dis. It won't mean much ta nobody else. No one else 'round here likes a good adventure like you and I does, Rose. Dat's why I took a job on a riverboat all dose many years ago. Seems like it was just yesterday."

Grandma B. closed her eyes momentarily, going someplace Rose couldn't tell where. She opened her eyes again, slowly.

"I wanted ta see things and do things dat my parents could never do sharecropin' cotton on dat God foesakin' Dixie delta. And day wanted me ta do betta, too, soes day lemme go. But my adventures were hemmed in by river bluffs, and lack a education. Den raising six children by myself didn't help none."

Grandma B. smiled. "But Rosie girl, I don't think yours is gonna be hemmed in by nothin'. You're gonna see things and do things dat I couldn't even dream of. You'll see. You're gonna be like dat flying lady. What's her name? Earhart somthin'?"

"Amelia Earhart, Grandma. Did you know she's gonna try and fly her plane around the world? Imagine that, around the whole world!"

"Yes-sir-re, dat's my Rose, another Amelia Earhart," Grandma B. smiled and closed her eyes once more.

"Maybe we should quit for now, Grandma B. Let you rest a while."

"Dat's prob'ly best, child," Grandma B. agreed. "But dere's just one more thing I gotta talk ta ya about." She lifted her head up so she could look straight at Rose. "I done heard dat ya think dat I's in dis pickle on account of you not gettin' da doctor after my second spell."

Rose's eyes welled up instantly just at the thought; the pain and guilt of it sitting just under her skin.

"Come over her, girl," Grandma B. said, lifting up her arms for Rose to fall into that familiar, soft place. Grandma B. let her weep a while before she began to speak, with Rose still nestled in her arms.

"Now don't you let yaself think for one minute dat I didn't bring dis here on myself. I knows what I was doin' when I told ya ta keep mum. It was my decision, not yours, and you was right ta let me make it. And beside, ya can't live your life around da what-ifs or da should-haves. Dat'll eat you up inside just as sure as dat hate for dat no good river scum woulda.

"Ya know somethin', Rosie girl, we's da only one'a God's critters dat pays more dan one time for our mistakes. Ya think a dog beats it self up for missin' out on a bone I throws out da back door 'cause he came around too late? No-sir-re, he sees his other dog friends enjoyin' da scraps, and he makes sure he's sittin' out dat back stoop whenever anybodies even workin' in da kitchen, 'fore we even done with dinner. God don't care if ya makes mistakes, child, he wouldn't let us choose if'in he cared about dat, he just care dat ya learns from 'um and does better next time.

"Our whole lives, dey be about choosing. Some times we choose right and sometimes we don't. Maybe I didn't choose right dat time on da boat, or maybe it's just my time, but listen here," Grandma B. said, holding Rose up by the shoulders so she could look into her eyes again. "I did da choosing, like it should be. Ya can't be choosin' for me. I's a grown woman. Ya owe me dat much, Rose.

"Ya'll see," she continued, pulling Rose back into her chest. "When you're a mother and ya have chill'in of ya own some day, well, den ya can choose for'um for a while. But den ya gotta learn ta let'em start choosin' on der own, even if dey skin der knee or get inta trouble at school. We all gotta learn ta choose for ourselves. Now, don't get me wrong, when dey's young ya gotta let'em know what's right and what's wrong, but den ya gotta let go; ya gotta let da good Lord watch over'em and let'em choose for der selves."

Grandma B. grasped Rose by the chin, putting on a serious face.

"Now ya promise me, girl, no more blamin' ya'self. I ain't a child who don't know no better. And I may be old, but I ain't senile, so I knows what I did. Ya gotta promise me!"

"I promise, Grandma," Rose said, a look of contentment all over her face—the burden finally lifted from her heart.

"Come 'ear and gimme some suga'," Grandma B. said, pulling Rose into her arms once more. This time, she was the one who needed a hug—the sweetness and energy that was her Rose flowing freely and unconditionally, filling her up with the precious, syrupy nectar of what was real. The conversation had drained her, but she knew it had to be done. She wasn't going anywhere if that child thought she had anything to do with her going. Grandma B. knew better, and now she was sure Rose knew better, as well.

As Grandma B. held her close, she soon felt the soft shaking of Rose's body as she began to weep.

"Now what's dis here nonsense?" Grandma B. said, lifting Rose up to look into her now damp face.

"I don't want you to die, Grandma."

"Oh, honey child," she replied, pulling her back down close to her again. "Everybody's gotta die. It's just part of livin'. God done blest me wid a good, long life, and now it's just my time."

"I know, but I'm going to miss you so much!" came Rose's muffled, wet reply.

"I know, child, I know… it'll hurt for a while, but any time ya be havin' trouble feeling old Gramma B. close, ya just open dat der box, and I'll be right der witch ya."

Rose could still feel her embrace as she sat in the pew. It was as real as if Grandma B. was there herself. The organ started up for the first hymn. Grandma B.'s presence filled her and fed that empty hunger which was inside her. Rose stood and made her way to the front of the choir. The family had agreed to let her sing a song for Grandma B., and now Grandma B. was there with her, holding her up, helping her feel whole again. The organ ended the introduction. Rose closed her eyes and began to sing.

> *A-maz-ing grace how sweet the sound,*
> *That saved a wretch like me,*
> *I once was lost but now am found,*
> *Was blind but now I see.*

When she opened her eyes again, she was in St. Mary's back home, standing up in front of the congregation, her brother Michael standing on her left singing, and to her right was Gerty and her other brothers and sisters. Her parents where sitting just in front of them, smiling contently. Rose's heart was lifted even higher.

> *'Twas grace that taught my heart to fear,*
> *And grace my fears re-lieved,*
> *How pre-cious did that grace ap-pear,*
> *The hour I first be-lieved.*

Rose smiled back at her parents, grasped Michael's hand, closed her eyes, and continued to sing.

> *Thru man-y dan-gers, toils and snares,*
> *I have al-ready come;*
> *'Tis grace hath brought be safe thus far,*
> *And grace will lead me home.*

Rose's voice cracked as she sang those last poignant words, a tear sliding down the outside of her cheek. She opened her eyes again to find Todd's hand in place of Michael's, and Aunt Tilley and Grace standing where Gerty and the others had been. When the love and compassion that enveloped her, and stood by her side, had suddenly struck her dumb; Todd, then Aunt Tilley, and finally Grace took up the tune until she was able accept the gifts which were standing next to her and join them for the last verse.

When we've been there ten thou-sand years,
Bright shin-ing as the sun,
We've no less days to sing God's praise
Then when we'd first begun.

~ ~ ~

Rose sat on the top stoop of Grandma B's small front porch, exhausted from the day's events. Folks were trickling out of the house now, which just hours ago was abuzz with family and friends laughing, hugging, reminiscing, and eating—there was lots of eating. The family had brought home all the wonderful dishes the ladies of Antioch had prepared for Grandma B.'s funeral luncheon at the church.

Rose looked out onto the quiet evening street, as the streetlights flickered on to illuminate the night. A tall, thin figure had just turned the corner across the street, carpet-bag in hand. Rose straightened up and blinked twice to make sure she wasn't mistaken. Her eyes went wide with excitement. She ran across the street and wrapped her arms around the lone figure.

"Oh, Lilly Mae, you're a sight for sore eyes!"

"I'm glad ta see ya too, Rose, but ya mind lighten' up a bit, you're crushin' my arms," Lilly Mae managed to get out, her voice strained from the grip Rose had around her chest.

"Oh! Sorry, Lilly Mae. I'm just so excited to see you!"

"I couldn'ta guessed," Lilly Mae joked, her face bright with the warm greeting she had hoped for but wasn't sure she would get. "What ya all gussied up for? Ya goin' out tonight?" she asked, looking at Rose dressed in her Sunday best.

Rose's features turned somber as she looked down at the ground then up again at Lilly Mae, not sure how best to tell her.

"Grandma B. died, Lilly Mae, just last week. Today was the funeral."

Lilly Mae stood staring slack-jawed at Rose, awestruck at the news.

"Here, I'll take your bag for you," Rose said as the two friends silently walked to Grandma B.'s house, arm in arm.

It took a few days for the friends to catch up on what had transpired in their lives since they had last seen each other. They stayed up late the next three nights telling stories, laughing, and even crying a bit about what had gone on those many months apart. To Lilly Mae's relief, Rose's affection for her hadn't changed. Rose was the same sweet, easily excited character she had left, though Rose had grown an inch or two, as she herself had done.

But something was different. They both could feel it. The two girls who had left each other some eight months ago were both different—Rose, a little more reserved and contemplative in speech; Lilly Mae, a little less reserved than she had been but no less deliberate. Their mannerisms had changed perceivably, as well as their dress; they sat more politely, interrupted each other less, and jeans were rarely worn by either girl. They were turning into women, a fact they had both observed.

Once they had caught up on all the past events, the question of future plans naturally came to pass.

"Actually, I'd come by because I wondered if ya wanted ta work together again this summer, on the river I mean. I decided not ta work on the Capitol 'cause I wanted ta be a little closer ta home. And now that Grandma B.'s…, well, maybe you could come work with me on the J.S. It's owned by the same folks, but it goes up and down the lower river 'tween St. Louis and NaOrlins."

Rose knew this question was going to surface soon after she had seen Lilly Mae. She had wondered about it herself. She didn't have Grandma B. or Todd to keep her in St. Louis now, but she hadn't seen her family in a long time, either. Spending another summer with Lilly Mae was awfully tempting though; seeing a whole new part of the river and making it down to New Orleans held almost as much sway over her as seeing her family again.

Lilly Mae continued. "I kinda toll'em already that you'd want a job, so if'en ya wanna go with me then we have to leave in a little over a week," Lilly Mae finished, holding her breath slightly, anxious for Rose's response.

"Oh, dear. I'm not sure about that, Lilly Mae. School's not over for another two weeks, and I'd really like to finish up the semester, since they decided that I could."

"Well…, if it don't work out…," Lilly Mae said, her gaze falling to the ground along with her hopes. "That's okay."

Rose looked at her dejected friend. She really wasn't sure what to do.

"I need to think it over, Lilly Mae. Since they already think I'm gonna work with you, why don't we just let them think that for now, and I'll let you know in a couple a days."

~ ~ ~

Rose and Lilly Mae didn't converse much the next couple of days. Rose spent her days in school, and a good share of her evenings were taken up by studying. Lilly Mae had more time to talk to Grace, Darrell, Todd, and the kids. She had figured out by some of Rose's stories, and by observation, that Rose had some sort of connection to Todd, but she couldn't quite figure out what it was, and she was too embarrassed to ask. She bided her time, did a little sight-seeing on her own, and nervously waited for Rose's response. She hadn't realized how much it meant to her to have Rose with her for the summer until the possibility of her not coming was dangled in front of her. She had missed Rose more than she had thought. She was very anxious when Rose asked her out to the porch that next Tuesday after dinner.

"I talked with my teachers at school, and they are willing to give me my exams this week if I want to take them early," Rose explained.

Lilly Mae's face brightened.

"But I really do want to see my family, Lilly Mae," Rose said looking down at the ground. Lilly Mae could feel her heart sink. "I decided I could send them the address of the Streckfus Co., so we could send letters back and forth. That way, I'd at least know how they're doing."

Rose looked back up at Lilly Mae, who had a lightened look of anticipation written all over her.

"Does that mean you'll go with me?"

"Yah, that means I'll go with you, Lilly Mae," Rose smiled.

Lilly Mae reached over and hugged Rose as hard as Rose ever did. That's when Rose knew she had made the right decision. Now, all that was left was finishing up school and saying goodbye to Grandma B.'s family; the most difficult person to leave, Rose knew, would be Todd.

~ ~ ~

"I suppose you heard," Rose started, looking up at Todd from the swing at the grade school playground. This had been the place they would come when they had to talk to each other without others listening in—before the Rosebud incident, that is. Todd stood instead of sitting on the swing next to her, knowing what was coming.

"Yeah, I heard. When are you leaving?"

"Day after tomorrow."

"Oh!" Todd said, eyes wide with surprise. He had a feeling Rose would probably leave after Grandma B. had died. There wasn't any reason for her to stick around anymore. He had made sure of that on his end of things, trying not to be alone with her in the same room, trying to spend more time away from the house than in it.

He may have told her it was over those many weeks ago, but he knew that it wasn't. He couldn't keep from watching her when she wasn't looking, catching a glimpse of her brushing her hair in the morning, or reading a book in the evening. The smile on her face when she came to a good part in her book, made him smile along with her, reminding him how easily he could get her to smile on their many excursions together. Her face, the color and wave of her hair, her bright blue eyes—they were all imprinted in his memory and inscribed on his heart. He knew she had to leave, but he didn't want her to go. He wasn't sure he was going to be able to let her go without letting her know how much he still cared.

He sat down on the swing next to her, eyes looking down, appearing to examine the nails on his hands.

"I just wanted to explain…"

"You don't need to explain anything, Rose."

"Yes, yes I do. You've given me so much; you all have," Rose said, looking straight into his deep, dark eyes. Todd wasn't the only one who wouldn't forget. The soft, warm color of his skin, the deep, brown oceans that were his eyes, these were the things Rose would never forget, and the way his eyes lit up when he showed her yet another amazing site in the city. He seemed to know what would excite her without her even saying a thing. She loved him for that.

Then there were those moments of just being together, whether studying or just sitting around on a lazy Sunday after church reading the paper. He was just so easy to be around, so comfortable. These were the times she would catch him looking at her. He'd smile when she would look up, then casually go back to whatever he was doing. She knew he loved her no matter what he tried to tell her and despite the space he was feebly trying to maintain these last couple weeks.

"I don't feel it's right for me to stay here living with your family," Rose continued. "Grace will be done with nursing school for the semester, so she can watch the kids, and with Grandma B.

gone, well…, it just doesn't seem right. And you and I…," Rose diverted her gaze briefly then looked back at him again. "I guess we just weren't meant to be together."

And there they sat, staring at each other, each wanting to say more, but they knew it would make leaving that much more arduous.

"I found you!" Marcus called out as he jumped out of nowhere and up onto Todd's back.

"Whoa!" Todd said, trying to recover from the surprise. "You found me all right. You nearly gave me a heart attack!"

"Momma said it's time ta eat," Marcus said. He pulled on Todd's hand to follow him back to the house.

Rose stood and followed the two out of the playground. Marcus reached up for her hand almost as quickly as he ran out in front of them, leaping into the air, knowing they knew the game and would both swing him skyward, only to guide him gently down to repeat the whole process again and again, as long as their arms would hold out.

~ ~ ~

Grace didn't go to the river to say goodbye with the others, but she pulled Rose aside the morning of her departure to say something to her in private.

"Rose, I never did thank you for what ya did for my mother that night; bringing the doctor to the house, I mean. That meant a lot to the whole family. It meant a lot to me." She smiled at Rose. "I know I really didn't deserve that, but I guess that shows who's the mature one is here."

"Well, you know what Grandma B. would say," Rose replied with a smile.

"The Lord don't give us half of what we really deserve," the two said in unison, laughing together at the thought.

Grace took Rose in her arms and gently gave her a hug. Rose gently hugged her back.

"You take care a yourself now," Grace said. "And come back and visit when you're in the neighborhood."

"I will, I promise."

But of course, Rose wasn't so sure that she could.

~ ~ ~

As they approached the levee, the children were the first to run down to the piers where the boats were moored. It was strange for Rose to pass by the Capitol and step up to the J.S. Deluxe. It was a boat of similar vintage as the Capitol, but to Rose, it didn't seem to have the same charm.

Lilly Mae said her polite goodbyes to the family, then waited for Rose to step onto the boat. For Rose, it wouldn't be so easy. She gave Darrell a hug, promising him she would come back and visit. Then there were the children. Darrell had to round them up from running up and down the pier long enough to say goodbye— a departure which was more painful for Rose, of course, than it was for them. They had come to enjoy Rose's company, but in the usual style of a child, there were new things to see, new places to explore. Rose understood, so she let them go with a brief bear hug and kiss.

Then there was Todd. Darrell used the pretense of run-away children to let them have a moment alone. The two looked at each other awkwardly, neither knowing what to say or do.

"You take care a yourself, okay Rose," Todd started.

"Yah, you too," she returned. "And write to me. Tell me how you and the family are doing."

"Yeah, sure!" he replied, both knowing it would never happen.

They stood facing each other, staring into each others' eyes. The silence on the busy levee was deafening to their ears.

"I better go," Rose finally said, composing a thin smile.

She waited a moment for a response, and when there was none, she turned and headed for Lilly Mae who was patiently waiting for her at the entrance to the boat.

Before she had gone two steps, a brown hand took hold of her own. She turned to stand face to face with Todd, a look of remorse, and longing, and love all there at the same time. He took her face in his hands, and he kissed her, gently at first, but when she yielded to his lips, he pressed in intently, taking in the full measure of her mouth, holding his warm, firm body tightly against hers. There were only the two again, alone on the dock, locked in an embrace that did not measure time or place.

Todd finally broke the spell and pulled himself away, still holding onto Rose by her arms and the steady intention of his gaze.

"I love you, Rose."

"I know," she said, smiling softly at him. "I love you too."

"Rose!" Lilly Mae called out. The pier was empty of passengers. Only family and friends were left on the dock, standing by the rail blowing last minute kisses and final waves of goodbye to loved ones on board.

Rose's ardor turned to surprise when she realized she was about to miss her boat. She turned back to Todd, gave him a kiss on the cheek, squeezed his hand then turned and ran for the boat.

Rose stood at the rail until Todd and the rest of the family were just specks in the distance and everyone else, including Lilly Mae, had gone inside to start learning her way around the new steamer. Rose stood there long after the city was out of view. She couldn't move. If she let go of the rail she felt as if she would float right off the deck. It was intoxicating. She stood there, basking in the sun on a cloud-filled day. She felt like she had never felt before—a sea of dichotomy, brimming with warmth and a luminous excitement that is the untainted joy of a first love, yet shrouded with the bitter knowledge that society didn't condone this love; in fact, it reeled at the mere thought of it. That made her angry, then ultimately sad as she looked out on the rippling water and the green vegetation which held it all in, not really seeing any of it.

She decided then and there, she wasn't going to let them deface her joy. It was hers always, to bring out on gloomy days such as this to shine and inspire, to intoxicate and remind her of the possibilities of things ahead. There was always ahead. That was just one of the many things she had learned during her time in St. Louis, a time which had changed her forever.

Rose smiled and said a small prayer of thanks before she stepped inside, on to her next adventure on the river that started it all. She had come home once more.

ಜಿ *12* ಲ

Friendships are like old, worn shoes; they feel so comfortable when you put them back on again. But what happens when you somehow lose them, and at a time when you need them most?

Like any good explorer, you take advantage of the first pair you come upon, and deal with the repercussions as they come.

~ ~ ~

The J.S. Deluxe was similar in size to the Capitol, but her paddle wheels were on the side, not in the back, and she was fancier inside. The ceiling on the main deck was entirely draped with large, green and white striped material hanging in billows from one side of the ship to the other, with ceiling fans and ornate Japanese lanterns everywhere. There were tables with blue wicker chairs on each side of the first deck, with the middle floor open, except for a small water fountain surrounded by plants. That was why she was known as the "Garden Steamer." The whole decor on the J.S. was set to depict a garden theme. The dinning deck had Windsor chairs, painted yellow, around each table, with the third deck boasting Heywood-Wakefield ocean steamer chairs. The ball room was on the second deck and as large as the Capitol's, but it didn't have the rainbow lights Rose enjoyed so much. And unlike the Capitol, each deck was completely open, except for the Texas deck, where the crew's quarters were. That's why she mostly ran on the Ohio and the lower Mississippi Rivers, where there was less chance of getting into cold weather.

Getting used to her was not a problem for Rose, but not having Grandma B. in the kitchen wasn't as easy. It helped Rose to have Lilly Mae there. They had more catching up to do, including the now-obvious romance between Rose and Todd, so the days and weeks just seemed to fly by.

Rose found out Lilly Mae had kept up with her reading. In fact, she had taken a night class to work on her skills. Her bag was half-filled with second hand books she had planned on reading for the summer. On nights when they weren't too exhausted from their labors or busy with passengers, they would sit on the upper deck and read together, taking turns out of the same book or reading silently out of different ones.

The two girls easily fell in together again—the old jokes, the comfortable likes, the prickly arguments—all slipped into place the minute they laid their bags on their beds. And they were an easy pair to gather around. In fact, some of the other girl's discovered their reading time, and they wanted to join in. Some didn't like to read or couldn't, so they would bring along their knitting, crocheting, or embroidery and work as the others took turns at the book de jour.

Rose, being the consummate teacher, wasn't satisfied with this arrangement, so she convinced Lilly Mae to help her teach those who couldn't read. In return, Lilly Mae and Rose had to agree to learn how to knit, crochet, or do needle work—all of which Rose had a hard time with. She seemed all thumbs. Lilly Mae lapped it up like cream.

The summer flew by this way—taking on passengers, cleaning up after excursions, reading and handiwork circles, making meals for the crew, tutoring groups on their days off, taking on more passengers.... All taking place on their floating island, cradled by the majesty that is the mighty Mississippi.

Captain Roy was right; the lower river was much different than the upper river. Besides the fact that the topography changed—backwaters, marsh and delta ran up to the river's edge along a good share of the lower Mississippi—the river was much more of a snake path. And after a large rain, the boats could tread waters they normally couldn't navigate. This could shave hours off a trip between destinations. There were also more homes—or perhaps, better described as shacks—and factories which lived along the edges of the lower river. Rose felt this spoiled the placid solitude she took for granted on the upper-river refuge.

There were still stretches of river where Rose could lose herself, planted at the bow of the boat as high up as she could get. There she would read the coveted pack of family letters she would get when the J.S. made its way back up to St. Louis. The trips back to the city were bittersweet for Rose; she would love to pick up the stack of letters from almost every member of her family, but stepping into the city brought back many memories of her time there with Grandma B. and the kids, of Grace, Darrell, Aunt Tilley, Pearl, and of course, Todd.

Rose would purposefully take her time walking to and from the Streckfus office downtown, hoping by chance, she might see someone she knew; most notably someone tall and thin, with the deepest brown eyes and the warmest smile.

Her pensiveness the days before and after these trips to St. Louis didn't escape Lilly Mae. She made an extra effort to distract Rose and try to take her mind elsewhere.

At the end of the summer, both girls were looking forward to spend some time in New Orleans. During the summer, the steamer would make its way to the Crescent City every month or so, but they were too busy with their work to spend any time on shore. Rose's interest was piqued however, by the comings and goings which went on in the Big Easy.

New Orleans was a true port city, but her commerce wasn't limited to boats and ships which could navigate the Mississippi. New Orleans was an international port, docking large, ocean-going vessels which took passengers and cargo to and from every place on the globe.

Rose was amazed at the large, ocean vessels and the vast array of different people who worked on them or stepped off them onto their new homeland. On the few occasions when Rose wasn't busy on the steamer, she would hang out over the rail and watch the many different people—black, white, Asian, Hispanic, and Europeans of all types, dressed in a myriad of clothing. Some were obviously part of the dock scene, others most evidently newcomers, anxious with their new surroundings, having just stepped off a boat onto foreign soil. Rose thought this was even better than the people-watching she did at the train depot in St. Louis. One could imagine even more elaborate stories of where these foreigners had been and where they were going to.

When the day finally arrived for Rose and Lilly Mae to step off the boat for the season, Rose could hardly keep herself in her skin.

She hadn't slept much the night before, but she had decided she shouldn't keep Lilly Mae up, so she slipped out to watch the night life by herself. She was up long enough to see some of the male crew stagger back to the boat at about three in the morning, already starting to spend the money they hadn't yet received.

"Lilly Mae! It's time to wake up! Last day on the boat, ya know!" Rose said excitedly, poking Lilly Mae out of a sound sleep.

Lilly Mae groaned, rolling over and pulling the sheet over her head, harking back to a similar morning a year earlier. Once awake however, she couldn't get back to sleep, her mind pulled toward the reunion with her family and a certain special someone. She was excited to introduce them all to Rose. She had warned her mother Rose was white, so there wouldn't be any surprises when she brought her home. It still made her nervous, none-the-less. Her family didn't associate with whites socially, so she wasn't sure how they would react to Rose.

The crew shared their last big meal together that morning, cleaned up and got things stowed away for the repair crew, which would be boarding the J.S. to fix her up for the next season's work.

~ ~ ~

"Come on, Lilly Mae!" Rose called to her friend outside the cabin window, peeking in to see what was taking her so long. Lilly Mae was primping herself just one last time. Rose stood outside in the warming midday sun.

September in New Orleans was even warmer than St. Louis, so Lilly Mae had put Rose's hair in her now-favorite style, a French braid, to keep cool and to keep her hair out of her way during the trip to the Martin home. Rose wore a three-quarter length skirt and a light rayon blouse, which she had picked up in Natchez on their way down river, and a pair of half-inch heeled sandal shoes. When she put the outfit on, it reminded her of Pearl. It made her smile; Pearl would have been pleased. But truth be told, Rose would have rather put on some shorts and a tee shirt, but she didn't think it would be the best attire to wear to meet Lilly Mae's family.

Lilly Mae stepped out onto the Texas deck, carpet-bag in hand, and headed for Rose, an eager smile on her face.

"'Bout time, girl!" Rose said, imitating a typical Lilly Mae expression. "If I didn't know any better, I would say you were fixing yourself up for some beau."

Lilly Mae smiled sheepishly.

"Lilly Mae Martin! You never told me about a man in your life!"

"Don't have ta tell ya 'bout everythin'!" Lilly Mae teased.

"You sure do!" Rose said, picking up her suitcase and carpet-bag.

On the three flights down to the dock, Rose couldn't get Lilly Mae to divulge any information about this mystery man. Instead, she was relegated to reviewing the names and ages of all of Lilly Mae's family. She knew every detail about each of them, of course, but her nervousness was getting the better of her memory.

"Then there's Matthew, he's the youngest, right?" Lilly Mae continually nodded her agreement. "He likes airplanes and ice cream."

"Rose, you're gonna be fine," Lilly Mae said, trying to quell Rose's anxiety. "They're all gonna like you just fine." Lilly Mae hoped she was telling the truth.

The boat had docked just south of Jackson Avenue, upriver from the French Quarter. Not the usual place they stopped when they were picking up or dropping off excursion passengers. Here they sat next to ships on one side, which were emptying and loading large bails of cotton and wooden crates off of large cargo ships, and on the other side, unloading passengers just off a sea-going, passenger vessel. As the two girls looked out over the sea of humanity to their right, and the wooden crates and cotton bales that lay ahead and to their left, they could scarcely see a way through the mayhem.

The wharf along the Crescent City ran for approximately fifty-two miles. This allowed any number and type of vessels to dock and do business along the river's edge. The wharf was built of large, black tarred timbers driven deep down into the silty, sandy soil; reinforced with large pieces of metal along the top edge where the numerous vessels moored. The north end was where the cotton and grain moved off the barges. They would be loaded onto trains, or moved further down the docks to waiting ships bound for Europe, South America, or Asia. Then came the freight and fruit docks, followed by the other excursion boats, which moored along the French Quarter, as the J.S. normally did. Then there were the Puerto Rican docks, and banana docks, where some four-hundred million pounds of coffee and twenty-three million stems of bananas where brought in to the city each year. The Army Store Houses came next, and just past the industrial canal and dry docks was a large sugar refinery. And because ever inch of useable river's edge was used up, they dredged an eleven mile industrial canal just east of the ninth ward, which allowed even more ships to dock, and connected the river to the large Lake Pontchartrain and Gulf of Mississippi through the intracostal waterway. There was humanity as far as Rose could see.

"We'll go straight home first ta meet my family, then I can show ya around the city a bit," Lilly Mae explained, as they stepped into the din of people and the large cotton bales piled up along the wharf. Lilly Mae took-off in the direction of home, deftly making her way through the crowd. This time it was Rose who was trying hard to keep up. She had two cases, to Lilly Mae's one, and there were so many interesting people to see; it was hard to keep track of the back of Lilly Mae's head. Lilly Mae looked back every now and again as Rose struggled along. When Lilly Mae finally stopped to let Rose catch up, she was startled to find she couldn't see her. Rose had bent down to adjust the strap on her sandal and was out of Lilly Mae's view. Lilly Mae quickly turned back in the direction she had last seen Rose, pushing people out of her way, her eyes wide with anxiety.

Rose stood up and discovered she too had lost sight of Lilly Mae. She stood on her toes, scanning the many heads which surrounded her with no luck at all. She picked her cases back up and headed off in the direction she thought Lilly Mae had gone.

The two friends walked within six feet of each other, but weren't able to make eye contact through the crowd and the cargo which filled the wharf.

Rose was starting to breathe heavier when she realized she had probably lost her friend. They had never talked about where she lived, so she had no idea where to even start looking. Rose was slowly walking backward, contemplating what she might do next, when she ran right into someone.

"Oh, I'm sorry," she said, turning around.

There, standing next to her was Peter.

≈ 13 ⋘

One day, when Rose was walking along a creek back home with her father, she noticed some water coming right out of the ground, about fifteen feet from the water's edge. Her father explained to her that it was a spring. The water ran deep underground and was pushed up to the surface from far below. That's why it was so cold and so clear and tasted like all the rock and sand it had just squeezed past.

Rose's memory of that night a year and a half ago was like that spring. It flowed deep down inside her; it stayed there undetected and unknown, even to Rose, until the stress and pressure of seeing Peter's face again brought it all up to the surface, bubbling over cold and crisp, sending a chill through Rose's whole body.

~ ~ ~

Rose's throat tightened and a knot instantly formed in the pit of her stomach. She felt as though her breakfast was going to make a second appearance. Rose was surprised by how just looking at Peter instantly conjured up that night so many months ago as if it had just happened the day before. The fear, the embarrassment, the feeling of violation—it was all there, easily accessible. She had no idea.

It took Peter a moment, but he finally recognized Rose too.

"Well, if it ain't the pretty Miss Rose," he said smugly, eyeing Rose up and down. "Now haven't you grown up nice!"

He stepped closer to her. She stepped back.

"Lookie here mates, this be a girl I once had a little thing with on a riverboat up North," he boasted to the dock hands, who had stopped to see what their friend was up to. "She's a pretty one, ain't she?" he said, stepping closer still. "You look like you're lost there, sweetheart. Me and the fellas, we can help ya out there. Can't we, mates?" Then he smiled that evil smile, which Rose had seen once before; her stomach twisted one more time.

Rose knew this time she was out numbered. And to top it off she had lost the only person she knew in the city. This was one of those times Grandma B. would have told her she ought to run rather than fight, and she knew Grandma B. would be right, but she didn't know where to run. At this point, Rose knew it didn't matter. She just needed to get away.

As she continued to step backward, trying to decide which way she was going to escape, she bumped into yet another person, this time someone softer and more genteel.

"Oh…," she said, looking around to find she had run into the most beautiful woman she had every seen. Her short, perfectly quaffed hair hung out from underneath her small-brimmed hat which sat at an angle on her head. She was impeccably dressed in a tan suit which fit snug in the bodice, hips and thighs, ending with a flare just below her knees, and she was just putting on her white gloves, despite the seventy degree temperature. There were two young Asian women standing meekly by her side, looking like they would spook and run away if you said anything to them at all. This change in character turned Rose's thoughts around, and suddenly she hit upon an idea.

"Aunt Margaret! I've been looking all over for you!" Rose blurted out, putting her arms around the woman and giving her a polite hug. Rose pulled away, still holding onto the woman's arms, looking her straight in the eyes. The woman was looking at her as anyone would if some stranger had unexpectedly come out of nowhere and given them a hug. "I'm *so* glad I found you!" Rose finished, diverting her eyes to the left and tilting her head back just enough to try and convey the predicament she was in. Rose's heart was still racing. She stood still, anxious and fearful, as a small bead of sweat rolled down the side of her face. Rose knew if she didn't get away from these men, she wouldn't be as lucky as she had been the first time. She said a silent prayer of supplication—*Please, God! Please, God! Please, God!*—repeating it many times over to herself before the woman reacted to Rose's advance.

The woman looked into Rose's face, then past her at the burly men standing just behind her. She pulled Rose back to her gently.

"I'm sorry, my dear. I didn't recognize you; you've grown so. Come, take your things, we have so much to talk about."

After Rose had picked up her cases, the woman grasped Rose under the arm and led her away from the men, one of whom looked particularly put out as they walked away into the crowd. She could feel Rose's body shaking under her grasp. The two young Asian girls following close behind. Rose had to blink away the water which was now pooling in her eyes.

Once they had walked far enough away from the men, the woman stopped and looked straight at Rose.

"All right now, are you going to tell me what that was all about?" she said in a kind voice.

"I am so sorry," Rose said.

She was still shaking, still blinking away the tears, the knot in her stomach just starting to unravel.

"I had a…, incident with one of those men a long time ago, and when I ran into him here on the dock…." Rose shook her head in disbelief. "I just got off the J.S. Deluxe. I've been working on her all summer with a friend of mine. We were heading for her apartment here in New Orleans, but we got separated, then I ran into…, him."

Since that incident, Rose had learned some other choice words to describe the type of man Peter was, but she didn't want to act impolite in front of a complete stranger, a woman who exuded manners without saying a word.

"Thank you *so much* for helping me! I would have been in a lot of trouble if I hadn't bumped into you."

Rose looked back in the direction of the men but didn't see any of them. She took a deep breath and relaxed just a little more.

"You're very welcome, my dear," she said with a kind smile, the two young girls staring at Rose from behind the woman. "So, will you be okay then?"

"Well, not exactly. I don't have any idea where my friend lives. She said she lives in an apartment complex with a lot of other families, but I never found out where."

"Well, you *are* in a pickle, aren't you? That could be most anywhere. I guess you'll just have to come home with me then," she said rather nonchalantly. "Just let me make sure my luggage is taken care of, then we'll be on our way. Watch these two for me would you?" she said, pushing the two young women gently toward Rose. "Stay here with…," the woman stopped, turning back to Rose. "I don't think I got your name, my dear."

"Oh, I'm sorry. My name is Rose, Rose Krantz."

"I'm Miss Edna Dubay, but most people call me Madam E."

At that, Rose started to giggle. Madam E. looked a little vexed at her reaction.

"Oh, I'm sorry. I just seem to attract women who only use initials for their name."

Madam E. shook her head slightly, somewhat confused, then turned and gave directions to some men who were loading large trunks onto a truck. Rose noticed the trunks had stickers with the word "Japan" plastered on them.

Rose turned toward the young girls, extending her hand in welcome.

"Hello, I'm Rose."

Both girls just stared at her, not making any sound or movement to return the greeting. Then they turned toward each other and whispered something which Rose couldn't make out, keeping their eyes on her suspiciously.

"Well, okay then," Rose said quietly to herself.

Madam E. returned to the silent group.

"Everything's taken care of. I'll hail a taxi, and we'll be on our way."

The troupe followed Madam E. through the maze of people and across two sets of railroad tracks to the side of the road. Rose made sure she kept close to the group of women. Madam E. held her hand in the air, and a taxi immediately pulled up right in front of her. She stood next to the car as the driver got out, came around to where she was standing, and opened the door for her. Rose looked around at the other taxis in front of them. They didn't seem to be opening doors for their passengers. She wondered if this driver knew Madam E. personally. The two Asian women sat in the back beside Madam E., leaving the front seat for Rose.

It took them a while to make it out of the busy traffic at the wharf, but once they were free of the congestion, the driver expertly, and with amazing speed, weaved his way through the city. Rose had to hold onto the dash frequently to keep from hitting her face on it, or falling in to the driver. Rose deduced that this man must have known Madam E., since he didn't even ask where she wanted to go.

Most of the streets they took were quite narrow with older-looking two-and-three story buildings, shops, and restaurants so close to the road that Rose thought she could probably touch them if she rolled down her window and stuck out her hand. That was until they pulled onto a wide boulevard. This road had two lanes of traffic going each way, with two lanes of track in the middle for the street cars which ran along its length. The sidewalks were wider here, so Rose could more easily see the shops and movie theatres which lined the street.

They turned right onto Rampart Street and stopped just a few blocks from the boulevard. Rose stepped out and looked up at the white-washed, wood, two-story building which they had stopped in front of. It had a second-story balcony with black, ornately decorated rails and an overhang which ran along the entire length. The metal work was covered with lovely, flowering plants.

Rose walked around the car as Madam E. paid the taxi driver. He tipped his hat and jumped back into his car and sped away.

Madam E. stepped into the building, with the Asian girls following close behind. Rose followed them in.

Rose stood in the entrance hall, which was long and tall, running up two stories. The second story was ringed three-quarters of the way around by a walkway, with an ornate chandelier hanging down the center. There was a narrow staircase which went straight in front of them and was covered in deep maroon carpet. The other side of the entryway was a hallway leading straight back to a door. The walls were covered with a dark maroon-colored wallpaper with a pattern which looked like raised velvet. To the left was a set of double wooden doors, which were closed, and to the right were two glass doors, which lay open to a large parlor filled with upholstered chairs, davenports, a fireplace, a small bar, and a piano.

"Ginny!" Madam E. softly called out, as she slowly removed her gloves.

A large black woman came out of the door in the hallway, wiping her hands on her apron. She wasn't as round as Aunt Tilley, or as short, but she was the blackest women Rose had ever met; *dark like cherry tree bark just after a rain*, Rose thought to herself.

"How was your trip, ma'am?"

"Very successful, thank you, very successful. Our luggage should be arriving soon. Please make sure that it's taken care of."

"Yes ma'am," she said, nodding slightly. "Malcolm!" Ginny turned and yelled back behind her. "Malcolm!" she yelled even louder.

"Virginia, you know how I detest yelling."

"Oh, yes'um, sorry ma'am."

Just then a young man Rose estimated to be a year or two older than herself came through the hall door. He wore light, kaki-colored pants, a white tee shirt, and a cap similar to the one Rose used to wear until just about a year ago. His skin had a nice tan color to it, and Rose thought he was rather handsome. He removed his cap when he saw Madam E., and his curly, dark brown, shoulder-length hair fell into his face. He took note of Rose and the two Asian women out of the corner of his eye.

"Yes'um Ma-dam. What can I be doin' for ya?" He spoke in an unusual accent Rose would find out later was called French–Creole.

"Our luggage will be arriving soon. Please make sure it's taken care of."

"Whatever you be needin' Ma-dam," he said, bowing slightly; then he flipped on his cap, turned toward Rose and the other young women, and addressed them. "*Bonswah*, Mademoiselles," he said to them, smiling and tipping his hat. He turned back to the other women and nodded his head, "Ma-dam E…, Miss Ginny," then flew out the front door and out of sight.

"Ginny, take these two young ladies up to the blue room, please. They've been attached at the hip since we boarded the ship, so it'll be a while before we can separate them. I'll be up later to get them settled, and Miss Krantz…," she paused, looking slightly puzzled at Rose. "Maybe we can put a cot up on the back porch for you, dear. We'll have Millie hang a few curtains. It will have to do until we can find your friend."

As Rose stood listening to Madam E. decide where she was going to stay, she noticed the raised wallpaper pattern which covered the walls held the figures of women across it's surface—naked women.

~ ~ ~

Rose followed Ginny through the swinging hall door which led into the kitchen, then on to the back porch, which was empty except for a broom, a broken chair, and a large sack of rice.

"You can sets your things down here, honey child. I'll get Malcolm an' Millie ta fix it up nice for ya. Ya ain't gonna be staying long?" Ginny asked. She had a deep southern drawl, like the one Grandma B. pretended to have when she was trying to get Rose into Soldan.

"No, I got separated from my friend Lilly Mae, at the docks, and Madam E. said I could stay with her until I found her."

"Well, I 'specks ya want'ta be gettin' otta those Sunday-go-ta-meet'in clothes," she said, as she stepped back into the kitchen. "There's a toilet just off the parlor. You can use that ta change if'n ya want." She pointed to a door to the left of the hall door. "I's got some breakfast ta finish up on. The girls'll be getting up soon, and they get mighty cranky if'in they don't get their breakfast on time."

Breakfast? Why would they be eating breakfast at almost three in the afternoon? Rose wondered. She shrugged her shoulders, opened up one of her suitcases, and pulled out a pair of shorts and a light blouse. It was even warmer here than it was by the river front. Rose was discovering that summer lasted even longer here than in St. Louis.

Rose opened the door which led to a small hallway just off the parlor. It was dark, lit only by a single covered bulb in the ceiling. The walls were covered with the same velvet-like wallpaper as the front-hall. Rose ran her fingers along the voluptuous curves of the ladies reclining there. She opened the bathroom door and was stymied by the sight.

The room was of medium size and framed by dark wood trim. It was painted in a dark maroon color which matched the wallpaper. The walls were adorned with photographs everywhere —they were pictures of naked women. There wasn't a place she could look where there wasn't a woman either standing, reclining, or sitting. Some were partially dressed, but most were totally naked. And all the women were looking at Rose with eyes which seemed to say with disinterest, *Yes, what do you want?* Rose didn't want to look at the pictures, but she was strangely drawn to them, like the feeling she got when she saw someone who was hurt—she didn't want to look, but she couldn't help herself. As Rose stood and looked at each picture, she wondered to herself, *What is this place?*

She finally pulled herself away from the pictures, dressed quickly, and went back to the porch to put her things away. She didn't want Ginny to wonder what she was up to, and Rose had a few questions for her.

When she came back into the kitchen, there was a young girl, probably eleven or twelve, sitting at the table in front of a plate of eggs and a large sausage. Her skin was lightly pigmented, and Rose would have mistaken her for being white if it weren't for her nappy hair, all done up in small braids which stuck out all over her head like porcupine quills. *That's what Lilly Mae's hair must have looked like when she was young*, Rose thought. But this little girl lacked the honey brown tone to her skin that Lilly Mae had. Rose did miss her so at this particular moment. The young girl looked up at Rose and stared.

"Oh, this here's Millie. She helps out 'round here. Millie, this here's Rose," Ginny said, not stopping what she was doing for the introductions.

"Hey," Millie said meekly, before she dove hungrily into the plate in front of her, looking up now and again as if to make sure Rose was still in the room.

"Now hurry up, Millie. The food's almost done, and the girls'll be wantin' their breakfast," Ginny said.

"I know, I know," she said, food slipping out of her mouth as she spoke.

"Are you hungry, Miss Rose?" Ginny asked politely.

"Oh, no thank you. I ate on the boat."

"Well, maybe some iced tea then. It's hotter than blue blazes taday."

"Yes ma'am, that'd be nice. Thank you."

Ginny smiled as she set a large, ice filled glass of tea on the table in front of Rose.

"I knew I was gonna like you the moment I saw ya," Ginny said, pleased at the respect Rose automatically gave her.

"Set down a spell. Make yourself at home," Ginny encouraged her, pulling out a chair across from Millie.

"What boat ya come in on?" Ginny asked as she returned to her work.

"I was working in the kitchen on the J.S. Deluxe over the summer with my friend Lilly Mae. We had just gotten off the boat when we got separated. She was taking me to meet her family."

"Well, good thing ya run inta Madam E.. There're some pretty sleazy characters down at those docks."

"Yes, I know!" Rose heartily agreed. She agreed with Ginny about the dock hands, but the verdict was still out on Madam E.

"All right now, Millie, take this here tray up to Sadie and Bridget. Then come right back down," she yelled after her. "I'll have Ruth and Tess's breakfast done by then."

Rose sat and watched Ginny deftly move about the kitchen, stirring a pot here, pouring a drink there. She obviously had done this many times before. After a few minutes, Millie came back into the room and stood in front of the second tray, as Ginny laid down the last slice of toast.

"Now remember, Ruth gets da tea, and Tess gets da orange juice."

Millie picked up the tray and shuffled cautiously back upstairs.

"That girl aims ta please, but she ain't cookin' on all four burners, poor thing," Ginny explained, hands on her hips, staring at the swinging kitchen door.

Rose sat in silence as she watched Ginny fill the sink with soapy water.

"Can I help you?" Rose asked.

"You don't want ta wash no dishes, child!" Ginny said, a little surprised by the offer.

"Yes, I do! I don't like just sitting around watching other people work."

"Well, if in ya wants to…I'll wash an you kin dry."

Rose hopped up and picked up the dish towel. As she stood next to Ginny silently drying a drinking glass, she almost dropped it from the loud, slow thump, thump, thumping noise which suddenly came from out in the front hallway.

"That's just the men bringin' in Madam's trunks," Ginny explained. "She like ta bring different things back from her trips. Keeps the customers interested, ya know. Didn't know she was gonna bring some girls back with her too, though," Ginny said with surprise. "Like there ain't enough girls right here that could use the work," she continued rather disgusted. "And those two are so thin they looked like a good stiff wind'd blow'em right over. Just ain't right,"she finished, shaking her head.

Since Ginny seemed to be in a talking mood, Rose thought this was as good a time as any to get some of her questions answered.

"Um..., Ginny, what kind of work does Madam E. do?"

Ginny stopped and looked straight at Rose. "Oh, child, didn't she tell ya? She runs a doll house." She could tell by the look on Rose's face that she didn't understand her. "A place where men come and have relations with the young ladies," she finished, sticking her hands back in the suds like she had just told Rose Madam E. was teacher at the local grade school.

Rose's face warmed at the realization of Ginny's words. She had seen women like that in St. Louis, peddling their wares on the street corners in various parts of the city, but she never dreamt she would ever be in a house where they lived. This answered her questions about the décor, and made her position more precarious.

"Well, aren't you sweet, my dear, helping Ginny out," Madam E. said, smiling sweetly at Rose as she walked into the kitchen. "I thought we could start work on finding your friend. Why don't you come with me to my office, and we can chat a while."

Rose instantly dropped her dishcloth and followed Madam E. out into the hall. Rose felt the sooner she was out of this place the better.

~ ~ ~

Madam E. opened one of the wooden, double doors at the base of the steps, walked into the room, and sat down on a davenport which sat against the back wall.

"Close the door, would you please?" Madam E. asked. "Come sit here, next to me." She set her hand gently on the davenport beside her. Rose tentatively sat down next to her. This woman had changed somehow, since Rose now knew what she did for a living; and she was less than comfortable being in a room alone with her.

"Now tell me a little about your friend. The more I know, the more I can help you find her."

Rose explained all she knew about Lilly Mae, everything she thought would be important to know—her full name, her age, the size of her family, and the fact that it was just Lilly Mae's mother and grandmother who took care of the family.

"Oh, and she's black," Rose finished, almost forgetting a fact which would make it considerably more helpful in the search.

"I see," Madam E. said, raising her eyebrows. "And how long have you two known each other?"

"Well, we met over a year ago when I took a job on the Capitol, an excursions boat on the upper Mississippi." Then Rose explained how she had stayed in St. Louis to help Grandma B. and go to school. She told her how they met up again, and worked together on the J.S. over the summer, going up and down the lower river.

"That's quite a story. You've been quite a few places and done quite a few things for such a young lady. What made you leave home in the first place, if I may ask?"

"Well, my mother was having another baby—number nine— and I thought that maybe it might be easier on the family if I just left." Then Rose looked down at her hands in her lap. "But honestly, I really wanted to see some other places before I had to go to school, and I didn't want to get married. I wasn't ready for any of that, so I took the job on the Capitol without my parents knowing about it."

"Oh, I see. And does your family know where you are now?"

"They knew I was coming to New Orleans with Lilly Mae at the end of the summer, but I haven't heard from them in a while, since the only address they know to write to is in St. Louis at the Streckfus Company office. The riverboat never stays long enough in one place for them to write to me any place else."

Madam E. stood up and walked over to her desk, pulled out a piece of paper and started writing.

"I know a few people in town," she said as she wrote. "I'll let them know some of what you've told me, and we'll see what they can do for us."

Then she reached over to a button on top of her desk and pressed it. Soon there was a knock on the door.

"Come in."

Millie quietly stepped into the room and stepped up to Madam E.

"Please, take this to Malcolm," she said, handing Millie an envelope. "He'll know what to do with it." Then she turned toward Rose.

"Well, I know a little about you, so I think it's only fair that I tell you a little about myself." Madam E. then stood and walked over to the front window and looked out as she spoke. "I'm originally from Chicago, and like you, Rose, I left home at an early age, but for a very different reason. I made my way south and ended up here in New Orleans. Madam Hamilton found me and took me in. She showed me how she ran her business and sold it to me when she decided to retire."

She turned and faced Rose, the details of her features hidden by the glare which surrounded her from the window behind her. All Rose could see was her shapely figure. It gave Rose an eerie feeling to look at her.

"Do you know what business I'm in Rose?"

"Yes, Ginny told me," she replied, looking down at her hands again.

Madam E. walked over and sat softly down next to Rose, placing a hand on top of Rose's clasped ones.

"I'm sorry it makes you uncomfortable, but I assure you, you aren't in any danger here. Quite the contrary; even though I make my money catering to men, my main job is taking care of the women that work for me. If my girls aren't happy, then my patrons won't be happy either."

She stood again and walked back over to the windows.

"I know what it's like, living on the street. It's rough out there and hard for a woman to make it on her own." She turned and faced Rose once more. "I give my girls a clean, safe place to work, and they make a decent income on top of it. We run a respectable establishment here; we're not one of those two dollar-a-trick cribs on Robertson Street"

Rose looked confused, not sure what a "trick" or a "crib" was.

"Well, enough of this nonsense," she said, acknowledging the blank look on Rose's face.

She walked back over and sat next to Rose one last time.

"You're too young to think about such things. What we need to concentrate on is finding your friend. I'm sure we'll find her in no time and have you on your way."

She stood and walked over to her desk, pressing the button once again, then she stood waiting for someone to respond.

"In the meantime, I bet you'd like to see a little of the city while you're waiting for your friend."

"Oh, yes!" Rose said cheerfully. "I'd like that very much."

Rose still wasn't quite sure about Miss Dubay. She seemed like she was a nice enough person, but Rose still couldn't feel quite comfortable in these surroundings, so the chance to get out of the building and see a bit of the city was all that more enticing. Millie stepped back into the room.

"Millie, please take Rose out, and show her a few of the sights. She's never been to New Orleans before, so you could take her to most any place."

Rose stood and headed out of the room behind Millie.

"Oh, my dear," Madam E. called out to Rose, "just to let you know, our patrons start arriving around nine o'clock in the evening. For your own comfort, it might be best if you stayed in the kitchen after that time."

Rose was grateful for the advice. She didn't want to be mistaken for one of Madam E.'s girls. A shudder ran up her spine at the thought.

~ ~ ~

Millie turned out to be a good guide, not as friendly and even less talkative than Todd had been on their first time out in St. Louis, but she did know the city and adeptly moved from one interesting sight to the next. They walked back to the large boulevard called Canal Street and hopped on a streetcar heading down to the river front. Rose was a little anxious about being at the docks again; afraid they might catch sight of Peter, but it was also a chance to look for Lilly Mae.

It turned out they were at a different place along the Mississippi River wharf, so she didn't get a glimpse of either. They stayed at the head of Canal Street long enough to watch a ferry leave with a deck full of cars and passengers heading for the other side of the river, heading for what, Millie explained, was the city of Algiers.

They walked along the wharf area, following the railroad tracks along the river's levee. Rose couldn't get Millie to talk much, but she did get her into a game of tightrope; trying to see who could walk a rail the longest without falling off. Millie was a wisp of a girl and easily scampered along the rail as if she was a carnival performer and had worked a tightrope all her short life.

They walked past a large brewery, smelling the sweet-sour aroma of fermenting hops. Then came Jackson Square, a park the size of a city block set between red, two-story buildings with the same ornate railwork balconies which adorned Madam E.'s place. On the north end of the square there stood the majestic St. Louis Cathedral. Rose read a plaque outside the church which explained it was built 1850, and was named for King Louis XIV of France. She asked Millie if she could go inside. They sat in back—Millie sitting, Rose kneeling—as Rose said a short prayer; a prayer to help her find her friend.

After they left the church, they continued north, past numerous shops, taverns, and restaurants; the last of which made

Rose's stomach gurgle from the wonderful smells emanating from their tall, narrow, open doors. They made it back to Rampart Boulevard and walked back west, just as the sun was setting. One of the few things which Millie did tell Rose, was you didn't want to be walking out on the streets after dark.

They stepped in through the front door and almost ran into Malcolm, who was obviously on his way out.

"There you two be. I was just fixin' to come out lookin' for ya," he said in his interesting accent. He stepped back and opened his arm, cap in hand, to usher them into the hallway. Rose thought the way he talked sounded like he was singing and talking at the same time. It intrigued her, and she wanted to hear more. "New Or-leans is not the place for two lovely Mademoiselles as yourselves to be walkin' at night unescorted."

Millie giggled and flapped her hand in front of him, tickled at the attention and the fact that he had called her "Mademoiselle." She walked right passed him toward the kitchen without saying a word, with Rose reluctantly following behind.

"If'in there's anythin' I can get you young ladies, just call on Malcolm. I'm at your disposal," he finished, bowing low, leg and arm extended as if he were a knight bowing to his ladies fair.

Rose was tickled at the performance and the attention as much as Millie. She had a big smile on her face as she stepped into the kitchen.

"Want some iced tea?" Millie asked, opening up the refrigerator and awkwardly pulling out a pitcher of the light brown liquid.

"No thank you, but a glass of water would be nice."

Millie pulled up a stool and reached into the cupboard for a couple of glasses. She filled Rose's with water, then hers with iced tea. She sat silently across from Rose, staring at her but not uttering a word.

"So do you live around here?" Rose asked.

"I live here," Millie replied.

"Oh, then is Ginny your mom?"

"No, Sadie is."

Rose knew from this morning that Sadie was one of the women who worked upstairs. Rose wasn't sure how to respond to that, so she didn't say anything. They sat across from each other, glancing at each other now and again until Millie had finished her tea.

"I specks I should put up some sheets in the porch for ya."

Rose stood up after her.

"I'll help you!" she said, eager to do something other than stare at this small, quiet girl.

So the two girls spent the rest of the afternoon tacking up old sheets, mismatched curtains and even an old table cloth all around the screened-in porch. Rose even figured out a way to tie them up during the day to let in some sun and some air. Ginny had moved the sack of rice into the kitchen, and the broken chair was missing, so all that was needed was a cot, and Rose would be set for the night.

"I'll find Malcolm to get ya a cot," Millie said then she went into the front hall and out of sight.

As Rose stood watching the door swing slowly back and forth, pondering her predicament, she was startled by the sound of a buzzer going off. She looked around the room to see where it was coming from. Then it happened again. Then shortly after the first couple there came a quick third and fourth. Whoever wanted attention was losing their patience.

Rose thought maybe it was Madam E., so she stepped out of the kitchen and gently knocked on her office door. There was no answer, so she slowly turned the knob and opened the door. The room was empty.

When she stepped back into the entryway, she was startled again, but this time by someone standing at the top of the stairs. The woman was dressed in a silky dressing gown which barely covered her important parts above and below, and a robe which was so shear it didn't add much to the concealment. Her hair was long, all the way down to her waist, and the darkness at the top of the steps concealed her age. Rose could clearly see the glow of the end of the lit cigarette that she held in her hand.

"Where's Ginny and Millie?" she sniped at Rose. "I've buzzed them twenty times now! I need my purple dress, and it's no where to be seen. Ginny drew my bath and just disappeared," the woman fumed. "I'm not stepping into that tub until I know my dress is ready!"

"Millie just went out to find Malcolm…Miss…, and I don't know where Ginny is," Rose replied nervously.

"Well, when you see'em, make sure to tell'em Ruth needs her purple dress," she blurted out, then turned with a flourish and walked out of sight, mumbling as she went.

Rose stood staring up at the top of the empty steps; the facts of her circumstances much more evident. Rose had never seen a woman dressed quite like that before.

Rose shook her head slightly and walked back into the kitchen. Soon, she heard the porch door swing open and shut and then a dull thud as something hit the floor. When she went out to see what was happening, she saw Malcolm sitting on a cot, bouncing softly up and down.

"Seems sturdy enough," he said, smiling at Rose. "Aught to hold a small thing like you."

Malcolm stood and looked around the room. "Room seem kinda sparse, don't ya think?" Then he cocked his head slightly and straightened his spine. "Wait here, Miss Rose, I've got just the thing."

He hastened out of the room and into the front hallway. Rose could hear him bounding up the steps. Soon he was back, carrying a small, floral-covered, stuffed chair. He set it in the corner of the room at the head of the cot.

"There! That perks it up a bit. But it's still missin' somethin'," he said, still not satisfied. "I know! You need a night stand. I know how you ladies like places to put your things."

Rose wasn't sure if she liked being lumped in with the ladies who Malcolm was probably referring to, but she thought he was sweet to think of these things for her.

"Well, thank you Malcolm, but this will be just fine. I shouldn't be staying long, anyway." Rose smiled. "Hey, how do you know my name?"

"Malcolm Connelly is all-seeing and all-knowing. I know a little of that voodoo magic too."

"Voodoo magic," Rose asked, skeptical.

"Oh, yes! An old Creole woman in the Bayou taught me. I can even predict the future. Want me to show you how it's done?" he asked, pulling out a set of well-worn tarot cards out of his back pocket.

Just then Ginny walked into the kitchen from a doorway Rose hadn't noticed before. She had a pile of brightly colored dresses draped over her arm.

"Excuse me, Malcolm. I have to tell Ginny something."

Malcolm tipped his hat as Rose exited the porch.

"Ginny, a woman upstairs by the name of Ruth is looking for her purple dress. She said she wasn't going to take her bath until she had her purple dress."

Rose notice a light purple color peaking out of the pile on her arm.

"That woman—bad enough I have ta fill her bath like she some sort a queen, but I have ta wait on her hand and foot. I swears, I don't know why the Madam just don't get rid a her. She's getting up in years, and I knows there's lots more out there that'd give their eye teeth ta work in a place like this," Ginny continued, shifting her load to both arms. "Madam E. takes care a her girls, yes-sir-re. Not all of 'em do, ya know."

Just then the buzzer went off, making Rose jump. Ginny didn't flinch. Then they heard it three more times in quick succession.

"Lord have mercy, old queenie must be close to her country time!," Ginny said, obviously exasperated.

"Country time?" Rose asked.

"You know, that womanly time of the month. She gets mighty nasty just before her time," Ginny explained, as she headed for the hall door. "I swear, she gonna be the death a me yet," she finished, pushing the door open with her ample back side and disappearing into the hall.

Rose's stomach growled. This brought an odd fact to her attention; it was getting to be about dinnertime, but there wasn't a thing on the stove. Rose walked back out onto the porch to chat more with Malcolm, but he was nowhere to be seen.

"Man, he comes and goes quickly," Rose said to herself. Then she sat on the cot and tested it out for herself. *It'll do for the short time I'll be here*, she thought. Then she walked back into the kitchen to wait for Ginny, thinking perhaps she could help with dinner, since Ginny was obviously behind schedule.

When Ginny walked back into the kitchen, she had her arms full of dirty laundry. She huffed and puffed as she carried the armful passed Rose, into the laundry room, then she plopped herself down on a chair next to Rose.

"I know Madam wants the girls ta keep'em selves clean, but she gotta get me samore help, 'specially with two more girls ta look after. Millie tries ta help, but she ain't much for workin'," Ginny lamented. "She's slower than molasses in January. She's too young ta answer the call phone, so when the Madam is busy entertaining, I ends up doin' that too. The last girl I had helpin' out didn't last but a week. She just couldn't handle the hours."

"Well, I can help you out. That is, until I find my friend. I don't like sitting around much, anyway. I can help you get dinner going."

Rose's stomach growled again at the mere mention of food.

"Oh, I specks you're hungry ain't ya? We keep kinda strange hours 'round here, child. Millie and me, we don't usually eat 'til around eight; then we make some finger food for Madam, the patrons, and the girls. But our big meal is around four in the mornin', just before bed."

Rose had never thought about it, but the hours these girls worked were usually the hours everyone else was sleeping. No wonder they couldn't keep help.

Ginny got up and went over to the refrigerator. "I'll make ya a sandwich after I gets the roast in the oven," Ginny said, setting a paper package of sliced meat on the table.

"Oh, I can do that, Ginny. Just point me to the bread box and the butter."

After Rose had made her sandwich, she pitched right in with some of the dinner preparations. Every so often, Rose could hear the muted sound of a phone ringing in the other room.

At about seven-thirty Rose could hear some commotion coming from the parlor. Soon after, a young woman walked into the kitchen from the door which led to the bathroom. She had a dark tan complexion, as warm and soft as silk. Her wavy, dark hair fell well below her bare shoulders. The white top she wore cut across her voluptuous chest, which stood out like two round mounds that could barely be contained by the cloth which attempted to cover them. They were accented by a small red ribbon weaved into the top edge of her blouse, the same ribbon which ringed the bottom edge of her short, puffy sleeves. Her skirt was brightly colored and had a slit along one side, to expose a good portion of her shapely leg as she walked. She stopped momentarily when she caught site of Rose sitting at the table cutting the buns for the small sandwiches.

She walked over to where Ginny was standing, slicing some cheese, and she stealthily stole a piece before Ginny was aware of her presence. Ginny swatted at her hand as it passed quickly by her.

"Ya git yourself outta her, Tess. That cheese ain't no good for your fig'ger, and you knows it."

Tess gave Ginny a big squeeze from behind, then quickly reached around her for another piece of cheese.

"Now you git!" Ginny swung again and missed, as Tess giggled and ran out of the room.

"Gotta watch those girls like a hawk. They'd all eat 'till they looked like me if'n given the chance."

Millie strolled through the hallway door, sat down across from Rose, and stared at her, not saying a word.

"'Bout time you showed up, girl," Ginny scolded her after she noticed her presence at the table. "We got laundry ta do. Now git in there and git busy! Dinner'll be ready right quick."

Millie stood up slowly and sulked over to the laundry room to begin the daily ritual.

Next, Madam E. came into the room. She had changed out of her suit, into a simple burgundy-colored evening dress, her short brown hair still perfectly styled. Rose stood when she entered the room, eager for some good news.

"Good evening, my dear. How was your tour?"

"Just fine, thanks. Have you heard anything about my friend?"

"Oh, I'm sorry, dear. I haven't come up with any leads yet on your friend..., what's her name?"

"Lilly Mae."

"Yes, Lilly Mae. Well, I'm sure we'll hear something by tomorrow." Then she strode over to the porch and looked in. "I hope your accommodations will be sufficient for this evening. I see Malcolm found a cot, and he even found you a pretty chair. That was nice of him. He's such a resourceful young man, isn't he Ginny?"

"He sure 'nough is, ma'am," Ginny chuckled. "Ain't nothing that boy can't find."

Madam E. could tell by the look on Rose's face she was greatly disappointed that she hadn't found her friend.

"I tell you what," she said, coming over and placing her hand on Rose's shoulder. "Tomorrow I'll take you out to dinner at Antoine's, one of the finest restaurants in New Orleans. My treat!"

"That would be nice, but that really isn't necessary," Rose said, trying to be polite, but still feeling rather blue.

"I insist. You can't make a trip to New Orleans without trying some of our special cuisine, now can she, Ginny?"

"No-sir-re, ma'am. Nothin' better than Antoine's crawfish étouffée with a side a red beans and rice! Um, um. My mouth be waterin' just thinkin' 'bout it!" Ginny closed her eyes and shook her head softly.

"Well, it's all settled then. Ginny, try and keep the noise in the kitchen to a minimum so Rose gets a good night's sleep. I'm sure she's not used to the unusual hours we keep around here."

Then she turned back to Rose. "I'll be busy most of the evening taking care of business, my dear, so I won't be available. If you need anything, just ask Virginia or Millie. I'm sure they can help you with most anything."

Then she turned and started walking back out toward the parlor before she turned around again.

"Oh, Ginny, I almost forgot. We're a little short on cocktail glasses. Could you send Millie out with some, please? Oh, and one more thing. The new girls won't be working this evening. Could you please send up some dinner to their room, and give them a little dessert? We need to fill them out a bit. I think the last place those two worked fed them but once a day, if that!"

"Will do ma'am, but the other girls'll be jealous!"

"They have nothing to be jealous about. If they complain, you just send them to me."

"Yes'um!" Ginny said with satisfaction and went back to her slicing.

~ ~ ~

Dinner that evening was delicious; almost as good as Grandma B.'s roast beef. *Funny*, Rose thought as she sat picking at her food, not really hungry but forcing herself to eat to be polite, *didn't I eat roast beef my first night on the Capitol?* Then she remembered she had tasted it twice that evening. That brought the sight of Peter back into view, and spoiled her appetite completely. She couldn't make herself eat another bite.

"You ain't so hungry, child?" Ginny asked, concerned.

"No, I'm sorry. It is very good, but I just lost my appetite."

"Well, you ain't et a slice a my buttermilk pie yet. I made it special just for you!"

"Oh, I'm sorry Ginny. I just can't. Perhaps tomorrow. I'll save room for it after dinner. Why don't I make up a couple plates for the new girls while you finish your dinner?" Rose suggested, wanting to keep busy.

"That'd be mighty sweet a' ya, Rose," Ginny said. "Millie's almost done, and she can take'em right up."

Rose dished up their food, including two large pieces of Ginny's buttermilk pie, poured a couple of glasses of milk, and set it all on a tray. Millie stood up and took hold of the tray to take it up stairs but nearly tipped it over. Rose stepped up to help without thinking.

"How 'bout I take up the tray, and you take the milk glasses?"

"Sure!" Millie instantly accepted.

Once Rose stepped out of the kitchen and into the hallway, she realized what she actually had volunteered to do—she was going to the bedroom of a call girl! And just as they were walking toward the steps, a small bell that hung above the front door rang, as two gentlemen in suits and hats stepped inside. They smiled widely at Rose and Millie, sending a rush of color into Rose's cheeks. Madam E. instantly appeared from her office door to greet them. She smiled and nodded at the girls then greeted the gentleman, took their hats, and ushered them into the parlor.

"Mr. C., welcome!"

The younger of the two gentlemen smiled broadly at Madam E., handing her his hat. The second gentleman was also smiling but timidly. He took off his hat quickly after noticing that Madam E. was waiting to take his, as well.

"This is William, Miss Dubay."

The middle-aged gentleman tipped his head slightly at the introduction. Madam E. repeated the gesture.

"He's in town from England. I'm sure you can find him a suitable escort for this evening. We are planning on going to the theatre after a quick bite."

"Well, of course. Right this way, gentlemen."

As Rose mounted the steps, she looked into the parlor and saw the stockinged leg of a woman just inside the parlor door. The Spanish-looking woman, Tess, who was sitting opposite the parlor doors, sat up straight in her chair as the gentlemen entered the room. Ruth stood to greet the new arrivals wearing her silky purple gown.

"Robert!" she called out with excitement, as she greeted the young man with a kiss on the cheek.

"Come on!" Millie called from half-way up the steps.

Rose pulled herself away from the scene in the parlor, stepping up just behind Millie. Rose could hear a phonograph begin to play. It was like the one in Monica's house, but Monica's mother would never have played a tune like the one that was playing now—a jazzy number which made a person want to tap their toes and dance.

When they got to the top of the steps, there was a door directly to their left. To the right there were two more doors. The balcony turned the corner where there were a second set of doors, then it turned once more, parallel with the front of the house, where two additional doors stood. This completed a three-quarter circle walkway around the inside of the second story with the sparkling, glass chandelier hanging down from a chain in the middle.

Millie stopped at the third door and set down one of her glasses of milk so she could open the door. Rose thought it was impolite to open the door without even knocking.

As they walked into the room, they saw the two young girls sitting close together on the bed, which sat against the wall to their right. Both wore pretty pink, chenille bathrobes.

"We…brought…you…some dinner!" Millie said, speaking loudly and slowly, as if the girls were deaf. "Here, set it over here," Millie instructed Rose, pointing to a small table under the windows on the left side of the room.

When Rose set the tray down, she took a better look around the room. The walls were painted a sky blue color. There were white, sheer curtains with a ruffled edge on the windows above the closed, white shades. The floorboards were painted a cocoa brown and covered by two oval, floral rugs, one on each side of the bed. The bed itself was larger than anything Rose had ever seen and was beautifully set; the comforter was a tasteful pink and blue floral pattern which matched the stuffed, cloth-covered chair that sat at the small table. Rose recognized it from the one that was now sitting on the porch next to her cot. There was a door on the other side of the bed that stood open to a small closet and a set of hooks all along the wall right behind the door. Underneath the hooks sat a wooden stand which held a white porcelain pitcher, basin, and towel.

Rose would find out later that all the girls' rooms had a similar pitcher and basin, despite a fully functioning bathroom just down the hall. They used it to wash and expertly milk the men they were entertaining to ensure they didn't have a venereal disease, which would put them in the hospital and out of a job. Penicillin, the treatment for VD, wouldn't be discovered until 1940.

The girls perked up when they saw the tray of food, standing but not daring to move toward it, eyeing Rose and Millie carefully.

"Go ahead," Millie said, walking over to them and gently nudging them toward the food. "You…can…eat," she said slowly and loudly again, making an eating motion with her hands and directing them with her eyes to the tray of food.

Rose took the plates off the tray, set them on the small round table, and looked around the room for another chair. There was a small wooden chair on the opposite side of the bed next to the basin, so she went over and got it. Now both girls could sit down and eat.

Why didn't Malcolm bring me this chair, the stinker? Rose wondered to herself.

"We'll…be…back…up…for the…dishes…later," Millie said, and she walked toward the door, motioning for Rose to follow her. Both of the new girls stood at the table watching Millie and Rose leave, not making a move to eat until they were out the door. Millie closed the door and stopped, putting her ear to the door to listen.

"Don't think they speak a word a' English," Millie said. "I can hear'em talkin', but I can't understand a word. They must be talkin' chink."

"Chink? What do you mean chink?"

"Mamma says they're chinks."

"You mean Chinese?" Rose finally understood what she was saying. "Actually, I think they're from Japan. At least that's where Madam E.'s trunks were from."

"Japan, China…, don't make no never mind ta me; they all chinks. Ya see'em all over the fish market and at the wharf talkin' chink to each other."

Then Millie squinted her eyes, pulled up her upper lip to reveal her not-so-white teeth and made a funny biting motion like a rabbit. Rose had to giggle at the funny face, but she stopped herself short, knowing it was impolite to laugh at other people just because they were different. She had learned that lesson a long time ago from her mother when the strangers would stop by the farm looking for food or work. They were usually different type of folk, but her mother reminded her they were all God's children and as such, deserved our respect. Rose had never forgotten that.

"Come on, Millie. We better get back and help Ginny with the rest of the food for the evening," Rose said in a more serious tone.

As Rose stood at the top of the steps, she could hear the music coming from below mixed with the din of voices talking and laughing. She took a deep breath and headed back down slowly.

As she gazed out of the corner of her eye toward the parlor, she noticed two more gentlemen in suits had joined the first two. They were each sitting with two girls whom Rose hadn't seen before. One of the women was colored. *She must be Sadie, Millie's mother*, Rose thought; she looked just like Millie except her skin color was a light, honey brown. She wore a frilly, light-green dress which showed off her generous bosoms. She had hiked the skirt up more than normal to show off her shapely, light brown legs. Sadie's hair was as straight as the young Asian girls, but it was stiff and curled smartly around her face to accentuate her perfectly proportioned features.

The last woman had to be Bridget. She had short blond hair and was younger-looking than Ruth, but she didn't have Ruth's pretty face, and she didn't have the same ease that Ruth seemed to have. Ruth talked and laughed with two of the men with ease, where as Bridget sat rigidly in her chair, smiling politely and nodding as she listened to the man sitting next to her. She was dressed in a white satin gown which showed off every lovely, shapely curve she had. Her ensemble was accentuated by sparkly, slip-on heels and a white, silk flower in her hair. She was ravishing. A fact that invariably distracted most gentlemen from her lack of finer social skills.

Rose took this all in within the few seconds it took her to come down the steps and slowly make her way around the staircase toward the kitchen. It wasn't as bad as she thought it might be; these women didn't look any different than some of the women Rose saw at the ballet in St. Louis. She didn't think about the fact however, that they were dressed for an entirely different reason. She breathed a small sigh of relief as she stepped back in to the kitchen, comfortable in her intentional ignorance.

Ginny was cutting up the roast beef to make into small, finger sandwiches for the patrons, when Madam E. stepped back into the kitchen.

"Is the tea ready?" she asked.

"Yes'um, it's in the frig," Ginny responded.

Madam E. removed the glass pitcher from the refrigerator. Its contents looked a little darker than the tea Rose had earlier in the day—a stronger brew to keep the ladies awake well into the evening. Then Madam E. went back into the parlor.

After Rose helped Ginny and Millie get the hors d'oeuvres ready for the evening, they cleaned up the kitchen, then Ginny and Millie returned to working on the laundry. Rose tried to help with that as well, but Ginny wouldn't hear of it, so Rose went out to the porch to read.

As she stepped out onto the porch, she noticed there were a few new pieces of furniture; her suit case was now sitting on a small chest, and there was a night stand on the other side of the bed, with a note sitting on top of it.

Rose walked over and opened it.

If there is anything else I can get the Mademoiselle, don't hesitate to ask. It would be my pleasure!

~ Malcolm

Rose smiled, went over to her suitcase, and pulled out a new book she had picked up at their last stop in Vicksburg, Mississippi— *Gone with the Wind*. She sat down on her cot and began to read. The distant sounds of music, laughter, and the occasional ring of the phone or the bell above the door faded between the lines of Miss Scarlet and Rhett Butler. Before Rose knew it, a couple hours had passed.

"Don't ya think ya ought to be headin' to bed, Miss Rose?" Ginny asked, surprising Rose out of her enchantment. "It's nigh onta ten o'clock."

"Oh, I suppose you're right," Rose said, yawning and stretching her limbs.

"I'll help ya get these here curtains down, so you can change with a little more privacy."

"Thanks, Ginny,"

"No problem, child," Ginny smiled, still tickled at Rose's politeness toward her.

~ ~ ~

Rose laid on her cot with just a hint of the city lights softly illuminating her room. She could still hear the muffled sounds through the closed porch door, but not enough to keep her awake, and not enough to keep her from finally recalling the day's events at the dock.

She had been able to keep her mind busy most of the day with all the new things she had seen and encountered, but lying there all alone in the dark, tired from a long day, she broke down and began to weep.

The sight of Peter's sinister face initiated the tears; then the thought of her predicament kept them flowing; she had lost her best friend in a city full of strangers, and she had been taken in by the owner of a bordello. She had no idea what she was going to do if Madam E. couldn't find Lilly Mae. Her fatigue and current predicament were clouding her judgment.

A blanket of loneliness crept over Rose, and she pulled her knees up tight to her chest. She had felt this feeling before, after Grandma B.'s death—surrounded by people, yet feeling very much alone. She got up out of bed, opened up her carpet bag, and pulled out Grandma B.'s metal starch box. She held it close to her chest as she crawled back onto her cot. She rolled on her side, clutching it like a doll. She didn't need to look at the contents; all she needed was someone she knew close by. Rose pulled the sheet up to her chin and wept silently until she fell asleep.

ℬ 14 ℭ

What do you do when given a bowl of lemons, or perhaps in this case, a crate of tomatoes? Well, in this instance, you make a pot of jambalaya, with a side of cornbread, please.

~ ~ ~

There was a clomp, clomp sound in the distant haze of sleep, then a louder squeak of a spring, and finally a slam of a wooden door closing abruptly, which made Rose sit bolt upright in bed, instantly awake. Ever since that night on the boat, noises in the night were an issue for Rose. It made sleeping difficult at times, especially in a strange place.

A figure stood at the door, leaning on the door jam in the shadows. Rose couldn't make out who it was. Her heart began to race. She could only think of one person who would try and find her in the night. She was trying to convince herself, without much success, that there was no way Peter could have found her here. *Maybe he asked the cabbie! Maybe he, or one of his friends, knew of Madam E.!* she thought frantically. *What am I going to do?*

Then it hit her—the smell she remembered from that night on the boat. He had been drinking again. Her body convulsed at the thought, her heart beat faster, and her stomach made a fist which pressed directly down on a bladder that needed instant relief. Her eyes strained desperately to make out the figure, just waiting for him to move. Finally, after what seemed like an hour, the person stood up and staggered toward her. But it wasn't until he almost fell across Rose's cot that she found out who it was.

"Damn!" a female voice exclaimed, trying to push herself back upright. The woman finally found the wall next to the cot to make it to a semi-upright standing position. "Who done put disss damn thing here?" she said with slurred speech. Rose moved slightly to try and keep out of her way.

The woman reeled around to face Rose when she saw the movement, leaning down just inches from Rose's face.

"Who...the hell...*are you?*" she said, sending rancid puffs of air at Rose with every word. The woman's eyes blinked and squinted to try and make out who was sitting in front of her, through the dark, which robbed her of light, and the inebriation that fogged her brain. She finally plopped down on the cot next to Rose as if her legs would no longer hold her.

"I'm Rose," she replied. Rose didn't feel the need to elaborate further to a drunk that she didn't know.

"Madam got so many girls now she be keep'em out here?" she said.

Then unexpectedly, she laughed out loud and stopped just as suddenly, as if the joke left her as quickly as it had come.

"I's got ta talk da Madam," she continued.

She stood, staggered forward, then fell over the stuffed chair Rose had pulled out from the corner of the porch when she was changing for bed. The racket she made caused Ginny to open the kitchen door to see what was going on.

"Roxie! What the hell you doin' here?" Ginny asked, bending down to help the drunken woman to her feet.

"I's come ta see da Madam," she said, stiffly brushing off her dirty, wrinkled dress, as if that would somehow improve its sorry state. "I needs a job, an' I knows the Madam can hep me out."

"Oh, you drunk ag'in, ain't ya? You know the madam don't take ta no drinkin' or no drugin', not from the girls and not from the help, neither."

"I know, I know, just git me some java," Roxie ordered, staggering into the kitchen. "An' I'll be right quicker than ya can shake a leg."

Roxie teetered over to the kitchen table and dropped herself down into one of the chairs. She dropped her head on her arms, as if it, was too heavy to hold upright. Rose stood in the doorway, not sure she should enter into this and not sure what she could do to help, anyway.

Ginny poured Roxie a cup of coffee, then sat down across from her. She tapped nervously on the table, looking toward the parlor door every so often.

"You best drink your coffee right quick. If the Madam catches ya here when you're like this, ya ain't gonna be getting' nothin' from her 'ceptin maybe her shoe on your backside."

"But I need a job somethin' fierce, an I know she's got connections."

"I been workin' for Madam E. for fifteen years now, and I knows ya ain't gonna get anywheres all pickled like ya is."

"All right, all right," Roxie said, admitting defeat. "But can I have a slice a that buttermilk pie?" She eyed the pie sitting next to her on the table.

Ginny got up hurriedly. "All right, but ya gotta eat it somewhere's else." She hastily sliced a piece of pie, put it on a plate, gave Roxie a fork, and shoved her back out the porch door. "Bring back the plate tomorrow!" she called out to her, before shutting the porch door behind her. Ginny walked hastily back into the kitchen and shut the kitchen door.

"Who was that, Ginny?" Rose asked

"That there be our last maid. She got ta drinkin' so's we never knew if'in she was gonna show up most days. The Madam gave'er plenty a chances too; even offered ta help her take the cure, but she wouldn't say she had a problem, the fool."

"Will Madam E. help her find a job?"

"If Roxie can stay straight long enough ta ask her, but not too many folks want'ta hire a drunk." Ginny walked over to the stove and started filling up plates full of food. A buzzer sounded, startling Rose.

"That's Ruth ag'in. I knew when Madam put in those damn buzzers it was gonna be trouble. Millie, come out here," she called to Millie who was working in the laundry room. "Take this here plate up ta Ruth, and hurry 'fore she drives *me* ta drink!"

"I can take one up for you, Ginny," Rose offered, feeling very awake for four in the morning.

"That's all right, child. Ya best be gettin' yourself back ta sleep. It's late. Sorry for that there nonsense with Roxie. She ain't a mean drunk, just a stupid one. Actually, everybody gets stupid when they get drunk," she chuckled to herself.

Rose went to the bathroom, then somewhat reluctantly went back out onto the porch. She opened up the porch door to make sure Roxie had left, then she latched the hook on the door, and laid back down on the cot.

~ ~ ~

Rose woke at eight the next morning, a little later than her normal six-thirty wake up on riverboat time, but then she wasn't usually woken up at four in the morning by drunks, either. *Well, only one other time*, Rose reluctantly recalled. She literally shook off the thought and got dressed for the day. She put on a dress, the lightest one she had. She was going out to dinner with Madam E. today, and she could tell it was going to be a warm one; the heat of the day was already seeping through her make-shift curtains.

Ginny had left Rose a note on the kitchen table letting her know where the bread and jam were, and the left over roast from the night before, so she could make herself some breakfast, since Ginny didn't get back to the house until about two in the afternoon.

"Boy, they do keep strange hours here," Rose said to herself. *I suppose that goes along with the business*, she thought.

As she sat down to breakfast, she heard a knock on the porch door. When she slowly moved away the temporary curtain which hung in front of the door, she discovered Malcolm standing there, one hand behind his back.

"*Bon maten*, Mademoiselle Krantz! May I come in?"

"How do you know my last name?" Rose asked as she unlatched the door to let him in. "No, no don't tell me: Malcolm Connelly is all-seeing and all-knowing."

"Mademoiselle is a quick learner."

"You can call me Rose."

"Then a rose for a Rose," he smiled, bowing slightly and pulling out a single red rose from behind his back.

Rose wasn't sure what she should do; she didn't really know Malcolm, but she didn't want to be rude. There was no harm in accepting a flower, was there? Or was that being too forward? She had never been given a flower before, and it was the most deep-colored, velvet red rose she had ever seen. He had been very kind and gotten her those things for her room…. The justifications ran endlessly through her mind, and all pointed to one conclusion—she timidly accepted the rose with a shy smile. She brought it to her nose and closed her eyes, inhaling the fresh, sweet scent.

"It's beautiful, Malcolm. Thank you."

"Now we need to find a vase," he said, walking into the kitchen and opening up cupboards in his search for a vase. "Ah, here's one."

He put water in it, took the flower from Rose, placed it in the vase, and set it on her end-table on the porch.

"I see I interrupted your breakfast. *Après vous*," he said, bowing slightly and sweeping his hand widely over the kitchen table.

He waited for Rose to sit down, then he sat down across from her.

"I think I'll try some of this wonderful bread myself."

He sliced a large piece of bread off the loaf, and proceeded to put large dollops of butter and jam on it.

"Thank you for the table and chest."

"Not a problem."

"If you came by to talk to someone, I think they're all asleep."

"Yes, I know. They keep different hours here, so I thought you might like some company."

"You know, Malcolm, I really don't know these people. Madam E. just picked me up at the dock," Rose started, then decided that didn't sound quite right. "I mean, I had lost my friend, and since I had never been in New Orleans before, she said she would help me…, find my friend, that is."

"Don't worry your pretty little head none, *mamzel*. I know you don't really belong in this here house. But even if you did, it don't make no never mind ta me. Let me assure you, these are good folks. They'll treat you right," he said, nodding his head with confidence. Then his countenance changed, taking on a somber appearance. "What's the name of that friend you're lookin' for?"

"Her name is Lilly Mae Martin. Do you know her?" Rose asked hopefully.

"Can't say as I do."

"She's colored!" Rose added for clarity.

"Nope, still don't know her."

Then he stopped, picked up his bread and started moving the jam around on top of it mindlessly with his finger.

"But Ma-dam knows some pretty important people in this town. A woman in her business makes a lot'a connections. She even knows the good mayor, Robert Maestri."

"Really!" Rose sat mesmerized by the melodic sound of his voice and the prospect of more information about the Madam. Living in a bordello was unnerving and interesting all at the same time.

"Yeah," he continued, perking up when he noticed he had Rose's undivided attention. "You'd be surprised at who walks through those doors. The Ma-dam runs a first class establishment," he finished, shoving the last piece of bread in his mouth. "But enough a this. How 'bout we see some sights!"

"That would be wonderful!" Rose agreed enthusiastically, grateful for some distraction and eager to see more of the city. "But I have to be back before noon. I have a dinner date with Madam E. that I don't want to be late for. Hopefully, she'll have some news about Lilly Mae for me. Let me just clean up these dishes, then we can go," she added, picking up the plate in front of Malcolm and placing it on top of her own.

"Now, let me do that!" Malcolm said, taking the plates from Rose and walking over to the sink to wash them.

Rose stood gawking at Malcolm. She had never known a man who volunteered to do dishes. She picked up her milk glass and gave that to him, then put the butter and jam away in the refrigerator, and stored the bread back in the bread box.

~ ~ ~

"Millie's already showed me around some yesterday," Rose said, as they headed out the front door.

"Yes, but I know places Millie has never even heard of. It would take me a year to show you everything I know in the city. The Connelly's are an old Na Orlins family. My great-great-great-great grandmother came over on a ship from Saint Domingue. She was a *gens de couleur libres*—a free person of color," Malcolm said proudly. "And a *placage* of a Frenchman here in the city."

"A *placage*?"

"A concubine. That was not uncommon back then."

Rose was enthralled as Malcolm recounted the history of his family and the wonderful city in which he lived, as they strolled along its narrow streets. He told Rose about its beginnings on the levee which was now the French Quarter, when it was surrounded by swamp and used by Indians as a portage to and from the Mississippi. He even knew about the city's inception in the early 1700s, when it was named Nouvelle Orleans after the then regent of France, Phillippe, the Duc d' Orleans.

Malcolm spoke with a love in his voice; this was his city, and these were his people. He had a connectedness to where he lived which Rose could not understand, but she still had to admire. Unlike Malcolm, she had never felt tied to anyplace; it was the people who held Rose to wherever she happened to be.

"The so-called owners of this land were many: the French, the Spanish, then finally the Americans in 1803 when the Louisiana territory was purchased from the financially strapped *Misyeu* Napoleon."

"Yah, I remember studying about the Louisiana Purchase in history class."

"At that time, it was inhabited by French and Spanish Creoles (native born), Indians, Blacks—both free and slaves—and Germans, some of whom were not the cream of the European crop, mind you." Malcolm continued with relish. "Ya see Rose, in the early years the, Europeans tried to clean out their cities by shipping over their prisoners and poor, men and women alike, so back then a lot of the people who lived here were not here by choice.

"Is that when your great-great-great-great grandmother came over?" Rose asked.

"She came over in 1791 during Haiti's slave revolt on the sugar plantations, when Na Orlins was owned by Spain."

"That would have been quite a time, wouldn't it?"

"I'd have loved to live in the city 'round then. But it's still a pretty busy place yet. You see, NaOrlins has the advantage of being both on the busiest river in the nation, and also being a major port for ocean going vessel. That's one of the reason's you see so many different people here abouts. It's quite unique that way. Always has been and probably always will be."

As Malcolm talked, it seemed to Rose that New Orleans had always been a place where a mix of people lived, and a place which had always been shaped by the river. Those many hundreds of years ago, that mighty brown river she had come to know and love had made the sandy, silty crescent which New Orleans still sat on to that day.

Before Rose realized it, they had walked many blocks and were standing in front of a pair of thin, weather-worn, white doors. Malcolm opened one of the tall, wooden doors and bowed slightly to let Rose in before him. They stepped into a small entryway. Malcolm raised his hand briefly and gave a quick, "*Bonjour,*" to a woman who was sitting behind a desk in an adjacent room, before taking Rose down a small hallway.

Rose was excited and scared at the same time. As she stepped into the narrow, dark hallway, she realized she didn't even know this young man she was following. He seemed nice enough, but she had learned a couple of important things living in St. Louis—things she would never have had to think about in rural Wisconsin—you can't believe everything you see, and you need to be on your guard when you're out and about in a big city. Now she was on her guard.

"Where are we going?"

"Someplace special. You'll see."

They went through another door, then turned right into another dark hallway. Rose noticed there were now bricks under her feet instead of carpet. When she looked behind her, she saw an opening which led to the street, closed off by a wrought iron door. *No way out that way*, she thought to herself, keeping her exist strategies ever present.

Finally, they stepped out into a large courtyard. Rose was transfixed. It was beautiful; there was vegetation everywhere: small flowering bushes, and trees reaching toward the opening above them, large planters with ferns and palms placed at every post of a wooden, white-washed balcony which ran along the left and front sides of the courtyard. There were steps to their left, leading up to the balcony, and to their right, a cement wall with a doorway in the center. The whole wall was covered with ivy and colored with the most delicate flowering purple and white orchids. In the center of it all was a fountain. Its base glittered from small bits of colored glass and tile embedded into it. It encircled a naked mermaid holding a seashell that overflowed with water, which trickled softly into the basin below.

"It's beautiful, Malcolm!"

"I thought you might like it," he said.

He grasped her hand and led her through the opening in the vine-covered wall. They walked into another courtyard, this one a bit smaller than the last, and it also had a fountain. This one flowed out of a bust of the sun, attached to a brick wall straight in front of them. It flowed into a half-circle cement pool which was attached to the wall beneath it, and it too was covered with vines.

This courtyard was also filled with plants, along with two small tables and chairs. There were three open doors, two of which led to staircases to the second and third stories. The air was heavy with moisture, which made the well-worn bricks beneath their feet damp and shinny.

Rose stood in silence gazing at the wondrous site, when she finally realized she was still holding Malcolm's hand. She quickly let go, her face flushing a flattering shade of pink.

"What is this place?" Rose asked, wanting to divert Malcolm's attention.

"It's a hotel. I come here when I want to escape the city."

"Yah, I can understand. I would never have guessed we were still in New Orleans," she said, admiring the well-hidden oasis. "Do you work here too?

"You might say that. I work in a lot of places, but I don't work for anyone but myself."

"What do you do exactly, Malcolm, if you don't mind my asking?" Rose said as she sat down on the edge of the fountain.

"Well, ya could say that I'm a one-man supplier. If there is something you want, most likely I can get it for ya. You need a nineteenth century settee—I can get it for ya. You'd like a bottle of 1889 French Champagne—I'm your man. There's a run in your last pair of stockings, and ya need a new pair—I know just where to get the best in town—all for a price, mind you, all for a price."

"You're amazing, Malcolm, truly amazing!"

Malcolm smiled and leaned against the brick wall next to Rose, pleased at the compliment

Rose gazed down into the pool of water, watching it ripple as the endless dribbles of water hit the surface and bounced back up again. Rose closed her eyes and listened to the droplets of water making their wet, tinkling music, pulling in a deep breath of the fresh, moist air, filling her heart and refreshing her soul. This was a magical place. She was glad Malcolm had brought her here.

Rose wasn't the only one breathing deeply; Malcolm was taking in the beauty that sat before him. He had never seen someone so lovely. The first time he saw her in the hallway, he thought he was looking at a goddess. But this Venus, he could tell, had a beauty which was more than just superficial. Beautiful women were a dime a dozen in New Orleans. Their face or their figure would make you turn your head, but once they moved or opened their mouths, the illusion would vanish. This one though, she had a way about her. The way she moved, the way she spoke; he could tell she had confidence and a caring heart which led directly to her brilliant blue eyes. This one he wanted to learn more about. This one he wasn't going to let go of easily.

Rose's meditation was interrupted by a gentle touch on her shoulder.

"We best be gettin' back, Mademoiselle Krantz," Malcolm said softly, looking at his pocket watch. "It's almost noon."

"Oh my, I forgot!" Rose said standing quickly. "And please, call me Rose."

Rose had to keep her eyes glued to Malcolm to ensure she didn't lose sight of him as he swiftly weaved in and out of buildings. She had lost one guide already, and she was determined not to lose another. He took this short-cut and that ally, at one point walking right through a hotel courtyard on their way back to Rampart Street. He would look back occasionally and smile, making sure Rose was still behind him. *No wonder he's as thin as a rail,* Rose thought. *He moves too fast to put on any weight.*

~ ~ ~

Madam E. was waiting in her study as the two entered the front door, the bell ringing above their heads as they entered.

"Come in," she said, somehow knowing it was Rose. Malcolm silently tipped his cap to Rose with a bow, then exited back out the front door without saying a word.

"Was young Malcolm showing you some sights?" Madam E. asked, as Rose stepped into the room, not looking up from the papers she was working on at her desk.

"Yes! He took me to the most beautiful place! It was a hotel with two lovely courtyards. It was filled with flowers and plants and had two splendid fountains."

"I'm glad you enjoyed yourself," she said, turning around to look at Rose. "Malcolm is a very nice young man, a bit rough around the edges perhaps, but I would guess that comes from taking care of one's self for so long."

"You mean Malcolm doesn't live with his family?"

"I suspect Malcolm hasn't lived with his family for some time. I'm not sure where the boy actually resides, but he is very resourceful and can take care of himself and others quite well."

"Who else does he take care of?" Rose asked without thinking her inquiry may not be any of her business. Her curiosity about this young man who was giving her so much of his attention was overriding her good manners. *Maybe he has other women he gives a lot of attention to,* Rose wondered.

"I know he keeps track of his grandmother in St. Bernard Parish."

"Oh," Rose said, a bit embarrassed by what she was thinking.

"Well, I hope you're hungry for some authentic New Orleans cuisine!"

"Oh, yes, very much so!"

"Shall we go then?" Madam E. asked, throwing down some papers she held in her hand. "I'm tired of looking at this bookwork, and I've only been at it for fifteen minutes."

Rose was quiet on the way to the restaurant. She had many questions she would have liked to ask Madam E., but most of them she thought were too impolite to ask. *How did the Madam get into this business? How many gentlemen come to the house each evening, and what kind of men are they? How much do they pay? How long has she been doing this kind of work?* All these questions and more were coursing through Rose's mind. But the most pressing question Rose had was about her friend, Lilly Mae.

After they had been seated in the restaurant, Madam E. finally broke the silence.

"You're very quiet this afternoon, my dear. Is there something on your mind?"

"Well, I was wondering if you had found out anything about my friend."

"No, I'm sorry. I have not. New Orleans is quite a large city, as you may know. I promise, I will let you know as soon as I find out anything."

Rose silently looked over the menu with disinterest, having lost her appetite at the bad news.

When the beautifully arranged dish was set in front of her she had to admit, she enjoyed the unique flavors, but she still had trouble making herself eat. She had decided on the crawfish étouffée Ginny had mentioned, not really knowing what anything was and not really caring much, anyway.

Madam E. tried to ease Rose's obvious melancholy by trying to engage her in conversation.

"So, what year are you in high school?"

"I started my first year in St. Louis," Rose replied without elaborating.

"Do you plan to continue here in New Orleans with your friend?"

"Lilly Mae hasn't started high school. She has to work to help her mother out, though she's taken a few night classes to work on her reading and writing," Rose said, brightening up just a bit, thinking about her friend's accomplishments.

"Smart girl. You can't get very far in this world if you can't read or write. I make sure all my girls can read and write."

"Yah, she's done very well considering I taught her to read just over a year ago."

"Well, I look forward to meeting this precocious young lady, and you let me know if the two of you decide you want to go to school. I can set you up at a very good Catholic high school not far from here."

"Thank you! I will."

Rose smiled and dug in to her dinner, suddenly finding her appetite again. Madam E.'s calculating conversation had brought back good memories and renewed hope of seeing her friend again, along with her hunger.

~ ~ ~

The evening rolled on by without a sign of Lilly Mae, then the next evening, and the next, until a whole week had gone by without any trace of her. Rose had even taken to wandering around town on her own during the day. She had turned down the wrong street on one occasion and was immediately turned back after she was propositioned by a scruffy looking gentleman who stepped suddenly out of a doorway, scaring her half to death. After that encounter, she thought it might be best to leave the searching to Miss Dubay. She had already decided not to look along the wharf, in case she would come upon Peter when she was alone. A second encounter with that roustabout, as Grandma B. would call him, was quite enough.

That Sunday Rose made sure she got up early in order to go to mass at St. Louis Cathedral. She wanted to say a prayer to help her find her friend. When she got back from church, Malcolm was in the kitchen, as usual. It was his new custom to join her for a late breakfast, since Rose was having trouble getting to bed much before midnight, despite Ginny's attempts at keeping down the noise in the kitchen. He was standing at the stove, stirring something that smelled spicy and sweet when she walked into the room; the odiferous mix of sausage, ham, peppers and tomatoes blended with the onions and Cajun spices to fill the room with an enticing aroma.

"Ah, back from *Leglis* already! I'm not quite done with the surprise," Malcolm said, turning around to reveal the lovely apron he was wearing. It was obviously one of Ginny's; it almost wrapped around him twice.

"*Leglis?*"

"Excuse me, Mademoiselle. I mean church. *Leglis* is Creole for church. Cooking Jambalaya always brings me back home again."

He turned back to his pot and started to stir it again.

"Oh, there I go, I spoiled the surprise. I thought I would make you a traditional Creole dish my father used to make. I even made some cornbread!" he said proudly, moving over to the skillet and lifting the lid to check on its progress. "This looks done," he said with satisfaction. "Just a few more minutes on the Jambalaya and *dinin* is *serv*! You can't put in the crawfish too early, my *popa* always says. It makes them too rubbery."

Rose smiled at the young man whom she had come to expect each morning. Besides the enjoyment she received from listening to his Creole accent, she was starting to understand what Madam E. had meant when she said he was an interesting young man. In addition to his vast knowledge of New Orleans history, he was an avid reader with an amazing memory. He would often quote famous writers such as Shakespeare or Hawthorne, Joyce or Dickens to name a few. And as it turned out, Malcolm hadn't even gone on to high school. He read the local paper, the *Times Picayune*, so he knew what was going on in the world, but he didn't seem to take world events as seriously as Todd had. And Rose couldn't help but enjoy the compliments and attention he gave her. It made her feel special and somehow more feminine.

Rose sat herself down at the table. She thought this would be a good time to ask Malcolm something that was on her mind.

"Malcolm?"

"Yes, *mo cher*!"

"I was wondering if I could ask you a favor."

"Anything for the flower of my heart!"

"Now, be serious," Rose said, scolding.

"I am serious!" he said, smiling and sitting down in front of her.

"It's been over a week, and Madam E. still hasn't been able to find Lilly Mae." Malcolm's face instantly lost its smile, and he looked down at the table briefly. "I was wondering, since you know so much about New Orleans, maybe you could find my friend for me."

Then Malcolm did something which Rose did not expect; he stood up without speaking and went back to the stove to stir the pot of Jambalaya. Rose looked at him perplexed. She wasn't sure what she had said to offend him, but she obviously had. She had no idea what it could have been; the question seemed innocent enough to her.

It took him a minute, but he finally did speak.

"I'm sorry, Mademoiselle. If the Ma-dam can not find your friend, then I will not be able to find her either," he answered without turning around.

Rose drooped in her chair at the blow his words gave, tears welling in her eyes. The now-familiar feeling of loneliness crept back to rekindle her deep-seated fear that she might never be able to find her friend again. She covered her face with her hands, wetting her palms.

Malcolm reeled around when he heard her soft whimper. He dropped his spoon in the pot and ran over to Rose's side. Kneeling down next to her, he took her in his arms. Rose did not resist; she needed someone to hold her, to make her feel safe and loved. Malcolm wanted to give her that safety, give her that love, but he hated that he was the cause of her obvious pain, a pain which was born of the lie he was obliged to tell.

~ ~ ~

That afternoon Rose knocked on the door to Madam E.'s office.

"Come in," came a soft voice from inside.

"Madam E., I was wondering if I could talk to you."

"Why, of course," she said, standing and moving over to the other side of the room. Rose sat down opposite her.

"I was wondering if I could take you up on your offer to help me get into a school here in New Orleans."

The Madam brightened at the news.

"Why, of course, my dear. May I ask what made to come to this decision?"

"Well, I do want to continue on with high school, and since we can't seem to find Lilly Mae—just yet anyway—I thought I might as well start back to school. I've already missed three weeks of it, so I'll have some catching up to do as it is."

"Very wise choice," Madam E. smiled broadly. "We'll go to St. Joseph's first thing in the morning. I know first-hand they have a first rate program. I've frequently hired some of their lay-teachers for my girls during the summer months."

"Aren't you sleeping in the morning?"

"Yes, you are correct. I usually am asleep, but this is important. I can manage just fine," she said. "The older I get, the less sleep I seem to need."

Rose looked at her. She didn't think she could be much older than thirty-five.

~ ~ ~

The two women stepped out onto the street promptly at seven in the morning, both sharply dressed for the occasion, though Rose thought Madam E. looked more put-together than she herself ever could, especially considering Rose had a full night's sleep, compared to the few hours that Madam E. must have had.

They walked in silence a few blocks before Madam E. spoke.

"Now Rose, I was thinking. A smart girl such as yourself could use a part-time job while she's going to school. I know you told me you had worked for a physician in St. Louis, managing his books and helping him with patients."

"Um hum," Rose agreed, nodding her head.

"And then, of course your experience cooking and cleaning on the riverboats the last two summers is invaluable, as well," she continued, looking straight ahead as she spoke. "I have a proposition for you. I will pay for your education, give you free room and board in exchange for your help with my books and helping Ginny out wherever is needed."

"That is, until I find Lilly Mae," Rose interjected.

"Yes, of course, until we find your friend."

Rose didn't answer immediately. She wasn't sure what she thought about living full time in a brothel. Everyone was nice enough; she had met all the girls at this point, and the others were much more pleasant than Ruth, though even she had seemed to soften a little the last couple of days. *No one has to know where I live,* she thought. *And I really don't have any other place to go at this point.*

Madam E. noticed her hesitation. "And I assure you, Rose. There is no other aspect of my business that you have to be a part of other than behind-the-scenes. And no one at the school has to know where you're living, other than the administrators. I'll see to that," she concluded, seeming to read Rose's mind.

"All right then, that would be fine," Rose agreed.

"Splendid!" Madam E. beamed. "Then we'll have to get you into a proper room, won't we?" Madam E. stopped talking a minute to think. "I know. I have a small room off of my office that would be perfect. It is out of the main flow of traffic, so you should be able to sleep better at night, verses off the busy kitchen."

And the busy parlor! Rose thought.

"We'll get Malcolm to help us move you in there later today," she said, turning her head slightly and smiling at Rose. "He seems to be spending a bit more time at the house than usual, hasn't he?"

Rose blushed slightly and looked down at the sidewalk in front of her. "He is good company," Rose admitted. "And I do so enjoy listening to him talk. He has so much to talk about! Did you know his great-great-great-great grandmother came from Haiti? Her parents sent her and her siblings to New Orleans on a boat in the 1700s to protect them from the slave revolt there!"

"I had no idea!" Madam E. smiled at the obviously smitten Rose.

"He also told me, in the late 1800s New Orleans was one of the major cotton ports in the United States. Probably two-hundred steamers were docked two and three deep along the wharf."

Rose talked all the way to the school, repeating everything Malcolm had told her about his family and his beloved Crescent City.

St. Joseph's was just inside the French Quarter, so it wasn't very far from Madam E.'s house. It was a large facility, taking up a whole city block in part because it had living quarters for some of its students, which included a laundry, dining area, and infirmary. Of course, the chapel took up a good portion of the floor plan along with the classrooms. When they stepped inside the entrance to the school, they were greeted by a young sister in a black habit.

"May I help you?" the sister asked in a pleasant tone.

"Yes, we're looking to enroll this young lady in the academy," Madam E. said as she took off her gloves.

"You'll have to talk to Mother Superior," the young nun said. She stood up from her desk and motioned to Madam E. and Rose. "This way."

Mother Superior was a large woman. She was also in a habit, though her headpiece went past her shoulder, where the young nun's went just to the base of her neck. She was sitting behind an equally large desk. She looked up from her papers as Madam E. and Rose entered the room.

"Mother Superior, this…, lady is interested in enrolling her daughter at St. Joseph's."

"Have a seat," the Mother Superior said, without so much as a crack in her obviously hard facade.

Madam E. sat down on the edge of one of the chairs in front of the desk. Rose imitated her in the other.

"Thank you," Madam E. politely replied.

"So you are interested in our Academy?"

"Yes. This young lady, who is not my daughter, by the way, has completed her freshman year at Soldan in St. Louis and would like to continue her education here."

"I'm afraid we won't be able to accommodate you," Mother Superior replied without feeling.

"She realizes the term has already started, but she is willing to put in some extra time to catch up with the others," Madam E. explained.

"That is of no consequence," the head nun replied curtly. "It is not appropriate for a young lady of her…, occupation to be part of our facility."

Both Madam E. and Rose flinched at her bold assumption. Mother Superior obviously knew of Madam E.'s business and did not want to have one of her girls studying at St. Joseph's. Madam E. deftly regained her composure. Rose looked at Madam E. with questioning eyes. Was she going to explain things? Was she going to tell Mother Superior, Rose wasn't one of her girls?

"This young lady does not work for me," she said, obviously struggling to moderate her reply. "She is not from New Orleans. She was in some difficulty, and I am helping her temporarily with a place to stay. That is all," Madam E. said with a hint of defiance in her voice.

"It matters little to me what circumstance brought her into your care. She is not appropriate for our school."

"I don't think you understand how much I have contributed to this church and your school…"

"I understand all I need to know," Mother Superior said, standing up behind her desk. "Now I must ask you to leave."

At this, the nun who was standing quietly in the back of the room stepped forward toward Madam E. and Rose.

Rose looked again at Madam E., whose cheeks had changed to a rosy pink. She was squeezing the gloves she had in her hands so tightly, her knuckles had turned white.

Rose didn't know what to do. Perhaps she should say something, let Mother Superior know what Madam E. was saying was the truth; she wasn't one of Madam E.'s girls; she had just arrived a week ago with her friend and gotten lost. But she didn't want to insult Madam E. by talking out of turn.

She looked back at the large nun who towered behind her desk with an impervious look on her face. Perhaps they should just leave and forget all about this. She turned back to Madam E.

"That's all right, Madam E...," Rose started with resignation.

The Madam held up her hand to stop Rose from speaking further.

"We are through here, Rose," she said in soft, strained tones. Then she stood and waited for Rose to follow suit. The Mother Superior looked pleased with herself at the decision Madam E. had made as she stepped around to the side of her desk.

Madam E. stopped at the now open door to the office and looked back at the nun.

"Rose, I think we'll have a talk with Father Michael," Madam E. said to her, though Rose knew her words were really meant for the Mother Superior, who was suddenly struck dumb, mumbling something incomprehensible as Madam E. hastily swept Rose out of the room, down the hall, and out of the building.

~ ~ ~

"That woman! How dare she!" Madam E. said through clenched teeth. "She has no idea who she's dealing with!"

Rose didn't know what to do. She had never seen the Madam in such a state before. She felt very uncomfortable with the position she had put Madam E. in and how it obviously upset her.

"I'm sorry, Madam E. I'm sure there are other schools I could get into. I really don't need to go here."

"I know, my dear. That isn't the point," she said as they sped along the sidewalk and around the block. "I despise hypocrites!"

she added angrily, her heels clicking loudly on the sidewalk as they moved briskly along. "She'll take my money for their school and for their charities, but when they themselves are asked for a little charity, they suddenly become selective." They turned another corner. "There's a good example why I haven't stepped inside a church in years."

Rose had to quicken her pace to keep up with Madam E.'s rapid steps.

"You see, Rose, religions—any religion you choose—they are just organizations run by people. And people...well, people like our lovely Mother Superior are flawed. So you have to take organized religion with a grain of salt. They can rarely live up to the doctrine that they profess!"

Before they made it to the end of the block, they turned in to a stately looking home which stood on the corner. Madam E. stood at the front door, straightened her dress, and took a slow, deep breath. Then she opened the screen door, picked up the heavy, metal knocker, and let it fall against the metal plate. She closed the screen and waited.

A few moments later a tall, gray-haired, colored gentleman in a white shirt and black jacket opened the door.

"May I help you?"

"Yes," Madam E. said, letting out another long breath. "I'd like to speak with Father Michael, please."

The colored man opened the door fully, then pushed the screen door open.

"Right this way. He is just finishing up his breakfast."

He motioned the women to sit in the parlor.

"I will let him know you are waiting. May I ask who's calling?" he asked politely.

"Yes, Adam, you may tell him that Madam Dubay is here to speak to him about a very important matter."

The old man grinned slightly at the mention of his name, bowed and walked out of the room.

Rose sat quietly with Madam E. waiting for the priest to appear. Rose busied herself with surveying the room. The parlor was trimmed in the same lovely dark woodwork which covered the walls in the entryway, with furnishings made of a straight, simple design, with dark brown leather upholstery. *This is obviously a man's home*, Rose thought to herself. No soft edges in this room.

There was a large cross on one wall and portraits hanging most everywhere else. The portraits were of old, stiff-looking men; all were in priest's garb, with the largest one being a full-length portrait of a man in what Rose recognized from pictures at St Mary's, were a cardinal's red robes. Rose wanted to look closer at the portraits, but Madam E. was still sitting stiffly on the edge of her chair, so she felt she should continue to sit.

After about five minutes, Adam came back into the room.

"The Father will see you now, Madam, in his study," he said, bowing slightly.

Madam E. and Rose stood to follow him.

"I think it best that you stay here for the moment, Rose," Madam E. said softly, back to her usual calm demeanor.

Rose sat quietly waiting for Madam E.'s return. Sitting in this room, surrounded by all these religious men, started Rose thinking about what the Madam had said to her. True, religions were created by people, but wasn't the basic message of religion—at least the two religions Rose was familiar with—wasn't their message about helping others? *Helping others is good*, Rose thought to herself. But she did understand some of what Madam E. had said; there were articles in the paper every now and then about the KKK, and that was supposed to be a Christian organization. Rose wasn't sure why churches just sat back and let the KKK terrorize whomever they pleased. That was *very* un-God like. Didn't Jesus even berate and cast the merchants out of his temple?

Madam E. had revealed to Rose a chink in the otherwise spotless armor of Rose's faith, a kink which would eventually led to a deeper understanding of how she defined herself and the world around her.

After about five minutes of sitting alone, Rose thought it was probably safe to stand and get a closer look at the men whose portraits hung on the walls. Rose stepped up first to the man in red.

Rose had always liked the bright red robes of the cardinals, with their funny little hats toped with a large, red pom-pom. As she looked at the smile on the pleasant looking man's face, she was struck by an amusing thought: *I wonder why the color of a prominent man of the church, is also the color that places like I am staying at are known for.* She also wondered which tradition came first.

Just then, Madam E. stepped back into the room, followed by a young man with short, very red hair.

"Rose, this is Father Michael O'Brien."

Madam E. gestured to the young man who stood next to her in black pants and a plain white tee shirt. Rose had never seen a priest in regular clothes. She was a bit embarrassed by the site. "He has arranged for you to go to St. Joseph's. Isn't that lovely?"

Rose was dumb-struck; how had Madam E. arranged this when the Mother Superior wanted nothing to do with them?

"Pleased to meet such a bonny lass." The pleasant young man smiled and extended out his hand to shake Rose's firmly. "Miss Dubay tells me you hail from Wisconsin."

"Yes…, that's right," Rose spoke hesitantly, still not sure about the arrangements.

"My mother's originally from Wisconsin, round about Milwaukee way."

"I'm from the Prairie Du Chien area."

Rose smiled. She was warmed by hearing the familiar accent of her mother and her mother's family.

"My mother's Irish too. She was an O'Leary before she met my father."

"Well, saints preserve us! It's a small world now isn't it, Miss Dubay."

"Yes, a very small world, father," Madam E. said with a smile. "We shouldn't be keeping you any longer, father. I'm sure you have work to do."

"Oh, my work is right here," he said, putting his arm around Rose's shoulders as he followed Madam E. toward the front door. "Helping young ladies such as Rose get the opportunities they need to help them on their way. That's why God put us on this here earth, now isn't it, Miss Krantz? He wants us to help others, that is, after we take care of our family and give thanks to the good Lord," he finished, letting go of Rose and looking her into her eyes.

Rose smiled widely, looking up at the handsome young man with strawberry red hair. She had heard these same words come out of her mother's mouth many times. *This must be a good omen,* Rose thought. *I must be meant to be here!*

"Now, you come by my home first thing tomorrow, and I'll walk you over to Sister Ann's office to get you enrolled," he said with a twinkle in his eye. "You do want to start right away?"

"Oh, yes! I'd love it!" Rose replied enthusiastically.

"Then it's all settled," he said, opening the door.

"Thank you, Father!" Rose said, beaming from ear-to-ear.

"Well, you're very welcome, my dear. You'll have to come by after you get settled in with your studies, and we can talk about our families. I still have family there in Wisconsin, ya know."

"Oh, I'd like that very much!"

"It's a date then." He turned to Madam E., "If there's anything else I can be helpin' ya with Miss DuBay, please don't hesitate ta call."

"Thank you, Father. And I'll have…, those papers sent by this afternoon."

"No need to rush, Madam. Take your time," he said with a smile. "Have a nice day now, and God be with you both." Then he lifted his right hand in that familiar sign of blessing—the index finger extended with the other fingers softly curled in succession.

Rose took the blessing to heart and sighed with a comfortable feeling of home renewed in her heart.

~ ~ ~

Rose's warm feeling for St. Joseph's was shaken however, after her second encounter with Mother Superior—Sister Ann Marie. Father Michael brought Rose to her office the next morning as promised and introduced her to the nun as if they hadn't already met. He made sure Sister Ann knew what was to happen and left Rose there alone with the nun and her assistant.

Sister Ann Marie was obviously put out by the fact that Rose was going to go to St. Joseph's after all, and she had a chip on her shoulder the entire time Rose attended the school. She even tried to block Rose from going in to the eleventh grade when the other Sisters recommended she be moved up, since the classes Rose had taken at Soldan had put her academically above her fellow tenth grade students at St. Joseph's. Rose didn't want to tell Father Michael about it, but when Madam E. found out – thanks to Ginny, who couldn't keep a secret to save her own soul—she paid a visit to the priest, and it was all arranged. Rose knew after that incident, Sister Ann Marie was just going to be one of those people who would never like her. So she tried to stay out of trouble and away from Sister Anna as best she could.

While Rose was getting acclimated to St. Joseph's, she was also learning her unusual, though interesting, part-time job with Madam E. It was part of her education she did not expect. First on Madam E's list of tasks for Rose was to straighten out her books.

"As you'll see, my dear, bookkeeping is not my strong suit. I can keep my customer cards up-to-date and accurate," she said, touching the box she had on her desk, with its large note cards neatly stacked behind alphabetized tabs. "But my finances are another matter."

To Rose's dismay, Madam E. opened an oblong box stuffed haphazardly with bills and small receipts. There was also a ledger book equally overflowing with small bits of paper. She happily handed it to Rose.

"You see, for me this is the last thing I am thinking about. Keeping my customers happy is what I excel at and what is most important to me. The financial end of things is important, mind you—it pays the bills—but if the customers aren't happy then the money means very little and, I have found, isn't forthcoming."

She sat back in her chair with a contemplative look on her face. "It may seem strange to you, but most men who visit my establishment are looking for more than just sex."

Rose blinked at her last word, which she said so matter-of-factly.

"Of course there are those who are looking for sex alone, but that is just part of it. Do you know the Bible verse, 'Where two or more are gathered, there I am also'?"

Rose nodded her head in recognition, remembering she had last read that verse on the back of a fan at the Antioch Baptist Church.

"I believe what God is talking about in that passage is relationships. He or she, if you like, knew that one of the most important things in life is to have a relationship with another person. In fact, I feel that it's the thing that truly gives our lives meaning. So if you are looking for meaning in your life, or you're looking for God, then you need to be with someone else to do that."

"You see, many of these men are like everyone else; they are just looking for companionship. Whether they are single or married, rich or poor, young or old, it varies little among them. Most are looking for a place they can be safe, a place where they don't have to worry about what others think of them, a place where they are accepted for who they are with all their foibles and idiosyncrasies."

Then she looked straight at Rose.

"That's what I provide for these men, Rose—a safe place for them to be with others who accept them for who they are. Strangely similar in that respect to Father Michael, isn't it?"

Rose sat silently, amazed at how the truth of Madam E.'s words were registering in her heart. Isn't that what we all wanted—to have a meaningful relationship with someone? And when you did, when you really connected with someone, *or just shared a handkerchief in an uplifting church service*—she recalled—it made you feel so good inside.

Madam E. continued.

"Luckily, while they are talking or dancing with the girls, we can serve them drinks or hors d'oeuvres for a fee. Of course, they are polite and buy a drink for their young lady, as well. Though, as you may have already noticed, the girls don't get anything stronger than iced tea," she said, changing her lesson from the ethereal to the more mundane.

Then Madam E. stiffened. "It is important that you know, Rose, that I insist that my girls act like ladies at all times, in my house and outside of it. So I would ask that if you notice any of them acting in an unladylike manner—swearing, drinking or doing any types of drugs—that you alert me at once. That sort of behavior is not what my clients are looking for. My girls are not common hookers that work for five and ten dollars a trick for some John. My customers expect more from my girls, and that is what I aim to give them. The girls may try and bribe you not to tell me when you notice these things, or may even try to get you to purchase something for them—Millie is an easy mark for them, I'm afraid—but I know you have more integrity, Rose, and will not give in to their childish whims."

Then she softened again and came over to stand next to Rose, opening the ledger and paging through it so Rose could see its contents.

"As you can see, I try and keep track of what comes and goes in the house, but I just can not seem to keep it all up-to-date," she admitted, as she pulled out receipts and small pieces of paper with figures written neatly on them. She showed one of them to Rose.

"This one is from one of Malcolm's visits. He supplies my girls with things that they need—and a multitude of things they do not. Unfortunately, most of my girls have a weakness for fine things, which Malcolm is more than happy to supply."

Rose looked over the piece of paper Madam E. was referring to.

Tess: evening shoes $ 15, evening bag $7
Ruth: 3 pair of hose, $3.50/pair
Sadie: 2 negligees, $20 each, 2 pair of hose $3.50/pair
Bridget: 2 pair evening gloves, $5/pair, 3 handkerchiefs
$1 each.

Rose's eyes widened at the exorbitant cost of each item— almost double what a person would pay in a store.

"As you can see, there is quite a mark up on these items. Unfortunately, they get no better deal if they go to local department stores such as Holmes or Maison Blanche. The sales women see my girls coming, and they mark up everything at least 100 percent; one of the downsides to my business, I'm afraid. And of course, I have to pass these costs on to the girls.

"Basically, this is how it works. Millie and I keep track of the things that the customers are purchasing each evening," she explained, pulling out another sheet of paper with a name at the top, obviously written in Madam E.'s hand. It had hash-marks next to items—such as drink, sandwich, dessert—hastily scratched in by Millie.

"I keep track of when a gentleman takes one of the girls upstairs. Then before they leave, I present them with their bill." She pulled out another, smaller piece of paper.

"So you would like me to put all your bills down in this ledger?" Rose asked.

"Yes, exactly. And some of my regulars prefer to keep a running tab. I keep track of them here."

She opened the ledger up to a section which had first names, last initials, and a list of figures next to them.

"They pay me every month, but most of my clientele pay the evening they're here. I pay the girls forty percent of the upstairs work and thirty percent of the downstairs receipts. I let them keep any tips they receive. I pay the girls each week and deduct expenses—the items they purchase—plus the cost of visits from Monty and any doctors' visits. I pay the incidentals—soap, shampoo, feminine products—plus room and board, but that is all. But I won't pay for their magazines, perfume, hair pins, or jewelry! Don't let them try and fool you into paying for things like that."

"Who's Monty?" Rose asked

"Oh, he's the hair dresser that comes every other week to do the girls' hair. On occasion, we may have him come by request, if one of the girls has been asked to go out for the evening to dinner or a show."

Madam E. then rummaged through the box and pulled out a stack of receipts in large, flowing handwriting, with each girl's name, a list of the services, and their adjacent cost.

"Here are Monty's bills. I pay him after each visit."

She sat back down at her desk. "I'm sorry this is such a mess. As you can see, I am in desperate need of your assistance," she said, smiling at Rose.

"I'll see what I can do."

✂ 15 ✂

Rose wasn't sure what she was going to see during the non-working hours in Madam E.'s house, never having been in a cat house before; actually, not even being aware of their existence. She had thought, perhaps, the ladies might sit around half-clothed, eating sweets, doing their nails and hair. She wasn't quite prepared for what she found to be the truth—assumptions we make about people are rarely accurate.

~ ~ ~

Rose's first morning at the house, she discovered later, was an unusual morning. Normally, on every day but Sunday, the girls came down to the kitchen for breakfast. Rose had missed out on this fact since she and Malcolm ate early each morning and were out of the house before the girls came down. But now that she was a regular part of the household and was going to school, she quickly became acquainted with the house routine.

When she arrived home from school each day the girls would be gathered in the kitchen eating their breakfast. That's when Rose received a different type of education altogether. After Rose's first day of school, she walked into the kitchen as the girls, bodies draped lazily over the kitchen chairs, were talking about the previous night's work. They looked up at her briefly when she entered the room but went right back to their conversations.

"Then he geev me de necklace!"

Tess smiled and pulled a delicate gold necklace, with a heart pendent hanging from it, from under her blouse.

Each woman stood up to touch it and get a better look—all talking at once, praising her gift and congratulating her on the acquisition. Ruth was the first to sit back down.

"That's almost as nice as the ring Eric gave me," Ruth said, waving around the gold ring which adorned the ring finger of her right hand.

"I bet he's gonna propose one a these days, Tess—you wait and see," Sadie smiled at Tess, shaking her finger in her direction. "I seen it many a time. A pretty thing like you from another country…, those white men, they go for everything but their own. They think that's ex…, exogic."

"You mean exotic," Ruth corrected her.

"I wish some man would come and take me away from here," Bridget said wistfully.

At that, Tess stood up and walked over behind Bridget and began to comb her fingers through Bridget's soft, blond hair.

"Don' worry none, Bridjet. You saavs you mawney, and you gets yourself a goo' job in a nice sma' town, away from dis beeg city, and you fin' a man real quick." Bridget closed her eyes, basking in Tess's soft, caring touch and her words of encouragement. "I come to dis cauntry wit nawthing, and after jus' two year, I have mawney and a goal' necklace."

Bridget reached a hand back to gently touch Tess's hand in thanks.

The two Asian girls sat next to each other, smiling softly at Tess and Bridget; the affection the two women obviously had for each other comforted the newcomers.

"Talk about jewelry!" Sadie piped up. "Did you see the ring that fat guy wore? It must a been worth at least two hundred dollars."

"I would guess more like five," Ruth corrected her again. "Bet he didn't give ya no tip, did he? Those rich ones never do."

She said this with the air of knowledge which, Rose would find out later, was from some fifteen years in the business. She decided Ruth must have started out at a young age, because she couldn't have been more than twenty-seven or twenty-eight.

"It's always the quiet ones. The ones you least expect it from. Those are the ones to look for."

"Yeah, and they like things nice and simple, not no strange requests from those types neither. Just screw'em the old-fashioned way, and they happy as clams," Sadie said with a smile.

At this point in the conversation Rose was helping Ginny wash up the breakfast dishes, and she almost dropped the plate she was holding. Ginny turned toward the girls and scolded them.

"Now watch your language there, Sadie. We got a proper young lady in the room. She ain't use ta such talk."

"Well, best she get use to it now. Ain't nothin' wrong with the word *screw*. Damn, I done heard a lot worse."

"Yeah, like the ever popular *fuck*," Ruth chimed in.

"Now listen here!" Ginny said, throwing down her wash cloth into the sink of hot water.

"Or the horizontal bop," Bridget added.

"And my favorite, tamin' the snake," Sadie giggled.

"In my cauntry, we say *domar el lagarto*—taming the lizard," Tess said with a smile, getting into the fun.

Ginny just stood looking at them with her hands on her hips, her eyes a fierce stare of reprimand. Rose was so beet red, she matched the strawberries which covered the apron she was wearing.

"If the Madam could hear you all now, you'd be in a heap a trouble."

"If I could hear what?" Madam E. asked as she stepped through the hallway door.

At Madam E.'s appearance all the women at the table sat bolt upright in their chairs, except the two oriental girls, who were already sitting politely on the edge of their seats.

Ginny scowled at the girls, not saying a word.

"I seems to forget," she finally said indignantly. Then she turned back to her dishes. Rose was glad she didn't say anything to Madam E. about what the girls were doing. She didn't want to be the cause of them getting into trouble; she had to work closely with these women, and she didn't want to get on their bad sides.

"I hope you are all ready for a review of table manners. May and Jolene need some practice," Madam E. said, walking up between the two Asian girls and placing a hand on each girls shoulder. They both looked up at her and smiled. "Ruth, please get some plates. Tess you get the silverware, and Bridget, would you please get everyone a napkin." Then she turned around to face the sink. "Ginny, I think they all could use a little practice with drinking etiquette. The way I saw some of you gulping your tea last night was just abhorrent. This is not Storyville girls. We will have a little more decorum in this house."

Ginny's face broke into a devilish grin, as she got the drinking glasses out of the parlor and set them down in front of each of the girls with obvious relish.

"Now, before we start, I want to let you all know that Rose...," then she turned toward Rose and motioned her to step over toward her. "Rose will be helping us all out here for a while. She will be in charge of the books." She smiled at Rose, putting her hands on Rose's shoulders.

"And she will be helping Ginny and Millie with some of their chores. Rose is new to this business and is not to be trifled with!" she added, looking sternly first at Ruth then at Sadie. "If I hear of anyone giving her a hard time, you will have to speak to me. Rose is doing us a big favor by helping us out, and we need to show her some kindness. Keep in mind, she is in charge of the books, and she may inadvertently over-charge you for something if she feels the need to." The girls all looked up at Rose with more serious expressions on their faces.

"Now Rose, would you mind getting a pitcher of water and filling up all the girl's glasses for us?" Then she turned to Ruth. "Ruth, would you be so kind as to explain to May and Jolene how we startout a meal."

"Well," Ruth started with a rather bored expression on her face, "when they bring the food out, you take your napkin and put it on your lap like this," she explained, taking her napkin from the side of her plate, putting it in her lap and gently opening it up to cover her thighs. Tess, Bridget, and Sadie all repeated the maneuver. May and Jolene looked questioningly at Madam E.

"Yes, go ahead," she encouraged them. And they picked up their napkins tentatively and set them softly on their laps. "Very good!"

Then she turned toward Ruth again.

"Ruth, you may take over," she said and started to walk out of the room.

"Um, Madam E., may I have a word with you?" Rose asked.

"Why of course, my dear. Follow me to my office."

"I'll be right back, Ginny," Rose said.

When Rose entered the office, she closed the door behind her. She didn't want anyone hearing what she was going to ask the Madam.

~ ~ ~

"I need to get the ledger," Rose explained and stepped into what now was her room, just off Madam's office.

Malcolm had moved her things from the porch for her, and found a small bed and table so she could do her bookkeeping there. It was a tight fit, but Rose kind of liked the comfy, cocoon-like feeling the room gave her. It was a good place to escape to when she wanted to be alone.

Rose picked up the ledger from the table and took it into Madam E.'s office. She opened it up and set it in front of Madam E.

"I found this section in the ledger that I don't understand. You have a substantial amount of money going out to a Mr. H. and a Mr. P. each month but no notation of what it is for.

I wasn't sure where to put this. Is it some expense for the girls that I need to deduct or perhaps part of your maintenance bills?" she questioned.

"Yes, I should have explained that to you. You see, prostitution is technically not a legal business, so in order to stay in business I have to pay certain…, you might call them, extra taxes. It goes to the local police that walk this section of the city. It is just part of my operational expenses in order to avoid being arrested and shut down. You understand?" she asked, raising her eyebrows. "This sort of graft is just an accepted part of my type of business."

"Yes, but the…tax keeps going up about every third month. If they keep that up, they'll run you out of business."

"You are quite correct, my dear. I'm not sure what to do about that. I'm really between a rock and a hard place on this one. I should probably have a talk with the gentleman and see if I can explain my dilemma." Then she smiled at Rose. "Thank you for bringing that to my attention. I knew you would be an asset to me. And speaking of assets, I have a favor to ask of you. I know you are quite busy with your studies, but I was wondering if you would like to earn a little spending money."

Rose's eyes widened. *She isn't going to ask me to do something with her customers is she?*

"I need to get May and Jolene up to speed on their conversational English. Ginny and I have been trying to teach them a few words, but I remember you telling me that you had helped your friend learn how to read, so I assumed you would be a good person to help them learn how to speak, and perhaps read, a little English."

"Sure. I could teach them right after they finish their dinner, I mean breakfast, right when I get home from school."

"That would be perfect. When can you start?"

"Well, I need another week or so to catch up on my classes; changing grades kind of put me even further behind the rest of the class."

"Yes, how is that going? Is that lovely Sister Ann Marie giving you any further trouble?" she asked with a wry smile.

"No, not at all. Mostly, I just try and stay away from her. The other Sisters are pretty nice. And Father Michael stops me once in a while after Mass and asks me how I'm doing."

"Mass, you have to go to Mass?"

"Yes, every morning. The only thing I don't like is, if you forget your head scarf, they make you put a handkerchief on your head."

"That is ridiculous!" Madam E. said in disgust. "Would you like me to say something to the Father?"

"Oh no, there's no need," Rose said anxiously. She didn't want to stir up any more trouble with the Mother Superior. "I really don't mind all that much. I just have to remember to bring my head scarf, is all."

"Well, all right. But remember, if you have any trouble, just talk to Father Michael. He'll set things straight."

"Yes, thank you. I will."

Rose did like Father Michael. He had invited her to his rectory as he had promised, after her first full week in the academy. They had a lovely supper in his backyard garden. He talked for hours about his summer vacation trips to Wisconsin as a boy to visit his grandparents' farm. He also enjoyed Rose's stories about her family and their farm. Rose always felt like she had a little piece of home close by whenever she would see the friendly priest.

Of course, Sister Ann Marie was a little nervous about the visit with the priest. After she had found out about it, she called Rose into her office to make sure there were no issues Rose needed to talk to her about.

"There is no need to get the Father involved in things that we can take care of ourselves, is there Rose?" She explained to Rose.

~ ~ ~

Rose worked very hard over the next two weeks to get caught up to the rest of her class. It was mid-October before Rose was ready to begin her lessons with May and Jolene. She enlisted Malcolm's help to get started.

"Here they are Mademoiselle, just as you ordered: three slates and a box of chalk."

"Wonderful, Malcolm! You're the best!" she said excitedly, taking the items from him.

"Anything for *mo cheri*," he said, bowing and holding out his hand in his now common gesture to Rose.

"You *are* a tease, Malcolm," Rose chided him.

"*O contraire*, I am very sincere. There is nothing I won't do for my *bel* Rose," he said, stepping up close to her. Then he took her hand and held it to his chest, looking deep into her eyes and making Rose blush.

After these many weeks, Rose still wasn't used to the closeness which Malcolm preferred when interacting with her. She enjoyed his company though, and was reluctant to give that up for the mere discomfort she had with his preference for intimacy. And if she had to admit it, she didn't mind the attention.

He was always a perfect gentleman and a perfect guide around the city, showing her the French Market and Café Du Monde—with its wonderfully sweet *begniets*—Canal Street and the lovely shops there. They even took a streetcar to the end of Canal and spent a whole day walking through a large cemetery looking at the well-kept burial sites. There she received a lesson in New Orleans topography.

Malcolm explained that all the graves were above ground because most of New Orleans was below sea level. This was important because of the hurricane season, which ran from June to September. If the bodies in the ground were not weighted down, they would be pushed up to the surface by the water-soaked earth, so most just avoided the issue and buried their loved ones above.

Then he showed her the levees and canals the city had built to keep the large Lake Pontchartrain and the Mississippi in its banks. The new Basin Canal was particularly impressive to Rose, considering it was dug by hand in the 1830s, and took the lives of thousands of Irish and Germans who labored and died there from yellow fever.

"Well, since you're so accommodating," Rose smiled, "take these papers and print the name—legibly, mind you—of every piece of furniture in this room, one name per piece, please."

"Oh, I think I hear Ginny callin' me!" he joked and walked toward the kitchen.

"I don't think so," Rose said, pulling on his arm and swinging him around to stand closely in front of him again.

"Oh *cheri*, I didn't know you cared!"

Then he took her in his arms and swung her around, dipping her like they were on a dance floor. Once Rose was over the surprise of being twirled around unexpectedly, she giggled and smiled at her happy Creole with the shaggy brown hair. Malcolm smiled broadly, getting the reaction that he had planned.

As Malcolm labeled the furniture, Rose went upstairs to get her pupils. Madam E. had put them in separate rooms two weeks after they arrived; Jolene stayed in the blue room, and she moved May to the first bedroom at the top of the stairs. She decorated May's room with items she had picked up on her trip to Japan. Both girls had beautiful, silk kimonos, which they only wore when they were in their rooms. They hung them on the walls for added decoration when they weren't wearing them. Rose knocked on May's door first. May opened it slowly.

"Come downstairs, May," she said, motioning her to leave her bedroom. "We're going to learn to read today." She moved her hands mimicking the opening of a book.

She stepped over to Jolene's door and did the same. The girls stepped softly out of their rooms and followed Rose down the stairs. Rose was amazed at how quietly these women walked. She had to turn around to make sure they were still following her. They would often enter a room and startle it's occupant with their sudden, undetected appearance. After a while, the two made a game out of it, giggling when their unsuspecting victim jumped halfway out of their skin.

Once back in the parlor, Rose gave them each a slate. She took hers and drew a letter on it.

"First, we're going to learn the alphabet." Then she pointed to the first letter on her board. "This is the letter A. It sounds like Ah. Can you say Ah? Ahhh...!" she said with a little more animation in her voice.

"Aahh," the two girls repeated together.

"Very good! Now write it on the slate, and say it at the same time." And so it went until they came to the letter F, when in the distance they heard the sound of a coronet playing a jazzy little tune. Both girls sat up straight, their ears turned toward the front windows.

Then, from out in the hall they heard Sadie's voice call out, "It's buglin' Sam!"

"The waffle man," Rose finished in mild disgust

"Da waffa maan!" May said excitedly. Then May and Jolene both ran over to the window to peer out.

"I didn't have to teach them that!" Rose said to herself. "Well, I guess the lesson is done for the day."

Malcolm stepped into the hall from the kitchen.

"Do I hear the melodious tones of the waffle man?" he asked. "Miss Rose, may I procure you a sweet confection?"

"Oh Malcolm, sweetie!" Sadie said from half-way down the stairs. "You'd get me a waffle, wouldn't ya?"

"Why, of course," he said, tipping his head slightly. "And it looks like these two ladies would like waffles, as well. Is that right May? Jolene?" he said a little louder to get their attention from the hallway. "Waffle for you?" he asked pointing to them then to himself. "I'll get them for you!" They both nodded their heads eagerly.

Out on the street, the bugling waffle man was attracting everyone's attention. He would stop playing now and again when his young male assistant would hand him a warm waffle. He sprinkled it with powdered sugar and gave it to the egar person standing beside his horse-drawn, wood-framed wagon. They'd hand him their dime, smile sweetly and lick their lips, and he'd be on his way belting out another tune. It was like the pied piper calling out all the mice in town, Rose thought.

"*Bonswah Misyeu!*" Malcolm called out. "Five waffles *ple.*"

Then Tess, Ruth and Bridget came out on the porch; the other girls wanted waffles too.

"I am mistaken, that will be eight!" Malcolm corrected himself.

Sam, the waffle man, looked up at the three women standing on the balcony and caught sight of Bridget from under his wood awning. He called out to her: "Yours is on the house!"

Bridget blew him a kiss. He grabbed it out of the air and softly placed it on his cheek; then he smiled a broad smile and got busy with his treats.

As they stood and waited for the waffles, Rose heard another tune coming down the street. This one was a slow dirge she vaguely recognized as *Just a Closer Walk with Thee.* As she looked down the street, she could see a group of colored musicians walking down the center of the street, coming toward them. Everyone else turned to look. Sadie made the sign of the cross across her chest and head.

At the front of the line of musicians was a man dressed in a suit and tie with a sash across one shoulder. He was playing a coronet. He was flanked by two other younger men in suits and hats—hats that looked like an unadorned policeman's hat—one playing a saxophone and the other a trumpet. Behind them came a smaller saxophone, a trombone, another horn, a tuba, and a large drum—with the words *Kid Howard's Brass Band*—which pounded out the slow beat. They were all stepping slowly along, rocking back and forth to the music, and moving their instruments up and down to the sorrowful tune.

Behind them was a horse-drawn wagon. The horse had a black feather plume on top of its head, which it would shake now and then as if the music made him sad too. In the open wagon was a coffin, and behind that was a group of colored people all dressed in black. Some of the women held handkerchiefs to their noses, occasionally wiping their eyes with them. An elderly, particularly distraught-looking woman stood in the middle of the first row of mourners just behind the casket. She was held on each side by two young men. It looked like, if they let go of her, she would fall right to the ground, her steps being particularly heavy and unsure. Rose said a silent prayer for the family.

After they had passed by, Rose asked Malcolm, "Do they always do funerals that way?"

"Oh, yes. It's even fashionable for the whites now-a-days. Then after they bury the body, they walk and dance back down the street playing a lively tune to celebrate the dead person going to their reward in heaven."

~ ~ ~

So the days turned into weeks and the weeks into months, each day being pretty much like the rest; Rose would get up early to a quiet house, get into her school uniform and head out for a day of studies; she would be home by three-thirty, get undressed while the girls finished their breakfast, then help Ginny clean up while she listened to the girls talk about their customers, or more often about what the latest movie star was wearing or what new item they were going to get that next week when Malcolm would come by with his wares.

Rose had all but given up on finding Lilly Mae, but she felt an obligation to Madam E. to at least stay through her first semester at St. Joseph's. She was also enjoying being back at school.

After the afternoon gab session, Rose would take May and Jolene to the parlor to work on their English. They were eager to learn and were very good students. Then it was off to her own studies before she helped Ginny with supper and preparations for the evening callers. She had made some friends at St. Joseph's, but because of her living arrangements and busy schedule, she never did cultivate the relationships. She was also anxious not to repeat the mistakes she made at Soldan.

It took Rose a while to get used to the doorbell and phone calls late into the night, but soon she learned to tune them out; she would just roll over and go right back to sleep. On weekends, she would catch up on the week's receipts and settle the books until every last penny was accounted for. She also helped with the cleaning and washing tasks. The washing was quite a big job, since there were six sets of bed sheets to wash most evenings, and every other weekend her sheets, Millie's, and Madam E.'s were also put into the mix.

Ginny required the girls to wash out their own stockings and undergarments, though quite often Millie agreed to do them for a small fee.

It was during one of these washing sessions that Rose's routine was disturbed, and she came face to face with the reality of what she was doing and where she was living.

~ ~ ~

It was a Saturday like most other Saturdays, except for the fact that Rose was in charge of the kitchen; Ginny had gone home ill. Rose decided she would surprise Ginny and make Grandma B.'s wonderful recipe for banana bread out of some inexpensive, over-ripe bananas she had purchased from a street vendor. One thing Rose had learned from her mother and Grandma B. was not to waste anything. There were many years that both women had to do with very little for their families, and even though the country was starting to stand on its own again, scrimping and making something out of practically nothing was still what most people did.

Millie, May and Jolene were in the washroom working on laundry. Rose had the radio on. They were all working gaily to the sounds of Marion Hutton singing *The Way You Look Tonight* with the Glenn Miller orchestra. They didn't hear what was going on in the other room until Millie opened the hall door to go upstairs and get more dirty laundry. Millie quickly closed the door and leaned against it, her skin blanching as she stared at Rose dumbfounded and bug-eyed.

Rose looked up from what she was doing. Millie just stood there staring at her.

"What's the matter, Millie?"

"There's..., there's po-lice men in the hall," she said nervously.

"What are you talking about?" Rose asked, not really believing what Millie had said. She walked over toward Millie and tried to get past her so she could look for herself.

"Don't go out there!" she whispered, stepping in front of Rose to block her access to the hall.

"Let me through, Millie," Rose said, a little more annoyed.

"We gotta leave!" Millie said anxiously, eyes wide and frightened.

"Let me see!" Rose insisted, trying to step past the frightened girl, but Millie stepped in front of her again.

"Oh, all right, I'll go through the parlor."

As she headed for the parlor door, Millie grabbed the back of her shirt and tried to hold her back. Rose stopped and looked at her in defeat.

"All right Millie, I won't go out there, I promise, but just let me go a minute. I just want to stick my head out a little and see what's happening."

Rose opened the door to the small hall which led to the parlor bathroom; then she opened the parlor door just a crack to see if she could see or hear anything.

There were police, all right. There was one standing in the parlor hall doorway, looking innocently around the room. But what scared Rose more was what she heard.

"Are there any girls upstairs, Madam?"

"Now Mr. Hamilton, there is no need for this nonsense. We can just go into my office and have a little chat and clear this all up. No need to get the girls mixed up in this," she heard Madam E. say with a slight strain in her voice.

"Sorry Madam, we got a new chief at the station, and he wants to make a good impression with the public. Ya know, show'em what good work he's doin' for 'em an' all. There's nothin' I can do about it."

Rose could tell Madam E. was getting upset. "But what about our agreement?"

"I'm sorry Madam, my hands are tied."

"This is ridiculous!" she said, exasperated.

"Mike, go upstairs and see who's all up there," the man ordered.

"Now see here!" Madam E. protested.

"Oh, no! You ain't goin' nowhere, ma'am."

"Let go of me!" Madam E. exclaimed.

"Oh, my God! They got the Madam!" Millie said, leaning into the wall next to the door, trying to melt into it and out of sight.

Jesus, Mary and Joseph! Rose thought, using an expression her Irish mother would say when there was significant trouble. *They are going to arrest everyone!*

Without hesitation, Rose grabbed Millie and pulled her back into the kitchen.

"Millie, you've got to go and find Malcolm. Tell him what's going on!" she said, pulling her toward the porch door. "And hurry!"

Millie ran out the door, down the alleyway, and quickly out of sight. Then Rose remembered May and Jolene were still in the laundry room. As she stood in the doorway to the laundry, she noticed someone was coming through the kitchen door!

She ducked into the laundry room and looked around the room with a discerning eye. She spied the two piles of sheets on the floor. *That'll do!* she thought as she grasped Jolene and May by the arms.

"Listen," she whispered softly, "There is trouble! You need to hide!" she said insistently pulling them over to the pile of linen on the floor. The girls could see by the look on her face that Rose was serious, so they immediately did as they were told.

Rose had just covered them up when a policeman walked into the room. Rose, hearing him come in, pulled a sheet from the pile, turned around and shook it out in front of him, startling him and making him step back.

"Damn! You scared the shit out of me!" he said, half in anger and half out of surprise.

Rose tried to regain her composure. She was only glad the man couldn't hear how fast her heart was beating.

"Excuse me," she said as innocently as she could. "Is there something you need?" She walked toward him, trying to push him out of the room with her close presence. He stepped back a step or two but wasn't dissuaded.

"Who are you?" he asked gruffly.

"I'm the maid," Rose lied. "Is there some problem?"

"I'm looking for any of the girls that work here."

"Just me and my laundry in here," Rose answered as sweetly as she could. The man pushed past Rose, making her stomach tighten. He looked around the room carefully, at one point standing right in front of Jolene and May. Rose noticed a small, pale foot slip slowly back under the sheets as the man stood right in front of them. She leaned back against the utility sink at the close call, then she straightened up again when she saw the man turning back around. He looked at Rose a few seconds, then left the room without a word.

Rose ran over to the pile of laundry. "Stay in there 'til I come and get you!" she whispered to the girls.

When she walked back into the room, Malcolm was standing in the middle of the kitchen.

"Oh Malcolm! It's awful!" she said, running into his arms. Malcolm held her for a brief moment then pulled her away, still holding on to her arms.

"Where are they, Rose?" he said hurriedly

"They're out in the hallway! They're rounding up the girls and Madam E.!" Rose said with tears welling in her eyes. "I hid May and Jolene in the laundry room. They already looked in there, but they didn't see them," she said, wiping away her tears. She knew she needed to be brave right this minute, but the sight of Malcolm had brought all her anxiety to the surface, and it was bubbling out of her eyes.

"I'm gonna go see what I can do. You stay here and make sure May and Jolene don't move!"

Rose held on to Malcolm's hand until he reached the hallway door. "Be careful!" she whispered to him, then she pulled him down toward her. In what seemed like slow motion, she kissed him softly on the lips.

There was a look of shock on Malcolm's face when Rose pulled away, which was soon replaced by a smile. "I will, *cheri!*" he whispered softly back. He squeezed her hand and slid out the swinging door. Rose stood with her back to the door to listen.

"Mike, Harry! What's all the commotion here?" she could hear Malcolm ask loudly. Rose opened the door slightly so she could hear better.

"We gotta take'em in, Malcolm."

"Now, there's gotta be somethin' we can work out."

" 'Fraid not. Chief's orders."

Then there was a brief silence. "Harry, Harry, Harry," Rose heard Malcolm start up again, his voice coming closer toward her. She closed the door quickly but didn't move. "You know that console radio you been asking me ta find for ya for your anniversary? I found it just the other day! You leave the Madam E. here," he whispered, "and I can have it dropped off at your place—no strings attached!" There was a brief silence. "Just think how happy the wife would be!" Malcolm added, trying to sweeten the pot. There was another brief silence.

"I can't let the Madam go, Malcolm," Harry responded. Then he paused, "but I can let ya have one of the girls."

"How 'bout if I throw in a case a champagne! Then you and the misses could really celebrate!"

"Sorry, it'll have to be one of the girls or no deal," he said finally.

"That's fine, Harry, that's fine," Malcolm agreed.

"All right Petie, lets tak 'em outta here!" Harry yelled down the hall. "Except this one."

Rose could hear his voice growing more distant. She pushed the door open again slightly. She could hear the soft whimpers of the girls as they were ushered out—all except Ruth, who wasn't going quietly.

"Get your hands off me you oaf! I'm not some slab a meat you can just throw around!"

Rose opened the door a little wider to see Malcolm standing at the base of the steps, holding on to Bridget as Madam E. led the rest of the girls out the front door. Rose tentatively stepped out into the hall and up to Malcolm and Bridget. They all watched Madam E., Tess, and Ruth being led to the police wagon. Madam E. stood by the door of the wagon comforting the girls and helping them each inside. She looked up to see the three standing in the doorway.

"You take care of things, Malcolm, Rose," she called out before she too stepped into the wagon. But she wasn't about to step in without assistance. She stood staring at the young man who was guarding the wagon door until he took her hand and helped her inside. *Always the lady,* Rose thought to herself; she admired Madam E.'s grace in the face of her humiliation. *Always the lady.*

Rose gained a new respect for Madam E. that day, and she decided she would try and emulate her tenacious style.

~ ~ ~

Madam E. and the girls were back home by about midnight. It turned out the Madam had an advantageous conversation with the new police chief. Now Rose entered only one name into the ledger for her monthly payments, letting the chief decide how the money was going trickle down to the men on the beat. And the sunny-side to all this was that the cost wasn't going to keep going up. This man realized it was in his best interest to keep Madam E. and her girls in business, so a set fee was decided upon—there would be no more raids on Madam E.'s house.

The sunny-side to this for Rose was the closeness which instantly developed between her and Malcolm. Emergencies either bring people together or tear them apart. This one had pushed Malcolm and Rose's relationship to a new level. Malcolm spent more time at the house now, even helping Rose with some of her tasks just to be with her, or so she could get her jobs done faster in order for them to have more time away together. He also became more openly affectionate; he would steal a kiss in the laundry room, or chase her up the stairs to capture her in his arms, giggling and squirming before she would submit to his advance and kiss him to gain her freedom.

The other women in the house became closer to Rose as well. She got pulled into their afternoon conversations, initially by teasing her about her new-found romance, but eventually they sought her advice or opinion on things. Since none of them had gone on past middle or grade school, they considered Rose the authority on most everything, deserving or not—everything, that is, except fashion and men.

One slow, rainy October afternoon, they conspired and decided Rose needed a lesson in how to best present oneself when trying to impress a man. They enlisted Monty, who, besides being their hairdresser, was also their fashion consultant. Madam E. got into the mix with her own surprise.

~ ~ ~

"Well, if it isn't Miss Rose!" Monty said gaily, when Rose opened the door for his usual bimonthly visit.

"Are we ready for our surprise today?"

He sashayed into the hallway, a garment bag over one arm, his satchel with all his beauty supplies in the other.

Rose had found out from Ginny a while ago that Monty was gay. Before that, Rose didn't know what gay was, but she knew Monty acted like no other man she had been acquainted with. She had Ginny doubling over with laughter when she tried to describe Monty's mannerisms to her with pantomime, displaying her ignorance and skill at acting.

Rose wasn't sure what Monty meant, so she just brushed off his statement and asked who he was here to see.

"Well, you, of course!" he said grinning.

Just then, Ruth came running down the steps, followed immediately by Sadie, Tess, then Bridget. May and Jolene stood at the top railing, smiling down at Rose, obviously not part of the surprise but wanting to be in on all the excitement. Ruth swiftly grabbed Rose by the shoulders and led her into the parlor.

"What's all this?" Rose asked in confusion.

"We have a little surprise for you, Rose," Ruth said happily. "Monty here is going to do his magic on you!"

"What?"

"We decided you needed a little lesson on how to keep your claws tight into Malcolm," Sadie said.

"You don' waan to lose dat one," Tess added, smiling.

"Look at the lovely dress Monty brought!" Bridget said. She had pulled up the garment bag to reveal a lovely wine colored, satin evening gown.

"No peeking!" Monty scolded, pulling the bag back down over the dress. "We need to do the face and hair first!"

Tess pulled a stool out from the bar and placed it in front of the large parlor mirror. Ruth gently nudged Rose onto the seat. Monty stepped in behind Rose and started manipulating her hair.

"So girls," he said, as they all gathered around the flustered, young girl, "should we do an up do or something more Lana Turner?" he asked cheerfully. First he piled Roses' auburn locks on top of her head, then he let them fall down onto her shoulders, curling it under at the ends.

Rose looked in the mirror at all the women standing around her who were looking back at her, expertly studying the different hairstyles Monty was proposing. The last time she was in a similar situation all the women around her were black. Now they were all different shades. She could even see May and Jolene, who had snuck downstairs and were poking their heads in the view of the mirror to see what magic Monty was planning to perform.

She was amazed at herself how comfortable she felt with all these women. Her amazement didn't come from the fact that these were women of ill repute. Rose knew better than that. It was that they were all women, and she was really enjoying their company.

Less than two years ago, she would rather have done a week's worth of extra chores than have Gerty play with her hair as Monty was doing just now, or she would rather have eaten dirt than hang out with most of the girls at her school. Now she looked forward to coming back to Madam E.'s and being part of the girls' conversations; she liked being their confidant, their advisor, or just another one of girls. She felt a strong tie to these women, which was somehow different than the tie she had with Silus, or Todd, or even Malcolm. It was something unspoken, it was different, it was deeper. She couldn't put her finger on it, but it was there. She had that same feeling with Lilly Mae and with Grandma B., but living with an entire house-full of women, the sentiment was that much stronger. She sighed and smiled at all these women she considered her friends.

"Oh, an updoo, definitely," Ruth decided.

"Yeah," the rest of the girls agreed.

"Sadie darling, here hold this," Monty said, holding Rose's hair back up on her head. Then he came around to Rose's face and looked at her seriously, playing with a few strands of hair which he had pulled down over her forehead.

"We most definitely need some bang action here though," he said, putting her hair this way and that across her forehead. "Tess sweetheart, get me my scissors and comb, would ya please?" Rose swallowed hard and prepared herself for the transformation.

"Okay girls, now shoo, shoo. I need room to work," he said pushing the girls away with a flick of his fingers. The girls took up their cigarettes, magazines, and dime-store love stories—the only literature Rose could get them to read beside the entertainment section of the newspaper—and perched themselves around the room in order to keep a close eye on the metamorphosis.

Just like in Aunt Tilley's chair, first came the hairstyle then came the makeup.

"Now, for the piece-ta-resistance!" Monty said in butchered French, as he pulled the wine colored, satin dress out of the bag. All the girls stood around ooing and ahhing over the lovely gown. "Now, we need some privacy," he said, grabbing Rose's hand and pulling her into the parlor bathroom. To Rose's surprise, he walked into the bathroom with her and stood looking at her, expecting her to start undressing.

"Um, excuse me, Monty, but I think I can do this myself."

"Oh, all right," he said a little disgusted, "but I'll wait just outside the door in case you need me!"

Rose carefully put on the beautiful gown and looked at herself in the mirror. She had to admit, she did look very nice. Monty had done a wonderful job with her hair; he put it up in a French twist, cutting her bangs so they hung parted at the side, with a soft curve over her forehead, and lose ringlets in front of her ears. Her makeup was also done tastefull—just enough to compliment the dress and her face but not so much to make her look like a floozy.

And the dress—it was gorgeous! It was a dark, wine color, with short, flowing sleeves, and a low pointed neckline, which complimented Rose's moderately sized breasts—even though Rose wasn't used to that feature of her body getting so much attention. The bodice fitted snugly from her chest to her hips, though the back was open down to the tips of her shoulder blades. This feature didn't allow Rose to wear a brassiere, which she wasn't quite comfortable with, but Monty assured her, through the door, that this was the way the dress was suppose to be worn. The skirt of the dress was full, sitting in soft, delicate rolls around her legs all the way to the floor.

Rose reluctantly stepped out into the small hallway. Monty gasped and placed a hand over his mouth, eyes wide in surprise.

"Oh, my Lord!" he said grasping both her hands. "You are gorgeous! All right, turn around," he ordered, making a circular motion with his finger. "Oh! I almost forgot—the shoes!"

He ran back into the parlor, not opening the door wide enough for anyone to see and returned with a lovely pair of black satin pumps with a small V-shape cut out of the toe. Once those were in place, he pulled the dress down on her hips and, much to Rose's chagrin, pulled it up on her chest. Then he decided she was finally ready for presentation. He stood behind her and pointed her in the direction of the closed parlor door. Then he squeezed through the door and shut it again quickly, in Rose's face.

"Attention, attention ladies, please!" he said clapping his hands. "I would like to present Miss Rose…," then he stopped and opened the door just enough to poke his head through. "What's your last name, dear?"

"Krantz."

"I would like to present, Miss Rose Krantz!" he said to the parlor full of eager women. He opened the parlor door wide and stepped aside.

There was a collective drawing in of a breath as Rose stepped through the door and into the light of the room.

Sadie whistled a cat call, and all the girls ran up to her goggling and gaggling over this curl and that neckline, her "womanly breasts," and her "shapely hips." As they were all standing around making Rose's blush grow even deeper, May and Jolene scampered out of the room and up the steps, only to return seconds later with a lovely pearl necklace and drop pearl earrings.

"For tonigh'!" May said as she put the necklace around Rose's cream-white neck. Jolene carefully put in the earrings.

"Tonight? What do you mean, tonight?"

"You didn't think we'd get you all dolled up for nothin'!" Ruth said.

"Go get Madam E.," Sadie ordered Jolene. Jolene bowed slightly and scampered silently out of the room.

Madam E. entered the room and stopped short when she caught sight of Rose. "My dear, you are lovely!" she said, beaming proudly as if it were her own daughter standing in front of her.

"We dee not tell her what she doing tonight," Tess explained to Madam E.

"Well, when I told the girls what I had planned for you this evening, it was their idea to call in Monty for some assistance." Monty stood next to Rose, beaming with pride at his creation. "Very nice work, by the way, Monty."

"Oh, it was nothing, really. When I've got such a lovely pallet to work with, my artistry is just the icing on the cake," he said, softly touching under Rose's chin.

"At any rate...."

Then she was cut off by the sound of the bell over the door. Madam E. looked at the watch pinned to her chest

"Ah, he's right on time, as usual," she said to herself. "Please show the gentleman in, May."

Gentleman! What gentleman? Rose thought, cowering behind Monty with her hands covering her bare chest. *I don't want to let any strange man see me like this!* But when she peeked out over Monty's shoulder and saw who stepped into the room, her mouth fell open and her hands dropped to her sides.

"I haven't missed the party, have I?" Malcolm asked gaily.

~ ~ ~

Rose hardly recognized him; he was wearing a dapper fedora hat instead of his usual cap; he had on a white shirt and tie, a dark brown vest and black dress pants, and when he took off his hat, Rose got an even bigger surprise—he had cut his hair! Instead of the long, loose waves which usually sat on his shoulders, his hair was cut up to his ears. Rose thought he was the most handsome man she had ever seen.

Then Malcolm caught sight of Rose. He stood there silent for a moment, slack-jawed and staring at what he thought was the most beautiful creature in the world. It took him a while before he could speak, which was truly a feat for the very loquacious Creole.

Everyone stood back silently, looking earnestly at the young couple. Bridget finally gave Malcolm a small nudge from behind. He walked up to Rose and gently took hold of her hand. First he said something in Creole; then he shook his head slightly and spoke to her again in mostly English.

"*Mamzel*, I am truly at a loss for words to describe your beauty!" he said, never taking his eyes off her face. Then he kissed her hand, stepped back and looked at the whole of her from a short distance, smiling broadly. "You are a Venus!"

"Well, I suppose you two are wondering what this is all about," Madam E. said. "I wanted to thank you for what you did for the girls and myself a while back."

"You paid me for the radio already!" contested Malcolm.

"That was not enough, Malcolm. You both did us all a great service, and I wanted to thank you formally, so I've arranged for you to go out to dinner this evening at Galatoire's; then you are to go to the St. Charles to see a show."

Both Rose and Malcolm looked silently at Madam E.

"There is no need to do such things," Malcolm protested.

"Yes, Madam E., it really isn't necessary!" Rose agreed.

"It's all set," she said, smiling and stepping between the lovely couple. She grasped each under the arm and led them to the front door. "Millie, run and grab my fur wrap and my beaded purse, would you please?"

Millie ran up the stairs and appeared quickly with the mink stole over her arm and the small black purse dangling out from underneath.

"There," Madam E. said, adjusting the cape around Rose's shoulders. "Now you're all set!" She opened the door and stepped aside.

Malcolm and Rose looked at each other and smiled. "Well, shall we?" Malcolm asked, holding out his arm. Rose took hold of Malcolm, and they both stepped out onto the sidewalk to a waiting horse drawn carriage.

"I was wondering why Ma-dam wanted me to rent this thing for the evening. Now I know why."

Malcolm held her hand as she stepped delicately into the carriage as the driver held the door open. Rose felt just like Cinderella going to the ball with her handsome prince, or one of the well-off girls at Soldan when they would have their coming-out party at the exclusive *Vail of Prophet* ball. Malcolm sat down next to the beaming young beauty, and they waved at all the faces squeezed into the doorway of the house. Monty had stepped outside and was blowing his nose in a handkerchief as he waved at the pair. Rose felt extremely happy and very loved.

"You look very handsome, Malcolm!" Rose said sincerely.

"Yeah! Who said ya can't make a silk purse out of a sow's ear!" he joked. "And you, *mo cheri*, what happened to that young *fly* that I saw those many months ago? All I see now is a beautiful, young woman in front of me," he said to her softly, looking into her bright, blue eyes.

Rose looked down and blushed.

"No need to be embarrassed *mamzel*. You are a vision." Then he leaned over to her and softly kissed her on the lips. When he pulled away, Rose giggled.

"What?" Malcolm questioned.

Rose opened Madam E.'s purse, found a handkerchief and tenderly wiped the lipstick off his lips. They smiled at each other, grasped hands, and silently sat back into their seat, basking in the rhythmical clip-clop of the horse's hooves on the pavement and the loving touch of the one beside them. This was a night neither would ever forget.

ဆ 16 ∞

The bud on the sturdy stem is unfolding with tender loving care, the pink blush compelling to all who gazed upon its beauty—particularly, one smitten Creole. But would all see the radiance; feel the softness of soul which lies within its petals.

A new, more personal, test was ahead to determine just that.

~ ~ ~

When November rolled around with no mention of a Thanksgiving feast, Rose learned that holidays at a sporting house were not happy times. Rose had never thought about it before, but when she asked Ginny why they weren't celebrating Thanksgiving, she explained that the girls weren't exactly welcomed back home, so they tended to ignore major family holidays. They did do a little something for Christmas, but just amongst themselves; the girls got each other small gifts: silk hose, hair clips, or perhaps a new pair of gloves. They also purchased something for Millie, Ginny,

391

Rose, and the Madam. Malcolm always managed to get special deals for the girls at Christmas. Because there wasn't much business on Christmas Eve or Christmas day, Madam E. shut down the house for two whole days. Ginny, Rose, and Millie worked all afternoon Christmas day on a big feast.

Luckily, Ginny had let Rose know about the gift exchange ahead of time, so she was prepared with gifts for everyone. Thinking of gifts for the girls was easy: a subscription to Vogue magazine had them all cooing, plus the forbidden fruit—chocolates for each one. She gave Millie a beginning reader, since she had just started teaching Millie to read, along with May and Jolene. And for Ginny she bought a delicate, though very demure, night gown. It took Rose quite a while to think of what to get Madam E. She finally decided upon a new pin for the watch which she always wore on her chest.

Everyone seemed to enjoy the day. They sat around the small tree Madam E. had put up in the parlor for the guests, reading and listening to the console radio. Then, after a large meal that evening, they opened their gifts to each other and sang Christmas carols, until Madam E. had decided they were all getting too melancholy and sent everyone to bed. Rose felt very close to all these women and hardly missed her family, until they started on the carols. The mixture of fatigue and past memories of family singing sessions made her, and the rest of the girls, homesick. The only ones who weren't affected by the lack of family were May and Jolene; while the Christmas holiday was enjoyable to them, there were no memories of Christmas-past to remind them of their social isolation. Most everyone went to their rooms with a heavy heart, including Madam E.

Rose was sitting on her bed writing a letter to her family when there was a quiet knock on her door. Madam E. poked her head into her cozy little room.

"Rose, are you up for a visitor yet this evening?"

"A visitor?" Rose questioned, unsure of who would be coming to see her at such a late hour. Then Malcolm stuck his head in behind the Madam's. Rose beamed at the sight. After Malcolm hadn't shown up for supper, she assumed she wasn't going to see him at all this day. It had dampened her spirits a touch, but she knew his family was in New Orleans, and she assumed he was spending time with them, which she thought was only right.

"Well, I'll be going up to bed now," Madam E. smiled. "You are welcome to use my office if you like."

"I'll wait for you out here," Malcolm said.

Rose quickly put on her robe and headed for the door. Just before she opened it, she ran back to her night stand, pulled out a small wrapped gift, and stuffed it in her pocket.

Malcolm stood up from the davenport as Rose entered the room. He stepped up to her, and before Rose could react, pulled her close and kissed her. This was not like any kiss he had ever given her before; Rose could feel a passion and a longing which she had not felt before, pulling her in and almost collapsing her legs underneath her. When he finally pulled away, she felt as if she needed to sit down before she fell down; she felt intoxicated and weak in the knees, though the only drink she had that night was for the toast Madam E. had given at the dinner table.

Malcolm seemed to sense Rose's wooziness, and he led her by the hand to the davenport, Rose not taking her moony eyes off of Malcolm since their lips parted.

"I'm sorry I couldn't get here earlier, but my *popa* showed up unexpectedly."

"*Popa?*"

"Oh, I'm sorry *Mamzel*, my father. *Gran-mer* cried like a baby; she was so happy to have all her family around her. I had to wait until she went to bed before I could sneak out."

"You didn't need leave your family!" Rose said, feeling a little guilty she had pulled Malcolm away from a father she knew he saw infrequently. But on the other hand, she was awfully pleased he was with her now. Until she had seen his head poking through her bedroom door, she hadn't realized how much she had missed him.

"Oh, *cheri*. I couldn't let Christmas pass without seeing the love of my life."

Rose blushed and looked down. She knew Malcolm was prone to exaggeration, but she hoped he wasn't over-stating things just now.

"I have something for you."

He grinned, pulling a small, velvet gray box out of his pants pocket, then a piece of paper from out of his back pocket. Rose recognized it as a box which usually held jewelry. Most of the girls had similar boxes, which they kept their special jewelry in. Rose took a deep breath, sitting up straight in anticipation.

"I hope you like it!"

Rose smiled at him and, without saying a word, cautiously took the box and the paper from his hand. She opened the paper and began to read.

"How do I love thee? Let me cou-court the wa-ways?" Rose looked puzzled at Malcolm.

Malcolm took over for the stuttering Rose who was unable to read his scratchy script. He read without looking at the paper.

"How do I love thee? Let me count the ways. I love thee to the depth and breath and height my soul can reach, when feeling out of sight for the ends of being and ideal grace. I love thee to the level of every day's most quiet need, by sun and candle-light. I love thee freely, as men strive for right; I love thee purely as they run from praise. I love thee with the passion put to use in my old griefs, and with my childhood's faith. I love thee with a love I seemed to lose with my lost saints, I love thee with the breath, smiles, tears, of all my life!—and if God choose, I shall but love thee better after death."

"That was wonderful, Malcolm! Did you write that?"

"No, it belongs to Elizabeth Barrett Browning."

"I bet you could have written it," Rose said sincerely.

Malcolm smiled at the compliment. Rose had no idea how hard it was to put down on paper what was in one's heart, but he liked the compliment all the same; he liked how easily Rose made him feel like he was worth something.

"Open the box!" he encouraged her.

Rose slowly lifted the velvet lid. Inside was a necklace; it was a small, delicate, filigree gold heart hanging from a thin gold chain. The gold was slightly dull, like it was very old. She looked up at Malcolm then grabbed him around the neck with one of her famous bear hugs, almost knocking him over.

Malcolm laughed and eventually peeled her away, with Rose still mute but beaming.

"I take it, that means you like it?"

Rose looked at him with that *of course I do, you idiot* look.

"It's lovely, Malcolm, thank you. And thank you for the beautiful poem," she said, kissing him gently on the cheek.

"The necklace, it belonged to my *gran-mer*," he said proudly.

"Oh, Malcolm," Rose said in a worried tone. "I can't take this!" she closed the box and handed it back to him.

"No," he said, pushing it back in her lap. "She knew I was going to give it to you. She knows how much I care for you."

"But Malcolm," Rose pleaded. But he stopped her, placing his finger lightly over her mouth.

"No more discussion," he said softly. "All gracious ladies accept gifts from their suitor with a smile and a kiss," he teased.

Rose looked at the closed box and the poem, leaned close to Malcolm and gave him a soft, wet kiss on the lips, which he instantly accepted. They both lingered there, pulling each other close, drinking each other in with equal passion and thirst, their lips opening and closing, touching and parting. He could feel her firm breasts through her light nightgown and robe. She could feel his taut chest and strong arms surround her. The slight touch of their tongues sent new heat rising in them both, until Malcolm stood suddenly, breaking off the embrace, leaving Rose feeling vulnerable and alone on the davenport.

"Is there something wrong?" she asked. *Perhaps I was too forward?* she questioned herself.

"No..., No...," he said, sitting back down next to her and taking her hands in his. "I just..., I just love you too much, Rose. If I didn't stop...," He looked at her with a very serious expression on his face. "I might not have been able to stop at all."

Rose was a little surprised at his disclosure, but then smiled in recognition of his gallant gesture.

"Can I put it on you?" he asked looking down at the box still in her hand, wanting to change the subject. Rose gently took the necklace out of the box, undid the clasp, handed it to Malcolm, and turned away from him, holding her hair away from her satiny, soft neck, waiting for him to put it around her. As he reached around her, he could smell the delicate lavender scent of her dark, auburn hair, the soft locks caressing his skin. He stopped a moment, closing his eyes, taking it all in. Clumsily he closed the clasp. Rose turned back around, touching it lovingly against her milky-white skin. Then she reached into the pocket of her robe.

"I'm almost embarrassed to give you this after this beautiful necklace," she said, shyly handing him the small package.

Malcolm took the small box and unwrapped it.

"A mouth harp!"

"Then you don't think it's silly?"

He kissed her softly on the cheek. "Of course not. It's perfect! Mine fell out of my pocket just two weeks back in a place…well, in a place that a person doesn't just reach into to retrieve it."

Rose giggled, knowing she had lost many an item in the same small room in their yard at the farm. That seemed like eons ago. She snuggled up close to Malcolm. He leaned back, reclining them both on the davenport. He combed his fingers lightly through her hair, moving it lovingly away from her face as she closed her eyes and dozed off to sleep.

As he watched her chest rise and fall, feeling the soft warmth of her body on top of his, and the silky strands running through his fingers, a twinge of fear crossed his mind; maybe this was too good to be true; maybe she would end up like the other girls he had known who had teased him and led him on only to drop him when someone better came along. And there was always someone better. What did he have to offer her? He was everyone's friend, but he could trust no one. He knew how to feed himself and get what he needed, but could he feed a family? Was what he did honorable enough for the obvious lady that Rose was? Would she come to look down on him for what he did and where he came from—a poor bayou family that learned how to make ends meet by their hands and their heads? He hadn't let himself dream of such things until now. But now she was in his arms. Now she was very real, and he wanted to be with her, always.

He looked down at her soft, flawless face. He was memorizing the curve of her chin, the shape of her nose, the fullness of her rose-colored lips. He gently touched her cheek. She stirred and snuggled in closer, contentment written all over her. Malcolm decided he needed to introduce her to his family. That would tell him what she thought of him; when she learned where he came from and who his people were. He knew they would love her. How could they not? She was an angel. He was content with the fact that she was lying in his arms. He could live with that, for now.

~ ~ ~

The opportunity to meet Malcolm's family came in the spring on Mardi Gras. Rose was a little disturbed by how busy the house was over the New Year's holiday; it wasn't the usual gentlemen who sat with the girls for thirty minutes to an hour, listening to music, dancing, and having a few drinks. It was men Rose had never seen before, men who seemed interested in only one thing. So when Ginny told Rose that, come Carnival, it would be that way for at least a whole week, she jumped at the chance to get away from the house.

Rose had heard about Mardi Gras the year before at Soldan. Monica's family, who were devote Catholics, even had a king cake sprinkled with sugar dyed purple, green, and gold—the traditional carnival colors. But Ginny had made a king cake for them just after New Years, which confused Rose, who thought it was a Mardi Gras tradition. Malcolm explained to her, as they were sitting down to Ginny's delectable coffee cake, that it is supposed to be served on Kings Day, the twelfth night after Christmas, when the three wise men were said to have visited the Christ Child. Everyone laughed and teased Millie when she found the small doll, which Ginny had baked into the cake, asking who she was planning to invite to her party, which Rose discovered, was another carnival tradition.

Malcolm also explained to Rose the other traditions of Carnival. He took her to the first parade of the season on St. Joseph's day, March nineteenth put on by the Italian community in the French Quarter, or *Vieux Carre*, as Malcolm called it. The main Mardi Gras parades and the associated balls started about three weeks later. Malcolm tried to explain to Rose all the different exclusive, white social groups, called krewes, which put on each event—Comus, Momu, Proteus, Rex.... But they all sounded like Greek to Rose.

What she did enjoy was watching the parades. It was a magical time in the city. Many of the spectators dressed in costumes or masks just to *watch* the parades. Spontaneous street dances where common when these costumed spectators gyrated without reserve to brass bands, similar to the one she had seen in the funeral procession. Rose lost count of the number of women she saw dressed as men and men dressed as women. A long carnival tradition, Malcolm told her.

Rose questioned Malcolm why some of the people on the floats would throw small bags of flour at the crowd, breaking and covering the unsuspecting target in white.

"It's an old tradition that's losing favor with the politicians," he explained. "It's not something the tourists particularly appreciate, so most of the kewes now just throw those cheap necklaces," he said, pointing to the brightly colored necklaces around Rose's neck.

When the major parades began, each krewe seemed to try and outdo the next; each parade having its own theme, elaborate costumes, and paper-mache floats. Even the Indian parade, on fat Tuesday, was a grand event. Negroes dressed in large feather headdresses and elaborate costumes made of intricate beadwork, rode on floats, or walked along the street. Horses and riders were all decked out, and bands played lively tunes as marchers waved and smiled at the crowd. Rose didn't understand why the people on these floats were called Indians since they were all Negroes, and not Indian at all. Another old tradition, Malcolm explained.

"Though until the depression, the different "Indian tribes," all dressed in costume, would take advantage of the situation and get into fights with each other. It was a way to cause a little trouble with a little anonymity. "Things really haven't changed much," he said with a smile.

The other parade entirely made up of coloreds was the Zulu parade, which started out on a tug on the Basin Canal. The participants were covered in black grease paint, black long johns and grass skirts, with white paint around their eyes and mouths. Malcolm explained that this parade was put on by the Zulu Social

Aide and Pleasure Society, an exclusively black krewe which helped other blacks with aid and credit when they needed it.

Rose particularly liked the night parades of some of the white kewes. They were illuminated by Negro flambeau bearers who dressed and danced along with the parade. It was quite a sight.

The river parade was also a spectacle. Rose gazed at the floating carnival of lights with the aw of a child; that is, until the Natchez and the Capitol steam boats floated by all aglow in their hundreds of lights, playing their calliopes, and blowing their loud whistles to the cheers of the crowd gathered on both sides of the river. It had quite the opposite effect on Rose; it reminded her of her long-lost friend and her inability to find her. When Malcolm asked why she had become so sullen, he became saturnine as well. They walked home in silence, holding each other close.

~ ~ ~

On fat Tuesday, Rose was invited to a meal at Malcolm's grandmother's home, in St. Bernard parish. Malcolm told her there was also going to be a community dance after dinner.

"You'll love it, *mo cheri*," Malcolm explained on their way to his grandmothers. "Zydeco music is music of the soul."

Rose didn't say much on the way there; she was nervous about meeting Malcolm's family. *Will they like me? I'm not Creole; maybe they won't like Malcolm going out with someone who's not Creole. Maybe they'll think I'm too young....* All these things and more floated through Rose's head. She was becoming very attached to Malcolm, so meeting his family and making a good impression meant a great deal to her.

Rose wasn't the only one with butterflies. Malcolm did all the talking for the both of them. By the time they pulled up to the small house on stilts, Rose had heard every relative's name—living and dead—knew how many children they had, and the name of every neighbor he expected to be at the party. There were so many names swimming through Rose's head, she wasn't even sure she was going to remember her own.

The house was a small bungalow style, built on stilts for the rainy season when the Bayou would overflow its marshy banks. That also explained the small rowboat leaning up next to the house. The yard was fenced with mismatched, wooden posts and bent and rusted chicken wire. There were some flowers on one edge of an expansive, newly planted garden; otherwise the only other vegetation in the yard was a few well placed trees.

The grass was tender and green underfoot as Rose and Malcolm stepped out of the car Malcolm had somehow procured. He didn't own his own car. He didn't need one in the city.

There were four elderly gentlemen sitting on the porch. As they approached the house, chickens scooted out of their way. The youngest man stood and stepped off the porch to greet them.

"*Bonjour*, Malcolm," the man said, stepping with some difficulty down the steps, saying something to Malcolm in Creole.

He grasped Malcolm's hand and pulled him in for a hug and a slap on the back. Then he turned to Rose.

"And who is this *bel moman*?" he said with a smile, taking Rose's hand in both of his and kissing it softly. Now Rose knew where Malcolm got at least some of his charm.

Malcolm stood proudly next to Rose. "This is Rose Krantz, *Nonk* Jean."

"Krantz? That's an interesting name. What is it?"

"It's German," was all Rose offered.

"Welcome, Rose!" he said, leading her up to the front porch. "Now we know why Malcolm has been spending all of his free time in the city."

He smiled back at Malcolm who walked behind the pair.

"Come meet our 'Shack Bully', Malcolm's *gran-mer*."

Malcolm's uncle chuckled softly, then called out something in Creole. He pulled aside the muslin cloth which covered the front entrance and guided Rose inside without following. Much to Rose's dismay, Malcolm didn't follow her in. She could hear his voice on the porch joking and talking in Creole to the other men.

She stepped into what was obviously a room for both eating and socializing. It ran the length of the house, front to back. There was a stone fireplace on the far right wall, blackened around the opening from many years of fires. Above it hung six or eight different bunches of plants, hung upside down to dry. There was a large table in the front of the room with benches along each side and a chair on each end. The glassless windows around the room were all open. The same muslin cloth that covered the door was pulled back, letting the warm spring breeze caress her skin. The rest of the furnishings in the room were very simple—a small table and oil lamp, a straight back chair sitting next to it, and a rocker by the fireplace. Everything was as neat as a pin. Rose could tell Malcolm's Grandmother was a meticulous housekeeper.

As Rose stood looking over the room, a short, rotund woman entered. She had wavy, black hair pulled back into a tight bun, with skin just a shade darker than Malcolm's, which shone with the same glow and confident wisdom that Grandma B.'s had.

"You must be Rose," she said with a broad smile. She walked up to Rose and enveloped the young girl in her arms. "Welcome, my dear. I'm Mary, but everyone calls me Gran-mer. *Vini an*, come in and have a seat." She kept an arm around Rose's shoulders as she led her into the next room.

The kitchen was draped with every nature of dried flower, plant, and root, and what wasn't hanging from the ceiling was kept in the numerous jars which lined the many shelves all around the room. Malcolm had told Rose that his grandmother was the local healer, but Rose had no idea what that might entail until now. What hit Rose first, though, was the spicy, enticing aroma of something cooking, which she had just a hint of in the other room.

"*Vini*, come, have a seat," Malcolm's grandmother said pointing to an open chair at the kitchen table. "Rose, this is Jean's wife, Julia."

"*Bonjour*," said the slight woman with long dark hair who was sitting at the table. She nodded her head in greeting. Her hands were busy shelling crawfish, so she couldn't take hold of Rose's to welcome her.

"Oh, let me get you an apron. You don't wanna get that nice party dress dirty," Grandma said, handing Rose an apron. She hesitated when she caught sight of the necklace around Rose's neck, then she looked into her eyes. Rose wasn't sure her expression was one of subdued pleasure or indifference. Rose swallowed hard, feeling a drip of perspiration roll down her side.

Rose wasn't sure what to wear to this occasion, and she had received much conflicting advice from the girls. Madam E. finally intervened and helped her decide on a full calico skirt, which belonged to Tess, and a white cotton blouse, which belonged to Bridget. Ruth supplied a pair of hoop earrings to match her lovely gold heart necklace. Sadie added the finishing touch with a dab of *Emeraude* perfume. Ginny supplied her recipe for corn muffins that she, Jolene, and May had made that afternoon.

"These are corn muffins," Rose said, exchanging her grease stained bag of muffins for the apron.

"How thoughtful," Gran-mer said sincerely. Then she set a bowl of greens in front of Rose. "Would you mind cutting this up for me?"

Malcolm's grandmother knew the best way to make a woman feel comfortable and get her to talk, was to give her something to do in the kitchen.

"Hey, Mama!" a lovely middle-aged women said as she walked into the kitchen and gave Malcolm's Grandmother a kiss on the cheek, pie in hand.

"And you must be Rose!" she said, turning to Rose.

Rose nodded.

"I'm Malcolm's Aunt Margarite."

Then she turned back toward her mother.

"Where do you want me to put this pie?"

"Just over on the counter is fine," Gran-mer said. "Here," she continued, shoving some pot holders into Margarite's hands. "Make your self useful; check on the biscuits."

"No sense in me just sitting and having a nice conversation with our guest now is there?" she teased her mother. "No, No…, don't tell me: idle hands are the devil's playground," she said, putting a hand up in front of her mother.

"Don't mock me, child."

"I'm just teasin', Mama. I haven't been in the devils playground for years now." She and Julia laughed. Gran-mer just looked at her sideways and went back to her pot on the stove.

"Malcolm tells me you be goin' to school," Gran-mer said to Rose, not taking her eyes off what she was stirring.

"Yes ma'am. I'm a junior at St. Joseph's."

"A good catholic school, that's nice. Then once ya done with school ya gonna settle down 'round here and start a family?"

"Mama!" Margarite scolded, with a pan full of biscuits in her hands.

"Well, ain't that what every woman wants—get married and have children?"

"Well, actually, I'm not sure what I'm going to do. I would kind of like to travel and see some different parts of the world."

"*Hou-wa*, you're restless like my Daniel. I hardly see the boy but twice a year. I don't know where all he goes off to."

"He's not a boy, Mama," Margarite said.

"He'll always be my boy, just like you always be my girl; don't be forgettin' that," she said, shaking her spoon at her daughter.

Margarite went over and gave her mother a big squeeze from behind. "I love you too, Mama."

"All I know is, ya can travel the world over, child, and you ain't gonna find anything different then what ya got right now," she said looking Rose straight in the eye. "Speakin' a children, where yours be, Margarite?"

"Mary's with her fianance's family, and Tommy and Willy, well they'd rather go to town for the festivities."

"That's the problem with young folk these days—they ain't got no time for family no more," Grandma said, shaking her head.

"You almost done with those crawfish, Julia?" Grandma asked.

"Yes'um, just two more."

"Ya put ya crawfish in your gumbo too early, girls, and it gets rubbery," Grandma instructed the small group of women.

Just then, Malcolm came into the kitchen. "How you ladies gettin' on?" he asked. "Um, um, that gumbo sure do smell good!"

"You been here how long and you ain't come give your *gran-mer* a kiss? I brought you up better then that, child!" his Grandma chided him.

Malcolm stepped quickly over to his grandmother, grasped her around the waist, picked her up, and swung her around in a circle.

"Put me down, child," Grandma scolded. "I's too old for such nonsense!"

"You're never too old, *Gran-mer!*" Malcolm said, still holding her tight.

Rose watched with interest at Malcolm's teasing affection for his grandmother. She knew she had helped his father raise him after his mother died, right after his birth. Rose wasn't sure what was worse, not knowing your mother at all, like Malcolm, or knowing her enough to miss her, as Todd did. Seeing the love Malcolm had for his grandmother, she thought maybe Malcolm's road was a little softer.

"Now let go a me, and get your no-good *nonks* to help ya get the dining table outside," she ordered, pushing him toward the door. "It's nice enough that we can eat out-a-doors, then we'll be that much more ready for when the dancing starts."

Dancing? Oh yes, the dancing. Rose had tried to forget about that. Whenever the girls tried to get her to dance to pass the time while they were waiting for the gentlemen to show for the evening, Rose always seemed to have two left feet. Grandma B.'s lesson on the riverboat hadn't soaked in.

The evening meal went fairly well for Rose. She didn't misspeak or say anything that seemed to offend anyone. Malcolm would try to steer the conversation away from Rose when she appeared to tire of all the questions about her family, her time on the riverboats, and what she did in St. Louis. It was a friendly group, but Rose felt a little like it was an inquest, especially from Malcolm's grandmother. Rose thought even the dance would be better than the Spanish Inquisition. Besides, she knew she didn't *have* to dance.

~ ~ ~

It was the fourth song before she convinced Malcolm to sit one out. The fiddle and spoons, accordion, guitar and washboard continued for two more songs before everyone else needed a break. Everyone filed outside, fanning themselves and laughing. Rose and Malcolm were already standing outside enjoying the cool which the evening brought. Rose remembered how it was always cooler on the farm at night than it was in the city. It was the same out here in the bayou. The melodic sound of the crickets and frogs, and the sweet smell of moist night air filled her nostrils in the dark night and brought her back to that familiar place for just a moment. She had forgotten how soothing and peaceful a summer night in the country could be.

When the music had first started, Malcolm swept Rose up in his arms and moved her around the room with such ease that it didn't take long for Rose to pick up the easy sway of his hips, and gentle coaching with his hand on the small of her back. Whether the songs were in Creole or English, it didn't seem to matter to anyone; it was the traditional three time waltz of *Valse, Bebe,* or the quicker one-two rhythm of *Flammes D'Enfer* which pulled everyone, two by two into the middle of the room.

"So what do you think?" Malcolm asked Rose, handing her a cool glass of well water.

"It's wonderful, Malcolm." She smiled at him, taking the glass out of his hand. "I've never heard music like that before."

"Let's go over here and sit down." Malcolm pointed Rose to a large tree stump.

Rose looked at Malcolm concerned. "I don't think your grandmother likes me too much, Malcolm."

"Why do you say that, *cheri?*"

"First off, she didn't like my idea of traveling around after high school. Then the fifty questions at dinner; it was like she was looking for ammunition to use against me."

"Oh, you've got it all wrong." Malcolm took her hand to reassure her. "She likes you very much! She told me so herself. She is just very direct about things. She doesn't like to play games with people. She likes to be very upfront; she wanted to find out about you, so she just asked you out-right. I tried to help you out, but my *gran-mer* is a very persistent woman. When she wants something, she usually gets it."

"I can tell!" Rose laughed nervously.

They heard the music start up again, and people started filing back into the small house. Malcolm straightened up and smiled at Rose, eyes sparkling and bright. Rose could not resist his boyish grin. She lifted her hand and he took it; in they went to dance the night away.

~ ~ ~

It took a week for the grin to leave Malcolm's face, and Rose, maybe just a day or two less. The Mardi Gras experience seemed to weave their two souls even closer together, so now Malcolm's visits to the house were daily and his departures always ended with a soft peck on Rose's cheek. The event and subsequent closeness the two had developed, vanquished any thoughts Rose had to return home before the school year was done.

The timing was perfect for the Madam. She had an unexpected visitor for Carnival. Someone, Rose found out from Ginny, who she once had a relationship with which didn't work out. It was the talk of the house the next day at breakfast.

"I think he stayed the whole night," Ruth said quietly, not wanting Madam E. to hear. "I heard the front door open and close about seven this morning when I got up to go to the bathroom."

"Is that the same man that left her two years ago?" Bridget asked the group.

"The same schmo," Sadie said, leaning back in her chair with a sly grin on her face. "I can't say I blame the woman for takin' him back, though—he's a real looker!"

"I sink dat suit he wears was from Spain. I have seen dis style der," Tess added.

"Ma'dam like dis man?" May asked.

"She likes him a lot! I think she would have married the guy if he would'a asked." Ruth said.

Then the conversation turned to Rose.

"Speakin' a romances, how was meet-the-family night Rose?" Sadie asked.

"Oh, it went off pretty well." She smiled a shy smile. "If it wasn't for his grandmother giving me the fifth degree, I would say he has a pretty nice family. And the Zydeco music was so much fun!"

"Yeah, your beau dropped you off pretty late!" Ruth teased.

"Thanks for noticing, *Mom!*" Rose teased back. All the girls laughed, each calling Ruth "Mom."

Rose picked up some of the girls' dishes and took them over to the sink, where Ginny was running the wash water.

Ginny spoke softly to Rose, so the other girls wouldn't hear her. "I assume Malcolm's been actin' as a gentleman. I know the boy's been around the block a few times, but if he ever tries ta take advantage of ya…, so help me God…," Ginny's face tightened and her knuckles took on a lighter shade of brown on the edge of the sink.

"He hasn't tried anything, Ginny," Rose whispered back "But I promise, I'll let you have the second crack at 'im if he ever does, right after me!" They both chuckled.

❧ 17 ❧

Secrets are funny things; there seems to be some sort of karmic force that surrounds them. If the secret is small and insignificant— say, you've dyed your hair since you were twenty-five, or you sneak a cigar every once in a while because you like the earthy smell of tobacco and the bitter taste it leaves on your tongue—these types of secrets seem to remain secrets. But if it's a bigger secret, something which impacts someone other than yourself in a significant way, it never seems to remain under wraps; it will eventually come out over time. There is some type of force which pulls together just the right moments and just the right people for your secret to be revealed. Rose was soon to be the recipient of such karmic forces. She was to learn a secret, which she never would have guessed on her own.

~ ~ ~

The next afternoon, while sitting in Madam E.'s office with Malcolm, Rose would confirm the house gossip.

"Malcolm, Rose, I have called you both here because I have a big favor to ask."

Madam E. sat statuesque, in a pristinely tailored suit with nigh a hair out of place.

"I have been asked to go out of town for a couple weeks on a boat to Nova Scotia, and I have decided to go, but only on one condition—I want you two to watch over my business for me."

She waited a minute for the surprising news to sink in, then she continued.

"I know this is a big responsibility, but I have complete confidence in you both. Of course, you will get paid handsomely for your services. If you decide you do not want to take this on, I will understand fully."

Malcolm and Rose looked at each other, both a bit dumbfounded at the proposition.

"When would you be leaving?" Malcolm asked.

"This next Monday," Madam E replied, then she paused. "I think you should talk this over before you make your decision, but I need to know as soon as possible if I am to make other arrangements. Could you let me know your decision by tomorrow?"

"I think if we have a moment, Madam, we could let you know now," Rose replied.

Madam E. brightened. "Well, then I'll leave you two alone to discuss the matter. I'll be in the kitchen." Then she left the room.

"Wow, that was a surprise!" Rose said, leaning back on the davenport.

"You can say that again!" Malcolm agreed.

"Well, what do you think?" Rose asked.

"You mean you're actually considering this?"

"What harm can it do? I've got Easter break next week and the week after...well, you can take the night shift, and I can take the day shift. The girls don't get up until I get home from school, anyway."

"Rose." Malcolm looked at her seriously. "This is not exactly something you want to put on your resume—'Managed brothel with six girls for two weeks with boyfriend'."

"That does sound seedy, doesn't it?" she laughed in agreement. "Though who but you and I are going to know about this? I don't have any family around here, and your family already knows you do business here, don't they?"

"Well, my *gran-mer* doesn't know, but then she doesn't ask, either." Malcolm shook his head. "The last time you did someone a favor, you ended up in the hospital with stitches in your head."

Rose looked at him sternly. "That was my own doing. It had nothing to do with helping Grandma B.," she scolded.

"All right, but even if we can do this, I'm still not sure it's a good idea."

"It'll be fine, and it's only for two weeks. The police have just been paid, so we shouldn't have any problems on that end."

"Well, if you think I'm going to let you run this place in the day by yourself, you're mistaken!"

"So you're going to stay up twenty-four hours a day for two whole weeks?"

"Well, I'll sleep on the davenport here, but I'm not leaving the house!" he insisted.

"Okay, Malcolm." Rose smiled at his concern. "But you're sleeping in my bed. I'll stay in Madam E.'s room."

Madam E. was obviously pleased and relieved with their decision. The girls were also quite happy. Madam E. would have closed the place down like she did during her last trip to Japan, and they all lost too much money to want that to happen again. And the tourist season was just beginning with all the northern businessmen making trips south to start their summers early. It was a busy time for them, before hurricane season and the heat and humidity of the summer set in.

When Madam E. was set to leave, the whole house made a day of it, packing her up and going down to the wharf to see her off. It was a perfect spring day; there wasn't a cloud in the robin-egg blue sky, the soft breeze off the river kept them all cool in the warming afternoon sun, and every flower along their way seemed to be in bloom. No one had seen Madam E. in a better mood. She wasn't her usual calm, collected self, either; she seemed to have let her guard down just a smidge.

"Ticket, ticket…," Madam E. said frantically searching her purse for her boat ticket.

"I think you told me that Mr. Wells had the tickets Ma-dam," Malcolm reminded her.

"Oh, yes," she said relieved. "I did say that, didn't I. I seem to have lost my head."

Rose smiled at her nervousness.

This man must mean a great deal to Madam E. for her to be so flustered, Rose thought. *I can't wait to meet him!*

"Last call, last call, all aboard the SS Triton to Nova Scotia! Last call!" a man in a crisp uniform yelled as he walked through the crowded dock. And, as if to add emphasis to his words, the large ship blew its loud whistle.

"Well, I better get going," Madam E. said, turning toward the group. "You all take care of each other." Then she uncharacteristically hugged each girl. "And Malcolm, you take good care of Rose," she said, holding Rose's hand. "She's a very special young lady."

"I know she is, Ma-dam."

Madam E. walked rapidly up the gang plank and disappeared into the crowd on the main deck. The group stood around waiting to see the ship leave the wharf. As they stood watching, Millie spied Madam E.

"There she is!" she said excitedly, pointing toward the ship.

"Where?" her mother asked.

"On the second deck! Standing with the man with the hat!" she explained.

The group scanned the second deck rail and the many men in hats. They finally saw Madam standing closely to an equally crisply dressed gentleman, politely waving to the group, an obvious smile on her face. They all enthusiastically waved back.

When the ship blew its whistle—three short burst to signal its pending departure—it stealthily pulled out of its slip and out onto the river. The group turned to head back home. As they walked toward the taxi stand, Rose was stopped by the familiar sound of a calliope.

"Hey, that sounds like the Capitol!" Rose said out loud. "I'd like to stay and see her come in if that's okay with you?" she asked Malcolm.

"Sure, Rose, if you really want to?" He knew seeing riverboats and hanging around on the wharf made Rose sad and nervous at the same time. But today, on this bright cheerful spring day, her long-lost friend and her encounter with Peter didn't seem to dampen her spirits. Seeing Madam E. so happy and obviously in love reminded Rose of her ever-growing love of the young man she was standing next to; it shielded her old pain from view and filled her with a new hope of better things to come.

She didn't have to wait long; the tall, black pipes and long, white, wedding-cake-like paddleboat came sliding into view as the song *Happy Days are Here Again* played on her calliope, merrily announcing her ever-closer presence, calling to all to come and join her for a leisurely ride. Rose walked closer to her slip to get a closer look and maybe see some of her old crewmates, if she was lucky.

Sure enough; there on the main deck, throwing out the rope to tie the Capital down was Martin. Rose grinned from ear to ear at the familiar face and the familiar memories which went along with him. She wanted to yell out to him and wave, but he was too far away yet. She scanned the other decks for more faces.

There was Mike, Samuel, and Lavenia getting things stowed or hanging out over the rail. Rose brightened even more. Why hadn't she come down to see her old friends sooner? Why did it bother her so? She hardly could remember. Then she stopped and almost fell back against Malcolm, her face losing its color and brilliance.

"Are you okay, Rose?" he asked.

When she didn't answer right away, he stood in front of her and looked into her now wet eyes.

"What's the matter, Rose?" he asked, taking hold of her arms.

But Rose couldn't talk. She just kept staring up at the Capitol. There, just off the third deck, was another familiar face staring down at her. Rose put her hands over her mouth; then she pulled away from Malcolm without an explanation and began to run, waving her hand frantically, not losing sight of the face which was looking at her with the same lost expression.

"Lilly Mae! Lilly Mae!" The tears were now streaming down the sides of her face.

"Rose! Rose!" she could hear faintly as she got closer to the docking steam boat.

Malcolm ran up behind her, searching the rails for Rose's long lost friend.

"I'm coming right down!" Lilly Mae yelled out, then ducked out of sight, only to appear again on the main deck next to Martin after what seemed like an eternity to Rose. Lilly Mae's face was equally streaked with tears.

Rose quaked up and down with excitement, then hugged Malcolm so hard she nearly choked him. She pulled away from him, grinning ear-to-ear. He handed her his handkerchief and she wiped her eyes and face.

Lilly Mae was off the gangplank only a few seconds after it was dropped down onto to the wharf, the two friends running into each other's arms. When they finally released their embrace, they both giggled at each other. Rose dug in her purse for her handkerchief to give to Lilly Mae, then blew her nose once more with Malcolm's. Malcolm just stood off slightly behind Rose with a somewhat somber look on his face; he didn't want to interfere with the happy reunion, though he was having trouble being totally happy about it himself.

"Oh, I'm sorry!" Rose said, stepping back to fully expose Malcolm to Lilly Mae. "Lilly Mae, this is Malcolm. Malcolm, at long last...," Rose sighed, "*This* is Lilly Mae."

"Pleased to meet you," Malcolm said, dropping his eyes to avoid Lilly Mae's direct gaze. Rose did not notice this mild avoidance, but Lilly Mae did.

"Nice to meet you," Lilly Mae replied.

Rose grasped both of Lilly Mae's hands in hers. "I just can't believe I've found you after all this time!" Rose beamed at her friend. "Where have you been? Madam had everyone looking for you!"

Lilly Mae looked over Rose's shoulder at Malcolm, who looked back at her blankly.

"I looked for you too, Rose, and when I couldn't find ya, I took a job on the Capitol so I could stay around the city. They do day excursions outta NaOrlins all winter."

"That's probably why I never saw you. I've been avoiding the wharf like the plague," Rose explained, grasping Lilly Mae by the arm and walking with her down- river. "Boy, have I got a lot to tell you!" She smiled.

"Me too, Rose," Lilly Mae said, but she stopped walking and looked straight at Rose. "But I have to finish cleaning up the boat yet."

Then she looked at Malcolm, who had stopped a few steps behind them, then back to Rose.

"Can we meet this evening, maybe over dinner?"

Rose looked at Malcolm then back to Lilly Mae.

"Oh, I'm sorry Lilly Mae. I have to work this evening."

"No you don't," Malcolm piped up. "I can handle things, Rose."

"That's not fair to you, Malcolm; our first night, and I'm running out on my end of the deal."

"Ginny, Millie, and I can handle things. And besides, it's your Easter break, you can stay up late with me on my shift if it makes you feel better." He smiled at her.

Lilly Mae stood there confused; she didn't understand a word they were saying.

"Yah, I forgot it's Easter break! That's perfect! Okay, I'll take you up on your offer." Then she turned back to Lilly Mae. "Where would you like to meet?"

"Well, Mama's a little tired from all the Easter guests, so it might be best to go to your place. Is that okay?"

"Well...," Rose hesitated, looking for the right words. "We probably shouldn't go there just yet." She looked at Malcolm and smiled. "It's a little hard to explain just now. How about we go to Delmonico's? They have great seafood!"

Lilly Mae looked at Rose with mild amusement.

"Looks like you're a regular native," Lilly Mae teased. Rose smiled. "Yeah, that's fine. How 'bout seven?"

"Wonderful! Seven it is!" Rose said; then she grabbed hold of Lilly Mae for one more signature squeeze. "I just can't believe you're real!"

"Well," Lilly Mae said in a strained voice. "I can see some things never change!"

"Oh, I'm sorry, Lilly Mae," Rose apologized and let go of her. "I'm just so excited!"

"I couldn't tell!" she chuckled, pleased as Rose was at their meeting, and Rose's enthusiasm. "I better get going. I'll see you later," Lilly Mae said as she turned and walked back toward the steamer.

Rose watched her walk away. Lilly Mae turned and looked back at the pair, waved, then stepped out of sight.

Rose grasped Malcolm's arm and squeezed as they headed for the streetcar. "I can't believe I've finally found her!" she said with excitement. "This is the best day!" Then she looked up at Malcolm, her face bright and beaming. Malcolm forced a smile. Luckily for him, Rose was too excited to notice his lack of enthusiasm. He quickly looked up the street, trying to spy when the next streetcar might be by to pick them up and take them home, conveniently avoiding Rose's direct gaze.

~ ~ ~

The dinner with Lilly Mae lasted well into the night. There was much to catch up on, especially for Lilly Mae. She couldn't believe Rose had stumbled upon Peter and now was living and working in a whorehouse. Lilly Mae told Rose about the night classes she was continuing to take; then the conversation made its way around to the gentlemen in their lives.

"So are you still going out with someone?" Rose asked excitedly. "If I remember correctly, when we were leaving the J.S. last fall, you were trying not to tell me about someone."

"Ya, there is still someone," Lilly Mae reluctantly admitted. "His name is Michael; he lives in the tenements where I live and works for the railroad."

"So..., are you going to tell me all about him?"

"There isn't much ta tell, really. He's eighteen, and he lives with his family right now, but he's saving up for a place of his own."

"No, I mean like, is he cute? Does he take you out for dinner or to the movies? Is he a good kisser?" she teased.

Lilly Mae shook her head softly at Rose's amusing questions. "We go ta the movies sometimes, but like I said, he's savin' his money, so most times we just go for walks along the river or the canal." Lilly Mae paused, then looked seriously at Rose. "How 'bout Malcolm? How long you been goin' out with him?"

"Well, we met the same day we lost each other, but we really didn't start going out until…, maybe just after Thanksgiving. The house was raided and he…."

"The house was raided!" Lilly Mae sat up wide-eyed. "Did you get arrested?"

"No, just some of the girls and the Madam, but Madam E. managed to strike a deal with the police chief, so we don't have to worry about that anymore. Madam E. is quite amazing, really; she manages that house and all those women and hardly ever gets flustered. In fact, I think she likes it. She knows a lot of influential people in this town—mostly men, of course."

"My God, Rose, I just don't believe ya stay in a place like that."

"It does seem strange when you think about it, but the women are really very nice, and Madam E. gives me room and board and pays for my schooling. In exchange, I help her keep her books, help around the house, and I'm trying to teach May and Jolene English. They are two new girls from Japan." Rose hesitated. "And I'm in my room by the time most of the gentlemen show up anyway."

"Gentlemen? I can't believe many of them are gentlemen."

"That's surprising, isn't it? I didn't think that would be the case either, but most of Madam E.'s clientele *are* gentlemen. Unfortunately, some are married men, but Madam E. runs a very classy place. You have to have fairly deep pockets to visit there.

Of course, around Mardi Gras and New Years there were a lot
of strangers that showed up, but most of the time the same men
come by."

"What about this Malcolm fellow? There's somethin' 'bout
him that doesn't seem quite right," Lilly Mae said in her usual
straight-forward style.

Rose furrowed her brow, a little offended by the remark.

"Really? Why do you say that?"

She had forgotten how blunt Lilly Mae could be at times.
And when it came to Malcolm, she felt like she needed to defend
him. *Yes, he hasn't gone on to high school, but neither have you; and yes,
he has kind of a strange occupation, but he makes good money; and most
importantly, he really cares for me,* Rose thought as she waited for Lilly
Mae's reply.

"Well, he didn't seem very friendly, and he hardly can look at
me straight."

"I think he was just fine!" Rose said, still a bit miffed.

"You only see what you want to see, Rose," Lilly Mae said,
then she looked down at the empty glass in front of her.

She was instantly sorry for what she said the minute she had
said it. It was true; Rose seemed to have blinders on when it came
to some things, especially people. But she knew she shouldn't have
said it by the lost look on Rose's face. She was trying to curb her
tendency to say exactly what was on her mind, but when it came
to her best friend, it was particularly difficult; she didn't want Rose
being taken advantage of.

"I'm sorry, Rose," Lilly Mae said. "I shouldn't have said that.
It's just that I don't wanna see ya get hurt."

Rose sighed. She could tell by the look on Lilly Mae's face she
was truly sorry.

"That's okay. Let's not fight about this." Then she perked up and smiled. "Once you spend some time with him, I'm sure you'll see that he's really very nice."

She reached out her hand and gently held onto Lilly Mae's forearm as it rested on the white table cloth.

"He really cares for me, Lilly Mae, and I care for him too."

Lilly Mae smiled and placed her hand on top of Rose's. "I'm happy for you, Rose."

~ ~ ~

When the girls parted, they promised they would meet up again that next Sunday evening. Lilly Mae had to work the rest of the week, and Rose knew she would be busy taking care of the house until then. Sundays were always their slow day, so that would work out just fine. Rose had invited Lilly Mae over to the house for dinner so she could spend some time with Malcolm, to get to know him. Lilly Mae somewhat reluctantly accepted, not sure about going to a whorehouse.

About six o'clock that next Sunday there was a knock on the back door. Rose rushed out to the porch to let in Lilly Mae.

"Hey!" she said excitedly, grabbing her friend in a tight hug the minute she stepped onto the porch. "Come on in!"

Rose grasped Lilly Mae's hand and pulled her into the kitchen. Malcolm was standing at the stove stirring up some wonderful aromas out of a large pot on the stove.

"Hope you like Jambalaya?" he asked Lilly Mae with a smile. He knew he had to be friendlier to her than the first time they had met. She was Rose's best friend, so he wanted to make sure he got along with her, even though it was a bit awkward, considering the circumstances.

"Yes, that'd be fine," Lilly Mae said, noting his change in mood.

The three talked for about three quarters of an hour while Rose and Malcolm worked around the kitchen preparing their meal. It was mostly Rose who talked, really; Lilly Mae was her usual quiet self. Malcolm seemed unusually quiet, Rose thought, and perhaps a little nervous as well.

Rose was watching him carefully, trying to see if what Lilly Mae had said was true. He seemed to be friendly toward Lilly Mae, but he didn't seem to want to sit down at all. That was a little odd. Rose couldn't be sure. She decided that when they sat down to dinner, she would be able to really tell what was going on between them.

They hadn't gotten many calls for the girls that evening, so Rose had given the ladies the night off. Ginny never worked on Sundays, so they wouldn't be disturbed until Sadie, Millie, May, and Jolene came down for dinner around nine o'clock. Ruth, Tess and Bridget had gone out for the evening to see a Clark Gable and Claude Colbert movie, have dinner, then maybe go dancing. The girls had a hard time changing their usual schedule on their days off, so they usually didn't try.

Before they left, and before Lilly Mae had arrived, Ruth made Rose promise they would join them at Pete Lala's Cafe later, to go dancing. Rose wasn't sure Lilly Mae would want to go, and she wasn't so sure about the idea herself. She had never been out to a club in New Orleans, and considering her last experience at a night club was a fiasco, the thought of going out made her nervous. Rose knew there was a more relaxed level of tolerance for Negroes and whites doing things together socially in New Orleans, but it still wasn't the norm. She agreed to meet them just so they would leave and let her finish preparing the house for her friend's arrival.

Rose had Malcolm sit right across the table from Lilly Mae when they finally sat down to eat.

"Rose tells me you've taken a night class to improve your reading," he said, looking right at Lilly Mae.

"Yeah, that was last year. This winter I took a class on writing, and now I'm taking one on history."

"That's wonderful!" He smiled pleasantly at her. "History is my favorite subject. I think a person should never stop learning."

"I keep telling Malcolm he should go back to school and get his high school diploma, but he prefers to study on his own," Rose added, pleased that the two seemed to be getting along just fine. Rose finely was able to relax a little and enjoy the rest of the dinner sitting with two of the most important people in her life.

As the three were cleaning up after dinner, Sadie, Millie, May, and Jolene came into the kitchen. Lilly Mae was a little nervous when they walked into the room, but Lilly Mae soon discovered that Rose was right, they seemed like regular people; they were dressed in regular house dresses and they were all very nice.

"I made enough jambalaya for everyone," Malcolm told them. "It's still on the stove. You might have to heat it up a bit though."

"And there's corn muffins and apple pie on the table," Rose added. "We're going to have our coffee in the parlor."

Rose took the coffee off the stove, placed it on a tray with the cups and saucers, which Malcolm had taken out of the cupboard, and they headed into the parlor.

They hadn't been in there too long when, much to Rose's dismay, Ruth, Tess and Bridget noisily came through the front door.

"Hey, here they are!" Ruth said loudly.

Rose immediately stood up and introduced her fellow housemates to Lilly Mae.

"Very nice to meet choou," Tess said, shaking Lilly Mae's hand.

"Yes, that's wonderful that Rose finally found you. I know they looked for you for a long time," Bridget said.

"All right now, enough of this chit chat. We're going out dancing," Ruth said; then she grabbed Rose behind the arm. "And so are you!"

"Yes, we all go dance," Tess said, taking Lilly Mae under the arm.

Bridget took Malcolm's arm, and they all went out the front door pulling their somewhat reluctant partners.

They walked noisily down the sidewalk as the wind whipped their hair about, threatening rain. Rose could tell by Ruth's breath that they had been drinking, which explained their boisterous behavior and loud voices.

Pete Lala's was a small place on the corner of Iberville and Marais, north of Rampart Street, in what Malcolm explained was the old red light district called Storyville.

Rose was amazed that the stately, three story brick buildings they passed along the north side of Basin Street were once beautifully kept cat houses. Most of the buildings in this area, including Pete Lala's, were now very run down and in a bad need of a coat or two of paint. Pete's was a two-story building which didn't even have a sign. In fact, if you didn't know any better, you would have thought it was a place which sold only Jax beer, for the Jax beer sign above the door, and the large one painted on one whole side of the building.

There was the distinct smell of cigarettes when they stepped inside the place, but it was still early, so there was not enough smoke yet to cloud the view of the dark wood bar, which ran the length of the inside wall. Behind the bar were three large mirrors reflecting different colored bottles of alcohol displayed on small steps just in front of them. The bartenders wore white shirts and black bow ties, with their sleeves rolled up, ready for a busy evening. Wooden round tables and chairs lined the wall opposite the bar, with just a few patrons scattered around the room. At the back of the room there was a slightly raised area where a colored, four piece band was getting ready to play.

"We'll get a table, why don't you get us a waiter to take our order," Ruth suggested to Malcolm, pointing toward the bar.

"Now, isn't this nice?" she said after they had all sat down. When Malcolm returned, he had to take a chair from another table to squeeze into the table with the rest of his party.

The waiter stepped up to their table. "What'll it be?" he said in a gruff voice.

"I'll have a brandy old-fashioned sweet," Ruth blurted out.

"I'll have a glass of red wine," Bridget said. "Two, please," Tess added.

"What would you like, Lilly Mae?" Malcolm asked.

"A Jax is fine for me," she said.

"Rose, would you like a soda?" Malcolm asked.

"A soda! No such thing!" Ruth interrupted. "Give her what I'm having," she ordered the waiter.

"Is that all right, Rose?" Malcolm asked.

"You'll love it, I swear. You hardly taste the booze!" Ruth pressed.

"Sure," Rose said tentatively.

"You don't have to," Malcolm assured her in a quiet voice.

Rose smiled at Malcolm's concern. "That's fine, Malcolm."

"I'll have a beer too," Malcolm said to the waiter who had a look of impatience on his face.

As Ruth started her inquires of Lilly Mae, the band began to play. It was a fast song of the jazz variety that Rose had heard Ginny listening to in the kitchen at the house. Ruth stopped in mid-sentence, grabbed Bridget's hand and pulled her out into the center of the room where they began to dance. After a few moments, Ruth sashayed over to the table and pulled on Rose's hand to join them, yelling to Tess over the music to join the threesome.

The four women danced to the tune all by themselves, since the bar was less then halfway filled, and most people hadn't had enough liquid courage to get them dancing this early in the evening. Rose was self-conscious as she moved hesitantly to the music. Ruth, Bridget, and Tess had no such inhibitions; their bodies expertly accentuating the rhythm and flow of the music, punctuated by the broad smiles on their faces. Rose couldn't help enjoy herself watching them, and she slowly was able to relax. Malcolm and Lilly Mae sat quietly watching the group. The next number was a slow, bluesy tune, so the ladies headed for the table.

When they sat down, their drinks were sitting in front of them. Everyone thirstily took a sip, including Rose. The concoction Ruth had ordered for her tasted better than she expected. There was just a hint of bitter dandelion on the back of her tongue, but the overwhelming sweetness of the drink made it very tolerable. They were able to make polite conversation during the slower, quiet tune, until the next louder, jazz number cued up.

And so the evening went, dancing to one or two songs, then sitting down for some light conversation and drink. Malcolm and Rose danced two slow songs together, and as the evening and the drinking progressed, Ruth, Tess, and Bridget danced with the men who would occasionally step bravely up to their table. Lilly Mae was even asked to dance by a young, colored gentleman, but she declined. The place was starting to fill with patrons, the smoky haze thickening, scratching Rose's throat, and irritating her eyes.

When Rose sat down after finishing a dance with Malcolm, she had a second brandy old-fashioned sitting in front of her. If it wasn't for the dryness of her throat, Rose wouldn't have considered starting in on a second cocktail. After a few more sips she was noticing her body temperature rising and a faint buzz in her head.

Another slow tune started up and Malcolm stood and asked Lilly Mae to dance. Much to Rose's surprise, she accepted. Rose watched them move slowly around the floor, Lilly Mae, rather stiffly, Malcolm, swaying softly to the music. Rose was happy Lilly Mae's observations had turned out to be false. She wanted them to become good friends, and it seemed that things were working out just fine. Rose sat looking at them through the haze, melting into her chair, content with the sight before her and the liquor inside her.

Rose turned back to talk to Bridget. When she looked back onto the dance floor, Lilly Mae and Malcolm had stopped dancing and were obviously in a heated conversation.

Rose sat up straight, almost getting out of her chair to see what was the matter, but soon Lilly Mae was resolutely walking over to the table.

"I need to leave!" she said in a huff.

"What's the matter, Lilly Mae?" Rose asked in confusion.

By this time Malcolm was standing next to Lilly Mae. Rose looked at him with questioning eyes.

"Ask *him*!" Lilly Mae blurted out, then she headed for the door.

Rose got up and quickly followed, nearly tipping into the full table beside them. Rose's head was spinning from Lilly Mae's sudden change in mood and her sudden change in position, the alcohol and the smoky haze making everything seem surreal. Malcolm followed Rose close behind. Rose caught up to Lilly Mae and grabbed her arm before she stepped out the door.

"Lilly Mae, stop! What's the matter?"

Lilly Mae looked at her friend, then at Malcolm standing next to her. Choosing her words carefully, she sighed, "I need to leave, Rose. I'm tired, and I've got a long way to walk home."

"Won't you let us call you a cab?" Malcolm offered. Rose looked at him then at Lilly Mae, nodding her head in agreement with the suggestion.

"No, I'd rather walk," she said, and headed out the door. Rose and Malcolm followed her out.

"But Lilly Mae...."

"I'll talk to ya later, Rose," she said as she stepped out into the light mist which was falling in the foggy night. Lilly Mae was soon out of sight.

Rose stepped out into the mist. She liked the feel of the damp spray on her face. It helped her partially wake out of her mental fog and cool her heated brow.

"Come back inside, Rose," Malcolm said.

Rose stepped back under the second floor overhang which was above the entrance.

"What happened, Malcolm?" Rose questioned. "Everything seemed to be going so well!"

Malcolm hesitated. "We should talk about it tomorrow, Rose. It's late. How 'bout we head home."

"No!" Rose insisted. "I want to talk about it now! What did you say to her that made her so upset?"

Malcolm hesitated again. "Well…, she asked me why someone who knows Na Orlins as well as I do would have trouble finding her."

"Well, you explained to her that it is a big city, and there are a lot of people in it, especially colored people, didn't you?"

"I tried," he said, then he looked down at the wet cement under their feet, "but she wouldn't believe me."

"I'll have to talk with her; explain how hard you and Madam E. looked for her."

"It was Madam E., Rose…."

"But you looked out for her too!"

"Yes…, but…."

"Well, I'll just have to make her understand," Rose said, interrupting him again with a determined look on her face. Then she looked at Malcolm with tired eyes. "Can we go home now?"

"Sure Rose, I'll tell the others that we're leaving."

Rose looked out into the dark, misty night. The street glistened in the street light and illuminated the waves of misty rain as the wind moved the small droplets like an undulating swarm of lake flies. *Why didn't Lilly Mae believe him? It is a big city, and she had been working on the riverboat, so she wasn't around all of the time,* Rose thought to herself.

Malcolm stepped out of the bar, and gave Rose a half-smile to reassure her. Now wasn't the time or the place to tell her the truth. He knew it would be coming soon, but not tonight. He put his arm around her and pulled her close. She put her arm around his waist, and they walked off into the wet darkness.

ಬ 18 ಛ

The truth is not always easy to swallow. For Rose, it wasn't just the truth which was hard to take but deciding what to do about it as well. A test of her maturity was on the line and ultimately much more.

~ ~ ~

The next day Rose woke determined to find out what had happened the night before. She had found out when the Capitol would be getting in that afternoon and decided she would meet it at the wharf to have a talk with Lilly Mae. With all the conversing with Lilly Mae the week before, she had failed to find out where Lilly Mae lived. Malcolm had left the house before Rose woke up, so she left Ginny a note letting her know where she was going, and that she'd be back soon to help her with the afternoon preparations. They didn't have many clients scheduled for that evening, so she wasn't worried about leaving Ginny and Millie for a couple of hours.

Lilly Mae was surprised to see Rose standing on the wharf when she stepped onto the gang plank. She forced a smile, knowing what conversation was ahead of her.

"Hey there, Rose!" said Mike with a big smile. "Long time no see! How ya doin'?"

"Just fine, Mike," Rose smiled back. "How are you?

"Can't complain." Then he noticed Lilly Mae walk past him. "Glad you two ladies found each other. Lilly Mae's been worried sick about you. Well, I best be gettin' back ta my work. You ladies enjoy your evenin'!"

"Thanks, Mike, you too!" Rose said cheerfully.

"Hello, Lilly Mae," Rose said brightly.

"Hey, Rose," Lilly Mae replied with a little less enthusiasm.

Rose grasped Lilly Mae under the arm and walked her away from the boat. "We need to have a girl-to-girl talk, my friend."

Rose led her to a bunch of wooden crates further upstream from where the excursion boats docked, just west of the French Market.

"I need to know what happened last night; how come you didn't believe Malcolm?"

"Oh, I believed him all right!"

"Then what's the problem?"

"Didn't you talk to him?"

"Yes, a little."

"And you're not upset?"

"Upset about what?"

Lilly Mae hesitated, not sure what Rose and Malcolm had talked about, not sure what she should say. What she did know was she didn't want this guy lying to Rose, making her believe something which wasn't true. She looked directly at Rose.

"That he didn't really try to find me," she said softly.

"Wha...."

Rose couldn't even finish what she was about to say. She sat there staring at Lilly Mae in confusion. After a few moments she finally spoke.

"He said that to you?"

"I asked him why a guy who grew up in the city didn't know ta look uptown for a colored girl."

Rose sat quietly, trying to understand why Malcolm would lie to her, trying every which way to come up with some excuse for him, but she couldn't. She knew her best friend wasn't lying; she knew Lilly Mae would never do that about something so serious. She felt something deep inside her breaking, the same feeling she had when Grandma B. died; she felt like she was losing something which was close to her heart.

"I don't know why he'd do that, Lilly Mae." Tears welled in her eyes, and she instantly blinked them away.

Lilly Mae stepped closer to Rose and put her hand on her shoulder.

"I don't know why either, Rose, but if you're really serious 'bout this guy, you best be havin' a talk with him about it."

As Lilly Mae spoke those words, something else stirred in Rose—anger.

"I'll have a talk with him, all right!" she said, standing up, looking straight ahead of her at nothing in particular. "Who does he think he is, keeping you away from me?"

Her words brought out the betrayal she now felt.

"I don't know what his excuse will be, but it better be good!"

Rose turned back to Lilly Mae and hugged her.

"Thanks, Lilly Mae, you've always been a good friend. I'm sorry I got you mixed up in this, but I need to find Malcolm."

"That's fine, Rose," Lilly Mae said, content with the way the conversation had turned out.

"I'll see ya later," Rose said as she turned and started walking away.

Then she stopped suddenly and turned back around.

"Give me your phone number, so I can call you."

"We don't have a phone, Rose, but I'll stop by your place on Saturday to see how things are going. If you need to see me before that, just come down to the wharf when I get out of work."

"Okay." Rose managed a small smile.

"Good luck, Rose."

"Thanks, Lilly Mae, but I'm not the one who needs the luck right now!" she said, incensed.

When she got home, Malcolm still hadn't come back, so the anger which built as she walked back home had no way to dissipate. Ginny had tried to find out what was bothering Rose, but when Rose told her she didn't want to talk about it, Ginny let her be. She had never seen Rose angry before, so she thought it better to leave her alone.

~ ~ ~

When Malcolm walked into the kitchen about seven that evening, he was his usual, jovial self. "How are my two best women today?" he asked Ginny and Rose, who were both sitting at the table peeling potatoes.

437

Ginny opened her eyes wide and turned away, not saying a thing. He hardly noticed her reaction behind Rose's heated glare.

"Ginny, can you handle things in here a moment? Malcolm and I need to talk."

"That's fine, child. You take all the time you need."

Rose walked out of the kitchen through the hall door and into Madam E.'s office. She didn't even look to see if Malcolm was following her, she just assumed he was. She had just sat down on the davenport, steam coming out of her ears, when he came into the room.

"So why did you tell me that you had looked for Lilly Mae when you never did!"

Malcolm was startled momentarily at the sudden barrage. It took him a second to speak.

"I never told you I had looked for Lilly Mae."

"Yes, you did! Just last night and that first week I was here!"

Rose stood up and started pacing in front of the davenport, then she stopped and looked straight at Malcolm.

"You lied to me, Malcolm."

Malcolm sat down in a chair opposite Rose.

"I didn't lie to you, Rose."

"How can you say that!" she yelled at him, tears welling in her eyes.

She turned away from him, so he wouldn't see her cry. Then she felt his hands gently touching her arms.

"I didn't lie to you. You just heard what you wanted to hear." Rose turned around and looked into Malcolm's eyes. "What I told you that first week you were here was, that if Madam E. couldn't find her, then I couldn't either."

Rose was silent for a moment, trying to recall what was said so many months ago.

"Well, okay, fine! Let's say you're right," Rose admitted haltingly. "But what about last night?" Rose sniffled and wiped her eyes with her hands. "You said that you had looked for Lilly Mae."

Malcolm held a handkerchief out to Rose. She didn't take it.

"What you asked me was if I was looking out for her, and I was. I just wasn't actively looking for her."

"And what is that supposed to mean?" Rose said angrily.

"It means that I was asked not to look for her, so I didn't, but once I knew how much it meant to you to find your friend, I kept my eyes open in case I came across her."

Rose's face became blank, and she dropped her hands to her sides. "What do you mean, you were asked not to look for her? By whom?"

Malcolm sighed. He knew if he answered her question honestly he would probably lose a very good client, but he knew if he lied he would lose much more. "Madam E.," he said, looking Rose straight in the eye.

Rose sat down, staring into Malcolm's face.

"I don't believe you!" she said, finally taking the handkerchief out of his hand. "Madam E. wouldn't lie to me."

He looked like he was telling the truth, Rose thought, *but then I thought he was telling the truth before.* She stood up again and began to pace once more.

Why would Madam E. want to keep Lilly Mae from me? She had no reason. Is Malcolm lying again just so I'll be angry at Madam E. instead of him? She shook her head and covered her eyes with her hands before she pulled them over her mouth. This was the man she had dreamt of marrying. She shook her head again, slower this time. *How could I have been so blind?* she thought. She dropped her hands from her face and looked seriously at Malcolm.

"I need some time to myself to think this over. I need to talk to Madam E."

Malcolm stood and walked over toward her. She stepped back to avoid his touch. His face and arms dropped, crestfallen at her cold response.

He spoke in a somber, serious tone. "I know you have no reason to believe me, considering I haven't been totally upfront with you," he said, taking a step back. "Take whatever time ya need, Rose, but I'm not leaving and letting you take care of this place by yourself."

"Ginny can help me. I'll be fine."

"We both agreed to take care of things, and I'm not walkin' out on my end," he insisted. "I'll try and stay outta your way until you decide you're ready to talk."

Rose looked at Malcolm standing there, obviously hurt by her aloofness, and she couldn't help but feel sorry for him. He was still acting the gentleman she always knew him to be. Maybe she was wrong. Maybe he was telling her the truth. But she couldn't be sure. He hadn't been upfront with her about Lilly Mae until now, but she couldn't see any reason why the Madam would try and keep Lilly Mae away from her.

She had to be strong. She had to be sure. She agreed with Malcolm's terms, and he left the room without saying another word.

The week went by slowly. Whenever Rose and Malcolm met while working in the house, Malcolm would politely nod his head and go about his business without saying a word. Rose didn't mind this the first few days, but by the third day she wanted him to bound into the room in his usual jubilant manner—broad smile on his face—and greet her with his wonderful, Louisiana Creole voice and a peck on the cheek. But she knew that would be a mistake; she knew she had to hear from Madam E. what had really happened. Talking more with Malcolm wouldn't help. The more he distanced himself from her, the more she wanted to believe him. She knew it was just her heart telling her what to do, not her head. Her heart had gotten her into this mess, and she wasn't going to listen to it again.

The rest of the house easily figured out there was something between the usually happy pair, and despite attempts at finding out what was up, neither were talking. It was a long week for everyone.

~ ~ ~

The day that Madam E. was to arrive home couldn't have come soon enough for everyone in the house. Everyone except Malcolm went down to the wharf to bring her home.

"So how was your trip, Madam E.?" Rose asked, taking her carpet-bag from her as she stepped off the gangplank.

The Madam looked up at Rose and beamed.

"It was wonderful, Rose. I'll have to tell you all about it. Nova Scotia is a beautiful place."

Then she turned and looked for the gentleman that she was with. He was looking after their luggage.

"Stay here," she said excitedly. "I want you to meet Thomas."

She headed out into the crowd which was pouring off the boat. Soon she returned, holding the hand of a very handsome man in a suit and tie.

"Girls," she said, looking at everyone standing around them. "This is Thomas, Mr. Thomas Moore," she said, glowing.

"Very pleased to meet you all," he said, taking off his hat and nodding his head slightly. "Edna has told me all about you," he said with a smile.

Everyone nodded and smiled politely back.

"Well, I must be off to make my train," then he turned to Madam E. "Will you walk me to the station?"

"Of course, dear," Madam E. said, looking deep into his eyes.

"Thank you for coming to greet us, but I'll have to meet you all back at the house. Thomas has to catch a train back to Washington in just a half hour, so I won't be long." Then she turned toward Rose.

"Is Malcolm here, Rose?" she asked, looking over the girl's heads.

"No, he stayed to do some last minute things at the house," Rose said somberly.

Madam E. smiled at Rose.

"I knew I could count on you two to take care of things for me. Did you have any troubles?"

"No, everything went just fine."

"Wonderful! You'll have to fill me in when I get home."

Then the Madam looked around and saw a porter with her luggage. She walked over to him.

"Rose, could you please make sure these get back to the house? I'll be along shortly."

"Sure," Rose agreed.

Rose hailed a cab and everyone squeezed into it for the ride home.

Rose was pacing in the office when Madam E. finally made it home.

"So, you had a nice trip?" Rose asked, her focus not really on the Madam's answer.

"Yes, a lovely trip. We even took a weekend trip to Martha's Vineyard," she said as she took off her gloves. "You really will have to go to Nova Scotia some time, Rose. I know how much you like to travel. You would love it there. There is so much to see!" She sat down in the chair across from the davenport.

"So tell me, how have things been?"

"Fine, I mean, mostly fine," Rose said, starting her pacing again.

"Have a seat dear, and tell me what happened," she said in a concerned voice. Rose sat down on the edge of the davenport.

"It has nothing to do with the girls or the house; that all went fine. It has to do with Malcolm and me."

Rose stopped and looked down at her hands clasped in her lap.

"Oh..., man troubles, those are the worst kind," Madam E. said sincerely. "Go ahead, dear, tell me what's happened."

"Well, I found my friend Lilly Mae," Rose said.

Madam E. blinked, startled by the news. It took her a moment to respond.

"Isn't that nice. How did you find her?" the Madam asked.

"It was just after we had said goodbye to you, actually. She has been working on the Capitol all summer, and it pulled up just after your ship left."

"Well, that's wonderful. And how is your friend doing?"

"Oh, she's just fine, but the problem is, well…, Malcolm told me that he hadn't been looking for Lilly Mae at all."

"That's interesting," she said in a curious tone.

"What's more interesting is that he said he wasn't looking for her because…, well, because you had told him not to."

Rose stopped momentarily, looking for a response in Madam E.'s face, but when her expression didn't change she continued.

"But I'm not sure he's telling the truth. I just can't think of a reason why you wouldn't want me to find my friend."

Madam E. stood up and walked toward the front windows without saying a thing. She looked out of the windows much as she had the first day Rose had arrived in her home. Then she walked back and sat back down in the chair facing her.

"Well, he is telling the truth, Rose," she said, looking at Rose with sincerity. "I told him not to look for your friend because I wanted you to stay and work for me."

Rose dropped back onto the back of the davenport as if Madam E.'s words had just pushed her over. She sat there motionless, her mouth open in disbelief. After a moment, she finally sat back upright.

"But why? You didn't even know me then."

"I knew enough about you to tell that you were a smart girl, and you were someone with the experience I needed to help me run my business."

She stood up and walked back toward the windows.

"You see, Rose, I believe in God as much as you do, and I believe God plans things to happen for reasons we don't always understand. So when you bumped into me that day on the wharf, and I brought you home and found out what a wonderful young

lady you were, a young lady with just the skills I needed, well...,
I thought perhaps our meeting wasn't just by chance." Madam E.
sat back down in front of Rose.

"So you see, I couldn't take the chance and let you go. I had to
do what I could to make sure you stayed here," she said. "Malcolm
was just doing what I asked, and he knew that if he didn't he would
lose a very good customer. You can't blame Malcolm, my dear. It
is all my fault."

Rose couldn't believe it. Malcolm had been telling her the
truth. It was Madam E. all along. Now she felt guilty for not
believing Malcolm, but that familiar feeling of betrayal returned.
She had trusted Madam E. She assumed because she was a
woman—a woman of some class—that she could trust her. But
she was wrong. What other things had she lied about? Rose didn't
even want to think about it. Now she had to decide what she was
going to do.

"I understand if you don't want to stay with us any longer,
Rose, but you are very welcome to stay as long as you like."

Rose looked into Madam E.'s kind face, a face she had come
to trust and even love, a face which had betrayed that trust. At this
moment she wasn't sure what she was going to do. Rose did know
she could think better when she was alone.

"I'm not sure what I want to do right now, Madam," Rose
said sincerely. "I need some time to think it over."

"You take all the time you need."

She looked down at her hands, then back up into Rose's face.

"I know I betrayed your trust, my dear. That isn't what one
woman should do to another, and I am sorry for that. I assure
you I have treated you fairly in every other respect, and if you are

honest with yourself, you may realize that you too have gained something from your time with us," she said with a fragile smile.

Then she stood, walked over to Rose and kissed her on the forehead.

"You're a wonderful young woman, Rose," she said, taking Rose's chin in her hand. "Whatever you decide to do, you are going to be just fine."

She smiled again and left the room. Rose sat there for many minutes in a daze, all the things Madam E. had said, and all the things she and Malcolm had said to each other playing back in her mind.

Suddenly she sat bolt upright, eyes wide with realization, as a broad grin spread across her face.

"Oh, my God!" she said to herself. "I almost forgot!"

Rose ran into the kitchen. She checked the laundry room. She ran upstairs and into the first open door she saw. There he was, stripping the bed. She ran up to him and threw her arms around him with such force they fell together on the half-stripped bed.

"What the...," was all Malcolm could say before she brought their lips together in a strong, passionate kiss. When Rose finally pulled away, she laid there on top of him, smiling from ear to ear.

"I take it you've had a little chat with the Ma-dam," Malcolm smiled.

They both sat up on the edge of the bed. Rose looked contritely down at her lap. "I'm sorry I didn't believe you, Malcolm. I just wasn't sure of anything or anyone."

"I'm sorry too, Rose. I should have told you sooner, but I was afraid of losing Madam E.'s business." He touched Rose's chin, turning it up to face his own. "I should have known what was more important. When you pulled away from me last week, I finally realized how much I had to lose. I promise never to keep anything from you again." Then he lowered his face to hers, grinned and kissed her softly on the lips.

Rose's decision wasn't a very hard one to make; she really didn't seem to have much of a choice. She wanted to finish school, but if she left Madam E.'s, then she would have to find another place to stay. She couldn't stay with Malcolm; that would not be proper. She couldn't stay with Lilly Mae—though she had offered—there really wasn't any room; Rose found out they lived in a two room tenement apartment not far from the river. And she couldn't really find a place to rent when she didn't know if she was going to stay in the city after the school year was done. She thought it best to stay put, finish her semester, then decide what she was going to do. So that is what she did.

~ ~ ~

Rose had changed and she knew it. She felt good about her decision to stay with Madam E. She had taken another step, another small leap into adulthood, and come out the other side more confident, more self-assured. Yes, a woman she trusted and admired had lied to her, but Rose couldn't totally dismiss her reasoning, and there was no real harm done. It had also brought her and Malcolm to a new understanding. Yes, Malcolm wasn't perfect like she had thought of him before, but Rose knew his love for her was sincere, and it was now deeper than ever. Making a decision on what to do at the end of the school term was going to be harder than anything she had done before.

~ ~ ~

The last month of school flew by for Rose. Summer arrived in New Orleans typically in May and everyone, even the Sisters, were eager to get out of the warm classrooms and on to summer vacation. Rose had written her family telling them of her upcoming graduation from eleventh grade and that she would decide after that what she was going to do. She had sent them an Easter card and gotten one back in return—the handiwork obviously done by little hands—but there was something missing on the card; Michael usually always put a small message somewhere in the family letter, but there was no message or any explanation why it was missing. She immediately wrote a letter home to find out why.

~ ~ ~

One hot June evening, Madam E. had left Rose in charge of the house, which always meant Malcolm came by to help out. Thomas Moore had arrived on the afternoon train to surprise Madam E., so she was going out for the evening.

Rose was standing in the parlor at the bar, going over the list of clients who were scheduled for the evening. The ceiling fan was on high and the windows were wide open to catch any breeze which might make it into the house, though by this time in the evening it was usually a warm breeze coming off the hot pavement which had been heated all day by the sun.

Rose was wearing one of Tess's hand-me-downs—the colorful skirt and white short-sleeved blouse with the red ribbon circling the over-sized neckline—which Rose had seen her wear that first day in the house. Rose wasn't as built up front as Tess, so the neckline annoyingly kept slipping off her shoulder.

The front bell over the door rang, as a group of boisterous young men stepped into the house. Millie held them in the hallway and came to ask Rose what she wanted to do with them, since they weren't on the schedule.

Rose glanced at the group, pulling her blouse back onto her shoulder—group of military men. Some were standing in the hall looking around, others were at the front door trying to coax an obviously reluctant comrade into the building. Rose rolled her eyes and turned back around to look at the schedule. She didn't particularly like it when these young men showed up—Navy, Army, Air Force—they were all the same: loud, obnoxious, and usually tapped out. At least it was the beginning of the evening, and they weren't totally drunk yet. They were even worse when they were drunk.

"Go find out how many of them there are. If there aren't too many, we should be able to squeeze them in," Rose instructed Millie, who had grown a couple inches this spring, along with the grass and flowers.

"Come on Bookie, it'll be fun!" one of the young men said, as he pulled on his friend's arm, and another one hindered his exit from behind.

"Listen Dave, I'm just not up for this sort of thing," he said while resisting their physical pressure. But the one behind him started to push while Dave pulled, and they had him in the house before he knew it. Once inside, he decided he would stop resisting for now; he'd find another way out.

As he stood looking at the strange red wallpaper, that his friends had discovered—to their amusement—was embossed with naked women, he couldn't help shake the strange feeling he had been at this address before. Not that he had been in New Orleans before; he and his Air Force buddies were on furlough for the first time, and since their base was only a couple hours away, they decided to take a trip to New Orleans. They had been told by the older guys on the base that there were plenty of women, lots of bars, good music, and good food to be had here. What seemed familiar was the street address of the house, but he couldn't place when he had been at 325 Rampart Street before.

The young colored girl stepped back into the hall and asked how many of them there were. Bookie looked passed her into the parlor, which was obviously laid out for entertaining, with stuffed chairs and davenports all around the room and a piano at the far end across from the bar.

"Check that one out!" Dave said, nudging him in the ribs with his elbow. "She's a real looker!"

"She probably as ugly as a dog," Bookie teased back.

Actually, she did look nice; she stood mostly on one leg, which thrust her hips out to one side, accentuating the soft curve of her pelvis above her shapely calves; she had wavy, dark auburn hair which fell down over her shoulders. She was a beauty all right, at least from the back. But what did she look like from the front? As Bookie stood staring at Rose, her blouse fell off her right shoulder. He blinked, poked his head forward to try and get a closer look and squinted in disbelief.

~ ~ ~

He pulled his head back, shook it slightly, and blinked again at the woman across the room. This was definitely a woman, not a young girl, and she was working in a brothel, so it couldn't be who he thought it was—that was wrong on two counts. But come to think of it, her birth mark *was* on her right shoulder, and her hair was auburn, though he couldn't quite remember if it was that dark. He was certain it never looked that nicely combed. He had to be sure.

"Rose?" he said softly as he stepped into the parlor.

"Hey, Bookie," Dave chuckled at his friend. "Mike!" he called out again when he didn't get a response. "Can't wait 'til we're invited?"

"Rose?" Mike said a little louder.

Rose heard her name being called, but she knew it wasn't Malcolm's voice she heard. She turned around to see who it was.

The two stopped and stared at each other, neither moving a muscle or saying a word. Then they both smiled, and Rose came running up to her big brother, throwing her arms around him and squeezing as hard as she could.

"Whoa, Girl, let me breathe a little here," he teased her, peeling her from around his neck.

Dave saw the two embracing, and he called to his friends, "Look guys!" He pointed to Rose and Michael. "We can't get Bookie in the building, and he's the first one to get a girl. Go figure!"

Rose looked over Michael's shoulder and shook her head at the comment, then she turned her attention back to her brother.

"I can't believe it's you!" Rose said in amazement, grabbing him around the neck again for another quick hug.

"*You?*" Michael questioned, eyes wide. "I knew you were in New Orleans, but I never figured I'd find my sister in a place like this!"

"I suppose!" Rose laughed softly. "Here," she said, taking his hand and leading him into the kitchen. "Come in here and wait for me. I'll explain everything."

"I can't wait!" Michael said chuckling, yet obviously uneasy about finding his sister in a bordello.

"Ginny, Malcolm, this is my brother, Michael!" Rose said excitedly, still holding his hand as they stood together in the kitchen.

"Well, I'll be," Ginny said.

Malcolm came over and shook Michael's hand. "Very pleased to meet you, Michael," he said with a smile.

"I have to take care of the young men out in the hall, Malcolm. Could you keep Michael company for a few minutes?"

"I can do that, *cheri*!"

"No, that's okay Sweetie, I won't be but a minute," she said. "And it'll give you two a chance to get to know each other." She smiled and stepped back out of the room.

"Have a seat, Michael," Malcolm said, pulling out a chair. "Can I get you something to drink? A beer, an iced tea?"

"Tea would be fine, thanks."

"Rose didn't tell us her brother was in town."

"Rose didn't know," Michael said, taking the glass of tea from Malcolm and taking a drink. "I joined the Air force three months ago, and this is the first furlough we've had. Since I knew Rose was in New Orleans, I thought I'd tag along, but I forgot to write down her address." Then he shook his head. "But I never thought I'd find her in a place like this!"

"So then she never told you where she was staying?" Malcolm asked.

"Nope," he smiled. "I suppose the folks wouldn't have looked kindly on the idea."

"Lord have mercy," Ginny giggled.

"Well, let me assure you Mr. Krantz, your sister isn't working in this house—not in the capacity you might be thinking. She works for the Ma-dam, keeping her books, cooking, cleaning and the like," Malcolm explained.

"Then why's she out there now?"

"Oh, she's just fillin' in," Ginny explained. "Madam E. has a gentleman caller, and she's out for the evenin'."

Michael looked at the Ginny and Malcolm, not quite sure he believed them but wanting very much to all the same.

"Yes, Rose is just scheduling the clients for this evening, and she takes care of them once they arrive. No, that didn't sound right. I mean she gets them drinks and introduces them to the girls, collects their money, you know, that sort of thing."

"Actually, I don't know. But I'll take your word for it," he said with a smile.

Ginny went back to making dinner, not wanting to get into this somewhat tense conversation. Malcolm sat across from Michael smiling and wishing Rose would get back sooner rather than later. He wasn't sure he was helping the already awkward situation with her brother.

Finally, Rose skipped back into the room and sat down next to her brother. She grabbed on to his arm, beaming brightly at him.

"I still can't believe you're here!" she said.

"Your friends here have been explaining to me why *you're* here." He smiled at his sister.

"Yah, it is a little strange isn't it? But I'm sure they told you I don't work here. I mean, I don't work upstairs. Well..., I work upstairs sometimes but just to clean up and stuff," she said, obviously flustered. "You know what I mean."

"Yeah I do. I'm just enjoying hearing you try and describe it!" he chuckled.

"Oh, you…," Rose said, slapping him lightly on the arm in playful disgust

"Boy, would Mom and Dad sure like to hear about this!" Michael said with a roguish grin on his face.

"Don't you dare, Michael!" Rose said excitedly.

"I wouldn't say anything," he said, wrapping an arm around her shoulders and giving her a slight squeeze. Rose noticed just then how much bigger and stronger her brother had become. He looked a lot like her father, only stockier.

"Wow, they've been working you hard, haven't they?" Rose said, squeezing his large biceps.

"There's not much else to do on base but work and drill."

"You still like to read, don't you?"

"Sure do. Why do you think they call me Bookie? I went through the three books I brought with me the first three weeks, twice."

"You can take some of mine!" Rose offered. "I've gotten some good ones from Malcolm." She turned and smiled at Malcolm. He smiled back at her. Michael watched as they lovingly exchanged glances.

"I need the tea, Malcolm," Millie said, walking into the room.

"Oh, *pardon mwa*, Millie. Coming right up!" Malcolm stood up quickly and picked up the iced tea pitcher.

"And we're runnin' low on beer, too," Millie said. "Those Army boys sure can drink!"

"I'll get those," Ginny offered.

"Very nice to meet you, Michael," Malcolm said, shaking Michael's hand. "Perhaps we can meet again."

"Yeah, sure," Michael said, half standing.

Malcolm rushed out to the parlor after Millie.

Rose turned back to her brother. "So when did you join the Air Force? I can't imagine Mom letting you go!"

"She didn't have much say about it really. I talked it over with Dad, and he agreed that if we got into a war in Europe or Asia, it would be better if I got into the service before it all started up, so I could maybe get a command position."

"But why the Air Force?"

"I'm training to be a fighter pilot, Rose," he said lifting up his chest.

"I'm not surprised. I remember you making that model airplane of The Spirit of St. Louis after Charles Lindberg flew across the Atlantic," Rose said. "Mom and Dad must be proud."

"Yeah, I guess so."

Then he looked around the room and noticed they were alone.

"Hey, what's with this Malcolm character? Are you going out with him or something?"

"Yes, we're seeing each other," Rose said with obvious pride.

"He works here too, does he?"

"No, he's just helping me out 'cause Madam E.'s out tonight, and I'm in charge."

"What's he do? I mean when he's not helping you."

"Well, I'm not really sure what you'd call what he does." Rose hesitated. "He gets things that people want, particularly things that are hard to find."

"Well, who does he work for?"

Rose looked at him questioningly. "I think he just works for himself."

Just then, Ginny walked back into the room.

"Malcolm's gonna take care a those boys, Rose. They're a little too much for Millie to handle."

Rose stood up with an anxious look on her face. "Oh dear! I probably should get out there."

"That's okay, Rose. I probably should leave."

"Oh, you can't leave yet, Michael. You just got here!"

"You've got work to do." Michael smiled and held her hand. "I can have visitors any weekend, if you want to come and visit me at the base. I'm done with basic training, but I've got a few months of pilot training, so I'll be there a while yet. Maybe you can take the train or bus up and meet me next weekend."

"Oh, that'd be wonderful, Michael. I'd love that!"

"I'm at Barksdale Air Force base, just outside of Shreveport. Ya know where that is?"

"I do!" Ginny interrupted. "Sorry, couldn't help over hearin'."

Rose and Michael looked at each other and smiled.

"I can get her there, no problem," Ginny continued.

Michael took one last gulp of his tea then stood up. Rose stood up next to him. "Then I'll see you in a week!" he said, taking hold of his sister and giving her a big hug. Rose sighed deeply, melting into her brother's arms, soaking in that familiar, comfortable family love, a love which comes from growing up with someone, from common experiences that don't need to be voiced but are felt and remember all the same. And, of course, from the family genes which bind from generation to generation. She had forgotten how much she had missed it until it was dropped on her doorstep.

Michael started walking toward the parlor door, then turned around suddenly. "Oh man, I almost forgot! Mom's been sick. Dad called me a couple days ago and told me Mom caught a bad cold that turned into pneumonia. She's in the hospital."

~ ~ ~

Rose stepped backward, a shocked look on her face. "Oh, dear!" was all she could say. Michael stepped up close to her and held her hand.

"Dad says she's gonna be all right, Rose. I don't think you have to worry," he said, trying to reassure her. He saw the tears welling in her eyes, so he put an arm around her shoulders. "Oh Rosie, she's going to be okay!"

"I know, Michael," Rose said through her sniffles. Michael handed her his handkerchief.

"Thanks." Rose blew her nose, wiped her eyes, then looked back at her brother with a serious expression on her face. "She could have died, and I wouldn't have even known it." Her eyes teared up again.

Michael looked back at her just as seriously. "But she didn't die, Rose. I wouldn't have been there either. We can't live our lives for our parents. They wouldn't want that anyway, would they?"

"I suppose not. But at least they would have been able to call you. It would have taken a week or more before a letter got to me." Rose sat back down at the kitchen table. "I need to go home, Michael."

"You know, you could probably just give Dad a call and find out how Mom's doing," he said, sitting back down across from her.

"It's not just that." Rose looked up at him, her eyes red and puffy. "I didn't realize how much I missed my family 'til you showed up. I really need to see everyone," she said, blowing her nose one last time. "You know, I've been away nearly two years."

"Yeah, we were all kinda surprised when you didn't come home from Marsha's that next day." He gave his sister a knowing smile. "I knew something was up when you had your shoes on for a simple overnight at a friend's house."

Rose smiled shyly and looked down at her hands. "Yah, that wasn't very smart of me, was it, running away like that?"

"You had us all pretty worried. Mom made us say a prayer for you every night." Then he laughed. "And I still do!"

Then they both laughed.

"What's all goin' on in here?" Malcolm teased as he walked back into the room.

Then he saw Rose's red and puffy eyes.

"*Cheri!*" He ran over to her side and knelt down next to her. "What's the matter?"

"Nothing, Malcolm," she tried to reassure him, but he wasn't buying it. "Nothing, really." She smiled at him lovingly and lightly caressed his worried face.

Michael rose from his chair. "Well, I can see you're in good hands, Rose."

Rose stood and stepped up to her brother and gave him one last hug.

"Say hey to Mom and Dad for me would ya, and all the kids!" he said as he headed for the parlor door once more. Then he turned one last time toward his sister.

"We still have a date, don't we?"

"I may have to delay it a while."

"That's fine. You know where to find me."

"I love you, Michael!"

"I love you too, kid," he said with a smile, then disappeared behind the door.

When Rose turned around to face Malcolm he was standing, staring at her with a blank expression on his face.

"Are you planning on leaving, *mo cheri?*"

Rose walked up to Malcolm and wrapped her arms around him. This was where she wanted to be; this was where she felt content. He held her close, not losing the forlorn look.

"I have to go home, Malcolm," she said, finally pulling away enough to look into his eyes. "My mother is ill. She's in the hospital."

"*Oh cheri!*" Malcolm's lamentation turned to concern. "Then you must go to her!"

Rose smiled at her thoughtful sweetheart.

"Michael said she's going to be okay, but I need to see her. I need to see my whole family."

Tears began welling in her eyes again. She wiped them away with Michael's handkerchief.

"Oh, I forgot to give him back his handkerchief!" Then she huffed out a small laugh, looking at the handkerchief. "I doubt he would have wanted it in this condition anyway," she said mostly to herself.

Malcolm moved Rose toward a kitchen chair and guided her to sit down. He pulled up a chair and sat down facing her.

"What's wrong with your mother, Rose?"

"She had a bad cold and caught pneumonia. Michael said she is doing better now, but I'd still like to see her." She looked into Malcolm's eyes; all she saw was compassion. "I haven't seen any of my family in two years! I just didn't realize how much I missed them until I saw Michael again."

"I understand, *cheri*. Family is very important," he said sincerely. "When will you leave?"

Rose thought a moment. "I'll have to see when Madam E. can make other arrangements for help."

"Not to worry, my love, I can take your place until she finds someone to fill in for you."

Rose brightened. "Oh, would you, Malcolm? That would be wonderful; then I could leave tomorrow!"

Rose wrapped her arms around his neck and squeezed as hard as she could, burying her face in his supple neck, drinking him in, swimming in the easy waters of his care and compassion. Already she felt a need to memorize every detail about him for her long trip home.

She pulled away suddenly. "Oh, I forgot about Michael's friends!"

"They're all taken care of, but you might want to take a look at the schedule. I don't know when the next client is scheduled to arrive."

Rose looked at the clock on the wall. "In about fifteen minutes!" She stood up and headed for the parlor. She stopped half-way, ran back to Malcolm, and kissed him vehemently, then she ran out of the room leaving him drugged and doe-eyed.

Ginny stood at the stove and shook her head.

"Um, um, um, you got it bad," she said, teasing him.

Malcolm gave her a sideways glance and a half smile. He knew she was right; he loved Rose more than he had ever loved anyone before. A worried look ran across his face. He also knew he had to let her go, but in doing so he was taking a big risk, the possibility that he could lose her forever.

❦ 19 ❧

For adventurers, departures are always bitter-sweet; it is hard to leave something comfortable and familiar, but the lure of what lies ahead, the unknown opportunities, the excitement of what might be next, is always present. The truly venturesome, such as Rose, know this, and it is weaved into their very being. Right now, it was pulling Rose apart.

~ ~ ~

"I'll miss you so much, Malcolm!" Rose said with tears in her eyes.

"I'll miss you too, *mo cheri*," he replied, not wanting to let her out of his arms. He liked the feel of her soft, inviting body next to his, the familiar smell of lavender in her hair, and the love she so easily gave him.

"Rose, it's time." Lilly Mae touched her arm gently. "The train's about ta leave."

Rose looked into Malcolm eyes. He smiled a smile of recognition; he knew she loved him. Rose reached her face up to meet his, and they touched lips in one last kiss of longing.

"All aboard!" the conductor yelled down the busy station platform.

The three friends made their way through the crowd to the nearest car. Once Lilly Mae had learned what had happened with Malcolm and Madam E., she had decided to give Malcolm another chance. She was glad she did; she had discovered why Rose liked him so much, and realized his love for Rose was quite genuine. They enjoyed a few happy evenings together laughing at some of Rose's antics – Lilly Mae supplying riverboat stories and Malcolm supplying sporting house stories. Rose felt a bit picked on, but she was mostly pleased that the two people she cared for so deeply were getting along so well.

Rose said her tearful goodbyes to all the girls, Ginny, and Madam E. at the house. Madam E. thought it was best that just Malcolm accompany Rose to the station, to give them some privacy. She assured Rose her job would still be waiting for her upon her return. There wasn't a dry eye in the house when Rose stepped out of the front door. Rose felt like she was leaving her other family.

The threesome stopped at the doorway to the train car. Rose gave Malcolm one last hug as a tear escaped down the side of her face.

"Come on, Rose," Lilly Mae prodded her one last time.

Rose pulled away and rummaged for her handkerchief in her purse while trying to hold on to the package which Malcolm had just given her. Lilly Mae took the package, and Malcolm pulled his handkerchief out of his pocket and gave it to her with a silent smile. Rose wiped her eyes, then held on to it reflexively. She took back her package and stepped up onto the railroad car as it started to inch forward. Rose blew Malcolm a kiss. Lilly Mae pushed Rose up to the next step so she could step up behind her. They both waved at Malcolm as he jogged a short distance down the platform, until they moved rapidly out of sight.

Lilly Mae nudged her friend into the car where they found an empty seat together and sat down in silence. Rose put her hand over Lilly Mae's and squeezed it gently. Having Lilly Mae along made leaving Malcolm a little easier; she was glad she agreed to come and visit. She was excited to show Lilly Mae her home and introduce her to her family. Leaving Malcolm was harder than she thought it would be; she had grown so close to him without even knowing it.

They had spent the last evening together, much of it in silence, walking around the city, each not wanting to say what they both feared deep in their hearts. Would their love stand the test of distance? Would it last the test of time? Both were old enough to know that either thing could change a relationship. Other things, other people could easily plant a seed of doubt, question the realness, voice concerns for their future. But both were too in love to let the thought appear in any form; too in love to live past the here and now.

So they walked together in quiet solemnity to all their favorite places—along the Basin Canal, among the bright lights and busy shops on Canal Street, into the garden district passed the beautiful, stately homes, beside the Mississippi, down to the unusually quiet French Market, sitting in Jackson square. They ended the long evening falling asleep in each other arms on Madam's davenport, not wanting to leave each other any sooner than they had to.

But Rose was going home, and that excited her as well. She wanted to make sure her mother was okay, to look into her father's deep brown eyes, and feel the roughness of his cheek against hers; to see all her brother's and sisters again, especially the baby she had never met. She was almost two now, not even a baby anymore. All these things were moving through her mind.

But there was something which still left her uneasy with this departure—would she want to stay once she was among her loving family again? The effect on Rose of that brief time with Michael was strong. But her love for Malcolm was strong as well, stronger than she had realized. She fretted about the decision which was yet to come.

Rose looked at her friend sitting beside her, her head down, working on her knitting. Unlike Rose, she hadn't stopped since she had first learned how last summer on the J.S. Deluxe. Rose already had two scarves and a vest she wasn't sure what she was going to do with, since there wasn't much use for such things in Louisiana, though Wisconsin did get pretty cold in the winter.

Rose knew one thing—no matter what happened, she would always have a friend in Lilly Mae. She thought about how different they were from two years ago; much different than the two young girls who had met that one early summer day in Grandma B.'s kitchen. That day seemed so long ago. It was hard to even remember. They looked different; they had grown. They acted different; they were young ladies now. But their love for each other had only deepened. They had taken that leap and they had made it, so far anyway. They both knew there were many more leaps and baby steps yet to come, but they also knew that if their friendship had made it this far—through so much turmoil, after so much time—they could always count on each other, no matter what the world dished out.

Rose had almost forgotten about the gift which Malcolm had surprised her with. She looked down in her lap at the neatly wrapped, brown paper package tied with twine. She recognized the wrapping and shape when Malcolm handed it to her on the wharf. She felt ashamed; why hadn't she thought of giving him something—something he could use or wear so he would think of her? But leave it to Malcolm, he knew just what to get her. A book.

She opened the paper slowly. The title read, *The Citadel*. She had seen it in the best seller list in the *Times Picayune* and commented to Malcolm about wanting to read it. She smiled. She liked how he always paid attention to little things like that.

She opened the cover to find a folded piece of paper inside. She unfolded it cautiously, not wanting to cry in public. It was inevitable.

My Rose

I stutter,
I stop,
I stare.

The beauty I see:
the milk cream of her skin,
the apple blossom in her cheek,
the mouth as sweet and soft as pillow candy,
the body of a sculptor's dream.

But these coverings
are mere shadow
to what draws us all so near.

Pretense drowns
- in the blue of her eyes
-in the warmth of her hands
-in the depth of her heart.

I dare not go there,
for I will surely drown as well;
a lover's bliss-filled sleep.

I close my eyes,
and wait until the scent of Rose
once more gives breath
to my heart.

> *With deepest Love,*
> *Yours always ~ Malcolm*

Rose picked up Malcolm's handkerchief and wiped her eyes. Lilly Mae turned toward her when she blew her nose. She handed the poem to Lilly Mae without a word. Lilly Mae looked at Rose after she had read it.

"You got a special one, Rose."

Rose nodded her head and wiped her eyes once more, bring the handkerchief to her nose as she closed her eyes and pulled the scent of him inside.

Rose rested her head back, letting the gentle sway and the quiet hum of the train lull her to sleep.

~ ~ ~

They arrived in Prairie early in the morning after many station stops. Rose hadn't told anyone that she was coming; she wanted it to be a surprise, so there was no one at the station to greet them or give them a ride. Rose and Lilly Mae headed out to Bluff Street where Rose set down her suitcase and put out her thumb. The only people who were driving around at this time of the morning were farmers, and picking up a white and black girl was not something a farmer in a small town would be apt to do. It wasn't until Rose's neighbor—her old friend Marsha's dad—rode by and recognized Rose that someone actually stopped. He had just picked up some feed at the coop and was heading home when he thought he recognized the tall, white girl standing on the side of the road. He had to stop and back up to make sure. She was wearing a dress, which Rose would rarely do, and she was standing next to a colored girl whom he did not recognize.

"Rose, Rose Krantz? Is that you?" Marsha's dad called out through the open window.

"Yes, it's me, Mr. Ripp! How are you? How's Marsha?"

"Oh, she's just fine. She's goin' ta school here at St Mary's, and doin' pretty good too!" he said proudly. Then he noticed their suitcases sitting beside them.

"You lookin' for a ride?"

"Yah, that'd be great!"

Mr. Ripp got out of the truck cab and walked around to pick up their suitcases and set them in the back of his truck on top of the feed sacks.

"Mr. Ripp, this my friend, Lilly Mae."

"Pleased to meet you," he said, tipping his feed-company hat at the obviously nervous young woman.

Lilly Mae smiled. "Nice to meet you," she replied softly.

Mr. Ripp got back in the cab, and Rose and Lilly Mae squeezed in beside him for the bumpy ride to the farm.

When they had said their thank-yous and goodbyes to Mr. Ripp, the girls picked up their cardboard and cloth suitcases and walked down the gravel drive toward Rose's house; both girls having a little difficulty, unaccustomed to wearing heels on gravel. Rose had asked to be left off at the top of the driveway, so as not to alert anyone to their presence.

The first out to greet them was Max, tail wagging, body wiggling, ready to give out sloppy kisses when Rose bent down far enough for him to reach her face. He didn't bark once. Rose bent down and dug her hands in the thick fur around his neck and gave him a long hug. He sat perfectly still. He pranced along beside them up to the house like it was just yesterday that Rose had left. It felt good to be home again.

Gerty had come up to the kitchen door when she heard the sound of gravel underneath moving tires, as Mr. Ripp pulled out of the driveway. It took her a moment, but when she recognized who it was, she threw open the door, pushed the screen door out of her way, and ran out to greet her sister.

"Rose!" she called out as she ran up to her, throwing her arms around her and nearly knocking them both over. It took her a moment to release her grasp.

"I can't believe it's you! You..., you look great!" she said excitedly, holding Rose away from her at arms length, blinking the tears from her eyes.

"Thanks, Gerty." She smiled at her sister. Even though she had been gone these two years, Rose felt that somehow she knew her better now. Rose had to try and blink the water out of her eyes too. She pointed to her friend. Lilly Mae put her suitcase down.

"Gerty, this is my good friend Lilly Mae."

Gerty grasped Lilly Mae's hand in both of hers and shook it gently and without hesitation.

"Welcome, Lilly Mae. It's wonderful to finally meet you," she said warmly. "Why didn't you tell us you were coming?" she asked, turning back to Rose.

"I wanted it to be a surprise."

"Well, you must be tired after your long trip. Leave your cases here, I'll send the boys out to get them," she said as she headed back toward the house. "Come on in. I'll make you some coffee. Dad just brought Mom home last night, and she'll want to see you right away!" she called back over her shoulder as she hurried into the house ahead of the girls.

Rose held back slightly as she walked up to the porch. The farm looked just the same as when she had left it; there was wash floating on the line to the north of the house; the barnyard was as neat as always. The rose bush under her parent's bedroom window was full of buds, and the faint sweet-sour smell of hay and manure hung in the damp morning air. It was all there, just as she had left it, but there was one thing which felt different, and she knew that it was her.

Rose slowly stepped up onto the porch and walked cautiously up to the screen door. She looked through the screen at the hazy scene within and saw her mother sitting at the kitchen table in her house dress, sipping coffee. She could tell she wasn't quite herself yet—she didn't have her apron on.

Her mother dropped her cup on the saucer when she saw her daughter standing there. Then, almost as quickly, she smiled a knowing smile and sat up straight with excitement, but she didn't stand. Rose opened the screen carefully. She stepped through the door, listening to the drawn-out squeak as the spring stretched out to accommodate the two passers-by; then the slap of wood meeting wood as it quickly pulled the door back in place. She remembered the sound, and she smiled at the simple familiarity and comfort it brought.

Without saying a word, Rose walked up to her mother who was now standing. She gently hugged her, taking in that familiar feel, that familiar scent, that familiar love.

Rose released her embrace, but her mother had hold of her hand; she wasn't letting go just yet.

"Mom, I want you to meet my good friend, Lilly Mae."

Rose's mother smiled at Lilly Mae. She walked up to her and gave her a gentle hug.

"Welcome, Lilly Mae," she said, smiling, holding onto her at arm's length. Then she motioned for them both to sit down. "Come, both of you, sit down! You must be tired from your long trip."

The three women sat down. Gerty placed cups of steaming coffee in front of Rose and Lilly Mae, then she sat down with a cup for herself.

Lilly reached out her hand and placed it on her daughter's arm, smiling contently.

"So tell me about your ramblin', Miss Rose."

❧ Afterword ❧

The vast majority of facts in this book are historically true. I have, per a writer's license, made some exceptions to this. For those like myself who like to know what is historically true and what is true fiction in a story, I will list here the instances where I have taken such license.

First off, there is no Catholic Church in Crawford County called St. Mary of the Hills. I just like the way that name sounded, and it seemed logical to me; there were a fair amount of Germans and Irish in the hilly Crawford county in the 1930s, and most, of course, where Catholic, so it only seemed to make sense.

I mention that Prairie du Chien was a port town, but I actually don't know how much, if any, commerce took place on the river at that point in time. There were various industries that were placed along the river on Feriole Island and railroad tracks that ran its length sat right next to the river, where they still do today.

Another small stretch of the truth was when Rose is in Prairie making her call to the Streckfus Steamer company. In my story she makes a call from a telephone booth. Marilyn and Roy Rybarczyk, who lived in Prairie du Chien at the time, don't remember any phone booths in town in the thirties. They were in existence in other parts of the country, however, so I put one there to fit Rose's need for one.

If you look closely at the picture of the Capital on the cover, you will see that the deck that the officers' and women's cabins were on—the Texas deck—was smaller than the decks below it. When Rose ran out to throw up after her upsetting encounter with Peter, she would have had to go down a flight of steps to be able to lose her dinner into the water. But then throwing up onto the deck below wouldn't be as poetic as leaning over the rail and seeing the moon reflecting in the water below. On the real river boat the other male crew (all of which were black) all stayed in the "hold," which was an area below the first deck. Mary Otte doesn't remember any black women working on the boat, only a small number of white ones, so the fact that Grandma and Lilly Mae sleep on the Texas deck with Rose is fictitious. I don't actually know where a black woman would have slept if she was a member of the crew. Mary remembers that the cabins were indeed small and held a bunk bed that she shared with another woman, not the two separate beds as I mention in my story. I couldn't have Rose and Lilly Mae on bunks beds; however, it wouldn't have worked for Rose's encounter with her night intruder.

The Orpheum Theater in Savanna, Illinois did exist, but from the picture I found of it I could not tell if it had a balcony. I also don't know what the lobby looked like—it could have been designed in art deco since that was popular in the late '20s—or if the ceiling had twinkling lights. I know older theaters of that era had such features, so I added them here.

Also in Savanna there was a Radke Hotel, but I don't know if there was a restaurant attached to it, though by the present interior design, I assume there was (as there is today). I also don't know if it would have been segregated.

When Rose buys Grandma a radio in Savanna, the only small radio around at that time probably sat a foot and a half high and a foot wide, not something that could be easily be wrapped or carried and would probably have been too expensive for Rose to purchase. In the 1930s most people had console radios. I had to speed up time here and allow Rose to purchase a smaller radio that hadn't yet been available to purchase.

As an aside, in the late 1930s on the excursion steam boats that piled the Mississippi at that time (and that is all the steamers did by this time in history—they were no longer packet boats, that is boats that hauled cargo and/or housed passengers overnight) all had their own musicians that stayed on the boat the whole season, and these bands were made up exclusively of black musicians. The Marable's Capital Revve (Louis Armstrong was a member) and the Mississippi Serenaders (directed by Walter "Fats" Pichon) were two such bands that played on the Capital at various times. Initially, the black players received room and board on the boats they worked on. Apparently, by approximately 1939 this had changed and became more the exception than the rule.

It was interesting how difficult it was to find out what was segregated and what was not during those years. I suppose it wasn't something you would want to keep a record of. For instance, I was not able to find out if the movie theatres or restaurants in Prairie du Chien and Savanna were segregated. I do know from talking to Earl and Marilyn Rybarczyk that the balcony of the Metro theatre was nick-named "nigger heaven," but the couple also did not recall any blacks who lived in town at the time. [If you personally have such information, I would love to know about it. I would be happy to make corrections in future editions.] In general, most things at this time were still segregated, though my personal source of information on St. Louis history—Lois (Colombo) Bryce, who was a teen in St. Louis in the late '30s—told me that many public places in St. Louis were not segregated: the street cars, and the soda fountain at Famous Barr department store, for example. But I am not too ignorant to know that blacks and whites did not mingle, just as the city at that time was very segregated by nationality: the Italians to the southwest in the "Hill," the Germans further south, the Irish in "Dog Town" just west of down town, and the blacks in the "Ville" and the "Mill Creek Valley" area.

It is correct that the people who worked in the kitchen on the Capital were black, but in fact, according to Mary Otte, it was all men. Most of the crew were men. When Mary worked the boat in the early '30s, the only women that worked on the boat worked in her job as purser—she handled the money and the payroll on the Capital—or in jobs selling tickets, candy and cigars or as cashier. I don't know how many people it took to run an excursion boat the size of the Capital on a regular basis (a few sources tell me different numbers). Mary thought it was thirty or so. One source mentioned that a different crew ran the day excursion than the moonlight excursions which could go as late as midnight. On its maiden voyage, on May of 1920, there was a crew of 125 aboard her.

In the 1930s Roy Streckfus, one of the founder's five children, was the captain of the Capital. All four of the Streckfus boys became captains, and they all knew how to pilot vessels, but I'm told that the captain rarely piloted his boat. He was probably too busy running things. (The founders, John and Theresa Streckfus, had five daughters as well, three of whom made it into adulthood. They also worked on their parent's river boats. It was very much a family business).

In St. Louis, the Rosebud Cafe on Market St. was a black establishment that Tommy Turpin and Scott Joplin played at, but I don't actually know if it was open in the 1930's.

When the Capital heads down to New Orleans for the winter, as it did each fall, it actually took on excursions as it made its way south, unlike what I have depicted here. But I needed to get Grandma B. and Rose off the boat, and that was an easy way to do this.

Kid Howard' Brass band that everyone in Madam E's house sees ushering a funeral service down the street did exist at this time in history. It was made up of 12 players vs the seven that I mention in the story.

The courtyards that Malcolm takes Rose to in her first days is New Orleans are loosely taken from the courtyards of the Historic French Market Inn on Rue Decatur, a stones throw from the Mississippi. I stayed at this old inn in 2003 when I was accompanying my husband on a business trip and doing research for my book (luckily, before hurricane Katrina). It does feel like a magical place.

And for clarity sake for those of you, like myself, who are under the age of sixty, dinner in this time period is our lunch, supper is our dinner, and a davenport is our couch. At least that's how it is in the upper Midwest.

I think that's about it. I hope these small bends and curves in the road of truth haven't dampened your enjoyment of Rose's story, for that is what this is primarily—a story.

ஐ Bibliography ௸

Wisconsin's Past and Present: A Historical Atlas – The Wisconsin Cartographers' Guild

This Fabulous Century 1930, 1940 Vol IV

Everyday Fashions of the Thirties

Best American Plays, Vol 1918 - 1958

Life on the River: a Pictorial History of the Mississippi, the Missouri and the Western River System – by Norbury L. Wayman

The River We Wrought, a History of the Upper Mississippi – John Anfinson

Upper Mississippi River History – by Captain Ron Larson

Villa Louis – Friends of Villa Louis

St. Louis and the Mighty Mississippi in the Steamboat Age: the collected writings of Ruth Ferris

Voices on the River – by Walter Havighurst

Excursion Steamboating on the Mississippi with Streckfus Steamers, Inc. – a dissertation by Dolores Jane Meyer

Savanna – Yesterday and Today – The Carroll County Genealogical Society

The Crisis – monthly magazine of the NAACP

Discovering African American St. Louis, a guide to historic sites – John A Wright

Central West End St. Louis – Albert Montesi and Richard Deposki

African Americans in Downtown St. Louis – John A Wright Sr.

Days and Nights of the Central West End – Virginia Publishing Co. 1991

A Post Card Journey Back to Old St. Louis and the 1904 Worlds Fair St Louis 1875-1940, postcard history series – Joan M Thomas

Where We Live: A Guide to St. Louis Communities – Missouri Historical Society

The Sidewalks of St. Louis Places, People, Politics in an American City – George Lipsitz
St. Louis – A found look back

The Ville St. Louis, Black America Series – John A Wright Sr.

The Ville: The Ethnic Heritage of an Urban Neighborhood

Color Me Dark: The Diary of Nellie Lee Love, The Great Migration North – Patricia McKissack

Native Son – Richard Wright

Twelve Million Black Voices – Richard Wright

The Women of Brewster Place – Gloria Naylor

Women and Minorities during the Great Depression

Mardi Gras, a Pictorial History of Carnival in New Orleans – Leonard V Huber

Masking and Madness, Mardi Gras New Orleans - Photos by Kerri McCaffety, text by Cynthia Reece McCaffety

All on a Mardi Gras Day, episodes in the history of New Orleans Carnival – Reid Mitchell

Belizaire the Cajun (movie) – 1986, Armand Assante

ROSE BLOOM

Creole New Orleans – Race and Americanization -Arnold R Hirsch and Joseph Logsdon

Dictionary of Louisiana Creole – Albert Valdman, Margaret Marshall, Thomas Klingler, Kevin Rottet

A House is Not a Home - Polly Adler

Call House Madam - Serge G. Wolsey

Storyville, New Orleans, being an authentic illustrated account of the notorious red light district – Al Rose

Pleasure Was My Business – by Madam Sherry and Robert Tralins

Great Bordellos of the World—Emmett Murphy

Beautiful Crescent, a History of New Orleans – John Garvey and Mary Lou Widmer

Offical New Orleans Harbor Guide and Souvenir of Steamer Capitol De Luxe – Streckfus Steamers, Southern Division, New Orleans, 1928

The Times Picyune – New Orleans, LA

The Courier – Prairie du Chien, WI

And too many web sites to mention…

Songs

Didn't Leave Nobody But the Baby – Written by T-Bone Burnett/ Gillian Welch/Alan Lomax/Sidney Carter/(c) 2000 Global Jukebox Publishing/Irving Music Inc./Say Uncle Music/Henry Burnett Music, (BMI)/All Rights administered by Global Jukebox Publishing, Bug Music, and Irving Music Inc. (BMI)/All Rights Reserved. Used By Permission.

You're Nobody Till Somebody Loves You – Written by James Cavanaugh, Russ Morgon and Larry Stock. (C) 1944, (R 1971). Used by permission of Shapiro, Bernstein & Co., Inc., Southern Music Publishing Co., & Larry Stock Musich c/o Larry Spier Music, LLC. All rights reserved including public performance.

Amazing Grace – Lyrics by John Newton, 1772, Music by William Walker.
This version is missing three verses of the original song. The last verse was added in the nineteenth century perhaps by John P. Rees.

Valse Bebe – Michael Doucet/Happy Valley Music, BMI, off of Beausoleil – Bayou Cadillac CD

Flammes D'Enfer – traditional: art., and words by Michael Doucet/ Happy Valley Music, BMI, off of Beausoleil –Bayou Cadillac CD

ཀ Louisiana Creole Glossary ങ

Après vous – after you. This is actually French. I couldn't find it in the Louisiana Dictionary I had access to or on line

Bonjour – this is the same both in French and Louisiana Creole

Bon maten – good morning

Bonswah – good day

Mamzel – lady

Misyeu – Mr.

Leglis – church

Dinin – dinner

Servi – serve

Popa – father

Mo – my

Cheri – sweetheart
O contraire – Oh, to the contrary

Bel – beautiful

Begniets – I don't know the origin of this word. My guess is that it is French. It is a puffy pastry covered in powdered sugar; a very old and delicious New Orleans tradition.

Ple – please

Fiy – girl

Gran-mer – grandmother

Nonk – uncle

Mardi Gras – fat Tuesday

Moman – young lady

Vini an – come in

Hou-wa – Oh!

Pardon mwa - pardon me